Samuel Bjork is the pen name of Norwegian novelist, playwright and singer/songwriter Frode Sander Øien. The Munch and Krüger series features three other books: the Richard & Judy Bookclub bestseller *I'm Travelling Alone*, *The Owl Always Hunts at Night* and *The Boy in the Headlights*.

Also by Samuel Bjork

I'm Travelling Alone
The Owl Always Hunts at Night
The Boy in the Headlights

THE WOLF

Samuel Bjork

Translated from the Norwegian by Charlotte Barslund

PENGUIN BOOKS

TRANSWORLD PUBLISHERS
Penguin Random House, One Embassy Gardens,
8 Viaduct Gardens, London SW11 7BW
www.penguin.co.uk

Transworld is part of the Penguin Random House group of companies
whose addresses can be found at global.penguinrandomhouse.com

First published in Great Britain in 2023 by Bantam
an imprint of Transworld Publishers
Penguin paperback edition published 2024

A CIP catalogue record for this book
is available from the British Library.

ISBN
9781529177152

Typeset in Sabon LT Pro by Jouve (UK), Milton Keynes.
Printed and bound in Great Britain by Clays Ltd, Elcograf S.p.A.

The authorized representative in the EEA is Penguin Random House Ireland,
Morrison Chambers, 32 Nassau Street, Dublin D02 YH68.

Penguin Random House is committed to a sustainable future
for our business, our readers and our planet. This book is made
from Forest Stewardship Council® certified paper.

THE WOLF

On 28 May 1993, two eleven-year-old boys were found murdered in a field near Fagerhult in Sweden, some ten kilometres north-east of Uddevalla. The farmer who found the bodies later described the scene *as if someone had opened the gates of hell*. One boy, Oliver Hellberg, was completely naked and lying on his back. The other boy, Sven-Olof Jönsson, was found a few metres away wearing only his underpants. An animal, a white hare, had been placed between the boys. Due to the complex nature of the case, a team of investigators from the National Crime Agency in Stockholm was dispatched to work with local police officers; however, it soon became clear that this arrangement was unsuccessful. In the years that followed, the senior investigating officer was replaced no less than three times and, in the end, even Sweden's Justice Minister, Eva Nordberg, had to resign. The investigative team was also accused of having leaked a diary belonging to one of the boys. The boy's parents, Patrick and Emilie Hellberg, went to court to stop the tabloid press from sharing their murdered son's private thoughts with the rest of the world. The couple won the first round in Uddevalla County Court but lost an appeal in West Sweden's Appeal Court. Some weeks later the boy's mother was found dead in the bathtub in the family home in Ekeskärsvägen. She had taken her own life. In what would later be referred to as 'the day of shame' in Swedish media history, *Expressen* and *Aftonbladet* published the boy's diary in full on 14 October 1993. For the first time both newspapers had the same front page: the last entry in the boy's diary. The page contained only a few words, written in cursive writing:

It's a full moon tomorrow. I'm scared of The Wolf.

The case remains unsolved.

ONE

NORWAY

APRIL 2001

Chapter 1

Thomas Borchgrevink was standing in the car park outside the old Fredheim School in Lørenskog, wishing the wind would pick up. He had no idea why she had chosen this particular spot for them to meet, but he had a hunch. To make it as difficult for him as possible. Was that why? It was, wasn't it? The thirty-six-year-old man glanced at his watch as a murder of crows took off from a nearby tree. The loud guttural sounds echoed across the emptiness because out here there was nothing but fields, a gravel pit and this white school building where he had once been a pupil. In another life. Before the incident. He hadn't been to this part of the world for over a decade. In fact, he had not been anywhere at all. Eighteen years inside. He had been released some months ago and was still struggling to adjust to the feeling. The feeling of being able to do what he wanted. Thomas Borchgrevink pulled his jacket around him, sat down on the steps leading to the old school and turned his face to a pale sun which was peeking out from behind a cluster of trees.

It was a quarter to nine. They had agreed nine o'clock, but he was taking no chances. She was capable of anything. *What did I tell you, we said nine and he didn't even bother to show up. Do you still think that he has a right to see his son? The last time they saw each other the boy was only two years old, for God's sake.* There was a sudden rustling in the treetops at the end of the road and he felt a small surge of optimism. Perhaps the wind would come after all? The kite had been a stupid idea, of course. He had racked his brains trying to think of some activity they could do out here. He had lingered in the toy shop for so long that the assistant had finally come up to ask him if everything was all right. All right? Of course things

5

were not all right. Why would she think they were? But none of this was her fault, and he knew it, so he had just picked the first thing that had caught his eye. A kite. Outdoors. Near his old school. They could fly a kite together. That was a good idea, wasn't it? He regretted it now, obviously, as the wind eased off in the treetops. A chessboard, that was what he had had in mind, teach the boy the rules, perhaps have a game, but he had dropped the idea when he was told that their meeting would take place outdoors. With a chaperone. That under no circumstances would she let him be alone with the boy.

Her attitude had been completely different when she had first come to visit him. He hadn't even remembered her name. *Borchgrevink, you have a visitor.* His first in three years. *It's a woman. Table number two.*

A visitor?

A female visitor?

His mum?

No.

Of course not.

She had dressed up as if it was a special occasion with flowers in her hair, rouged cheeks and a short summer dress. Siv Johnsen. They had been in Sixth Form together. The few months he had managed before he had finally given in to the voices in his head.

And he had to admire her persistence, every two weeks for almost three years, and in time he had almost grown to like her. Pictures from the labour ward. From their son's first birthday. *Martin misses his daddy!*

But then, no. No more.

Another man, he had realized eventually.

Not that he minded about her. But about the child?

The finest boy in the world.

His son. Martin.

No, no way.

Thomas Borchgrevink got up from the steps and started to pace up and down to shake off his anger.

Easy now.

Don't get mad.

Even though she had suddenly stopped coming and several letters had arrived instead, typed sheets of paper from faceless lawyers telling him he would no longer be allowed to see the little one.

He kicked a small stone across the playground and checked his watch again.

A quarter past nine.

Not a soul in sight.

There was practically nothing on Losbyveien, the road that led up here from Finstad; hardly any people lived this far out. There was a shooting range near the bend in the road. A gravel pit behind the trees further up; he knew every stone. He had loved this school, this area, coming early every morning rather than be at home in the dark house with the cold people who were supposed to have taken care of him. The sound of the clock on his bedside table and the arms of Mickey Mouse indicating he should get up if he wanted to get out in time, tiptoeing softly in his socks across the floor so that no one would wake up, the lunchbox he would fill with whatever he could find.

He hadn't impressed at school, but he hadn't been one of the worst either. He had done OK.

A quarter to ten and the first car arrived, a slightly rusty Toyota Corolla, a blonde woman with round glasses nervously shook his hand.

'Astrid Lom, Children's Services.'

'Thomas.'

A slight clearing of the throat over a file which presumably contained the same information that had been sent to him.

Convicted of manslaughter.

At the age of eighteen.

Good behaviour.

Early release.

Mother has agreed to him seeing the boy.

Under supervision.

Five to ten, finally the car arrived.

White. Expensive, obviously.

She had found someone better, not that it mattered, not now.

Thomas Borchgrevink felt himself grow warm all over as he walked with clammy hands to meet them.

'No, no, wait.' A hand held him back.

'Yes, of course, sorry.'

One step at a time. On the boy's terms.

Martin.

There he was.

Thomas smiled broadly as he saw the car door open.

A confused-looking boy with dark hair and a brown jumper got out of the car with no sign of the adults in the front wanting to help him.

Bloody idiots.

Don't you see that he's . . .

Fortunately, the social worker had a better understanding of children. She strode briskly across the ground, put her arm around the boy's thin shoulders and suddenly there he was. Thomas Borchgrevink had to steel himself in order not to cry.

'Hi, Martin.'

'Hi . . .'

Beautiful blue eyes reluctant to look at him properly. The boy stared at his trainers instead.

'How are you?'

'Eh?' A gaze now, some curiosity.

'That's a cool jumper.'

'Er . . . thanks.'

The boy peered up towards the social worker as if to ask her who she was and what she was doing here.

'Is that a robot?'

'What? No. It's Bionicle.'

Thomas took a tentative step forwards.

'Bionicle. Cool name.'

The boy laughed after some hesitation. 'No, he's not *called* Bionicle, he *is* a Bionicle.'

'Oh, right, sorry. So what's his name, then?'

'This one?'

'Yes.'

The boy seemed to retreat into himself for a moment. Then he said, 'His name is Makuta.'

'Cool. Is he your favourite?'

The boy peered anxiously at him for a second time.

'Er . . . no. My favourite is Ehlek, but they didn't have a jumper with him on it.'

'That's annoying.'

'Yes. But I have the action figure.' He glanced briefly over his shoulder at the white car.

'It's a shame I didn't know you like Bionicles or I could have brought you one.'

'It's all right.'

The boy blew his fringe away from his forehead and glanced expectantly at the bag by the steps.

'What's in the bag?'

'Nothing very exciting, I'm afraid, I had hoped it might be windy.'

'Windy? Why?'

'So we could fly it. There's a kite in the bag. But I don't know, perhaps you think that's boring?'

'Oh no,' the boy said, and smiled a little. 'I like flying kites.'

Once again the trees rustled, so there was someone up there who was looking out for him after all.

'You do?' Thomas smiled. 'So how about we give it a go?'

'OK,' the boy said.

'Perhaps we should try the fields? I think it might be windier out there.'

He took the kite from the bag and looked towards the social worker.

'Is it all right if we . . .'

She nodded.

'Why did you ask her?' the boy wondered out loud when they had walked away from the old school building and the kite was lying on the ground between them.

April in Norway.

The smell of freshly ploughed soil.

Soon grain would be sown, and in the summer it would turn yellow.

He was struggling to hold back his emotions now.

'She's here to watch out.'

'Watch out for who?'

'For you. Do you want to have the first go? I'll hold the string and you can run?'

'OK.'

The boy smiled again and picked the kite up from the ground.

And now it no longer mattered. The two faces in the car. The social worker and her thick file. All the years disappeared.

There was only a young boy running across the field, grinning from ear to ear as the kite finally took off, billowing proudly in the sky.

'Look! Wow!'

Twenty beautiful seconds before the kite plunged and crashed into the hill at the end of the field.

And then – the moment Thomas Borchgrevink would never forget.

The boy ran back to him, this time with a completely different expression on his face.

'What is it, Martin?'

'There's someone lying over there.'

'What do you mean?'

A small hand shamefully trying to hide the wet stain at the front of his trousers.

'They're not moving.'

Chapter 2

Forty-two-year-old Holger Munch was sitting in his black Audi with Bach's Cello Concerto no. 1 in G major on the car stereo, feeling guilty at having abandoned his family in the middle of Sunday lunch yet again. Not that they had complained. They never did. No matter what time these phone calls came. Late at night. In the middle of their summer holiday. Christmas Eve just as the pork roast was being served up. Totally supportive, no matter what. He had worked as a homicide investigator for almost twenty years, and Marianne, his high-school sweetheart, had always been there. It had been love at first sight and they had married young. Nine years later, their daughter Miriam arrived, finally. Miriam was fourteen years old now and she was nowhere near as bad as people claimed teenage girls were. His family was always there for him, celebrating his promotion last autumn knowing full well that he would be even busier now. A new homicide unit, with its very own offices away from Oslo Police headquarters. Not only had Holger Munch been entrusted to lead this historic new creation, but he had also been given free rein to pick his own team. For the first time in as long as he could remember, he had had an uplifting winter. He was usually plunged into deep gloom behind his frozen red beard, cursing everything and everyone, especially the idiots who went skiing and loved the snow, but this year he had had more positive things on his mind. He was an entrepreneur founding a new venture. That was how he had felt. And yet, there had been something in Marianne's eyes, hadn't there?

He shook off the thought and showed his warrant card to the officer who had stopped his car at the police cordon; he could tell even at this point from the face of the young man.

11

This was something else.

He saw the same nervous glance hidden behind a tough uniformed facade a minute later when he parked his car by the white school building.

'Nilsen, head of operations.'

Munch nodded and took out a packet of cigarettes from the pocket of his beige duffel coat.

'Is anyone from my team here yet?'

'Er, yes . . . a blonde woman. The lawyer?'

'Goli.'

'And a guy in a suit . . . Fredrik?'

'Fredrik Riis,' Munch said, lighting his cigarette.

'Forensic officers were first on the scene, and they've been here for a while,' the muscular police officer told him, and pointed across the field.

'Pathologist?'

'Here too. He arrived not long ago.'

The officer pulled off one glove and placed his finger on a map.

'We've blocked the road here and here. The road is called Losby-veien. Not many people live out here. There are a few farms where we have had to keep access open so we ran the cordon down along this road, which is called Vålerveien. Is that OK?'

'What about the boundaries of the fields?' Munch said.

'I've people out there,' Nilsen said with a nod. 'It should be sorted now.'

'What else do you have?'

Munch studied the map, then turned towards the trees that surrounded them.

'It's a bit of a nightmare,' Nilsen said. 'The boys are out there, which is *here* on the map. As you can see, there are fields in every direction, and trees everywhere. We're thinking the killer might have entered here and then left the same way. If you ask me, I think we'll be lucky if anyone has seen anything.'

'What's this?' Munch wanted to know, pointing to a building indicated on the map.

'A shooting range.'

'Have we cordoned that off?'

'Er, no, not yet . . . because it's located . . .'

'Do it,' Munch said wearily. 'And send a team up to it. And this?'

'A big gravel pit,' Nilsen said, pointing towards the trees in the east. 'Do you want us to—'

'If you haven't done it already, then yes. Have you?'

He looked at the police officer, who didn't know what to say.

'So you want a team up there as well?' the man said eventually.

'I do,' Munch nodded, then headed towards Anette Goli, who had just emerged from the old school.

His first hire.

He hadn't had a moment's doubt.

'Have you been up there?' the skilled lawyer asked as she raked a hand through her blonde hair.

'Not yet. What's it like?'

'Bad. I had Wik on the phone just now. He wants to know if they should cover them up or if you want to see them as they are.'

'Leave them as they are,' Munch said, lighting a new cigarette with the previous one. 'Who found them?'

'A motley crew, to be honest.' Goli sighed, and nodded towards the school building. 'I'm just trying to unravel the family situation.'

'Go on?'

'A custody battle, as far as I can gather. A man had come here to meet his son. Mother was present with her new boyfriend and we have a chaperone from – Children's Services, would be my guess. I'm not sure. I've had to separate them. I've got the father in there and the others in different rooms. Do you want to talk to them?'

'Not now. Just make sure we get all the details.'

'OK, Katja can deal with that.'

'Is she here?' Munch exclaimed in surprise, and then he smiled. 'I thought that she—'

'Turns out working for Kripos wasn't her dream job after all,' Goli said with a wink. 'I picked her up on my way out here. Is that all right with you?'

'Of course.' Munch nodded, and then he smiled again.

His second hire.

13

Katja van den Burg.

That choice had been just as simple and as obvious as his first one.

'Right, do you want to get going?'

'Yes, where are they?'

'That way,' Goli said, pointing. 'But I recommend you change your shoes. It's quite muddy out there.'

'OK.'

Munch dropped the cigarette butt on to the ground and headed to his car to fetch his wellington boots.

Chapter 3

Twenty-one-year-old Mia Krüger was sitting at the back of the auditorium in the basement of the National Police Academy, struggling to keep her eyes open. She had been out all night. Again. Her head hadn't hit the pillow until six in the morning, was it? She suppressed a yawn as the lecturer with the crew cut and the shiny boots clicked to produce another slide from the projector. Damn it, why hadn't she given up and gone home earlier? After all, she had been looking forward to this lecture. An introduction to Delta, the police force's tactical unit. It was the sole reason she had decided to become a police officer in the first place. Despite her parents' objections. The obvious disappointment in her mother's eyes when Mia announced that studying Literature at the University of Oslo ultimately was not for her. That she had already quit her studies. That she had decided to do some travelling and then start at the Academy in the autumn.

A police officer, Mia? No, but . . .

Never mind.

First woman in Delta. She had read a feature in a magazine about how tough it was, that no woman had ever met the entry requirements, and had made up her mind on the spot. Yes, you heard right. Delta. That was where she was going.

So fuck the lot of you.

Mia Krüger stifled another yawn as a list appeared on the screen. The basic entry requirements. And that was just the start. After that came hellish weeks of physical and mental tests, and this was where the few women who had attempted to get in before had failed. But not her. Of course not. Easy-peasy. She would be the first woman to

15

succeed. And that would show them once and for all, wouldn't it? The male chauvinist pigs who were now glancing at her with contempt, wondering what the hell she thought she was doing here. The only woman in the room.

She heard a snort from the first row, a blond moron who regarded himself as God's gift to women. He had come on to her in the gym only a few weeks into their first year, and she groaned at the memory. Chat-up lines from some crib sheet for losers as he flexed his muscles in front of the mirror with a Neanderthal belief that they might help his case.

You have beautiful eyes . . .

They're as blue as the sea . . .

Oh yes?

Poet, are you?

Yours are too close. And you know there should be a forehead between your eyes and your hairline, don't you?

And your hair, it's so exotic and dark . . . It's really classy the way it falls over your slim shoulders . . . So what kind of girl are you? Are you up for a bit of fun?

Puke.

Seriously?

What an idiot.

She had cut it off in her room in Torshov that same evening. Her hair. She had stood in front of the bathroom mirror with a knife, hacked it off furiously and watched it fall into the sink; whenever it grew too long, she would repeat the ritual.

The fitness tests were now displayed along with the requirements she knew inside out, and she regretted not having picked up a coffee on her way here. Even though it would have come from a machine and tasted like crap. Anything to escape the strong urge to sleep.

She pulled herself together as everyone's eyes finally turned to the slide.

3,000 metres in less than twelve and a half minutes.

Tick.

Back home in Åsgårdstrand, she had been able to run that distance in eleven minutes and fifteen seconds at the age of fifteen, and the disgusting coach who liked to comment on how girls looked in tight running leggings had scratched his head, checked his stopwatch and asked her to run it again because 'there must be some mistake'.

Really?

Fuck you.

Fifty sit-ups.

Seriously?

Tick.

Fifty push-ups.

Now that had taken her a little longer, but not much. She had screwed a bar to the ceiling of the attic flat she shared with two other girls from her year, who were more interested in how they looked and who had done what with whom after the Friday beers that the student union organized. Every morning, before the others got up, she had pulled herself towards the ceiling, until her arms could no longer support her.

Ten pull-ups with chin-ups.

Two birds with one stone.

Tick.

400-metre swim.

Seriously?

Tick.

Free diving to a depth of 4 metres.

Tick.

He had noticed her now, the man from Delta with his shiny boots, and she could feel it coming from him too.

What do you think you're doing here?

Mia had always had an ability to almost feel other people's thoughts.

You see things other people don't see, don't you? Don't you, sweetheart?

Her grandmother, who wasn't her real grandmother, and yet was so like her. Eccentric. At times borderline mad. At the age of almost eighty, she continued to sit in her garden until late at night, smoking a pipe, drinking whisky, howling at the moon, and never giving a toss about what other people thought of her.

Mia's mobile pinged, and she reacted automatically, pulling it out of her bag with nimble fingers.

Sigrid?

No.

Of course not.

She hadn't heard from her twin sister in months.

It was the reason she went out at night.

To wander the streets with print-outs she had made.

Have you seen this girl?

Sigrid Krüger.

Please call me if you know something!

Sigrid and Mia.

Sleeping Beauty and Snow White.

Twins.

One fair, the other dark.

Born to a sixteen-year-old girl who couldn't and didn't want to raise them herself. Adopted by Eva and Kyrre Krüger from Åsgård-strand. She was a teacher, and he had a paint store in Horten. Mia instinctively touched the bracelet she wore on her left wrist. A con-firmation present. An anchor, a heart and a single initial. S on Sigrid's, M on hers. And then, one night under the duvets in their bedroom:

You'll take mine and I'll have yours?

She hadn't taken it off since.

Damn it, Sigrid?

Where are you?

Mia forced herself to set aside her fears and was dropping her mobile into her bag when the door suddenly opened and the secre-tary from the principal's office popped her head round.

'Sorry for the interruption, but is Mia Krüger here?'

Murmuring across the auditorium now.

Everyone's eyes back on her.

'Eh, yes, that's me.'

'The principal wants a word with you.'

'OK?'

The secretary merely waited.

18

'Now?' asked Mia.

'Yes, now.'

Scornful laughter rippled across the front row as Mia packed up her things and walked down the steps as quickly as she could.

'What's it about?' she said when the door was closed and the two of them were alone in the corridor.

'I don't know,' the grey-haired secretary replied. 'But I think it's important. Do you know where to go?'

'Sure.' Mia nodded, slinging her bag over her shoulder.

She took the lift up then crossed the tarmac square to the main building on the other side.

What was it this time?

She had been to the principal's office before.

To be lectured in front of his large desk like a schoolgirl; his stern gaze, which she just couldn't take seriously.

Discipline, Mia. Several of your tutors have complained . . .

So what?

It's not my fault that you people think we're still living in the 1950s.

Are you sleeping on school premises, Mia? Wendelbaum said he found you curled up on the classroom floor again.

Whatever.

She had gone to Frogner Park to look for Sigrid. Behind the monolith where the junkies tended to hang out, only a few hundred metres from the National Police Academy. Afterwards, she hadn't bothered to walk all the way home.

It was a different reaction this time around when she knocked on the door and heard the deep voice.

'Hi, Mia. Come in, come in.'

She paused in the doorway, wondering what she was walking into. The principal, Magnar Yttre, had got up from his chair and was beaming at her as he ushered her inside.

'Can I get you anything? How about a cup of coffee?'

Chapter 4

Munch was sitting by the window in the coffee shop on the corner of Bernt Ankers gate and Mariboes gate, a few hundred metres from his new office, having switched both his mobiles to silent. The investigator was old school and had yet to get used to their constant beeping. He preferred being left alone to think, but no chance of that now, obviously: both phones had rung non-stop in the last twenty-four hours. One of the calls – from an old colleague who was now the principal of the National Police Academy – he had answered only to say that he was too busy to talk, but Yttre had been euphoric, barely letting him get a word in edgeways. *I think I've found someone for you, Munch.* The timing was extremely inconvenient, but he had allowed himself to be persuaded.

He had heard Yttre talk about this test before. It had been developed by UCLA researchers. The National Police Academy tended to run it on all second-year students, who were told that it was just a bit of fun so they wouldn't feel pressured. Some photographs from a crime scene. *What do you see?* This girl was believed to have aced it.

Fine. He could spare Yttre half an hour. It would also give him a chance to get a bite to eat. Marianne had called him again just now, worried about him, as always – did he get enough sleep and, especially, did he get enough to eat?

She's quite eccentric, Munch.

But give her a chance, OK?

He had just carried his coffee and sandwich to the table when the door opened and there she was.

Twenty-one years old.

She was young, but Munch's experience had taught him that youth need not be a problem in itself. Several members of his team, some of the best ones in fact, were under thirty. Not that he was thinking of hiring anyone else. He already had the people he needed, but Yttre, who was normally hard to impress, had been so excited. *We have never seen anything like it before, Munch. Not even close. This girl is unique.*

It had obviously piqued his interest.

'Are you Munch?'

She was dressed in a black polo-neck jumper, skinny black jeans, black Converse trainers and carried a black rucksack, but the first thing he noticed about her were her eyes.

Bright blue and remarkably clear. Light brown skin, almost like that of a Native American. Shoulder-length, pitch-black hair, oddly uneven; it looked almost as if someone had attacked it with a blunt pair of scissors, not that it seemed to bother her. The young police student stopped in front of him as if this meeting was the most natural thing in the world and extended a slim hand towards him.

'Mia Krüger.'

'Hi, Mia. Welcome.'

'Thank you,' was all she said, and sat down without showing any signs of taking off her rucksack.

'Would you like something to eat? Or drink?'

She glanced briefly at the menu behind the counter.

'No, thanks.'

'Perhaps you don't drink coffee?'

'I do, but not here.'

'Is that right?' Munch said. 'Are you a connoisseur, a coffee expert, perhaps?'

He had intended to be ironic. Oslo had recently been invaded by coffee shops, each one trendier than the next – young, ridiculous hipsters practising coffee brewing almost as a kind of religion – but his comment didn't seem to provoke her.

'Is that what you want me to look at?' the young woman said with a glance at the two buff files lying under his mobiles.

'Yes. Did Yttre say anything?'

She shook her head.

'Good,' Munch said. 'All I want you to do is look at some photos and tell me what you think, all right?'

'All right.'

'This one,' Munch said, pulling out one file, 'contains pictures from a crime scene we visited yesterday morning. And this one . . .'

He placed the second file next to the first.

'Is pictures from a crime scene in Sweden, eight years ago. I want you to take a look at them and tell me what you see, OK?'

'If it's the same killer?'

'I didn't say that.'

'But it was what you meant?'

She looked at him quizzically, and Munch had to suppress the urge to smile. Yttre had been right, this girl really was quite something. Unique even in his experience as the head of the homicide unit in 13 Mariboes gate. He was used to people looking at him with something bordering on awe, but this young police student didn't seem intimidated at all.

'Yes, that was what I meant.'

'Then why didn't you say so?'

'Because it might block your thinking. I want you to keep an open mind. You might see something, something I've missed.'

'OK, I get it,' Mia Krüger said, and turned the files so they were facing her.

She didn't open them; she just continued to sit there, waiting.

'Could you leave me alone for a while?' she said, and looked up at him again after a pause when he still hadn't taken the hint.

'Of course. How much time do you need?'

'I don't know. Twenty minutes?'

'Very well. I'll be right outside if you need me.'

Munch got up, picked up his lunch and found a bench across the street.

Nine missed calls. Most of them from Anette.

'Hello, it's Holger. What's going on?'

Anette Goli heaved a sigh down the other end.

'Well, what's not going on? The commissioner wants to be

22

briefed. I reckon the Department is putting pressure on her, she thinks we ought to hold a press conference—'

'We'll wait. I've already said so.'

'That's what I told them, but it doesn't seem to be good enough.'

'Good enough for whom?' Munch grunted irritably.

'Don't take it out on me. You know what she's like.'

Hanne-Louise Dreyer. She was the newly appointed commissioner of Oslo Police. There had been considerable internal opposition when it became known that the minister had set up a separate homicide unit in the capital without consulting the police force. Senior management had rattled their sabres; they viewed the new unit as an expression of dissatisfaction with their own work. Munch had hoped that the situation might change with the appointment of this new commissioner, but oh no. It would seem to be his lot in life. Never to have a boss he got on with. Never mind. The ball was in his court now, and there was nothing they could do about it, which was obviously why they were so tetchy.

'Just tell her to wait,' Munch said. 'We won't release the names of the victims until we have spoken to both families; what is it about that she doesn't understand?'

'Like I said, don't take it out on me. Tommy's mother's plane lands at one o'clock. I've asked Katja to pick her up from the airport. Who the hell goes to Spain on holiday and leaves an eleven-year-old boy home alone?'

'She might have had her reasons. Let's not go into that now.'

'Leaving the neighbours to look after him? Turns out they didn't even know they were responsible for the boy.'

'We'll deal with it once she gets here. What about the van?'

Their only lead so far. A white van had been spotted near some trees by Losbyveien.

'Oxen has gone to talk to Traffic Control. The road ends at the golf club, so the van can't have left in that direction. We're concentrating on route 159 east and west, and the toll barrier on the E6. They're getting hold of the footage as we speak – I think we have found seven cameras. I have him on the other line and he will let me know the moment they find something. But, even so—'

23

'What?'

'A white van? How many of those are there in Oslo?'

'It was a Sunday morning,' Munch said to encourage her. 'Let's keep our fingers crossed. What about the Lundberg family?'

'Very helpful,' Goli continued. 'And weirdly calm. I don't think they have really taken in what has happened yet. Fredrik is with them now. He'll call me soon. Are we still planning a team briefing at four o'clock?'

'Yes, will you let everyone know?'

'OK. Listen, I have to go, it's Dreyer calling again.'

'No press conference until—' Munch began, but Anette had already rung off.

Bloody idiots.

Surely it must be possible for him to get five minutes of peace.

As if he and his team didn't have enough on their plate already.

Three cigarettes later he decided that the young police student had to be done by now. He had watched her through the window the whole time. She had barely moved, but now the files lay closed in front of her.

'How did you get on?' Munch asked once he was back at the table.

She didn't seem to have registered his return. Her blue eyes were wide open, but her thoughts were far away.

'Sorry,' she said eventually, and ran her hand through her dark hair.

'It's all right,' Munch reassured her, and checked the time.

It was almost forty minutes since he had left his office. Time to wrap this up. It was all very well, an educational test – he had come here as a favour to Yttre and because it had piqued his interest – but there were limits. He had more important things to do. And yes, the same thought had crossed his mind.

Who goes on holiday to Spain and leaves an eleven-year-old boy home alone?

'Some pictures are missing,' the young police student said tentatively.

'I'm sorry?'

She placed her finger on one of the files.

24

'From this one.'

'What do you mean?'

'What I said. Some pictures are missing.'

Munch frowned.

'I'm not sure I quite understand—'

'Well, he would need to be higher up, wouldn't he?'

'Who?'

'The killer.'

The girl looked at him strangely.

'He must have been standing on something.'

Chapter 5

Fredrik Riis parked his car outside the detached house, number 18 Timoteiveien, got out and looked towards the low housing blocks on the other side of the common. Finstad. Between Oslo and Lillestrøm. Near Lørenskog. Not quite a town. Not quite countryside. The twenty-seven-year-old investigator lived in Briskeby, in the heart of Frogner. When he was seventeen his parents had given him his flat, with a view of the iconic old fire station, in the same apartment block where he had always lived. As if they were relieved once he got old enough to be given this gift. *Here you go, a flat for you. From now on you're on your own.*

He had a flashback to a good childhood memory. Family trips to Finstad. His cousins had lived out here, and they would visit often. When Fredrik was a boy, he had loved life out here. So different from the silence in the apartment at home. Rows of big, colourful detached houses with lush gardens and idyllic street names. Timoteiveien, Kløverveien, Tulipanveien, Konvalieveien. As a ten-year-old, he had felt envious of everything this area had to offer a child: sports fields, playgrounds, meadows and not least these almost magical woods in which you could roam free. Children squealing with laughter as they ran through the sprinklers in the large, sunny garden. A place where it seemed as if everyone genuinely cared about each other and actually liked doing things together. He had sat excited in the back of the car every time they returned to the city, listening to the discussion between his parents about whether perhaps they should move out there. His mother was very much in favour, but his father had been against it. *We're not moving to the country.* And that had been the end of it.

The view in front of him now prompted another memory, one not quite so comfortable. *The poor*. That was what his cousins had called them. Those who didn't have a house of their own but lived in the low tenement blocks on the wrong side of the tracks, a stone's throw away. He had felt strange when Munch had asked him if he could be the one from the homicide unit to act as the family liaison officer for the family of Ruben Lundgren, 18 Timoteiveien. *I've been there before, haven't I?* A boy they had played with, a friend of his cousins – Fredrik couldn't remember the name – had lived there, though it was a long time ago, of course.

A new family lived in the big, grey house now. Four new names on the floral nameplate by the door. *Sanna, Ruben, Vibeke and Jan-Otto Lundgren live here.* Cars were parked a little further down the road. Photographers with long lenses. Discreet, but at the same time not. They had yet to release the names of the two boys, but the media already knew them. *There's never any privacy out here, nosy neighbours, busybodies poking their noses into everything*, had been some of his father's rather misanthropic arguments in the discussion in the car.

Ruben Lundgren. Eleven years old.

Found naked in a field less than one kilometre from his home.

Next to another boy.

Tommy Sivertsen. From the housing blocks on the wrong side of the tracks.

Fredrik rang the doorbell, then took a few steps back on to the gravel.

'Yes?'

A face appeared behind the door, which was opened only a little.

'Hello. Jan-Otto Lundgren?'

'Yes?'

The man behind the door gave him a strange look, as if he was struggling to understand that he had a visitor.

'Fredrik Riis. I called earlier?'

'Oh, yes. Hello. Come in.'

An ordinary house. An ordinary galvanized-steel doormat which quivered slightly as he stepped on it and followed the man inside.

An ordinary hallway. Boots and shoes lined up neatly on an Ikea shoe rack. Coats in different sizes and colours on colourful pegs, underneath them a shelf with storage boxes where someone had written *Hats*, *Scarves* and *Gloves* in neat handwriting on sticky labels. The mother, Vibeke Lundberg, aged thirty-eight, is a sales manager for a software firm with a head office near Strømmen shopping centre. The father, Jan-Otto Lundgren, aged forty-two, is a systems engineer working for Telenor. Sanna, aged five, was in the older children's section at Løken nursery school, only a few hundred metres from here.

An ordinary family.

An ordinary life.

Right until that phone call twenty-four hours ago.

Jan-Otto Lundgren attempted something which might be a smile when Fredrik took off his shoes and followed the dazed man into the living room. They had laid the table by the window that overlooked the garden. A Thermos flask. Small, white coffee cups. A bowl of biscuits. The mother, Vibeke, was sitting on one of the spindle-backed chairs with the same dead expression as her husband, and got up slowly when they entered.

'Vibeke Lundgren.'

An almost lifeless hand met his.

'Fredrik Riis. Homicide unit.'

On hearing that, the slim woman recoiled, and he regretted it immediately. He should have opted for something more neutral, just said *Police* and left it at that, but he had spoken automatically – it was his first time acting as a family liaison officer, and he had braced himself for the task on his way here.

Nothing could have prepared him for this, of course. The large house was so quiet that he could hear the ticking of the oval clock hanging by the door to the kitchen. The chair scraping against the parquet flooring when he pulled it out to sit down. The teaspoon clattering against the bottom of the coffee cup when he stirred in the sugar lumps that Vibeke's trembling hands had offered him.

The sound of someone hushing a child further down the passage.

Who is it, Granny? Is it Ruben? Has Ruben come home?

'I'm sorry for disturbing you,' the young investigator said when both parents had sat down. 'I know that we visited you yesterday, but we need to confirm every detail. From now on, I'm going to be your family liaison officer, and if you need anything, I'm here for you, any time, OK?'

He put his hand into the breast pocket of his suit and carefully slid two business cards across the white tablecloth.

'Any news?'

Her voice was thin but still hoarse, like air from feeble lungs catching against the sandpaper in her throat. She had tried to put up her hair in a bun and yet it hung limply on one side. The cream blouse had been buttoned wrongly and sat crooked over her slumped shoulders.

'No, not at the moment. I'm sorry.'

'But you are . . . working on . . .'

Jan-Otto Lundgren was unshaven, had dark brown eyes and spoke in a very soft voice. Like a robot on low battery that didn't know how or why it needed to finish its sentences.

'What's important for us now is to map all Ruben's movements,' Fredrik explained, and opened his notepad. 'I know that you spoke to a police officer yesterday, but I would like to double-check a number of things so we can be sure that everything is correct.'

Jan-Otto Lundgren nodded softly.

'The last time you saw Ruben was Saturday evening, about ten o'clock, is that right?'

'I know we said ten,' Vibeke said, running a hand across her forehead. 'But wasn't it closer to ten thirty? I think—'

'No, it was ten o'clock,' her husband said, putting his hand gently on top of hers. 'After we had watched *The Reunion*, right?'

'*The Reunion?*' Riis echoed.

'Yes, the TV show, do you know it? *The Reunion?*'

Fredrik Riis didn't watch much television, but even he knew what Jan-Otto Lundgren was talking about. Classic Saturday-night entertainment on Norwegian television. The whole country gathered in front of their screens. Two celebrities were reunited with their schoolfriends and had to try to remember who they were.

'He was mad at me,' Vibeke Lundgren said, and was lost to her thoughts once more, this time behind a faint smile. 'He wanted minced beef on his pizza. But Sanna doesn't like it; she just wanted ham. So I fetched him a cola from the basement even though we don't really drink it these days. It's so bad for the teeth, isn't it? All that sugar?'

Her husband stroked her hand again.

'Ruben went to his bedroom after dinner. He was going to play on his computer. But only until eleven – that's the rule.'

'Did you look in on him?' Riis continued. 'Later that night? Did you check that he was asleep?'

There was a moment of silence.

'I really don't know . . .' Vibeke Lundgren began. 'Surely I must have done . . . I always do . . .'

'Sanna had a tummy ache,' her husband said apologetically. 'And she couldn't settle. I read to her in bed, and I must have nodded off as well. When I woke up, it must have been, well . . . half past midnight?'

'So you were with Ruben all evening. You watched TV together. And afterwards, he went to his room. He had no plans, so far as you were concerned?'

'Plans?' Vibeke Lundgren said. 'What plans?'

'No, I'm only asking. He hadn't arranged to meet anyone? Friends? Or maybe a girlfriend?'

'A *girlfriend*?' the slim woman snorted. 'He's only eleven years old. He was at home with his family. Then he went to bed. As he always does. Plans? What plans would they be?'

She looked up confused at her husband, who gripped her thin hand more tightly.

'His window was half open,' Jan-Otto Lundgren said, looking him in the eye now. 'When I went to wake him up for breakfast on Sunday. He must have climbed out.'

'And you don't know when . . .'

'Sometime during the night. That must be what happened.'

'Was this something he was used to doing? Had he run away from home before?'

'No, no, no . . .'

30

She was mumbling now and pulled back her hand.

'He has never gone anywhere. Ruben is always at home. Ruben is the nicest boy in the world. Ruben doesn't climb out of his window. Ruben is always in his bed. Clean bedlinen with a Pokémon design. That's his favourite. I bought two sets so he always has one on. I've just washed the other.'

The mobile in Fredrik's pocket rang. He took it out and glanced at the display.

Anette Goli.

He switched it to silent and placed it on the table in front of him.

'And this Tommy Sivertsen? Was he a friend of Ruben's? I mean, did they usually . . .'

Vibeke Lundgren had got up now and was standing in the middle of the room, looking lost. She was shaking all over and her eyes were unfocused.

'Ruben?'

'I think it might be better if we . . .' her husband said cautiously, and put his arm around her.

'Of course.' Fredrik cleared his throat and put his notepad and mobile back in his jacket pocket.

Back on the crunching gravel, he did what he could to shut out the sound of the desperate howling coming from inside the house.

His mobile vibrated in his pocket.

'Yes, Fredrik here.'

'It's Anette. Where are you?'

'I'm with the Lundgren family.'

'Is it possible for you to leave? I need you.'

'OK, what—'

'We've found something by the shooting range. A well house. It looks as if the boys might have been there. Can you get here? Now?'

'Of course,' Fredrik Riis said, and slipped the phone back into the pocket of his suit jacket as he practically ran down the gravel drive to his car.

Chapter 6

The old man with the white hair knew that some of the people hanging on the wall might get *quite cross* at not having been invited to the dinner party, but it was a proper celebration today and only the inner circle would take part. He had been planning it for days, even ironed the tablecloth. The strange thoughts wouldn't trouble him today. It was a double celebration. Seventy, imagine that! And he had got a new job – that was much more important, wasn't it? And people had said that his acting career was over? Oh, no, it wasn't. The old man smiled, then he let his towel fall to the ground and waded into the cold lake.

He had made his debut at the age of only eighteen in Uddevalla Sixth Form College's annual nativity play. And yes, of course he had wanted to be cast as Joseph, but the innkeeper was nowhere near as small a part as people said. Because who was really the most important character here? The poor guy standing outside the inn begging to be let in? A man who couldn't even make his own wife pregnant? Or the man who was in charge, who decided who could come inside and get a place to sleep? Exactly. There was no contest. He smiled again as he rubbed the bar of soap against his loofah, dipped it in the water and started scrubbing his back. Oh, how beautiful Lake Lilla Köperödssjön was in this light. He had lived here for sixty-four out of his now almost seventy years, first with his mother and grandmother. Then with his mother. Then alone.

Even though . . .

No, he didn't have the energy to think about this now. Soon it would be time to celebrate. With 1.6 kilometres of shoreline, Lake Lilla Köperödssjön was nine metres at its deepest, not five point one, as they claimed at Ray's Garage when he had gone there to ask how much they would charge him to fix up the old Volvo. And they had been angry with him when they had come the long way into the forest and the Volvo hadn't been there after all. Much swearing had ensued. I beg your pardon? How was that his fault? But even so, that moron had shaken his head and spat on the ground in front of him. It was a pity really. Having a car would have been useful, of course. He had carried his bicycle through the forest instead, ridden it all the way to the off-licence in Uddevalla, just for this occasion. Hallands Fläder aquavit: 38 per cent, with notes of elderflower and cinnamon. The old man finished scrubbing himself and dived under the water to rinse off the suds.

What did Stockholm matter now? No, he was not going to think about that.

Allan Edwall, the actor. He would be invited.

He was his first choice, no contest. Because he had to prioritize, decide who would be sitting at the table and who would continue to hang on the wall.

No, thank you. He much preferred the forest outside Uddevalla to dirty Stockholm. This was the place to live.

His second great performance, perhaps the one of which he was proudest, was in prison. As an inmate. Number 112-452311. Sent to prison for indecent exposure in Vasa Park and for handling stolen goods. That production had enjoyed a long run. Fourteen months. He had been very popular in that role.

Ingmar Bergman? A seat at the table?

The old man shook his head and laughed to himself as he got dressed and walked up the small path towards the yard.

Definitely not, for obvious reasons. The idiot didn't even hang on his wall any more.

There were thirty-six pictures on the wall. All of them were genuine Swedish heroes he had met personally. Some only in his dreams, but that made no difference.

Oh bother, he was back at the door and he had quite forgotten to do his seating plan, so he had to walk back down to the lake again.

There was a fine reflection of the sun in it, orange and April yellow in the pretty surface. Lake Lilla Köperödssjön. With 1.6 kilometres of shoreline. Nine metres at its deepest, not five point one, as they had claimed.

Thirty-six pictures on the wall. But he only had room for six at the table. Six pictures. Each would be placed on a chair because he had six chairs.

Did I say chairs?

Eh?

No, places to sit, I said.

He shook his fist in the air.

What do you say to that, Allan? Were you worried you were about to lose your seat?

Eh?

Are you afraid you'll hang on the wall, friendless, while the rest of us knock back Hallands Fläder?

I'm just joking, it's just a bit of fun. Of course, you'll get a seat at the table. You shall have the yellow chair.

He returned to the cottage and stopped deep in thought in front of the pictures on the wall.

Cornelis Vreeswijk. Yes?

Yes.

He carefully removed the drawing pin from the photograph and carried it solemnly across the floor to the table.

The red chair.

Tomas von Brömssen. Maybe.

No, what was he thinking?

Yes.

Yes, obviously.

Tomas von Brömssen.

The blue chair. Three to go, three to go . . .

Why don't we have a drink?

Allan Edwall had already opened the bottle of Hallands Fläder and was about to pour himself a couple of fingers – *it's time to get the party started* – but he managed to stop him at the last moment.

We're not drinking yet, OK?

The old man shook his head and was just putting the bottle as high up as he could in the cupboard over the cooker when the room filled with ringing.

What on earth was that?

He was alarmed and couldn't understand where the sound was coming from before the penny dropped.

The new phone. The mobile.

The job.

He ran across the wooden floor and pulled open the drawer.

A text message on the display.

Act 1. Scene 1. OK?

He typed his reply, smiling.

OK!

The white-haired old man went over to the shelf under the window, pulled out the black ring binder, opened it on page one and took a deep breath.

Then he sat down in front of his other mobile.

Chapter 7

A double-height entrance with columns. Two sliding doors of glass and grey metal opened into a foyer which looked recently renovated. Mia could see that he was trying hard not to make a big deal out of it, except he didn't quite succeed, the investigator with the reddish-blond beard and the warm smile. There was a mixture of curiosity and joy in the otherwise steady and intelligent gaze, as if he couldn't quite believe what he had just witnessed while at the same time he was wondering what to do with it.

It's not always a good thing, Mia. Being able to see more than other people.

Her grandmother was having one of her bad days. She had been ill for a long time but refused to see a doctor; so typical of her. Thin and almost black-eyed, curled up on a mattress on the floor. No bed for her, of course not, this elegant and headstrong woman whom Mia loved so much.

It can make you frightened. And lonely. Other people don't understand what you understand. About life. About people. About how it's all connected. Think of me when I'm gone, promise me, Mia? If you get lonely?

It was just like her grandmother. She might be ill, but she still wanted to be there for Mia. Fortunately, she had recovered some weeks later and would soon be turning eighty. This weekend, in fact. Mia Krüger was looking forward to it. And dreading it. Because she knew how it would be. How her mother would be. If Sigrid didn't turn up.

Which she obviously wouldn't.

Where are you, Sigrid?

Mia Krüger sneaked a peek at her mobile as the cheerful homicide investigator smiled and pressed the button to call the lift.

'Our offices are on the third floor. The unit was formally moved here last autumn, but we're still renovating. Builders – what can you do?'

She had taken to Holger Munch immediately. You can tell instantly if you like someone. Or at least she could.

Holger is someone you can trust, he is honest, you are safe around him, he will help you with anything you might need.

It wasn't always this specific; sometimes it was just a hunch, a good, warm feeling, in contrast to a horrible, bad one. No mumbo-jumbo. At least not as far as she was concerned. Mia had been like this all her life, but she had never imagined that her ability might be useful. As a child, she had believed that everyone was like her. It wasn't until her teens that she realized she was different.

She would turn twenty-two soon.

In six months.

In November.

Sigrid and her.

Last year, she had celebrated on her own.

This year, they would be together.

She had made a vow to herself.

I will find you.

Whatever it takes.

Mia stifled a small yawn as the lift doors opened and a sign appeared.

Oslo Police
Homicide Unit

'Right, welcome to our home.' Munch smiled again, entered a code into a keypad on the grey wall and opened the door to her.

An ordinary office scene, it was almost disappointingly dull. Bits of carpets on the floor in the corridors, partly replaced with parquet flooring. Offices with glass walls, initially an attempt at an open-plan office, the most recent trend in the world of business – synergy, being together, but at the same time not. The obvious need for private conversations had not been compatible with the architect's vision; creamy, rectangular plastic vertical blinds covered the windows in most offices, except for a few which were empty, with room to grow, as Munch had said after their conversation in the café had more or less finished. He had eyed her with the same inquisitive gaze.

'So name your price.'

He had chuckled to himself after he had said it; it was just a joke. She had smiled, but had still realized that his offer was genuine.

Will you come and work with us?

A change of tactic. Why don't you come and see the offices? Say hi to the other members of the team. Did she fancy that?

Right in the middle of a murder investigation.

Even though his phone was flashing constantly.

It was almost thirty hours since the bodies had been found.

Two eleven-year-old boys.

In a field.

The first forty-eight hours are the most important, aren't they?

She had read that in a book.

She was no fool. The apparently casual attitude the lecturer had adopted when they took the UCLA test. *Oh, it's no big deal. It's just for fun. To give you a little training in reading a crime scene. There's no pressure.*

Nor had Mia felt pressured, but the photographs had surprised her. They came alive. It was as if they were talking to her. She had glanced around to see if any of the others in the room were having the same experience, the same thrill, but it didn't look like it. Excited as a little girl given her first picture book, she had let herself disappear into them, and she hadn't come round until the lecturer placed a hand on her shoulder with a pile of sheets to be filled out.

'So this is my office.'

Munch was acting as her tour guide around the rooms, still gently inquisitive, the gravity of the situation on hold for now.

Several more glass cubicles, most of them screened off with long white blinds, but then a change: they turned the corner and arrived at something which genuinely was an open-plan office. Two slightly stressed people looked up from large screens; four in total, placed back to back on a big desk in the centre of the room.

'This is Anja and Ludvig,' Munch said.

A man, possibly in his fifties, rose from his chair and stuck out his hand. He wore half-moon glasses in a steel frame and a burgundy waistcoat with a red knitted tie underneath. He had a broad smile and a warm handshake, with eyes that caught hers.

'Ludvig Grønlie.'

'Hello, Mia Krüger.'

'And this is Anja.'

'Hello.'

The young woman with the tortoiseshell glasses didn't get up; she just glanced at Mia before sighing and turning her attention back to her screen while her busy fingers flew across the keyboard as if playing a piano.

'Are you serious, Munch?'

'Anja Belichek. Our impatient IT wizard. Straight from Harvard.'

'No, still not. Harvard is for low-intelligence posh kids who only get in because they have rich parents. I went to MIT.' The young woman sighed again and ruffled her short brown curls.

She wore a tartan skirt and a pretty white blouse that looked vintage, possibly from the fifties. She had a tattoo of a small, red heart on one wrist.

'We're up to fifty thousand pages now,' the young woman continued, finally turning away from the screen.

'She's right,' said the man called Grønlie.

He took off his glasses and cleaned them on his pale blue shirt, which stuck out from underneath the waistcoat.

'We need more people on this.'

'It's from the Swedish investigation,' Munch explained to Mia. 'We have requested all their case files.'

'And they just keep coming,' the young woman muttered.

With something that looked like a small smile of resignation she scrunched up her nose underneath the thick-lensed glasses and eventually seemed to notice that Mia was there.

'And you are?'

'This is Mia Krüger,' Munch said.

'OK?'

'But seriously, Holger?'

It was Grønlie again, his glasses back on his nose.

'Of course,' Munch said. 'It has already been taken care of. I've asked Wilkinson to put together a team for you down at Police HQ. Seven or eight staff, will that do?'

'Anything is better than nothing,' Anja said.

'You don't want me to go down there?' Grønlie asked. 'To check that they're doing their job? That they're looking for the right information? There's a hell of a lot of material here.'

'Wilkinson will take care of it. I need you here.'

Munch ushered Mia out of the room but stopped in the doorway.

'Yes, come to think of it. Draw up a list of priorities for him.'

'OK.'

Grønlie pulled out a notepad and a pen.

'Leads. Suspects. Witness statements. Families. In that order. All red flags directly to me. I want a report emailed to me every night before midnight.'

'Are you joking?'

Anja was addressing Munch, but Mia could see that her facial expression was friendly.

'There's a bottle of Dworek in it for you if you find anything,' Munch said with a wink.

'Make it a case and we have a deal,' the young woman retorted, and turned her attention back to her screen.

'She's Polish,' Munch said by way of explanation once they were back in the corridor.

He showed her into a large room, and Mia could see it now. The pressure. A clock ticking somewhere behind his eyes. It was just a front. The smile he had plastered on to his face was for her sake.

Thirty hours.

Of course, she had seen the newspapers.

She had read enough books to know what was going on.

It wasn't a game any more.

After the experience she had during the test, she went down to Deichmanske Library straight after the class, and since then she had spent every afternoon there for weeks. She had read everything she could find about crime scenes, serial killers, criminology, pathology and forensics. An attempt to understand what had happened in her head and in her body. And down among the dusty shelves, a fascinating world had opened up to her; it was almost as if she . . .

No, no.

She had to stay focused on Delta, the police force's tactical unit.

It was what she had trained for.

It was what she wanted to become.

The first woman.

She was going to show those bastards.

The jovial, jokey expression on Munch's face had gone now as he turned on more lights and Mia found herself surrounded by the work they were doing here. The facts of the case as opposed to the newspapers' speculation. The photographs he had shown her were displayed on one wall, but there was so much more. Captivated, Mia looked around.

'This is our incident room. This is where it all happens,' Munch explained, still with that burdened expression in his eyes.

Suddenly Mia felt that she was in the way. She had looked at some pictures – so what? – but this was real. More than anything, she wanted to make her excuses, take the lift down, walk back into the street and leave these people in peace to do their job, but the room was so compelling that she stayed where she was.

'I want to remind you that what you're looking at now is confidential.'

'Of course.'

'I'm probably breaking a million rules by just letting you in here.'

'I understand.'

'But after what you told me . . .'

He looked at her as if in agony. Dejection and seriousness written all over his face. It was almost as if she could read his mind.

Two families have lost a child. They will never see their boys again. The whole world is watching us now.

And it's my responsibility to make sure that we get him.

That they get justice.

Do you understand?

'I understand,' Mia said softly.

'What?'

'Sorry, I just—'

She broke off as the door behind them opened and a woman in her early thirties rushed inside. A stern gaze, blonde shoulder-length hair and clothes which made Mia place her in a bank rather than with the police.

'Where have you been? I called you a hundred times. We think we may have found the van. Oxen has—'

Munch interrupted her.

'Anette, meet Mia Krüger.'

The blonde woman stopped in her tracks and gave her an odd look.

'Mia, this is Anette Goli. My right hand.'

'Hello,' Mia said cautiously.

'So what?' the woman who had just arrived wondered out loud as she threw up her hands. 'We have two sightings of the same van, one by the Metro Centre in Lørenskog and the other just outside Lillestrøm harbour, we ought to—'

'Just give us two seconds,' Munch interrupted her again, and turned to Mia.

'Please would you take another look? For Anette's sake? Tell her what you told me?'

The friendliness was back in his eyes.

'Now?' Mia said.

'Yes.'

Munch smiled faintly and gestured towards the pictures on the wall.

Chapter 8

Fredrik Riis held up his warrant card, was allowed through the cordon and parked his car near a sign saying *Lørenskog Rifle Association. Founded in 1891.* Two old, brown rifles decorated the oval logo that greeted him as he got out of his car.

He was met by a familiar face, an encounter he could have done without. Erik Brun. An old classmate from the National Police Academy. Though calling him a mate would be an exaggeration – an idiot from his year would be more appropriate. The burly police officer waddled across the yard, and his face, too, fell when he saw Fredrik.

'If it isn't the Posh Boy as I live and breathe.'

Brun ran a hand over his chin and made a point of not extending it to Fredrik.

'Hello,' Fredrik said, ignoring the other man's rudeness.

It was the best way with people like that. They had patrolled the streets together for several months, which explained the surly face he was now met with. Envy, pure and simple. There had been a vacancy in the Violent Crimes Unit at Police HQ. A dream job. He knew that Brun had also applied for the position, but Fredrik Riis had got it.

You're still in uniform, I see?

But he was not going to stoop to Brun's level. Good manners. It was the only positive quality he had taken away from his home.

Oslo was a small town. Fredrik Riis knew the origins of his nickname perfectly well and how fast it had travelled through the ranks. Excited and a little nervous at having got the job in the Violent Crimes Unit, he had called the duty officer before his first day at work and enquired about the dress code. The duty officer had played a practical joke at the stupid rookie's expense. *Suit and tie. The Violent Crimes Unit absolutely insists on it.* Perhaps he should have smelled a rat, but then again, he was young, gullible and, more importantly, nervous. He had turned up in his best suit and a freshly ironed shirt. He had spent hours on it; he had even gone out to buy a better iron. Italian shoes polished until they shone. A small handkerchief neatly tucked into the breast pocket. Even a tie pin, solid gold, which he had inherited from his grandfather. So proud that he couldn't stand still, his first team briefing in his new job. He had stepped out of the lift, only to be met by several smiling faces. Like a clown. That was how he had felt. Super-awkward. Very tense. The room had been eerily quiet. The only sound was the squeaking of his new leather shoes against the linoleum. He had run the gauntlet to the desk with his name on it, and then the laughter had erupted.

Never mind.

It had worked out fine in the end.

People were friendly.

And then, in a moment of madness, of defiance, he had decided to embrace his nickname.

Why not?

With his head held high, he had turned up for work, smartly dressed, every single day ever since. It was the only way to shut them up. He had stuck to this style of dressing. A little more relaxed now, he had dropped the tie, but kept the suit.

'What have we got?'

'A well house, right down there.' Erik Brun pointed. 'Forensics are still there. We were told to stay away. They think they're better than us, keeping us away so we don't *contaminate*. Who do they think we are?'

Brun looped his thumbs through his belt and spat into the gravel.

A bunch of morons, probably.

'Good to see you, Erik.'

He patted the bulky officer on his shoulder and continued down to the shooting range towards three forensic technicians in white coveralls.

44

Spring had finally arrived. Trees in various shades of green lined the gravel road. Two gulls took off from the roof of the range and disappeared across the fields with a screech. Fredrik Riis hated winter. Something he and Munch had in common. They were city boys – that might explain it. Out here, it was probably different, white, with snow-covered hills good for sledging or ski jumping. Not like the centre of Oslo, only a slushy darkness, wet streets and shivering people. He had read somewhere that they had stopped teaching schoolchildren that snow was white, because everyone could see that it was grey. If it settled at all, that is. He had some friends who pestered him to come skiing with them every year. In the Alps. St Moritz. Seefeld. Slalom. Or snowboarding. But it held no appeal for him. He stayed mostly indoors during winter, in front of the fireplace with his stamps and his pet bird, waiting for the sky to grow lighter again. So he could breathe. There was a ping from the pocket of his suit jacket and he stopped halfway down the gravel road to check his phone.

Hell.

Will I see you tonight?

Fredrik considered the offer for a brief moment, but he already knew what the answer would be.

No.

He waited a few seconds for the reply which he knew was coming.

Why not?

He shook his head in despair and dropped the phone back into his pocket.

'Are you from the Homicide Unit?'

A forensic technician came walking up the road towards him.

'Yes, my name is Riis.'

'Hello, I'm Janne.'

She slipped off one blue latex glove and shook hands with him.

'What have we got?'

'An old well house. A member of the search team discovered it some hours ago. I fear they may have trampled all over it, but we've done what we could to save any evidence there was.'

45

She pulled the hood from her head and nodded irritably up towards the officers he had just left.

'You would have thought they taught them better at the Academy, wouldn't you?'

She gestured for him to follow her down to the trees.

'But you're finished now? So I'm good to enter?'

She nodded. 'We have collected prints from the lock and everything else we could find.'

A small metal padlock lay on the ground in front of the dilapidated well house, which had once been painted red.

'It was locked?'

'No. The lock was hanging from the bolt.'

'OK,' Riis said, slipping on his gloves.

'You'll need this,' the forensic technician said, handing him a large torch. 'It's strangely dark in there. It's so old you would think light would slip through the gaps between the planks, but someone has insulated it on the inside. With black roofing felt. It looks like someone has used it for . . .'

The technician pulled out a packet of cigarettes from a pocket underneath her coverall.

'Used it for what?'

'That's the thing. For something. It's not often that a crime scene sends a shiver down my spine. Oh, yes, that reminds me . . .'

She went over to a large suitcase and took out a clear plastic evidence bag.

'Underwear?'

'We don't know if it belongs to one of the boys, but the chances are high, wouldn't you say?'

The blonde forensic technician shuddered, then nodded towards one of the other technicians, who was approaching her with a lighter and lit her cigarette.

'Is it all right for me to go inside?'

'Be my guest.'

Fredrik Riis turned on the torch and ducked as he entered through the small door.

Bloody hell.

Chapter 9

Click. And the world around you disappears. Nothing but these photographs now. Take all the time you need. There's no one else here. Only you and the pictures. Place the pictures next to one another. Vertically and horizontally so that they form a square on the desk in front of you. Don't pick too many. Pick the pictures which give you the most complete impression. Don't swap them around once you get started. The entire process must take place in one go, no pausing. Have you got the pictures you need? Can you see the big picture? The detailed shots you think you need? Use a sentence, a sound or the taste of something in your mouth to remove the last remnants of reality around you. If you meditate, you'll know what I'm talking about. It can be something completely absurd. As long as your body and your mind know what is at stake. Are you ready? Then we'll begin.

Think about Granny.

Mia shut out the world and concentrated fully on the pictures, which lay carefully arranged on the desk in front of her. It felt better this time. She had been inside their world recently and she didn't have to dread them or be scared of what she might find. She could really enter into it now. Even more deeply than the last time. Because there was something she hadn't seen, wasn't there? Not only that some pictures were missing. No, it was more than that. A gap. In the story. In the pictures she already had. Something that was wrong. Something she hadn't picked up on initially which screamed out at her and yet she still couldn't see it. Mia closed her eyes and tried not to let herself be irritated by the blonde woman, who had switched her mobile to silent, as she had been told, but had forgotten to switch off its vibration mode. In her jacket pocket. A suit jacket for a woman. Tailor-made, not mass produced, or if it was, then it was not from a high-street shop. Sky blue. A neutral and serene colour. No impulsive decisions. I am calm. Reflective. That noise from the jacket again. Wool and viscose. Three buttons. Pockets on either side, just above the hips.

'Sorry, do you mind . . .'

Mia turned to the woman called Anette and nodded in the direction of the quivering mobile.

'Of course. I'm sorry.'

A stiff smile around pursed lips, a quick glance at Munch, followed by a light shaking of the head.

What the f—, Holger?

You know the clock is ticking, don't you?

OK, Mia.

Easy does it.

Think about Granny.

Two practically naked boys are lying in a field. One has short, blond hair. He is lying on his back. With one hand on his chest. The other is at an angle further away. The face of the first boy appears calm. Some freckles on his small nose. My first impression is that he reminds me a little of a cherub. The kind they put on stickers. Leaning over a cloud. This boy is naked. His penis is small and he has just a few pubic hairs above it. They are also blond, the same shade as the curls on his head. No hairs on his testicles. You already know his age, but if you had to guess, you would have said that he was ten years old. He is eleven. He is short for his age. Skinny. Fragile. Could easily pass for a nine-year-old, in fact. His limbs are slim. His legs seem too long for his short body. You can imagine him running now. He is a fast runner. He is like the wind, smiling and breathless as he crosses the finishing line before the others. Delete that. You don't know that. If he competes. But he is a fast runner. He has a blue line around his neck. He was strangled. From behind. With something thin. Not a metal wire, it would have left different marks on his skin. A fishing line? Possibly. You can feel that he is struggling to breathe. His chest starts to gasp for air. Why doesn't he raise his hands to defend himself? No injuries. Not on any of his fingers or on his arms or anywhere else on his white body. Yes, a few bruises. One on his elbow, one on his left knee. But they have nothing to do with this. The photograph of his fingers. You would have liked to have seen them even closer up, under a microscope, but this will have to do. Because this is the first thing you notice. His killer took his time with him. No boys have nails that clean. He has cut them. Cleaned them. Arranged the fingers attractively, carefully, in a small fan as if on a painting. A portrait of a hand. A still life. Perhaps a Rembrandt. Or a Caravaggio. This boy. You know his name is Ruben now. The hand on his chest is covered by a white plaster cast. The fingers just about stick out from the opening, but they are just as well groomed as on the other hand. What did you do, Ruben? Did you fall off your bike? Punch the wall with your fist? No, you're not the type. Your shoulders slump a little. Perhaps you are ashamed of your long legs. No, maybe it's not that. But there is something. Have you been bullied? Over a long period of time? By adults? Have you been very scared? Only such children end up with hunched shoulders; they protect you against the outside world. The other children like you. They write on your plaster cast. With different felt-tip pens. In different colours. There's a girl you have a crush on, or she has a crush on you. Sylvia. There is a red heart around her name on your plaster cast. What happened to your hand, Ruben? Is it related to your hunched shoulders? You are certainly the main character in this scene. The protagonist. The other boy is merely a supporting character. He isn't as handsome. He hasn't been cleaned as carefully. He isn't even completely naked. He wears old, dark blue underpants. The elastic is limp. They have clearly been washed countless times. They are practically falling apart. He has been dumped next to you. His face hasn't even been turned towards the sky. A glimpse of the two other boys now, the boys from Sweden. The same positions. One completely naked. The other not. The boys found on Sunday were not killed in the field. They were placed there for a reason. It's no coincidence. It has been carefully planned. All of it. Down to the smallest detail. An animal has been placed in between them. A small, red fox. It looks peaceful. As if it is asleep. Its eyes are shut. Its paws are stuck out in front of it. Its face is turned towards the boy who

49

looks like a cherub. Why didn't the people who took these photos understand that this is important? That we need to be higher up? To see the full picture? That is what matters.

Mia Krüger suddenly felt unwell, almost nauseous, and had to retreat from the pictures; she stayed on the chair with one hand covering her face, struggling to breathe properly.

'Everything all right?'

Munch with his kind eyes back in the real world. The clock by the screen on the end wall showed that only three minutes had passed. It had felt much longer.

'Sure, yes, fine,' Mia mumbled, and exhaled calmly through her nose in order to quell the pounding heartbeat under her black polo-neck jumper.

Why had she agreed to this? Being treated like this? A circus freak? Made to perform in front of two complete strangers?

Hell no.

That's enough.

Go home. Back to her own life. Get some sleep.

Then out into the dark streets.

To find Sigrid.

'Now what . . .' the blonde woman said.

The woman who was called Anette Goli was perched on a desk with her arms folded across the blue jacket, her body language indicating clearly that she thought this was a waste of time.

'In short,' Munch said, and went up to the photographs on the wall, 'Mia thinks that there's a place . . .'

He pointed to one of the pictures.

'Where there must have been a stool. Or a stepladder. Something like that, isn't that right?'

Mia nodded briefly.

'And that's important because . . .' Goli heaved a sigh.

'The boys weren't killed in the field. Their bodies were laid out there, isn't that what you're saying, Mia?'

'Yes.'

'The killer was meticulous,' Munch went on, eager now. 'The fingers. Cleaned. The bodies posed just like he wanted them. Killed in such a way that they have no injuries, damage or bloodstains; they're as clean as possible, except for the lines around their necks. And then . . .'

He looked towards Mia now, as if to give her the credit, but she made a dismissive gesture: the mood didn't feel quite so hostile any more.

'It's a painting,' Munch said triumphantly. 'A work of art. Two dead boys in a field. He needs to get higher up in order to document it.'

'OK?' Goli said in an inquisitive voice, having set aside some of her scepticism now.

She looked at Mia with interest, then back at the photographs.

'But what about the animals? A fox? And the hare? From the Swedish crime scene.'

'I don't know,' was all Mia said.

'You say *he*,' Goli said. 'We're sure it's a man?'

Munch looked at Mia.

'Yes,' she said quickly, and got up from the chair. 'Anyway, I have to go, so, that's me signing off. Good luck with it all.'

She left the room as quickly as she could and she was halfway down the corridor before Munch caught up with her. He really wasn't in good shape. He was panting over his round belly while he looked at her with the same curious gaze as in the lift.

'You're sure you don't—'

'No, thank you,' Mia said firmly, and opened the door.

He continued to follow her on her way out.

'Here,' he said, giving her his card. 'Call me. Any time. If you change your mind. Or if you remember something else. OK?'

'OK,' Mia said, stuffing the card into the back pocket of her jeans as the doors to the lift beeped and then opened slowly.

Back in the street, the spring air seemed even more refreshing than usual.

Mia stood very still on the pavement until the pounding under her jumper finally subsided.

Then she walked as calmly as she could on towards Hausmanns gate.

In order to catch the tram home to Torshov.

Chapter 10

She had set the alarm for nine thirty that evening, but she woke up as early as nine. The wall was pounding with music from another bedroom and Mia realized she had forgotten today was Monday. The second-year students started late on Tuesdays so this had become a habit. Monday beers. Pre-loading in Vogts gate. A dozen tarted-up, giggling police students. Squeezed into the small living room. Mia considered saying something but quickly abandoned the idea. They were already giving her strange looks as it was. If they wanted to drink themselves into a stupor, well, that was up to them. But did they have to do it where she lived? In the tiny flat which was already cramped as it was? Three of them shared it, but sometimes it felt like there were many more. The bathroom was never free. You never had any peace to cook in the kitchen. Mia had lived in Torshov for almost eighteen months now and, when the weather allowed, she spent as much time outdoors as she could. She liked sitting in Torshov park with a book. Or riding a bike to Maridalen to swim. Rather that than sit in the claustrophobic flat and listen to their wittering. Chatting about nothing. She was practically allergic to such people. Solitude was infinitely preferable. Roam the streets. Also at night. Two birds, one stone. Alone with her own thoughts.

And she could look for Sigrid at the same time.

She felt a strong urge to have a shower, but that was obviously out of the question tonight, so instead she put on her tight black jeans, found a black T-shirt and a thin but warm black jumper. She pulled out her big rucksack from its hiding place in her wardrobe and packed it with what she needed. Gloves. Torch. More flyers. How many? Fifty? The bag started to fill up.

52

Have you seen this girl?
Sigrid Krüger.
Please call me if you know anything!

She would have to drop by the Academy office soon, plead her way to more photocopies. Mia attached the arm holster so that the handle of the knife would fit right under her left armpit. A black EKA Nordic knife in solid metal throughout with a rubberized handle which made it light while still providing a good grip. Carrying a knife on the streets of Oslo was illegal, obviously, and if she was caught, she risked losing her place at the National Police Academy, but there was no way she was spending a whole night in this city without something to defend herself with. People were so naive, weren't they? The tram to and from work. Dinner with family and friends. In the daylight. Mediocre entertainment on the television, stupefying but good enough before going to bed feeling pleasantly contented. Nice Oslo. Safe Norway. Where everyone smiled as they wandered around in their anoraks. *Hi, hi. How nice to see you.*

Right until darkness fell.

And the cockroaches came crawling out.

Mia slipped the knife into the arm holster, laced up her Doc Marten boots, put on a black hoodie and pulled the hood over her head. Then she took one last look at herself in the mirror next to the wardrobe before she left.

She liked what she saw. It was almost a disguise. A shield against anything she might encounter in the streets.

She bowed her head, made her way through the noise and was soon on the tram heading into the city centre.

Oslo Central Station.

Plata.

She always started there.

It was where the junkies hung out.

Heroin?

Mia couldn't believe her own ears when her sister had blurted it out. Sigrid hadn't meant to tell her, but Mia had cornered her.

What the hell is going on with you, Sigrid? I hardly ever see you these days. I thought we were going to hang out together. Have fun?

Be students. In Oslo. I called your college – yes, I actually did – and they said you're not a student there any more. That you had stopped showing up. A nurse. I thought you were going to be a nurse. What the hell is going on?

I'm not shooting up.

We only smoke it.

Her sister, exhausted and gaunt, her eyes glazed underneath the once beautiful long blonde hair.

Shooting up?

Smoking?

What the hell are you talking about?

Sigrid.

The nicest, loveliest, most conventional girl in all of Åsgård-strand.

Who played handball, went horse-riding, did well at school and volunteered at an old people's home.

No.

At first she had thought it must be a joke.

That someone would appear with a camera, wash the matte make-up off her sister's hollow face, throw confetti in the air, applause and laughter, that the whole thing was just something they had made up in order to play a prank on her.

I will quit, you know.

Christ, Sigrid . . .

Of course I'll quit, only not right now. And yes, I owe people money. Not a lot, just a few thousand kroner. Could you tide me over? Just for a few days? Please?

They had gone there together.

To the ATM.

Mia had withdrawn practically all the money she had.

Ten thousand kroner.

That was three months ago now. The last time she had seen her.

Where are you, Sigrid?

Mia Krüger pulled a couple of flyers out of her bag and mingled with the crowd. Christian Frederiks Plass, known as Plata. Halfway between the railway station and the Oslo Stock Exchange. Named

54

after a Danish king who once ruled Norway and drank his tea in the well-tended palace gardens. Where the city's junkies now met. It wasn't very regal these days. The dregs of humanity. The losers. The tourists had complained. It was where they stepped off the airport train to visit beautiful Oslo, and this was their first impression. Horse, H, hero, smack, heroin. Trembling, thin, filthy fingers over torn jogging pants and threadbare puffa jackets. A thousand kroner per gram. Five hits per gram. Scrunched-up tinfoil with a lighter underneath. Bubbling, hissing. The tip of a syringe sucking in the amber fluid. A red rubber tube around a skinny arm to make the veins stand out on the skin. Cut-down drinking straws from Burger King just up the road. For those who preferred smoking it. Shivering figures, humanlike zombies, circling the cold tarmac, hunched over the precious substance with these white, home-made pipes in their mouths. Mia had almost thrown up the first time she caught a whiff of the strong smell. Someone had lit up right next to her. A young lad and a young girl. No more than fifteen or sixteen years old. Why, God, why? She had been distraught. It had felt as if all the decency in the world was sucked out of her. All the goodness. All the beauty. Gone in an instant. The sight of these young people in the street. Practically dead already. The degradation. And then the smiles that spread across their young faces as the drug kicked in and brought them a few brief moments of escape from their miserable lives.

'Hi, Polly. How are you?'

She had been here many times now. At first they had avoided her. Junkie instinct. They could see it in her eyes. That she wasn't here to score. That she was an outsider. But in time they had grown used to her, let her into their circle.

She's just looking for her sister. Hey, has anyone seen her sister? What's your name again? Does anyone know anything?

Do you have any cash? For a bus fare? A cup of coffee? Spare some change?

Sigrid – does anyone know her?

Sigrid? The new girl from Horten?

The exhausted-looking girl in front of her nodded slowly. She was struggling to keep her eyes open, yet somehow she managed to stay upright. World champions in endurance, these junkies. Zero food. Zero sleep. Zero nourishment. And yet, day in and day out, they kept going like a perpetual-motion engine with no fuel other than a fix from time to time.

Polly's eyes seemed to light up a little when she saw her.

'Hey, is that you? What are you doing here?'

The junkie glanced about furtively, then pulled the grey cardigan more closely around her body. A mumbling, lethargic voice came from her dry, cracked lips.

'We agreed?' Mia ventured cautiously. 'That I would come here tonight. With a present for you. Remember?'

The cogs turned slowly in the head under the filthy baseball cap.

'Oh yeah. Shit.'

The young girl's face suddenly erupted in a hopeful smile.

'So did you bring it?'

'Yes,' Mia said, with a nod of her head to the rucksack on her back. 'You're going to help me, remember? You said you might know where Sigrid was?'

Polly furrowed her brows and looked about her again. 'Not here. Follow me,' the young junkie said, and led the way with shuffling footsteps towards a corner of the railway station.

Another glance around. Paranoia.

Then again, Plata wasn't the safest place in the world.

'Can I see it?' The girl smiled with curiosity and briefly scratched her face.

'Sure,' Mia said, taking off her rucksack. 'But you were going to help me, remember?'

'Yes, sure.' The girl nodded nervously. 'What colour is it?'

'You wanted a pink one, didn't you?' Mia said, and took the doll out of her rucksack.

Polly. From Bergen. The first to come up to her. With a leaflet in her hand.

I know who she is.

Sigrid.

I've seen her.

That was three weeks ago now, and Mia had been here every single night since, but to no avail. The young junkie with the matted hair seemed to have vanished into thin air, but tonight she was finally back.

I can help you. I think.

But I want something in return.

A present? Can you do that?

Mia's bank account was almost empty. Again. Naively and like an amateur, she had given people money. For tip-offs. *Yes, I know her. Give me three hundred kroner and I'll make a phone call.* They weren't Good Samaritans, these junkies, it was purely a question of survival, as well as finding suckers to con, and in time she had wised up and stopped her charity, but this girl's request had been so unusual that Mia hadn't had the heart to say no.

A Cabbage Patch doll.

I had one when I was a little girl.

She looked after me.

Do you think you can get me one?

Mia rarely cried, hardly ever, but on her way home that morning she hadn't been able to stop herself. She was exhausted. Sleep deprived. No sign of Sigrid anywhere. All this misery. And then this poor girl wanted a doll?

How pitiful.

And yes, of course. Of course you can have a doll.

She had gone to a toy shop the moment she woke up – she hadn't even eaten breakfast – and spent the last of her money. She was now behind with her rent, but sod it, it could wait.

It was as if a shining light had been turned on in the young girl's tired eyes as she took the doll and clutched it to her cheek. Two brief seconds, and then her old expression returned before she quickly unzipped her cardigan and slipped the doll inside it.

'Thank you so much.'

'You're welcome. But you said that you knew something, remember?'

The girl nodded nervously and glanced anxiously about herself again.

'But you didn't hear this from me, OK?'

'No, of course not.'

'They'll kill me.'

'What?'

The girl was mumbling now, whispering. Mia could barely hear her.

'They say she's one of the new ones. Who travels. Diamonds in Majorstuveien.'

'Travels? What do you mean?'

Suddenly the girl jumped. Something was happening across the street: a loud disagreement, feet stomping across the tarmac, something flashing.

And it stopped being safe.

Faces making their way across the square towards them.

Hey, Polly, what are you up to?

'Markus Skog,' the girl mumbled, and she bowed her head and tightened her cardigan around her waist before half running out into the darkness, and then she was gone.

What?

Mia could feel the rage surge in her. She had to retreat from the questioning faces coming towards her so she wouldn't harm them.

Markus Skog.

Markus *fucking* Skog.

She was frothing at the mouth as she left the square and the junkies, and stopped, panting, at the entrance to Byporten while she tried to calm herself down.

Easy now, Mia. Don't get angry.

Even though you want to kill him. Even though he deserves to rot in hell. Because that's not going to help Sigrid, is it?

Mia pushed down her hood and took some deep breaths.

Suddenly she felt so tired, having no strength left.

Even though it hadn't been long since she had woken up from a long sleep.

A car drove past her with open windows. Young people waving bottles and screaming to music, on their way to the big city to party in the streets of Oslo tonight. She had a sudden flashback when she heard the music they were playing.

Weezer.

A geek rock band from California which Sigrid had insisted that she listen to.

It was the first time Mia had thought: *Something is wrong*.

Lovely Sigrid.

Who liked Celine Dion and Whitney Houston.

Who had posters of Backstreet Boys and NSYNC on her walls.

'Listen to this, Mia, isn't it cool?'

One summer evening in the garden in Åsgårdstrand. Just the two of them. Their parents were out and they had the house to themselves. Sister party. Champagne, strawberries and that pink fish soup Sigrid always made which didn't taste of very much and yet it wouldn't be the same if it did.

The car with the whooping young people disappeared down the street, but the music lingered in her ears.

Weezer.

The first time she had talked about him, they had been in the garden underneath the lamps.

Markus Skog. A musician from Horten, whom she was in love with.

Mia mustn't tell their parents because they wouldn't like him.

Because he was different and had a hard life. But he was going to change and she had promised to help him. He was ever so clever, really, and sensitive.

This music, listen to this.

Look, look at the logo . . .

Dancing barefoot in her white dress on the warm grass while she smiled in a way Mia had never seen her smile before, almost as if Mia weren't present, so happy, holding up her fingers so they formed a W.

Weezer.

Bloody Markus Skog.

This was all his fault.

Mia pulled the hood back over her head and stomped towards the traffic lights. She was just about to press the button when a thought suddenly came to her.

Shit . . .

She patted the back pocket of her jeans, shaking almost as badly as Polly had, then she remembered that her mobile was in her rucksack; she pulled it out and entered the number with trembling fingers.

'Munch here?'

'I think I've got it.'

'Who's this?'

'Mia. Mia Krüger. I think I've discovered what it was I didn't see earlier.'

'Go on?'

'The plaster cast. The boy's plaster cast. He had broken his wrist, hadn't he?'

'Er, yes—'

'He wrote on it.'

'Who?'

'The killer. He signed it.'

'Everyone else wrote their full name,' Mia continued. 'Except him. He only wrote a capital letter. Check for yourself. I'm an idiot for not spotting it sooner.'

'Can we talk about it tomorrow morning?' Munch sounded sleepy. 'We have a team briefing at nine a.m. Will you be there?'

'I'll think about it.'

'OK, great.'

Mia smiled to herself and dropped her mobile into her rucksack as the light in front of her changed from red to green.

TWO

Chapter 11

Twelve-year-old Lydia Clemens was squatting on her haunches in the forest with a firm grip on the taut bow, feeling sad that the world was about to end. That the beauty which surrounded her would soon disappear. The liverleaf by the tree stump. The deer grazing on the moor. The green leaves on the tall birch tree underneath which she would often rest when she was out on one of her trips. Soon it would be gone. And all because the people out there weren't good and had wrecked the planet. She didn't know precisely when the world would end, but it wouldn't be long, her grandfather, William, had told her. That was why the two of them lived alone out here and had learned to survive without needing anyone's help. It would be like a long, dark winter. *The long time*, he called it. Everyone would have to fend for themselves until Mother Earth had got rid of all the bad people, those who couldn't take care of each other and the planet.

She had counted fourteen different spring flowers just on her way up here. In addition to liverleaf, which was her favourite. Like all the other flowers and plants around her, liverleaf also had a Latin name, or its real name, as her grandfather had explained during the lessons in their cottage. *Hepatica nobilis*. Hepatica because it meant liver, a large organ behind the rib cage on the right-hand side which the body used to cleanse itself. The leaves of the plant were shaped like a liver.

Her grandfather had taught her about the Doctrine of Signatures, an ancient belief that *like* cures *like*. Since liverleaf had leaves shaped like the liver, these had been used to treat liver disease. Other plants in the forest were also named after their usage, such as the mandrake. Its root resembled the human body and, for that reason,

63

people believed that it could cure anything, and before people had wrecked the planet with their new technology, these roots had been very expensive and regarded almost as sacred.

They had given her some funny looks, the two teachers she had to talk to once a year. They had shaken their heads on their first visit to the small cottage and she had overheard their conversation when they thought she wasn't listening: *Surely this is no place for a child?*

Her grandfather had become incredibly angry. He had almost thrown a fit when she told him what she had overheard and asked him what Child Protection Services were. Normally, he was nothing like this. He was friendly and kind and very funny, and Lydia felt lucky that she would get to spend *the long time* with him. No one was as clever as her grandfather. He was like a walking enyclopaedia. Lydia herself hadn't been to many places, but she had been to Vassenden when they ran out of goods they couldn't grow for themselves, such as sugar.

However, she knew a great deal about the world from her lessons. History. And Natural Sciences. They were Lydia's favourite subjects. And Physics. Oh no, she had almost forgotten Maths, which really was her favourite subject. Her grandfather was the nicest teacher in the world because he made everything he told her exciting, unlike the people who came to check on her once a year, who hadn't known what the Doctrine of Signatures was. Mathematics. The numbers in everything. In the bowstring, which she now pulled tight in front of her right eye. In the leaves of the ash trees at the far end of the moor, which had now also turned green. Once when she had put her arms around a tree, she had almost heard it whisper: *You're the princess. Of the long time.* And ever since then she had visited them almost daily, unless there was too much work to do in the cottage. Which there often was, because preparing for what was coming was no mean feat. The cottage was too small for them to store everything there. They had only the kitchen, the washbasin, her grandfather's room, her room and the schoolroom. So it was a stroke of luck that her grandfather had spent nearly his whole life digging a secret bunker which had a concealed entrance no one could find unless they knew where it was.

There was so much room there! It was also furnished so that they could sleep there and be safe when the bad people started their wars. Because that was how it would begin. Wars had already broken out in other parts of the world. Most evenings, once she had read a little in one of the books which her grandfather borrowed for her from the library in Vassenden and was getting ready to go to bed, he would tell her the latest news from the world outside. Lydia knew what newspapers and the Internet and TV were, of course she did, but they didn't have them out here in the forest. Because they only spread lies. But her grandfather had a radio. Not one of those with a tiny aerial sticking out of it, no, this was a proper radio. A long-wave radio. It had its own room in the bunker and her grandfather would use it to talk to other people like them. Who were also good, who were preparing, and once it was all over, they would travel and meet up on a planet which was clean, good and beautiful.

They're fighting in Sri Lanka now.

Her grandfather was standing behind her while she brushed her blonde hair so it wouldn't get tangled.

They're fighting in Angola now.

When she washed off the ash she had put on her cheeks to go hunting so the sun wouldn't reflect too strongly in her eyes.

They're still fighting in Afghanistan.

When she cleaned her teeth.

They're killing each other on the West Bank again.

Lydia had never seen a war; she had only read about them and heard what her grandfather had told her. War meant that ordinary people like them started killing each other with weapons because they disagreed about something. They didn't seem to be able to make up their minds and so they killed each other instead. And sometimes they couldn't agree on who owned which parts of a country or if a mountain or a river belonged to this one or that one, and then they would start to kill each other to decide.

Lydia lowered her bow and felt sad again that the beauty all around her would disappear. She had no friends, she knew no other children, so this was pretty much all she had. Not that it wasn't enough, oh no, she loved the trees, the river, the birds, and she would really be very sad the day the darkness reached this place. Strange, really. How fragile everything was. Like now, for instance. The deer had been in her sights. If she had let go of the string, the arrow would have flown across the moor, pierced the heart of the beautiful animal and its life would be over. It would no longer breathe, its heart would stop beating in less than a second purely because she had moved her fingers and released the string – how strange was that? Why wasn't everything around them a bit – well, tougher? She had asked her grandfather about it one day and he had scratched his big beard, shaken his head and looked at her with his warm, brown eyes and said: *I wish I knew, sweetheart.*

And that was when she realized that although her grandfather was probably the cleverest man in the world, he didn't know everything.

For example, he didn't know that she missed other children. Having someone to play with.

Or about the other house deep in the forest. He knew nothing about that.

And that she was making her way to the house now, going there as often as she dared to look through the windows.

Sometimes the man who lived there would have his TV on.

She felt bad about it and yet she couldn't stop herself.

Oh, it was so exciting.

She had seen a puppet frog talking to a puppet pig who seemed to be a kind of princess because she wore a really pretty pink dress and she could make things disappear by waving a magic wand.

Lydia glanced up at the faint sun and calculated the time.

Yes, it would be fine.

She could be back in plenty of time for dinner.

Chapter 12

Tuesday morning. Forty-eight hours had passed. Fredrik Riis couldn't remember the last time he had slept so badly as he stepped into the lift to go up to the third floor. Normally an investigation didn't trouble him. The first time he had seen a body, yes, of course he had reacted – an old lady had been killed in her own bed in Sagene, and he had been one of the first people on the scene – but this? He pushed the lift button and tried to pull himself together. He caught a glimpse of his face in the shiny doors, but turned away. He couldn't bear to look at himself right now. It had been the same at home in the bathroom earlier this morning as he fumbled for the toothbrush. Fredrik couldn't get the images out of his mind. What he had seen in the small, red well house. It was almost unreal, the kind of crime scene you only saw in the movies, so evil, so dark. He had tossed and turned in his bed, almost desperate; he knew what the next day would bring and that he would need all the strength he had. The team briefing after the first forty-eight hours. A turning point, always, once these first two days had elapsed. He had worked with Munch on five cases now, and his experienced chief always followed the same procedure. No theories during the first two days. Just gather information. Unless they had facts, something concrete to investigate. Riis had protested during his first homicide investigation. Munch had been calm whereas Fredrik had been outraged and desperate. An old woman murdered in her own home – why didn't they *do* something? *It's a marathon, not a sprint.* Fredrik Riis glanced at the mirrored surfaces anyway as the lift pinged, just to check that he didn't look a complete wreck, which was how he felt. Was it his turn this time? To get it? He had heard stories of the most

67

hard-boiled investigators who had worked for decades without ever reacting, but then suddenly, completely out of the blue, a case would arrive which would get to them so badly that it broke them. Was this case going to break him?

He had bowed his head and entered through the small door to the well house.

The smell. He hadn't known what it was, but there was something. Something rotten. Inhuman.

Magazines on the floor. Topless women on the covers. Some kind of bait, porn magazines, exciting to eleven-year-old boys.

Bottles along one wall.

Cola. Fanta.

Empty bags of sweets.

He had felt a hint of nausea.

Fredrik Riis stuffed his shirt into his trousers, swept his blond fringe to the side and attempted an expression that looked vaguely normal as the lift doors opened.

The incident room. He tried not to look directly at the new photographs pinned up on the end wall and took a seat at the back. Was it just a brief episode? A minor shock? It was bound to pass.

Everyone was here, and he felt strangely better now. They were in it together.

'OK, everyone,' Munch said impatiently up by the large screen; he didn't look like he had slept much either.

His hair was messy. The same grey jumper and brown cord trousers he had worn yesterday. The chubby chief scratched his beard before reaching for the remote control for the projector.

A picture of the two boys emerged.

'Ruben Lundgren. Aged eleven. Tommy Sivertsen. Aged eleven.'

A new photograph, from the field this time.

'Found in a field a few hundred metres from their homes. Ruben had been stripped naked. Tommy was wearing only his underpants.'

A new picture. A close-up this time.

'Both boys were strangled, probably with a cable, possibly a fishing line.'

Another photograph.

'According to the pathologist, there are no signs of sexual abuse and no external damage to any of the limbs.'

Munch pressed the remote control again and Fredrik had to look away for a moment. The interior of the well house.

'Four hundred metres from where we found the bodies, we discovered this.'

New pictures. Close-ups of various objects.

'In the bottles containing fizzy pop and these miniatures of alcohol, we found traces of Rohypnol and Valium.'

'Evil bastard.'

It was Karl Oxen who broke the silence.

Anette Goli glared at him and raised her finger to her lips, but the beefy investigator couldn't stop himself.

'I mean, for fuck's sake? Sweets, booze and porn? And then he murdered them once he had drugged them?'

'Karl—' Munch interrupted him.

'I know, but come on? Who the hell . . .'

Karl Oxen.

Fredrik's least favourite colleague. His heart had sunk when he heard that the former boxer would be joining the team. He had no idea why. Munch normally valued brain over brawn, didn't he? Take Grønlie, for instance. Anette Goli. Katja van den Burg. Yes, even Fredrik himself, for that matter. But Oxen? He was nearly two metres tall, broad-shouldered, with a moustache and a tattoo of an anchor, and dressed as if he were a Canadian lumberjack. Fredrik knew Karl Oxen's achievements, of course. Oxen had contacts among practically every organized crime gang in eastern Norway. For some reason they regarded him as one of their own. They normally avoided police officers like the plague, but they were willing to talk to Oxen. If there had been a burglary or a trailer of drugs had been stopped by the border police, Oxen needed only to make a phone call and moments later he would at least know who *hadn't* done it. He was remarkable, of course, and a considerable resource as a police officer. But in this unit? No, Fredrik was still struggling to get on with him.

Nevertheless, Oxen had undeniably said out loud what they were all thinking.

'Let's not jump to conclusions, but it looks like it,' Munch said, and clicked the remote again.

A bird's-eye view of the area.

The field.

The old school.

The gravel pit.

The shooting range.

'As you can see, the well house is here. Hidden by the trees. You can't see it until you're very close. As Karl said, it looks as if the killer enticed them to go there and then drugged them. Later he strangled them, undressed them and moved them to the field, where they were posed in the way he wanted us to find them.'

'He moved them in the van?' Ludvig Grønlie asked. He was sitting along the wall with his laptop on his knees.

'Possibly,' Munch said, and clicked once more. 'As you all know, we have a total of four sightings of a type of van. A Peugeot Boxer.'

A photo of a white van appeared on the screen.

'The sightings were *here*, Saturday, at approximately four p.m. And *here*, Saturday, at approximately eight p.m. And then again *here*, very early Sunday morning, at approximately one a.m., and finally *here*, Sunday morning at seven a.m.'

'So we think he held them all night? In the well house?'

This time it was Katja van den Burg speaking, her face graver than he had seen it for a long time. While he found Oxen problematic, Fredrik had been delighted at the chance to work with the tall Dutch woman. They had hit it off immediately down at Police HQ. He didn't really know how she had ended up in Norway, but rumour had it that she had met a Norwegian man during military service in Afghanistan and later discovered that she loved her new country more than she loved him. She spoke excellent Norwegian with this clumsy, slightly stilted accent that foreigners often had. She was strikingly attractive in a typical Dutch way, tall, slim and with high cheekbones. Arms and legs in every direction, and always ready with a sarcastic comment. They had had a good laugh on many occasions and Katja was the only member of the team he saw outside of work. She didn't share his love of stamps though. She had shaken her head and asked him how old he really was when he happened to mention that he had just acquired a teal King Haakon from 1910, and was waiting for a postmarked 20-øre Lærdal stamp from 1885.

They shared a love of movies, however. He had had such a good time in her company that for a while he thought he might have a crush on her, but one evening when he had moved a little too close to her on the sofa she had brushed him off almost ironically. *Seriously, Freddie?* But she hadn't stopped hanging out with him. Fortunately. It was a while ago now. They were showing Kubrick's *2001: A Space Odyssey* at Gimle Cinema and he was thinking of asking her if she fancied going, but that was obviously out of the question now.

They had more important things to do.

'Again, we can presume so, but we can't be sure,' Munch said, and clicked to produce a new slide.

The words *Usual Suspects* appeared.

'Ludvig?'

'We have compiled a list of fourteen candidates who were within a reasonable distance at the relevant times. Convicted paedophiles and others on our radar.'

'As you know, we have a team down at Police HQ,' Anette Goli interjected, 'which logs observations and tip-offs from the public.'

'When we cross-referenced them with our list,' Grønlie went on, 'we found one person of significant interest.'

Munch clicked and a new picture appeared on the screen. 'Philip Pettersen.'

The photograph showed a man, possibly in his mid-fifties, with slightly greying hair and bushy eyebrows. The picture was grainy and it looked as if it had been taken with a telephoto lens.

'His name was mentioned by several individual callers,' Anette Goli explained, checking her papers. 'He's a former caretaker at Finstad School, which is the school the boys went to, but he was dismissed some years ago after countless complaints of what was said to be inappropriate behaviour. We haven't been given access to all the complaints, but according to several local residents, i.e. our callers, he filmed children in the showers and tried to contact them outside of school hours.'

'Like I said, when we checked out Philip Pettersen in our files, we found some reports,' Grønlie went on. 'No convictions, true, but four entries in total.'

'Relating to?' Katja wanted to know.

'Same type of behaviour. Inviting children to his home, hanging around playgrounds, and so on, but like I said, no convictions.'

'Surely you're allowed to hang around a playground?' Oxen said with a hint of acidity, his arms folded across his chest.

'Precisely,' Goli went on. 'And that's why he's not inside, but there were concerns and, as I said, he lost his job at the school.'

'So,' Munch said with another click. 'Philip Pettersen.'

He looked over his team.

'We have had him under surveillance for almost twenty-four hours. And we're thinking of paying him a visit today.'

'Sorry,' Anette Goli interjected. 'I forgot to mention that Pettersen lived in Gothenburg eight years ago. Just one hour from the scene of the earlier killings. He reported his change of address. Let me check . . .'

Another look at her documents.

'Yes, he reported his change of address back to Norway, to Lørenskog, in August 1993, just over two months after the killings in Sweden.'

There was murmuring across the room.

'So, again,' Munch took over, 'Philip Pettersen, aged fifty-one, a former caretaker. We need to have a chat later about how hard to go at him; I'll let you know how we should approach him and who will do it.'

Excitement and a kind of relief. Fredrik Riis could feel it himself: a faint smile had spread across his tired face.

They finally had something to go on.

'Can—' Oxen began, but he was interrupted.

'Like I said, I'll let you know how we'll do it and who will take part, but I must say that I'm cautiously optimistic.'

Munch was almost smiling in the light from the projector.

'Meanwhile, let's move on. Demographics relating to our victims. Family. Friends. Teachers. Does anyone have anything?'

Katja's hand shot up in the air.

'Yes, Katja?'

'Tommy Sivertsen lived alone with his mother, Hanna Sivertsen. As I'm sure you've all heard, I was due to meet her at the airport, but she fell ill while still in Spain so they wouldn't let her on the plane. She is currently . . .'

She flicked through her notepad.

'At the Hospital Vithas Alicante. I spoke to a doctor down there last night. He didn't want to say very much, but I've also been in contact with a representative from the Norwegian Foreign Ministry who will travel there today, and he will keep me updated.'

'Fine.' Munch nodded.

'As far as any other next of kin goes, I haven't found many. No one seems to know who the father is, and Hanna, the boy's mother, has a sister who lives in northern Norway, but they haven't been in contact for a long time, I believe.'

She turned the page in her notepad.

'When it comes to the neighbours, the ones who were meant to be looking after the boy, they've changed their story slightly. Now it is: *Yes, we were supposed to, but we didn't know that it was this week . . .*'

The Dutch woman shook her head and raised an imaginary bottle to her lips.

'Off their faces. I could barely get inside their flat because of all the empties.'

'OK. Good, thank you,' Munch said, and was about to move to the next point on the list in front of him when his phone rang.

He looked at it and broke into a smile.

'Let's leave it there for now. We'll break for five minutes and then I have someone I want you to meet.'

Chapter 13

Mia Krüger was sitting in Munch's office, a little overwhelmed by what she had witnessed in the last hour. She had paced up and down Majorstuveien all night without finding anything vaguely reminiscent of diamonds. She had collapsed exhausted into her bed, in an empty flat, thank God – her party-loving friends had already finished off their evening – again with this nagging feeling of having been taken for a ride by Polly, the drug addict from Bergen. Mia was still rather naive, wasn't she? Thinking that people who hung around Plata might want to help her. It was, ironically, one of those very same people who had told her one night: *You can't trust junkies. We'll do anything, say anything for a fix, it's the only thing we care about. Sorry.* A wry smile across their brown teeth and an outstretched hand into which she had put a bit of money. *One of those who travels?* What on earth did that mean? It was probably something Polly had made up.

She had fallen asleep with images of the plaster cast going through her head. All the names. And then the capital letter, on its own, near the edge, followed by a full stop.

W.

There's a team briefing at nine a.m.

Will you be there?

She had woken up feeling strangely rested.

For God's sake, Mia.

What do you think you're doing?

Of course you're going to say yes.

The tram was filled with faces that didn't seem as if they were looking forward to the new day. But she had smiled all the way

74

down to the office. Her heart had raced under her leather jacket. She had stood, almost awestruck, beside the columns as she looked up at the tall, cream building. She had been a little late, but it didn't seem to bother him. A big smile as he stepped out of the lift, looking almost as if he was about to give her a hug.

Welcome, Mia.

Great.

I'm really happy to see you.

Right, let's go say hi to everyone.

Strangely shy, she had run the gauntlet inside the large incident room. New pictures on the walls. Pornographic images. Bottles of fizzy pop.

She had struggled to concentrate.

Handshakes, nodding, smiles.

Katja.

Tall like an Olympic athlete.

Hello, hello.

Fredrik.

Dressed in a suit, he had a nice smile.

Hello.

Karl Oxen.

A booming voice and an anchor tattooed on his forearm.

Ludvig and Anja.

Hi, we've already met.

Anette Goli.

Still dressed as if she worked in a bank, but infinitely more welcoming today.

I've drafted a contract for you. We can take a look at it after the briefing.

And then she had to go through it again.

For the whole team this time.

Interpret the photographs once more.

Munch had selected a series of pictures especially for her. He looked almost like a proud father as he stood by the screen clicking and commenting along the way. The projector lighting up his face.

But she hadn't felt like a circus freak.

Thank God.

Everything had felt strangely right.

As if it was true this time.

For real.

They had welcomed her with open arms and she didn't know how to deal with that. It had almost been too much.

'I gambled.' Munch smiled from behind his desk after the briefing, an unlit cigarette dangling from the corner of his mouth as he took something from a drawer.

He placed a card with a lanyard on the desk.

'For me?'

'If you're going to be working here you need a warrant card. But more importantly, one of these.'

He unlocked another drawer and then placed a pistol on the desk.

'You're familiar with this one?'

'Yes.'

He didn't look entirely satisfied with her reply, so she continued: 'It's a Glock 17, safe action, 9mm. Seventeen bullets in the magazine, with an option of up to thirty-three. Produced in Austria by Glock Ges. Favoured hand weapon, especially by armies all over the world. Popularized by Bruce Willis in *Die Hard 2*.'

'Ahem . . .'

'Yes. Yes, I know it says there that it's a Glock 7, but it's a 17. Fourth-generation, this one.'

Mia nodded towards the pistol and found a lozenge in her pocket. Munch chortled.

'What I meant was, do you know how to use it?'

'Oh, yes, sorry. Yes, I do. But Norwegian police officers aren't usually armed, are we?'

He smiled again and produced a magazine from the drawer.

'*We* are. You'll discover that we have many privileges up here; that's the reason we're separate from the rest. Well, one of them.'

He scribbled something on a piece of paper and slid it towards her.

'What's that?'

'Your salary.'

It was her turn to fall silent now.

'Will it do?'

Munch smiled again and leaned back in his chair.

'Er, yes, absolutely—'

'Anette will stop by later with your contract. Do we have a deal?'

Another smile as he stuck his hand across his desk towards her.

'Welcome to the team. We have prepared an office for you – it's in the corner at the far end of the corridor. I've asked Ludvig to extract the most important information from Sweden so you have something to start with. There should also be a file marked *Philip Pettersen*, what we have on him so far. Something tells me that he might not have anything to do with this, but we have to start somewhere.'

She followed her new boss out into the corridor.

'Just let me know if you need anything else, OK?'

'Will do.' Mia nodded and made her way tentatively down the corridor to find her new office.

Chapter 14

Fredrik Riis was sitting outside the staffroom at Finstad School, feeling quietly pleased with the job Munch had given him. The school. The teachers. The pupils. The people who had known the two dead boys. A sad Norwegian flag was at half mast in the mild spring breeze outside and the mood inside the yellow building was equally subdued. Silent shock. The headteacher speaking quietly in her office. *Silje will look after you. She's just finishing a lesson and I have freed her up to speak to you afterwards. Silje Simonsen is the head of Year Six. She knows most of what goes on with them. We have discussed the issue of confidentiality, but the police officers who came here yesterday said that it ends when someone dies. Is that really true? We need to be considerate, don't we? Towards our other pupils. And the parents. By the way, do you know anything about the funerals? Everyone would like to attend, of course, but we have three hundred pupils and thirty teachers, and I don't suppose there will be room in the church for everyone, will there?* Under normal circumstances she was probably quite a strict woman, in her mid-fifties with short hair and white-framed glasses. Her eyes were distracted now, displaying a fake authority she didn't have the energy to maintain. *She shouldn't be more than ten or fifteen minutes. Would you like something to drink?*

Fredrik Riis had declined and was reminded that he had promised to ring the Lundgren family.

Ruben's funeral.

The pathologist had pretty much finished his examinations, but Munch had told him he wasn't satisfied yet and that it would be a few days before they could release the bodies.

There was a ping from the mobile in his pocket as the school bell rang. Doors were opened quietly, and silent children put on their coats and made their way towards the exit without the usual noise.

Will I see you tonight?

Riis heaved a sigh and shook his head.

'Hello. Are you looking for me?'

An inquisitive gaze over arms cradling a pile of books. He got up and nodded.

'Fredrik Riis.'

'Silje.'

'Do you have somewhere we can—'

'Yes, of course.' The blonde teacher smiled at him and showed him to a room a little further down the corridor.

Three desks arranged to create six workstations. The desks were piled high. The Norwegian school system was probably one of the best in the world, but still under-resourced; he had read in the papers a few days ago that a strike was planned. Not for higher wages this time, but for money for new schoolbooks. In some of the worst examples, King Olav still reigned and Ronald Reagan was the American president, and in a textbook on Home Economics pupils could read that it was important for *a woman to know how to organize her kitchen*. So, yes. He understood why. No strike at the moment, evidently – there were still teachers in the small room – but they seemed to have been warned and it didn't take long before he and Silje Simonsen were alone.

'Would you like something to drink? Coffee? A cup of tea?'

Fredrik Riis didn't have this police gaze everyone talked about, the ability to notice every detail, to describe a face down to the tiniest mole. He had struggled the few times they had covered this at the National Police Academy. He always ended up focusing on how he felt in the presence of the people he met; he would immediately start to wonder who they really were. Why and how they had ended up where they were now. What had made them choose this path in life. What they had been like as children. As teenagers. Things like that. What they were like in private. When no one else was watching them.

There had been no actual reprimand but a heavy sigh from Munch when Fredrik had once been asked to describe an elderly man he had interviewed in a case from some years ago, so he had pulled himself together and practised.

Silje Simonsen was an attractive woman, probably in her early thirties. Blue eyes and medium blonde hair cut so it just touched her shoulders. No ring. So probably not married? He glanced quickly down at the laden desk and couldn't see any photographs of a husband or children. A beige cotton jacket over slim shoulders. Jeans with slightly worn knees, trainers: red Adidas. Freckles.

'This won't take long,' Riis said, and took out a photograph from the pocket of his suit jacket.

She looked at it, somewhat surprised.

'Why—'

'It's confidential, so I must ask you to keep this to yourself. Do you understand?'

'Of course.' She nodded meekly.

'I'm asking you to identify all the signatures on it, if you can.'

'Everyone who signed the cast?'

'Yes. Do you think that's possible?'

She picked up the photograph and studied it closely.

'Do you recognize some of them?'

'Pardon? Yes, of course. Here we have Trond, Sylvia, Bente, Einar . . . but why?'

He could tell from the look on her face that she had already worked out the answer to her own question.

We think the killer may have signed it.

'Am I looking for . . .'

She frowned gravely and pursed her lips.

'We don't know. We just want – well, it's just something we need to clear up. I'm not allowed to say much more than that.'

'Of course,' Silje Simonsen mumbled, and studied the picture again. 'I think I recognize all of them. They tend to hang out in groups, you know? In their year. The boys all play for the same football team. Three of them also go to fencing.'

'Ruben had fencing lessons?'

'Yes.'

Riis took out his notepad and borrowed a pen from a cup on the desk.

'I'm guessing this is his sister?'

She smiled cautiously and placed her finger on the picture.

Sanna.

The handwriting was unmistakable, a five-year-old's first encounter with the alphabet.

'The only one I can't place is this one, I guess.'

Another finger against the picture, her eyes looking at him inquisitively.

'W?'

'No one from his class?'

Simonsen thought about it for a moment.

'No, we don't have anyone whose name starts with a W.'

The door opened to reveal a somewhat surprised face. The man apologized and went to close the door again.

'Hang on, Konrad, do you have any pupils with a W?'

'Say what?'

'Do you have any pupils in your class whose name starts with a W?'

'No.'

'How about the other Year Sixes?'

'Er, I don't know. Why?'

Riis took the picture from her and placed it face down. He smiled and nodded briefly at the newly arrived teacher, who took the hint and closed the door as he left.

'Like I said—'

'Oh, sorry,' Silje Simonsen said. 'I wasn't thinking, I got carried away—'

'That's quite all right. But you know that news travels fast, don't you? Rumours. We would like to keep this to ourselves for as long as we can.'

'But you're looking for someone whose name starts with a W?'

'I didn't say that. We're just trying to work out who signed Ruben's plaster cast. It might not be important. It might be nothing at all. It might have been signed by some homeless guy he gave some money to. Or someone who works in the corner shop where he buys chewing gum. Once we find out who it is, we can start thinking about other things. OK?'

'I understand.' Silje Simonsen nodded gravely and slipped the photograph into a book on the desk as if to show that this would stay between them.

'So how did it happen?' Fredrik asked.

'What?'

'His arm? How did he break it?'

She looked at him with surprise.

'You don't know that?'

'No.'

'Right, well, it was big news at the time – before this . . . I mean . . .'

'Go on?'

'It made it into the papers and everything. It turned Ruben into a minor celebrity, or at least it did here at the school.'

'Because?'

'Because he was so lucky, of course.'

She frowned again, almost suspicious that Fredrik didn't already know this story.

'Right? Did he fall off something or—'

'Oh, no. He was in a car that someone drove into. He was very lucky that it wasn't worse than it was. He had to be cut loose.'

'Where did it happen?'

'Over by the Burger Bar.'

'Where's that?'

She laughed briefly.

'Sorry, I forgot that not everyone knows everything that happens around here. This is a very small town.'

'So the Burger Bar?'

'Yes, at the junction of Gamleveien and Nordliveien. His father was reversing the car. Ruben was in the back. Apparently, another car was speeding across the car park and just slammed into them. It drove off without stopping. It was a big deal here some weeks ago. As I said, he was extremely lucky. Only breaking his arm. It could have been very, very nasty.'

'So it was a hit-and-run?'

'Yes.'

'And they never found the other driver?'

'Not as far as I know. But . . .'

She hesitated.

'But what?'

'Well . . .'

Her eyes looked unsure now. As if she didn't know whether to voice her thoughts.

'You have . . . oh, I don't know. You know about Ruben's father . . . or perhaps you don't?'

'What do you mean?'

'That he—'

The teacher was interrupted when the door suddenly opened. It was the headteacher with the white glasses.

'I'm so sorry for disturbing you, but Ragnar had to go home. Do you think you could take his class? They've already been in there for ten minutes and I can't find anyone else.'

She flashed an apologetic smile.

'Of course,' Simonsen replied. 'Which subject is it?'

'Religious Education, but just do what you can.'

Another apologetic look before she disappeared.

'I'm sorry,' Silje Simonsen said, and got up.

'I completely understand,' Riis said, and produced a card from his pocket. 'Please would you ring me later? Tonight? Or when you have a moment?'

'I will, absolutely.'

Silje Simonsen smiled and headed for the door.

Fredrik was back in the car park in front of the grim sight of the flag at half mast. The mobile in his pocket had vibrated several times. Every time the same message.

Why not?

Why not?

Fredrik thought about it for a moment before he reluctantly replied.

Because you're married, OK?

Then he started his car and drove to the Burger Bar.

Chapter 15

Ludvig Grønlie was wearing the same clothes as yesterday and Mia realized why after he yawned and remained standing, staring into space in the small office. He had been here all night. Mia almost started to feel bad once she understood. It was because of her. Munch had already known it when she called him last night. That she was going to be here. That she was going to take the job. Grønlie smiled a weary smile and ran his hand through his thinning hair, then nodded towards the files he had arranged neatly on the desk in front of her. The red knitted tie hung limply below his shirt collar and the light blue shirt stuck out crumpled over the waistband of his trousers. He wore chequered slippers, something which told Mia that Ludvig Grønlie was unlikely to run through the streets brandishing a gun; he probably spent most of his time here at the office.

'Just ignore them,' Grønlie said, leaning his backside against the edge of the desk.

'Who?'

'If anyone makes any comments about the speed of your employment. Not everyone here is nice. Jealousy. You know what it's like.'

'Not really,' Mia said cautiously.

Grønlie laughed briefly.

'No, of course not. Remind me how old you are?'

'Twenty-two. Nearly.'

'Oh, twenty-two,' Grønlie said in a dreamy voice, taking off his glasses. 'Youth. A carefree time. No responsibilities. Naivety. Chasing love. Believing the world is still a good place. That you can make a difference. Enjoy it while you can.'

'Er, thank you, I think,' Mia said, and laughed a little.

Grønlie chuckled and put his glasses back on. 'Don't listen to me. I become existential when I'm overtired.'

'He kept you up?'

'He called me at half past midnight. Told me you would be joining us. Wanted me to get everything ready.'

'Oh gosh.'

'No, no, don't worry about it. You make your choices here in life. And you have to live with the consequences. I could have been a fisherman. Got up every morning at five, been my own master at sea. Or a vicar perhaps. Preached about people's sins, then taken the rest of the week off. But I am where I am. Munch is my boss. I obey. It's my choice so I can't really complain about it.'

Grønlie winked at her and scratched his forehead.

'Where was I?'

Mia smiled and offered him the coffee she had bought for herself on her way to the office.

He took it and again he stopped and looked around the room with some vagueness.

'The files?'

'Yes, of course. Munch wanted me to give you a short summary, but I haven't actually got that far. The Swedish investigation went on for eight years. Dear God, I can't imagine what it must have been like for them. Fortunately, brains bigger than mine have sorted all the documents in order of priority.'

'So what have you brought me?' Mia wanted to know, and looked at her desk with curiosity.

'Our most important discoveries so far,' Grønlie said, and took a sip of the coffee. 'In the first pile, we have potential suspects. There are quite a few of them, but we have managed to boil it down to three – the three men the Swedes focused on over the years. They tried to charge two of them, but the public prosecutor stopped it both times. Desperation, Mia. Now I know that you're extremely new to this and it might seem great right now, but give it a week. Two weeks. A month. A year . . .'

Grønlie raised his eyebrows.

'I get it.'

'The first investigation I worked on, almost thirty years ago now, took us five years.'

'Right.'

'And to this day I still can't say that we actually solved it in the end. It was a complete fluke. He turned himself in. Couldn't cope with the guilt. If he hadn't said anything, who knows if we would ever have cracked it.'

'He's not going to do that this time,' Mia said, and opened the first file.

'Do what?'

'Turn himself in.'

'Oh? And what makes you so sure?'

'Just a hunch.'

She placed the photographs next to one another on the desk.

'Is it these three?'

'Yes.' Grønlie nodded. It looked as if the coffee had revived him a little. 'I've taken everything off the walls here in case you want to make your own system.'

He nodded to the tape dispenser which was next to the turned-off computer.

Mia put up the first picture on the wall by the window.

'Steinar Svensson,' Grønlie said, putting down the cup. 'Pipe layer. He had carried out work in the Hellberg family home some weeks before the murders happened. He was also seen near the scene the night before they found the boys. In his home, police found a room with magazines, pictures – yes, you can imagine. It turned out he wasn't quite your average guy. Nine trips to Thailand in recent years. Except they hadn't been able to link him to anything downright illegal over there, only allegations.'

'No forensic evidence?'

Grønlie shook his head.

'Strange, isn't it? These clean crime scenes? Not a single strand of hair? It's almost as if he knows what he's doing, isn't it?' he said, raising his eyebrows inquisitively and reaching for the coffee again.

'Go on?' Mia said, intrigued.

'This is very rare, I would say. It's usually what catches them out in the end. Blood. Semen. DNA from a single hair. In a case I worked on once, the perpetrator spat on the victim. Even I was impressed by what the forensic team was able to do. You can forget everything you have read or seen on TV, Mia. We're *even* better than people think. Finding a needle in a haystack, no, that's nothing. I've seen . . . Well, you get the idea. But this time?'

He gave her a rather odd look.

'So nothing to go on?'

'No.'

'Not in Sweden? And not this time in Norway either?'

Grønlie shrugged and again had this odd expression in his eyes.

'Now, Munch isn't willing to throw in the towel just yet and he has asked them to go over everything again, but—'

'Why do you keep giving me that look?' Mia said, finding a lozenge from a packet in her jeans pocket.

'What?'

'You say one thing and then you give me a strange look at the same time?'

Grønlie laughed out loud now.

'Munch did mention it.'

'What did he mention?'

'That you're quite unlike anyone else.'

Grønlie walked towards the door, then glanced out into the corridor before closing it.

'What I'm saying, since you asked me directly, is that there's something unsettling about this whole investigation.'

'OK?'

'These clean crime scenes? No forensic evidence?'

He stopped as if he was waiting for her to say something.

'I don't think I quite—'

Grønlie took a step towards her and lowered his voice.

'It seems like he knows what he's doing. Really knows what he's doing. As if he knows what we're looking for. Properly. Procedures you can't read up on. Things only we know—'

'Oh, you think that he is—'

Grønlie placed his finger on his lips and glanced towards the door a second time.

'We don't say things like that out loud.'

'A . . . police officer?' Mia whispered.

'It's not impossible.'

Grønlie shrugged again and took a sip of his coffee.

'So, shall we take a look at the other suspects?'

Chapter 16

Fredrik Riis entered the Burger Bar and was overcome by the acrid smell inside. He had been a pescatarian since he was fifteen and couldn't remember the last time he had been to a place like this. The faded menu on the counter told him that this wasn't the place for you if you wanted to keep your cholesterol down or follow any kind of healthy lifestyle. The server was a young man wearing a red shirt and red visor with the restaurant logo, the capital letters BB resting on something that looked like a triple burger, surrounded by two curved yellow French fries, which could easily be mistaken for the better-known fast-food chain. The customer base consisted mainly of young people who looked like they had nothing better to do than sit in here and smoke and possibly spend their meagre resources on twelve chicken nuggets for only 29 kroner and perhaps a mega Løren cola, not the branded stuff, now only 8.99 kroner, one krone extra to eat in. Riis waited patiently for the young man behind the counter to take orders from the customers in front of him.

'Next customer?' The young man behind the counter waved Riis forward.

'Fredrik Riis, police,' Riis said, showing him his warrant card. 'Please could I speak to the manager?'

'Do you mean Laila?' the young man said reluctantly, wiping sweat from his forehead under the visor.

'If she's the manager, then yes,' Riis replied.

'She's not here.'

There was a pause across the stained counter.

'All right. When will she be in?'

'I don't know.'

Another silence until the bell over the door rang out behind him.

'Are you going to order something?'

'No, I just have a couple of questions. Perhaps you can help me?'

'Er, OK,' the young man said, scratching his cheek. 'But I've customers to serve, so—'

'They can probably wait. This is about the car accident, a hit-and-run in the car park outside a few weeks ago. You didn't happen to be at work that day, did you?'

'Er, yes.'

'Did you see what happened?'

'No. I just heard a bang. Is it about that boy?'

'Yes.'

'Well, I did think it was a bit strange,' the server said, and shook his head.

'What do you mean?'

'That he wasn't allowed in here.'

'So they came here often? The whole family?'

'No, just him and his dad. But, yes, the boy always had to stay in the car.'

'That's not unusual, is it? I mean, Dad buys the food and later the family eat together—'

'Oh no,' the young man interrupted him. 'He only ever bought food for himself.'

'The father?'

'Yes.'

'Every time?'

'Er, I'm not going to get into trouble or anything, am I?'

'No, what makes you think that?'

'Well, talking to the cops . . .'

He picked up a cloth and started wiping the counter without paying attention to what he was doing.

'Definitely not. I saw some cameras out there. You wouldn't happen to have the incident on CCTV?'

The young man shook his head.

'They don't work. They're just for show.'

'OK, and as for Laila, do you happen to have a number for her?'

'No.'

'No? She doesn't have a phone?'

The young man hesitated.

'Ask me to show you something,' he then said in a low voice, and went back to wiping the counter.

'Eh?'

The young man nodded towards the door and said in a loud voice: 'All right, all right, but you'll have to be quick. I have customers waiting.'

He flung the cloth over his shoulder, came out from behind the counter and shook his head on his way to the door.

A group of young people at the corner table laughed.

'Sorry, but I would like to keep my teeth,' the server said apologetically when they were out of sight. 'Cops aren't popular around here, if you know what I mean.'

'I get it.' Riis nodded. 'So this is where it happened?'

'Yes. The car was parked there and then, yes, Christ knows how, but the other car suddenly came off Gamleveien and drove right over the grass here.'

The young man indicated the spot.

'There was a hell of a commotion. The police, the fire service, a tow truck and I don't know what, and we were forced to shut – people couldn't get through the doors. In the end, they had to cut him loose.'

'Ruben?'

'Was that his name? Poor kid.'

'And the other car simply drove off?'

'As far as I know.'

'And those don't work?'

Riis nodded towards the cameras on the wall.

'No, like I said, they're only for show, but . . .'

'Yes?'

The young man glanced about him and took a step closer to Riis.

'Now, I'm not some snitch who talks to the cops, but if I were you, I would pay a visit to Kruppel in the grey house up there.'

He nodded discreetly towards a house across the street.

91

'Kruppel?'

'Yes, he's an oddball. But he has cameras.'

'Oh, yes?'

'He rarely leaves his house. People say he's scared of something. I think he got beaten up in his own home once and now he has security equipment everywhere – you know, alarms and plenty of cameras. You can see them from here. If you . . .'

He nodded towards the house again as one of the customers stuck out their head.

'Can I get a burger here or what, Kenny? Or are you too busy jerking off your new boyfriend?'

Laughter from the open door.

'Kruppel,' the young man said again in a low voice before he rushed back across the car park.

Riis was sitting behind the wheel of his car when his mobile rang; a hushed Munch was on the other end, returning his call.

'Munch here, you called me?'

'Yes, where are you?'

'We're outside Philip Pettersen's house. He has just come home. We're about to go in. Was it important?'

'No, it can wait.'

'OK, good,' Munch whispered, and rang off.

Kruppel?

Hadn't he heard that name somewhere before?

Fredrik Riis dropped his mobile into his suit pocket and stuck the key into the ignition.

Chapter 17

Munch entered the offices at 13 Mariboes gate with something of a guilty conscience, which passed when he caught a glimpse of the young woman through the glass walls in the vaulted corner office. Her first day at work and he had thrown her in at the deep end, but fortunately it didn't seem to bother her noticeably. She had pushed the desk right into a corner, removed the chair, put the computer out of sight and pretty much plastered the walls: sheets of A4 paper, notes and photographs were neatly organized over and under each other. He couldn't work out her system from where he was standing, but he had no doubt that she had one. She was muttering under her breath, moving pictures from one place to another, sitting down on the floor with her face in her hands for a moment then suddenly leaping to her feet and running towards the wall to change something she had just done.

Munch had to knock on the door frame twice before she noticed that he was there.

'Am I disturbing you?'

'Yes,' Mia said.

She covered her mouth with her hand and squinted at a point on the wall as if she was trying to make it come alive.

Munch smiled at her response; he couldn't help but really like this girl. Her behaviour. The way she didn't seem to care about manners. As if other rules applied in her world.

It was refreshing. He could feel his mood improving already. The wasted trip to see Pettersen had irritated him all the way back here, but this dissipated now as he watched Mia move yet another picture to a different spot on the wall.

93

'Are you saying you would rather be alone?'

'Eh . . . what?'

She spared him a brief, absent-minded look, as if she was once more surprised at his presence.

'Oh, no, I was just . . .'

Mia continued to stand with her blue eyes turned to the wall; it looked like she was trying to capture something invisible in front of her, but eventually, she let it go with a small sigh and returned to the present.

'Are you making progress?'

'What? Yes, or rather . . .'

She ran a hand through her hair and shook her head.

'Many things are quite clear, I think, whereas others, well . . .'

Munch took off his duffel coat and leaned against the wall.

'Talk me through it. Tell me what you're thinking.'

'OK.' Mia cleared her throat and went up to a cluster of pictures.

The hare. The fox. Pictures from every angle, and several he hadn't seen before; she must have asked Ludvig for direct access to the police photographer.

'The animals,' she said, and turned to him. 'I think I know why he placed them there.'

'Go on?'

'You remember the boy's diary, don't you? One of the Swedish victims?'

'OK?'

She took a sheet from the wall and gave it to him.

'The diary which the newspapers published. *It's a full moon tomorrow. I'm scared of The Wolf.*'

She marched across the floor to the pictures of the animals again and tapped them both.

'I don't think I quite follow—'

'The Wolf?' she said, again, her eyes once more trained on the pictures of the animals. 'Don't you think . . .'

'Think what?'

Munch was starting to smile now.

'I think you will have to . . .'

'Oh yes, sorry. If the killer sees himself as The Wolf, then this makes sense, doesn't it?'

She pointed swiftly to the head of the hare.

'And this?'

The fox.

Slowly he realized where she was going with this.

'The hare and the fox are prey? For the wolf? Is that what you're saying?'

'Yes, exactly.'

She smiled triumphantly.

'Prey. That was the word I was looking for. He's showing us, isn't he? Have you ever had a cat?'

'A cat?'

'Yes, a cat. We had a pet cat and it would always bring us mice. It would place them on the floor in front of us. To show us how clever it was, what it was capable of.'

'So you think they were put there for our benefit?'

She looked at a loss for a moment. She turned towards to the wall again and drifted off once more.

'Maybe not for our benefit,' she said after a pause. 'Or maybe yes, I don't know. It might be mostly for his own sake. *Look, I'm The Wolf. Look what I can do.* Does that make sense?'

Mia suddenly looked a little hesitant. She glanced at him and scratched her forehead.

'It sounds plausible,' Munch said, failing to hide quite how impressed he was.

How many hours had he been gone?

Three?

And this young woman had already . . .

'OK, good.' Mia smiled. 'So that's the first thing.'

She walked quickly towards another cluster of pictures arranged beside a map of the crime scene and the surrounding areas. The victims this time. She had selected pictures taken from a distance, no close-ups. Munch followed her with curiosity.

'The second thing I've been thinking is . . .'

She frowned for a moment.

'OK, so this isn't as tangible, it's more a feeling I have. Is that all right?'

'Yes, of course.'

'OK. Take a look at this. There's something about the optics. There is an element of beauty, isn't there? It looks as if that's important to him. The aesthetics. And the thing about, well, the optics, I've said it twice now, but I'm not quite sure how to—'

'Not a problem. Please continue.'

'Right. I'm quite sure that this has been laid out to be savoured. Visually. So I've been thinking . . .'

She walked up to the map.

'He must have been watching.'

'What do you mean?'

She turned to him.

'The crime scene, I mean. In order to enjoy his creation. He must have. Think about it. To have created all this. And then we find it. For the thrill. He must have been there. So I got a map from Ludvig, and take a look at this—'

She placed her finger on a point on the map and looked at him.

'This is the only location which is higher up, so I'm thinking maybe there, or there, or yes, even there, but I would start—'

'By the gravel pit?'

'Yes, or is that a little too exposed? Perhaps the forest is better – there, for example? He couldn't be seen from there.'

'So you think he was watching us?'

'I do.'

Her blue eyes were shining now.

'Wouldn't you? Enjoy it? Watch us discover your creation?'

Munch nodded and walked closer to the wall. 'This is good, Mia.'

'Yes?'

'It's very good. I'll send people up there immediately. So you're suggesting here?'

He put his finger on the map.

'Yes. Or possibly there. I don't know; all we have to do is look for somewhere with a good, unobstructed view of the place where the bodies were lying.'

'That's good, Mia. Really, really good. For a moment I was worried that I had left you in the lurch up here.'

She looked at him blankly. 'Why? I'm fine on my own.'

'Absolutely.' Munch smiled. 'Well done. Was that everything?'

'Yes. Or rather, no.'

'Go on?'

'It's just a small thing.'

She started moving again, this time to the other end of the room.

'I've only just started on this, but it's important, I think.'

A list with only two entries.

'And this is?'

'In 1993, two murders in Sweden. In 2001, two murders in Norway. A gap of eight years.'

'Yes?'

She threw up her hands.

'Where was he all that time?'

'Exactly. That has been bothering me as well.'

'Right?'

She nodded and brushed the fringe away from her forehead.

'So what are you thinking?'

She mulled it over before she replied.

'It's hard to say. Perhaps he didn't feel like it. Maybe he didn't find anyone he liked. But, yes . . .'

'What?'

'It's most likely that he was prevented, don't you think?'

'As in?'

'Now, that I don't know. The man isn't well. He thinks he is, but he certainly isn't according to our yardstick. I mean, if he is The Wolf—'

'What are you thinking?'

She hesitated.

'OK, so this may be too simple. But could he have been locked up somewhere?'

'In prison?'

'Yes? Or in some sort of treatment facility?'

'An asylum?'

She smiled faintly.

'I don't think we call it that any more, but yes, somewhere along those lines.'

'Good job, Mia, really good.'

'Oh, I nearly forgot to tell you the most important thing.'

Mia shook her head and returned to the pictures of the animals. She removed one and handed it to him.

'Do you see it?'

She took an apple from her pocket, bit into it and pointed eagerly at the picture.

The fox. A close-up of its head.

'Not really?'

'Take a better look,' she said excitedly, and pointed again. 'Notice its ear.'

'All right?'

'Do you see it? Those marks? Right near the edge?'

Munch saw what she was pointing to and then he realized it.

Wow.

Brilliant.

'You think it might have been . . . tagged?'

'Yes. It looks like it, doesn't it?'

She smiled again and carried on eagerly.

'A tag in its ear. It means someone would have been monitoring it, doesn't it? Which area it moves in? It looks like the killer removed it, but even so. What if it had an active transmitter? One with GPS? If it was removed—'

She looked at him, almost teasing him now.

'Bloody hell,' Munch said, and smiled.

'Right? If it stopped transmitting when it was removed, then we know where—'

'Well, I'll be damned.'

Munch chuckled to himself.

'Have you—'

Mia was already walking across the floor towards her notes, the apple in her hand.

'I've made a few phone calls and, when it comes to red foxes, I believe we need to talk to the Inland Norway University of Applied Sciences in Lillehammer, certainly in relation to eastern Norway. They run a project in collaboration with the Norwegian Institute for Nature Research, I got a name . . . where is it? Yes, Nina Dobrov. She was busy, but I can visit her tomorrow morning.'

'This is bloody brilliant, Mia.' Munch smiled again, and had just taken his cigarettes from his pocket when there was a sudden knock on the door and a breathless and excited Fredrik Riis popped his head round.

'Am I interrupting you? I have something you absolutely must see.'

The besuited investigator didn't wait for a reply, but rushed ahead of them to his own office and stuck a memory stick into his computer.

'Right, I need to give you some background first. I went to the school to ask about the plaster cast, and then it occurred to me that we didn't know why Ruben needed it in the first place. I hadn't imagined that it could have anything to do with our investigation – I mean, an eleven-year-old boy, there could be all sorts of reasons – but something his teacher told me made me curious.'

He had their attention now. Munch pulled out a chair and put the cigarettes back in his pocket.

'It turns out that Ruben was something of a local celebrity. The plaster cast was the result of a traffic accident. Quite an unusual one. His teacher, Silje Simonsen, said they were all relieved that he had escaped so lightly. That it could have been much worse. So I decided to check it out. What I'm about to show you took place outside the Burger Bar. Ruben and his father went there to get some food. Or rather, his father went there to get some food, Ruben stayed behind in the car, in the car park around the corner—'

'And it was caught on a car park camera?'

'No. The cameras weren't hooked up, they were just for show. But an employee gave me a tip-off. Do you remember Roy Kruppel?'

Munch nodded. 'Wasn't he the guy who—'

'Exactly.' Riis smiled knowingly.

'Who?' Mia said, and looked from one to the other.

Munch was about to explain, but Riis beat him to it.

'Roy Kruppel. It was a nasty case some years ago. Highly unusual for Norway. Very brutal. Which was why it attracted so much attention. Roy Kruppel was an ordinary man who worked in insurance, and his wife taught in a local nursery school. They had two children, both of whom had left home, a house, a car, a dog – you get the picture: ordinary people living an ordinary life. Right until one evening in, well, let me think, in May, some years ago, yes it was the eighteenth, I remember it because I had been celebrating Constitution Day with—'

Munch cleared his throat.

'Yes, of course, I'm sorry.'

Riis flashed Mia a shy smile.

'That night three men broke into his house. Completely for no reason, it would appear. A burglary gone wrong maybe, we're not sure; he didn't have anything particularly valuable, not according to the reports I've read. Husband and wife were both tied up and gagged, the dog was drugged, they lay there for hours and then, again we don't know why, the burglars started beating them up. First the dog. Beaten to death. Then they started on Kruppel's wife. Again it was very aggressive, very violent, the whole thing seemed pointless—'

'She was left disabled after the attack,' Munch interjected, somewhat impatiently. 'And this is important because—'

'Yes, I'm sorry. Roy Kruppel was a changed man after the attack. Completely understandable – who wouldn't be? Nevertheless, he was terrified that something similar might happen again and since then his house has been almost like a fortress. A fence with barbed wire on the top and cameras everywhere—'

'So he recorded the crash down by the Burger Bar?'

'Yes, but not only that—'

'Can't you just show us?' Munch said, and took out his cigarette again.

The young investigator looked like he had intended to say more, but took the hint, turned to the computer and pressed play.

The image was grainy. Black-and-white. The camera had clearly been positioned to cover the outside of the house rather than the building across the road, so what they saw took place in a corner of the screen, almost out of sight. A light-coloured car was parked behind the Burger Bar. Riis paused the film and pointed.

'This is the Lundgren family's Volvo. We can just about see Ruben in the back there.'

He pressed play again.

Nothing much happened. For several seconds. The light-coloured car just sat there. The boy in the back didn't move.

'Now watch this.'

Completely out of the blue, a white van cut across the grass, drove at high speed across the car park until it crashed into the back door of the Volvo.

'Christ.'

Mia jumped.

'And now look.'

Riis pointed to the screen and turned eagerly towards them.

'He doesn't even stop.'

The wheels of the white van spun briefly on the tarmac.

'He's struggling with the gears, it would seem.'

The white van slammed into the door behind which the boy was sitting twice more.

'And then he finds reverse.'

The van shot backwards before coming to a standstill.

'He starts it again.'

The white van swerved, wheels skidding on the tarmac before it disappeared from the screen and was gone.

'Jesus,' Munch muttered to himself.

'Weird, isn't it?' Riis said, turning to them. 'It comes out of nowhere. Crashes right into the Volvo. Wheels spinning as he panics, and then he does a runner? He doesn't even get out of the van to check.'

'Was it investigated?'

Riis took a notepad out of his suit pocket.

'Yes. I spoke to an officer from Traffic. Reported, investigated and shelved. No fatalities, so not a priority.'

'But a child was injured?'

'Yes, that's what I said, but that was the answer I was given. He didn't seem that organized, but he said he would email me the report.'

'And is that all we've got?' Munch wanted to know with a nod at the screen.

'No, no,' Riis said. 'Kruppel had all day – all week, for that matter. He showed me his office. A fully equipped basement. It looked like a situation room. The CIA would be envious.'

'Poor man,' Munch mumbled, and stuck the cigarette in between his lips. 'And that's all we have of the crash itself?'

'Yes,' Fredrik said, clicking on a new file from the memory stick. 'And then there's this.'

'And what's that?'

'That's what happens afterwards. The police arrive. The fire service with the heavy-duty bolt cutters they use to cut people loose. The tow truck arrives quite quickly. The ambulance gets there eventually, strangely late, come to think of it. They get the boy out of the car and place him on the ground; he's there for quite a while. Plenty of spectators.'

Riis shrugged his shoulders.

'The boy is moved into the ambulance. Everybody leaves the scene. The truck tows the Volvo away.'

Munch got up.

'Great job, Fredrik. Excellent.'

'Thank you.' The investigator smiled and glanced at Mia, whose eyes were glued to the screen.

'A white van,' she ventured cautiously. 'Didn't you have sightings of a white van at the crime scene?'

'*We* did, yes.' Munch winked and produced a lighter from his pocket.

'Oh, sorry. Weren't *we* looking for a van like that? A white Peugeot Boxer? Have we found it yet?'

'No.'

'I don't know if you noticed, but it was missing its front number plate,' Riis interjected.

'But not the number plate at the back, right?' Mia said, leaning closer to the screen where Riis had paused the footage as the van was leaving the scene. 'Are we able to read the registration number?'

'Sadly, no. But I've sent the footage to our new e-group. They'll try to enlarge it. If we're lucky, we'll be able to see it, unless the pixels are too big.'

'Great job, Fredrik,' Munch said again as his mobile rang. He stepped out into the corridor to answer it.

'Yes?'

'It's Anette. Looks like it was a waste of time, unfortunately.'

'Pettersen?'

'Yes. His alibi checks out.'

'Damn. OK. Are you coming in here?'

'I'm on my way there now.'

'Good. Listen, how many officers do we have out there?'

'In Finstad?'

'Yes. Doing door-to-door inquiries?'

'Not sure, about thirty, why?'

Munch wedged his mobile between his chin and his shoulder and went into Mia's corner office.

'Could you dispatch ten or twelve of them to the forest?'

'OK. Any particular reason?'

'Mia thinks he might have been watching us. I have an exact location. Do you have a pen?'

Chapter 18

Lydia Clemens crept quietly through the trees. She had been playing this game for some time now, pretending to be a tiger creeping undetected across the forest floor. The twelve-year-old girl had become an expert at this, like everything she put her mind to. Archery, for example; it hadn't taken her long before she was even better than her grandfather, firing off three arrows in quick succession, straight into the bullseye in the meadow behind the cottage. Now she could hit anything. Her grandfather had made the sharp tips of her arrows in the forge, just as he had made the knife he had given her for her birthday. She would never forget his face when he saw how happy it made her. Her grandfather never cried, but a tear had rolled down his cheek in front of the fireplace in their little cottage.

It's amazing, she had cried out, and rushed over to give him a hug.

Really? Are you sure? You like it?

I do!

And it was true. Because she had used her old knife to butcher reindeer and gut fish and cut grass for the goats and clean fox pelts and carve wooden dolls. She had used it for everything, but it really was on its last legs now. *Just look at my knife. There's practically nothing left of it.* She had become a little angry when all he had said was: *Oh no, it'll last you a long time*. And then he had made her a new one after all, so that explained all those mysterious trips to the forge. *I'm just nipping out to the forge, Lydia. You stay in here and do your homework.*

Homework, always homework. Sometimes it was almost too much, but Lydia Clemens knew how important it was and put up with it. Because after *the long time, the eternal summer* would come, and the Earth would need people like her, who knew many things. So civilization wouldn't have to start from scratch. They would need smart people who had read a lot and were knowledgeable. History. The Natural Sciences. Maths. Chemistry. But also people with practical skills such as the ability to build a shelter and make their own candles and hunt. Because it would take time to rebuild society, several centuries perhaps, because of everything the evil-doers had destroyed.

Lydia had composed a small poem which she always recited to herself before she killed anything, just to show the world around her that she respected the life she was about to take. *I apologize, my darling.* With her eye near the taut bowstring. *I love you. I hope that there is a heaven for* – here she would insert the name of the animal, say, a hare – *and that when you go there, you will be happy for ever.* She would have preferred to close her eyes, but she couldn't, following her arrow all the way to its target. That was the secret behind archery.

The twenty longest rivers in China: Chang Jiang, Huang He, Amur, Pearl River, Mekong, Tarim, Argun, Han Shui, Wujiang, Selenga, Nen, Liao He, Hai He, Yalong, Kherlen, Orkhon, Yarlung Zangpo, Dadu He, Jialing, Huai.

The first twenty elements of the Periodic Table: hydrogen, helium, lithium, beryllium, boron, carbon, nitrogen, oxygen, fluorine, neon, sodium, magnesium, aluminium, silicon, phosphorus, sulphur, chlorine, argon, potassium, calcium.

The Russian Revolution in 1917: major landowners and factory owners held most of the wealth in Russia while the people starved and lived in poverty. The rich refused to share and the people rebelled. Led by Vladimir Ilyich Ulyanov, better known as Lenin, the people seized control of the country so that everyone could get enough food and proper jobs without having to bow and scrape to the capitalists.

A recipe for home-made soap: 150 grams animal fat, 360 grams rapeseed oil, 150 millilitres cold water, 71 grams lye, if you have it.

Quiet as a mouse now, she was a supple tiger as she approached the small house across the moor. She crouched down carefully in the heather behind an old pine and took out her binoculars. It looked quiet. No smoke from the chimney, which there had been last time. A stupid waste, really; it wasn't cold enough outside that you needed to light a fire inside. She stuck her small binoculars into her leather belt and crept cautiously across the yellow wisps. She loved the smell of moorland. It was almost magical, as if the moist cracks in the soil contained rusting metal. She had to watch her step, of course, and always place her feet on the solid peat and not be tempted to try the muddy holes where you could disappear and be gone for ever. It wasn't a problem for her, obviously. She knew this landscape inside out and had made friends with every plant. The house was old. Brown. Not very nice. The paint was flaking off in several places. An unpainted, grey barn across the small yard. No garden. No vegetables or flowers or anything. The man who lived here didn't look after his things. He didn't respect himself or his belongings, as her grandfather would have said. A quad bike was parked on the track by the house, but there was total silence everywhere. Lydia lay down on her stomach for the last stretch and elbowed her way to the wall, where she crouched down as she felt her heart beat under her deerskin jacket. She already knew that the television wasn't on because the last time it had given off a glow and she could hear sounds from it through the thin walls, but she raised her head and had a quick peek nevertheless. It was as she had thought. The black screen was completely lifeless. *Bother.* She heaved a sigh and sank on to the brown grass by the wall in disappointment. The sun almost reached the treetops now, casting long shadows across the ochre landscape, which was probably just as well. It was time to head home.

Lydia had just stood up when she heard a strange, whining sound. And a rattling. And a kind of thumping. She crept around the corner of the house. Then there was silence.

Had she . . .

No, there was the sound again.

She darted across the yard. Her leather shoes made barely any noise on the gravel and suddenly she was face to face with it.

A badger. Trapped in a cage.

Two tiny eyes and a small snout trying to force its way through the mesh door.

The rage surged in Lydia.

Animals in cages were unforgivable.

She sent a hateful thought to the man who lived in the dilapidated house and opened the latch that kept the animal trapped.

The badger looked at her gratefully before it scurried away to freedom.

Lydia glared at the front door and spat scornfully into the gravel, then crouched down and made her way home across the damp moor.

Chapter 19

Fredrik Riis let himself into his flat after a long day at work. He needed to check on his pet bird. Not that he had said so to the others, obviously. It was bad enough that they viewed him as the posh boy who always wore suits; he didn't want to be called a pigeon fancier as well. He kicked off his Italian shoes, carried his briefcase into the kitchen and was met by the small cockatoo sitting on the extractor fan over the cooker, looking at him mournfully. He smiled and offered the bird his hand. With some scepticism it eventually strolled on to his fingers, up along his arm, across his shoulder until it was close to his cheek, its favourite place. Sjöberg. A grey-and-white cockatoo with a yellow head and orange cheeks. He had named it after the Swedish high-jumper Patrik Sjöberg, who set an impressive world record in Stockholm in 1987. He chatted to the bird as he went to the feeding tray and let the cockatoo see him refresh the water and bird seed, an extra snack in the small ball under the little bell. It was important, he had read, to interact with the bird as much as possible. The grey cockatoo fluffed its wings and emitted a small sound of contentment. Fredrik fetched the sushi he had picked up on his way home, and for a while they sat in companionable silence, eating together in the kitchen.

He had just stepped out of the shower when his phone rang. He didn't recognize the number and answered the call in his bedroom.

'Yes, Fredrik Riis?'

'Hello, Fredrik. It's Silje Simonsen.'

He searched his tired brain before finding her. The blonde schoolteacher.

'Yes, hi. How are you?'

'Oh, I'm fine.'

She sounded as if she was smiling.

'I'm sorry for calling you so late, but it has been a busy day. My daughter was cross with me for picking her up late from nursery and she refused to go to sleep.'

'No problem,' Fredrik said.

'It was about the plaster cast,' the teacher continued. 'W, wasn't it?'

'Exactly. What did you find out?'

'I can't find anyone. There's a boy called Walter from fencing, but he had already signed his name, so I think you might be on to something there.'

'You called a student you don't teach?'

'Yes. Was I not supposed to?'

'Sure.' Fredrik smiled. 'It was kind of you, but really there was no need.'

He went to the kitchen, fetched a bottle of water from the fridge and took it with him to the living room.

'I really wanted to help,' she said in a friendly voice. 'It's fun, isn't it? Playing detective. It's not often I get the chance to do that. My job isn't as exciting as yours.'

'Oh, I don't know,' Riis said, and flopped on to the sofa.

'Well, that was all I was calling to tell you.'

'OK, great. Thanks for your help. You have my number, so if there's anything else—'

'Yes . . .' She hesitated.

'Was there anything else?'

She fell silent for a moment.

'Oh, I don't know.'

'Go on?'

'It's just that . . . I have a couple of boys in my class who – well, how can I put it? – they've started to act differently.'

'I see. How?'

'Well, it's a bit difficult to explain. It might just be the current situation, that recent events have affected them, but I don't know. They're usually forthcoming, but recently they have been avoiding me, if that makes any sense?'

'Yes, absolutely,' Fredrik said, and went to his bedroom.

'And earlier today when I was on playground duty, I came around the corner and, when they saw me, they stopped talking. They looked almost guilty, if you know what I mean?'

'I do,' Fredrik said. 'Perhaps I should pay the school another visit?'

'Yes, perhaps.'

'We need to have the parents' permission in order to interview minors, but we could just have a chat with them and see if it leads to anything?'

'Great,' the teacher said in a warm voice. 'I would like that.'

'That's agreed then. I'll call you tomorrow.'

'Super. Again, I'm sorry for calling so late.'

'Don't worry about it. I was awake anyway.'

'OK. Good night.'

'Good night,' Fredrik Riis said, and put his mobile on his bedside table.

Good night?

A little intimate, perhaps?

No, he was too tired to think about that now.

He had to get some sleep.

He had just returned from the bathroom, putting a blanket over Sjöberg's cage so that he could have a quiet night, and had finally slipped under his warm duvet when his phone, which lay below the bedside lamp, suddenly vibrated.

Can we meet up soon?

He heaved a sigh and texted back reluctantly.

No, bad idea.

Only seconds passed before the next message came.

Only a quick meeting? Please?

He thought about it for a moment, feeling almost sick, but then again, he had made up his mind.

No, we can't.

A new message straightaway.

Why not?

He sat up in his bed for a moment and buried his face in his hands. How the hell had he got himself mixed up in this?

He bit his lip and typed his reply as quickly as he could.

Because you're married. To one of my colleagues.

110

THREE

Chapter 20

Susanne Hval Pedersen peered nervously out from behind the curtains of number 13 Timoteiveien, wishing that she could remember where she had put her pills. She knew they were in an unusual place because she didn't really need them. The doctor had given her the prescription some weeks ago. Valium? Her? Don't be ridiculous. She was certainly not the type who needed artificial help to sleep. Yet her doctor had insisted. So she could relax a little. Her husband had lost his job and was acting strangely. She barely recognized him these days. He was out at night. And when he woke up, he would disappear again without saying a word. Without telling her where he had been. Or where he was going. *Where did I put those pills? In the first-aid box? But no, you have already checked in there. Three times.* There was nothing but paracetamol and Nora's asthma inhaler.

Susanne looked out of the kitchen window again, but quickly stepped back when she saw an unfamiliar car drive slowly past the house. As if she didn't have enough on her plate. Ruben from down the road. Murdered in a field nearby. Dear God. How incredibly brutal. It made no sense. It couldn't be true, but the whole country was talking about little else. In the local paper lying on her doorstep when she let out the cat. On every radio station in the car on her way to nursery with Nora, and later as she drove to Lillestrøm to open the shop. On the TVs lined up in the display window of the shop, Elkjøp, next door. Which normally showed cute wildlife programmes or fancy music videos, but not any more. Extra news bulletins. All day long. On NRK and TV2. Senior reporters with grave faces above the microphones. Tickers scrolling across the screens. BREAKING NEWS: POLICE RELEASE NAMES OF

MURDERED BOYS. There seemed to be no escaping it. Rows of tabloid newspapers. Screaming front pages. NO SUSPECTS. NORWAY MOURNS. As if they were at war. As if a whole nation had lost these two children. The people queuing in front of her in the supermarket, gossiping.

Did you hear that the mother of one of the boys had gone off to Spain? Left the kid home alone.

Yes, that's what they're saying.

Eh? Some neighbours, apparently, only they didn't know when they were meant to be keeping an eye on him.

Imagine that there are people like that! Yes, in council housing, obviously.

Eh? No, I've no idea who it is. But we know Ruben.

Oh, you didn't know? He's in the same year as my Anita. In fact, he came to our house once. Handsome boy. Freckles. Blond hair. A little angel, he was.

Susanne Hval Pedersen closed the curtains and looked at the clock above the kitchen counter. It was a quarter past nine. She had just put Nora to bed. On her own. Again. Even though the little girl had kept asking for him, poor thing. *Where is Daddy? I want Daddy to read to me.* The Very Hungry Caterpillar. *No, not you, Mummy, I want Daddy.* She had to sing for twice as long as usual before the girl finally went to sleep. She had stopped calling his mobile, as he didn't answer it anyway. The last time she had seen him was – well, when was it really? Last night? Sunday morning? No, she hadn't seen him; she had only heard the front door open. She had lain awake under her duvet hoping he would come to their bedroom, lie down next to her, hold her like he used to, and whatever this was would all be over. But he didn't come to the bedroom; she had only heard heavy footsteps on the stairs leading to the guest room. And in the morning footsteps going down, then the slamming of the solid front door. The car starting and driving off.

Where had she hidden those pills?

She went down to the basement and into the workshop. It was not a place she came to often and it took her ages to locate the light switch. This was his territory; it was where he kept his tools. A small

114

stereo in one corner. Vinyl records from his childhood, from his teenage bedroom, and his posters, the ones she had banned from the living room. Led Zeppelin. Rolling Stones. Jimi Hendrix. Thin Lizzy. The kind of music she hated. No, not hated, that was the wrong word. She wasn't used to it, not in the house where she had grown up, where people had looked down on it, and she had taken this attitude with her into adult life. Classical music. That was what mattered. The grand piano in the living room where they would gather when her mother played. A huge Christmas tree. Pretty dresses. Comfortably middle class. She had loved her childhood. She herself had played the cello. Not professionally, of course, but she was fairly competent. She had been picked several times to perform at the Oslo Conservatoire's annual summer concert. And then she had met him. A man who didn't know which fork to use. Who dressed as if he had just grabbed the first thing he saw in H&M. Had they grown apart: was that the problem? Everything had become humdrum. Routine. First, their son, who was now twenty-three, had left home, gone to Bergen to study medicine. And then the little one, wonderful Nora, had arrived, and they hadn't even been trying. Sex was no longer a regular occurrence in the blue-painted bedroom, something that was completely normal for a couple their age, as far as she could gather from her friends, but then one day. Pregnant? Incredible. Was she going to keep the baby? Of course she was going to keep the baby. She had only been thirty-nine at the time. It was no age at all. Her diabetes? What did that have to do with anything? She had been outraged, even changed her GP. And now Nora was sleeping in her little bed. *Where is Daddy? I want my daddy!*

Susanne heaved a sigh and stopped in the middle of the floor. She didn't know what she was doing down here. After all, she couldn't have hidden her pills here. She hadn't been down here for three years. Wenche, one of her friends who lived in Kløverveien, had told her about another woman, whose name she refused to mention, who had found a secret room behind her husband's gym in the basement. Susanne hadn't believed the story – it had to be made up – but her friend had insisted that it was true. A closet. With a hidden switch like you only saw in the movies. And it had contained – no, it sounded utterly sickening – equipment for S&M. Masks and chains and whips and leather costumes, big dildos, and Wenche had not spared her any of the details, but Susanne had shut her ears and thought of something else. In this neighbourhood? Where every street was named after a flower? No, she refused to believe it. But now she no longer knew what to think.

Susanne Hval Pedersen was just about to turn off the light when she noticed something in a corner. A bundle of clothing. Wasn't that his shirt? She approached it slowly. And his trousers? The ancient tracksuit bottoms he refused to let her throw out. She picked them up from the floor and studied them curiously. What were they doing down here? He always left his clothes in the laundry room like she had asked him to so she knew where everything was. She didn't mind doing everyone's laundry, but she had her system, and he knew that. Don't just dump your clothes all over the place; she had made that very clear, hadn't she?

Irritably she snatched the shirt from the floor, and that was when she noticed them.

The dried, rust-coloured stains. Everywhere.

What on earth was this?

Dear God, what have you been doing, Gunnar?

I've had enough. We need to talk about this.

She made up her mind.

She wouldn't wait in their bed any longer. But in a chair by the door.

She took his clothes to the laundry room, and put them into the washing machine on a hot wash.

Then she made herself a cup of strong coffee.

Chapter 21

The Norwegian Institute for Nature Research was housed in a red-brick building close to Ullevaal Stadium, and Mia Krüger couldn't help but think of her father, of their telephone conversation last night, and how horrible it had been to lie to him, even though, ultimately, she had had no choice. It was only a white lie, but it was still a lie. Ullevaal equalled football and Norway's national team. Mia couldn't have cared less about it, but she loved her father and years ago had gone to a match with him because he so wanted her company. Hers, not Sigrid's. He had asked her, and that was her overriding memory from their visit to Ullevaal Stadium. Companionship. Her and her father. For once, Norway had done well. Their team might possibly qualify for the World Cup for the first time since – 1938, was it? Something like that. It certainly was an awfully long time ago. A new coach had made things happen. Even Mia had heard of the man whose nickname was Drillo. An oddball who was very left-wing, wore wellington boots; a complete geography nerd who referred to all types of music as noise. He had invented a new approach to playing football which the rest of the world ridiculed but which seemed to deliver results. She hadn't paid much attention to what happened on the pitch, but she remembered how good it had felt to sit close together, surrounded by flags, plastic Viking helmets and people with their faces painted. Norway versus England. Baby brother against Big Brother – no, not really. A nobody versus the country where football was invented was probably more accurate. But who would have thought it, they had actually won. Little Norway had beaten England 2–0. She had been such a happy fourteen-year-old. Because everyone else was happy. Thirty thousand people happy together. On their way home in the car, she realized she had never seen her father like that before. He had been singing with the windows open, as had the whole country, for days.

Please have a word with Sigrid. Tell her Mum didn't mean it like that? That we miss her, we both do.

His frail voice on the phone, and she had bitten her lip in order not to say anything.

The argument that her mother and sister had had was, in fact, convenient because it bought Mia time. To find her sister, to fix this. Before her father discovered what Sigrid was really doing. The grief would kill him, it would, she was almost sure of it.

As long as you're with that waste of space, I don't want to see you under my roof, understand?

Their mother, stern and strict, as usual, would say things like that and, even though she often regretted them later, she still would not back down. No, if her mother had said that Sigrid couldn't come back as long as Markus Skog was her boyfriend, that was how it was going to be. And now her father, the diplomat who always ended up stuck in the middle, assumed that Sigrid was merely being equally stubborn.

She doesn't answer her phone. Not even when I call. What have I done? I miss my girls! Can't you tell her to come home? Please?

Mia hadn't planned to tell him her news. She was going to wait until her next visit home, but she had blurted it out, mostly to change the subject.

I've got a job, Dad.

What? But you're still at the Academy?

So proud of her.

That was typical of her wonderful father.

She could hear how emotional he had been; he couldn't stop singing her praises.

We have to celebrate this!

Because you're coming on Saturday, aren't you?

Saturday.

Her grandmother's eightieth birthday.

She hadn't asked Munch yet about taking time off; she wasn't sure how to go about it. Everyone in the team seemed to work at least 24/7, but she had promised her father to be there all the same.

The head of research at the Norwegian Institute for Nature Research, Nina Dobrov, was a woman in her mid-forties, and she looked exactly the way Mia had imagined her. Metal-rimmed glasses. Shoulder-length, medium-blonde hair. Colourless trousers below an equally colourless jumper. A face without any make-up and distracted eyes whose attention was caught by other things several times during their conversation. Not all scientists were stereotypical boffins, but this woman was. She was absent-minded, completely unbothered by her appearance, her office was a total mess and she spoke with warmth and passion about her work.

Mia was given the grand tour while the enthusiastic woman gestured and explained.

'The Norwegian Institute for Nature Research is also known as NINA, like me – funny, isn't it? The head of NINA is called Nina.'

The woman had a smear of something that could be yoghurt on her cheek, but Mia couldn't make herself say anything. She had just nodded politely as she was shown down narrow corridors and in and out of many, mainly empty, offices.

'The head of everything isn't quite right because our actual head office is in Trondheim, but there are quite a few staff based down here. I guess we're thirty-two in total, including students. Our areas of research are ecology and diversity in woodland areas, mountains, wetlands, rewilding, and everything, really. Daniel here – well, he's not here right now – works with entomological taxonomy. Then there's Vibeke, she works with terrestrial wildlife monitoring. Arnt – well, as you can see, most of our scientists work outdoors, in the forests and in the fields; after all, that's where we belong, not in tiny little offices. His specialism is insect monitoring. Berit, who normally sits *there*, is working on a very exciting project on the health of roach and small trout in lakes with high sulphur levels. NINA was set up by the Norwegian Parliament in 1988, marking the end of an incredibly long process. It was a question of separating research from management. To finally move scientists out of the Ministry for the Environment.

119

It's almost like the separation of Church and state, do you see? We can't have the Ministry dictating our research. That has to be free. Take, for example, farmed salmon . . . it's extremely important to the Norwegian economy, isn't it? But is it good? For the environment? For people? We can't have the government setting the agenda, can we? A government that only looks at financial considerations. No, our—'

It was undoubtedly all very interesting, but Mia stopped her at that point. It seemed as if the passionate head of research had almost forgotten the real reason for Mia's visit.

'About the fox?' Mia said, patting her bag gently.

'Oh. Yes, of course, I'm sorry,' Dobrov said, and finally rubbed the yoghurt stain off her cheek. 'Lars was supposed to be here, he's the expert, but he has gone to Lillehammer. As you can see, we're scattered to the four corners of the earth. The University of Lillehammer is responsible for most of the wildlife tagging here in eastern Norway. The admin side, however, happens mostly here, but after all, I'm the boss, so I do know something.'

She smiled and ushered Mia into a small meeting room.

'You said you had some photographs, didn't you?'

Mia sat down and took them out of her bag.

'It's about this red fox,' she said, sliding a picture across the table. 'As you can see, there are some dents in its ear, and I was wondering—'

'Hmmm, yes, exactly. Wilfred, now he should have been here, you see.'

The woman smiled at her again.

'Aha? And this is—'

A man in a lumberjack shirt and with tousled hair popped his head around the door.

'Weren't we supposed to have a meeting today?'

'No, it was moved to next week. Ottar has had to go to Vadsø.'

'Vadsø? But I only came in for this.'

'Weren't you told?' Dobrov smiled.

'No. As usual. Why does nobody ever . . .'

The man muttered to himself, shook his head in despair, and then he left.

'Where were we?'

'You mentioned someone called Wilfred?'

'Wilfred, yes.' Dobrov smiled again. 'One of our clever PhD students. A big fan of foxes. I wanted to offer him a permanent job, but love got in the way, sadly. He's in Australia now. Oh well, it happens.'

'OK, but do you think . . .'

Mia placed her finger on the photograph again, a little more firmly this time.

'It definitely looks as if there was a tag there,' Dobrov agreed, squinting through her thick lenses. 'Odd, though, in my opinion.'

'Why?'

'Because we have more or less stopped this.'

'Stopped what?'

'That kind of passive tagging. At least when it comes to red foxes. We got new transmitters last autumn. I mean—'

She gestured to her neck.

'Collars. GPS transmitters. They're better for the animal, and also for us; now we can follow them wherever they go. Every single step. We can see on the computer where they are at any given point in time. Exciting, isn't it? This new technology.'

'Passive tagging, what's that?'

'There are several ways to tag animals,' Dobrov began, in her professorial voice again. 'Leg rings, for example, which we use on birds. In the past we would sometimes use radio transmitters; they were surgically implanted into the animal, can you believe it? We actually found two brown bears killed by them. The implant reacted to moisture and rusted, causing the batteries to short-circuit. Tragic. So we've stopped doing that. The idea was that—'

'So that's passive.' Mia cleared her throat softly. 'As in this picture. Does that mean that you don't know where this one has been?'

'Yes. For that, we would need a collar. Unfortunately.'

'And that's what you're using on red foxes these days?'

'Yes, we started that a year ago. Funny, really—'

'So you're telling me that this fox was tagged before that. More than one year ago?'

'I would say so, yes?'

'So this is a case of passive tagging?'

'Yes.'

'Which means we have no way of knowing where it has been?'

'If we tagged it, it would be in eastern Norway. If someone else did, well, then it could have come from anywhere. Sweden, for example. We work closely with them.'

'OK, thanks for your help anyway,' Mia said, trying to hide her disappointment as she put the photographs back in her bag.

Her mobile rang just as she was leaving the building. The display showed an unknown number.

'Yes, Mia speaking.'

'Hello?'

A familiar voice that made her smile.

'Granny?'

'Hello? Mia? Hello?'

'I can hear you, Granny.'

'Hello?'

There was mumbling on the other end before the call ended abruptly.

Mia smiled as her mobile rang again.

'Hello?'

'Hello, Granny.'

'There you are. I must have pressed the wrong button. Why do these buttons have to be so small? What's the point of that?'

'Have you got yourself a mobile phone?'

'I have. How did you know?' the warm voice said proudly. 'It's red and it lives in my skirt pocket.'

'Very nice, Granny. How are you?'

'Me? Oh, we're not going to talk about me. I hear you've got yourself a new job? Congratulations.'

'Thanks, Granny. I hope to be there on Saturday.'

'What's that? Saturday?'

'Your birthday?'

The old woman snorted down the other end.

'No, thank you, I don't want a party.'

'You don't? Why not?'

'Instead I want to give you a present.'

'What?'

'I've thought about it for a while and now the time has come. I'm in Oslo tomorrow morning. Can you meet me?'

'Why?'

'So that I can give you your present. Can you meet me at noon?'

'I'm not sure.'

The old woman went quiet for a moment but managed to speak again.

'Can you, Mia? Behind the Royal Palace? At noon?'

'I'll do my best.'

'What?'

'I'll be there.' Mia smiled again. 'But I can't stay for very long.'

'It won't take very long.'

'Good. Then I'll see you there.'

There was silence once more, but she could hear that the old woman was still there.

'Granny?'

'Yes?'

'Are you going to ring off?'

'Oh, yes?'

'Press the red button.'

'Yes, dear, thank you.'

'I'll see you tomorrow.'

'You will.'

Chapter 22

Munch was in the gravel pit in Finstad, looking for the red marker that had been placed on the ground. He had been rather excited about his new hire, he had to admit, but he had taken flak from Anette Goli. The lawyer was known for her plain speaking and this time had been no different. *You offer her a permanent position after having known her for – what – fifteen minutes?* But that soon stopped. Both his own doubts and any criticism from Anette, who, after just two days, had gone from being deeply sceptical to being one of the new arrival's biggest fans. *What did she find? Seriously? On the ear of the fox? What did she suggest, did you say? What a mind. I wouldn't have thought of that.* Goli was walking towards him now. She had swapped her office clothes for something more practical, and that was yet another reason for him picking his team. They didn't just do the bare minimum. They went above and beyond. Because they wanted to. He had worked in places where the energy was so low that it felt like being in the dining room of an old people's home. But 13 Mariboes gate was the exact opposite. It could also be a little too much at times, but so what. Mia had suggested that the killer might have been watching them when they discovered the bodies. His team had regarded this as a personal insult. *Oh, he was, was he?* Anyone who didn't already have a job to do had put on their outdoor gear and were now searching the forest above them for evidence. Munch lit a cigarette from the previous one as Anette reached him, and pointed.

'You have to go all the way up to that row of trees to see the spot Mia suggested. From there I reckon you have around three hundred metres in either direction from where the view is good. You would need binoculars, obviously, but I'm guessing he had a pair of those. Anyway, I need to go: Dreyer called. I did tell you that she wants to see you in her office, didn't I?'

'I'm too busy.'

'Sure, but I did tell you, didn't I?'

'Oh, you did.'

'Great. At least *I'm* in the clear when she next kicks off.'

Goli smiled and turned to climb down the gravel pit, but soon stopped and made her way back up to him again.

'I almost forgot. I've had a telephone call from the National Crime Agency in Stockholm. They wonder if we would like some assistance.'

'Really? Which one of their teams who failed to solve the case do they want to send us?'

He hadn't intended to be sarcastic, but that was how it came out.

'They have a man who has been involved with the investigation from the start. A psychologist. He works as a profiler. Patrick something or other. It would save Ludvig and Anja from having to read every file from Sweden. It's a good idea, don't you think?'

'Absolutely.'

'That's what I thought you would say, so I've told them that he would be more than welcome. His plane lands tomorrow morning. I'll organize a flat for him, if we have one available. But you'll meet with him regardless, won't you?'

'Of course.'

'OK, great. I'll text you the time and place when I know more.'

Goli nodded and started once more to make her way down the gravel pit as Munch's mobile rang.

Marianne.

He glanced up towards the trees where fifty or so men and women were busy searching the forest floor.

He tried to avoid this.

His home life disturbing his work.

It was another world. And the two couldn't mix.

Not only so that he could concentrate, and enter his mind as deeply as he could, but so that he could live a normal life when he came home. *A life where no one found dead eleven-year-old boys in a field.*

His mobile stopped ringing, but her name stayed on the screen.

And then it hit him.

Was it today?

The 23rd of April.

Yes, of course it was.

Munch pressed the green button.

'Hello, Marianne.'

'Hello, darling, how is it going?'

'All right . . .'

'I didn't mean to disturb you, but you know what day it is today, don't you? Shall we visit this year, as usual, or do you want to leave it?'

Munch took a deep drag on his cigarette and let Marianne's question linger in the air.

The 23rd of April 1992.

Nine years since his father had lost his life. They had honoured him every year since with the family visiting his grave. A fine tradition.

Munch suddenly realized how tired he was. He hadn't slept much since they had found the two boys, and he was starting to feel it. A hint of frailty. A crack that let in tiny, negative thoughts under his armour.

Eight years.

That was how long the Swedes had worked and still not solved the case.

Would he, too, be standing here in eight years' time?

With no answers?

'Holger, are you there?'

'What, yes, of course. Listen, I think perhaps we should drop it this year. We're busy up here . . .'

His wife sounded a little disappointed.

'Yes, of course. Or perhaps we could postpone it? How about the weekend?'

A faint hope on the other end of the line, but he couldn't make any promises.

126

'Let's wait and see, OK?'

'All right. Will you be home tonight? Do you want me to cook you dinner? Put out some clean clothes?'

And then the memories came, although he tried to brush them aside.

His father.

Unresolved issues.

He imagined him in his mind's eye now.

Big and smiling.

On one of those never-ending skiing trips they always had to go on. Munch had grown up in a modest apartment block in Larvik, and these Sunday outings had been obligatory. His father, strutting ahead, with hot chocolate and oranges in his bag. His mother, more patient, fortunately, as her clumsy son tried to organize his legs on the journey to some destination far ahead. *Just a little bit longer. We're nearly there.* Norway. Patriotism. Finally he would arrive at some hilltop and his father would be grinning like a king surveying his realm. *Look at our country, Holger. The cradle of giants. It belongs to the people, do you see? We will never let capitalists take it from us!* His father had worked on the railways and been high up on the candidate lists for Norway's Communist Party. He had obviously never been elected to anything, for the simple reason that no one voted Communist any more, not that his father had ever seemed to notice. Every election night he would force his son to stay awake, always excited, always hopeful: *Tonight's the night, Holger, we're going to show them this time!* The poster of Lenin in the hallway and the strange green cap with the peak with the red star, which his father had been told by his mother to keep in the furthest corner of the wardrobe but which came out whenever there was a general or a local election. Accompanied by a wee dram; it had taken him years to realize that his father was an alcoholic. His father had never hit anyone and he was never visibly drunk when the children were around. It was his mother who had to put up with it, and Munch hadn't realized that either, not until it was too late, not until he saw the autopsy report after the car crash. A blood alcohol level way above the legal limit. A truck on the other side of the road. No one ever said outright that it might have been suicide; there was just a hint from their family doctor, whom Munch had subsequently visited. His father had had cirrhosis of the liver and the doctor had given him less than a year. His mother seemed to disappear afterwards. She turned into someone else. Now she was in a care home and had found Jesus, and she barely recognized her son when he dropped by, something which had sadly resulted in his visits growing ever rarer.

Munch had got drunk once in his life, at the age of fourteen, on his father's cherry brandy.

He hadn't touched a drop since.

'Did you lose the signal again, Holger?'

'What? No, I'm here. I'll try to swing by home.'

'Good. I'll leave you out some food.'

Something was happening up there now.

He could see Katja waving her arms.

'Thank you. Listen, I have to go. We'll talk tonight, all right?'

'All right.'

'Holger!'

He could hear the Dutch woman's voice echo across the gravel pit.

'We've found something! I think this is the spot!'

Munch dropped the cigarette on the ground and started moving his heavy body up the steep slope.

Chapter 23

Fredrik Riis was aware of how pleasant it was to see her again as Silje Simonsen closed the door behind them. They were alone in the classroom. It felt a bit odd to be back in a school as an adult, almost as if he had done something wrong. Silje took down the class photo from the wall and placed it in front of him. Fredrik was no fan of authority; perhaps that explained it. His father had been strict, very strict indeed. And young Fredrik had carried this with him into adulthood, exhibiting exaggerated respect for everyone who was senior to him in age and rank. The teachers at his school had been of the old-fashioned type, almost like a hangover from a 1950s teaching style – you couldn't call that a teaching philosophy, could you? Children were certainly not at the heart of it. Children simply needed turning into nice adults, to answer correctly and otherwise shut up. Fortunately, progress had been made since. He had visited a cousin's school on an open day recently and had been pleasantly surprised at how much more relaxed and welcoming everything had been compared to just fifteen years ago. The world was changing for the better, thank God.

'These are the two boys I was talking about,' Silje said in a low voice, placing her finger on the picture. 'Lasse. And Karl-Martin. Usually quite lively boys, but like I said, recently their behaviour has changed.'

'Have you tried talking to them?' Fredrik asked, turning the picture so it faced him. Twenty or so children were lined up, squinting at the camera, united in a community which would disperse in a few years.

'Perhaps I should have?' Silje wondered out loud, and chewed her lip. 'I just wasn't sure. After everything that has happened, you know? And I didn't want to spook them either. It's bad enough, what they have already been through, don't you think?'

'Absolutely.' Fredrik nodded. 'I'm glad that you decided to speak to me first. I checked the legal situation back at the office, and I think I was wrong. It's true that we need parental permission, but only for a formal interview. Chatting as we are now isn't a problem.'

'OK, good,' Silje said. 'Do you want me to fetch them?'

'Is now a good time?'

'Yes, I've already spoken to Bente, another Year Six teacher. She told me to just let her know when you arrived.'

'Great,' Fredrik said.

Silje Simonsen got up and headed for the door.

'Together? Or one after the other?'

'I don't know. Perhaps together? I don't want it to be intimidating for them. They'll probably feel more comfortable if they're together.'

'OK.' Silje smiled and disappeared out into the corridor.

His phone vibrated in the pocket of his jacket and he walked across to the window to take the call.

'Riis speaking.'

'Hi, it's Bernhard from the e-group. You sent us some footage and you wanted a registration number?'

'That's right. Any luck?'

'Do you want the good news first? Or the bad news? Or perhaps a mash-up of both at the same time?'

The young voice laughed.

'A what?'

'A mash-up? Good news? Bad news?'

Fredrik Riis heaved a sigh and glanced out into the playground. The new cyber department. The police force had finally acknowledged how far behind they were in terms of cybercrime and everything to do with electronic investigation. In a panic, they had scoured the internet for people to hire and had ended up with mostly nineteen-year-olds still wet behind the ears. This department was known as the e-group. Well, perhaps he was being unfair to them, but not much.

The situation was starting to improve, he had heard, but he had a hunch that the guy he was talking to still lived with his mum.

'So good news? Bad news?'

He could hear that Bernhard was munching on something and that he had his mobile wedged between his cheek and his shoulder while his fingers pounded a keyboard.

'Can you read the registration number on the plate or not?'

'Affirmative.'

'Pardon?'

'Yes. We can read it. I'm 99.7 per cent sure of it.'

'Go on?'

'But . . . we're currently experiencing a systems crash. Another one.'

'Windows?' Riis remarked dryly.

It was a standard joke in the department. He had been in contact with them before.

'Exactly,' the whippersnapper said. 'Weird, isn't it, how boomers insist on riding the Bill Gates horse even though the old nag is on its last legs?'

He laughed at his own joke, and then it sounded like he was taking a sip from a drink.

'Yes, really weird. Why don't you just run everything on Linux?'

'Exactly!' the boy exclaimed. 'I could do this so much more easily at home, do you get me?'

'I do. So will you be working from home now?'

'Eh, what? Er, no . . . I—'

'When do you think you'll be up and running again?' Riis sighed as he watched a ball in the playground bounce towards the window.

A dark-skinned girl ran to pick it up. She stopped for a moment, then she noticed him behind the window and studied him with her head tilted to one side before winking at him and running back to the other children with the ball.

Very cute.

Fredrik smiled. He had had the same reaction the last time he had seen his cousin. He wondered if men had a biological clock. Like women. Which announced that now was the right time to have a

131

child. He didn't know, but it certainly felt like it at times. Recently he had caught himself glancing longingly at people pushing prams.

'Could be an hour, could take us all night; the latter is more likely. You know, the Gates horse, it—'

'Call me when you have the registration number.'

'Sure. I—'

Riis rang off as the door opened and two apprehensive boys appeared.

'There he is,' Silje said, having reactivated her reassuring teacher's voice. 'His name is Fredrik and he's a police officer, but it doesn't mean that you're in trouble. He just wants a chat with you. *We* want a chat with you.'

The boys crossed the room and held out their hands.

'Lasse.'

'Karl-Martin.'

'Fredrik.' He smiled. 'Please sit down, and Silje is right. We just want a quick chat with you.'

He perched as casually as he could on the teacher's desk while the boys sat down behind their tables. They glanced briefly at each other, still nervous, and sat with their backs so straight that Fredrik almost felt sorry for them.

'You were friends with Ruben, weren't you?'

He smiled and tried to make his voice as gentle as possible.

'Yes,' they replied in unison, and looked briefly at one another.

'Was Tommy also his friend?'

'No, not Tommy, not so much,' said the boy called Karl-Martin.

He had tousled blond hair and bright blue eyes, and he looked a little like Emil from the Astrid Lindgren books.

'Any particular reason for that?'

The boy called Lasse hesitated.

'Well, he wasn't . . . wasn't really a part of the gang, I don't know . . .'

He stole a glance at Silje Simonsen, who offered him a supportive smile in return.

'He wasn't that interested in Tommy,' said the boy called Karl-Martin suddenly.

His friend reacted. 'Hey, Karl—'

'I know, but shouldn't we—'

'*He?*' Fredrik frowned. 'Who is *he*? Another boy?'

The boys shook their heads in silence.

'The man,' said Karl-Martin.

Fredrik could tell from looking at them now. The tension. Initially, he had thought it had to do with him being a police officer, but he realized now that its source was much more serious. The boys seemed quite simply terrified. But of what?

'Boys,' Fredrik said calmly, and leaned towards them. 'First, I want to say that if you've seen something and not told anyone yet, then it's quite all right. I don't want you to feel bad about it. Second, if you have—'

Lasse suddenly burst into tears.

'He said he was going to kill us,' he sobbed. 'If we told anyone.'

'The man?' Fredrik ventured cautiously.

They both nodded.

Karl-Martin's voice also wobbled.

'He wanted us to help him get Ruben up there.'

'Up where?' Silje asked.

'To the well house,' Lasse sobbed, running a hand under his nose.

Fredrik glanced quickly at Silje, whose eyes were widening.

'You met a man? Who wanted you to come with him to the well house? The little red one next to the shooting range?'

The boys both nodded, then shook their heads.

'Not us. He wanted Ruben to go up there.'

'OK? You're sure of that?'

They looked up at him for a moment.

'Eh?'

'I mean, you're sure that he specifically wanted Ruben. Not just any boy?'

'Yes.' The blond boy nodded vehemently. 'That was exactly what he said. He said he would give us money. If we agreed to help him. It was going to be a surprise. He had a present for Ruben. Up there. And he would give us a hundred kroner each if we could get Ruben to go there.'

Fredrik could see their small hands in their laps under the tables.

'This well house,' Fredrik said. 'Is that the place everyone knows about?'

'Not everyone, I guess, but most people. Teenagers go there to make out. And we have been there to spy on them. We haven't done anything wrong, have we?'

'Definitely not,' Silje reassured them.

'Of course not,' Fredrik echoed. 'Proper detectives, that's what you are. You should be proud of yourselves. For telling us this now.'

The boys peered cautiously at one another.

'Could we take it from the start? Can you manage that, do you think?'

They both nodded. They seemed to be less frightened now. Fredrik Riis took out his notepad from his jacket pocket.

'Where did you first meet this man?'

'Out by the football field.'

'No, it wasn't there,' the blond boy said. 'We first saw him down at the Burger Bar, didn't we?'

'Did we? I don't remember that.'

'Yes, think about it. Mum had given me fifty kroner and we were getting chips.'

'No, that wasn't me,' Lasse said.

'Yes, you were there,' the other boy said. 'And Else-Karin was there. And she said that Tove wanted us to go round to hers?'

'And did you go to Tove's house?'

'No, we never did, but you were there—'

'No, that must have been Mats.'

'Whatever,' Fredrik interrupted them gently. 'About the man you saw by the football pitch.'

'And at the Burger Bar.'

'And at the Burger Bar. Can you describe him to me?'

Both the boys were eager now; it seemed as if their greatest fear had relinquished its hold on them.

'He had a moustache,' Lasse said.

'And his teeth were weird,' Karl-Martin said.

134

'Yes, they were really weird.' Lasse nodded. 'As if the front ones were on top of each other.'

The boy opened his mouth to show them.

'Was he old?'

'Yes.' Lasse nodded.

'How old do you think he was?'

'About as old as you are,' the blond boy said, pointing to Fredrik.

'So, about thirty?'

'Yes. Or maybe forty.'

'He was really funny, like he wanted to be our friend, even though he was old. He talked about football, asked if we liked Manchester United and—'

'And Solskjær.'

'Yes,' his friend said eagerly. 'He asked if we liked Ole Gunnar Solskjær, and said that if we did, then he could get us his autograph.'

'His autograph?'

'Yes, his autograph.'

'OK?'

'Yes, he had been at school with Solskjær. He boasted of having dribbled past him, he said that he was actually a much better striker and that he was supposed to have played for Manchester United, but then something happened to his foot—'

'To his knee,' Karl-Martin corrected him, gesturing to his own leg.

'He was staggering a bit, so I guess that must be true.'

'Do you mean to say that he was limping?' Silje interjected.

'Yes, sorry, I meant limping.'

'So he would get you Solskjær's autograph. Did he also talk about Ruben?'

The boys looked at each other briefly.

'No, not the first time.'

'So you met him again?'

'Yes, over by the bus stop. He stopped us when we were out riding our bikes. That was when he asked us.'

'He showed us a photo,' Karl-Martin added.

'A photo of Ruben?'

'Yes. He asked if we knew him. And so on. If we could help him—'

'By getting Ruben to go to the well house?'

Both boys nodded now.

'And what did you say?' Silje asked them in a friendly voice.

'We said no.'

'OK,' Fredrik said. 'Can I ask you why? Why didn't you want to help him?'

It took a moment before the reply came.

'He wasn't being nice any more.'

'He wasn't? In what way?'

'He was different. Much more like, well, grown-up and strict, a bit like . . .'

Lasse glanced briefly at Silje.

'Like me?'

'Yes. Or no, not exactly like you, but you know how teachers get when they are cross—'

'Aggressive?' Fredrik suggested.

'Yes, exactly, he was practically spitting.'

'And that was when he said it,' Lasse stammered. 'That he was going to kill us. If we told anyone that he had talked to us.'

'And his moustache was different.'

'What?'

'Well, it was like . . .'

The blond boy drew his finger under his nose.

'The first time it was like this, but the next time it was more like that . . .'

'Do you think,' Fredrik said calmly, 'that if I got a sketch artist up here, then perhaps you might be able to describe him to us?'

'A sketch artist?'

They looked quizzically at one another.

'Yes, it's something we in the police use from time to time. If we don't know what someone looks like.'

'Do we have to draw him?'

'No, no, you just tell us what you saw and the sketch artist does the drawing.'

'OK?'

They glanced briefly at one another again.

'Maybe,' Lasse replied.

'But he was a bit different each time,' his friend said.

'That doesn't matter. Can we agree to that? That we send somebody up here? And then you can describe him to that person?'

'OK,' the boys said, looking almost a little excited now.

'Just one last thing: you're sure about this? That he was looking for Ruben? And not anyone else?'

'Yes. That was what he said.'

'Did he tell you why?'

They both shook their head.

'Good,' Fredrik said, getting up. 'Listen, boys. Thank you so much. You have done really well. And we're here to protect you now so you don't have to be scared any more. Will you promise me that?'

Smiles spread across their little faces.

'OK.'

He shook their hands firmly and watched as Silje ushered them back outside into the corridor.

He took his mobile from his pocket with trembling hands the moment the door had closed behind them.

'Yes, Munch speaking?'

'It's Fredrik. We have a description of the man.'

'What?'

'Two boys. They met him several times. Can you get me a sketch artist?'

'Of course.'

'Great, and listen to this.'

'Yes?'

'He was looking for Ruben.'

'What?'

'The victims aren't random. He knew exactly who he wanted.'

'Oh, shit.'

'Quite.'

'Well done. Are you coming to the office?'

'Soon. I just need to finish off here first.'

Fredrik Riis dropped his mobile into his pocket and headed eagerly out of the classroom to look for Silje Simonsen.

Chapter 24

The old man with the white hair had been expecting something to happen, but he had never in his wildest dreams imagined that they would be on to him so soon. It was daring of him, obviously, to invite six of Sweden's most famous personalities to a party, but why not? Live life on the edge, was his motto. An explorer, that was who he was, wielding his machete through unexplored jungles. He had taught himself that as a boy because he had often slept outdoors like a fox in a den, whenever he wasn't allowed in the house. Two fingers on his left hand still didn't work properly due to frostbite, but if his mother had said that he was a little devil who deserved to sleep outside, then she must have been right. Because you had to listen to your mother, even if her voice came out of the radio sometimes, and even when it wasn't turned on.

The party had been a huge success. Mikael Persbrandt had got drunk, as usual, and insisted on playing spin the bottle, but Allan Edwall had absolutely refused, and that was a relief because Persbrandt just wanted to talk about Maria Bonnevie all the time and how he would like to punch that smarmy Fredrik Skavlan in the face. But fortunately Cornelis Vreeswijk had taken out his guitar at this point and sung the 'Ballad of Fredrik Åkare and Cecilia Lind', and everyone had shed a tear and raised their glasses of Hallands Fläder aquavit until Ingmar Bergman had arrived, despite being depressed. A real party pooper. In the end, they had ganged up on him, all of them, and shut him in the basement.

The old man peered out from under the tinfoil-covered parasol and wondered how the authorities had discovered him so quickly. He had woken up on the floor covered by Max von Sydow's jacket, and that was when he had heard them. Voices coming through the planks that made up the kitchen wall. It wasn't hermetically sealed. He had stuffed newspapers into the worst cracks, but they had blown out. And the noises. But he had soon realized they weren't the usual noises. No, these were foreign powers who had come down from the moon and other places, and so it was better to make yourself scarce. Tinfoil. He had heard it would help. So he had ridden his bicycle as fast as he could to the supermarket in Göteborgsvägen and hidden in their stockroom behind boxes of crisps, right until they turned off the lights and he was free to help himself. To tinfoil.

The new job.

It might explain why the authorities were out to get him.

The fine new mobile. Which kept beeping in his kitchen drawer. Blasted thing.

He made up his mind. It had to go.

No more acting jobs.

The mobile.

He had to get rid of it.

The old man with the white hair braced himself, counted to three and then he ran as fast as he could across the yard.

Once inside the house, he stopped with his back against the door.

Good.

No noises now.

He covered his ears with his hands for a moment when he heard that Ingmar Bergman was still in the basement and banging on the ceiling with the broom, but finally he had arrived.

In front of the kitchen drawer.

Now how was he going to do this?

He looked around the kitchen. Fortunately, the answer was staring him right in the face. The yellow washing-up gloves.

Perfect.

He carefully put on the gloves and had just opened the drawer when the mobile beeped again.

Damn it.

He looked at the small blue mobile with apprehension.

Act 2. Scene 3. OK?
He thought it over for a moment.
He didn't want to let the director down.
Act 2. Scene 3. OK?
All right then.
It was do or die.
One final conversation.
The old man went over to the folder lying on the bench under the window and entered the number on his other mobile.

Chapter 25

Mia had slept well for the first time in a long time and immediately detected a similar optimism among the rest of the team as they gathered in the incident room for the first case review of the day. A beaming Munch entered the room and took his place by the projector.

'Welcome, everyone. Brilliant day yesterday, so we want to keep it up today. There's a lot for us to get through so I suggest we get straight to it.'

He pressed the remote control and the first photo appeared on the screen.

A large pine tree in the forest above the gravel pit.

'The killer was watching us.'

Another picture, from the ground underneath the tree this time.

'I know that this has upset quite a few of you, and that's good. I think we need to make the most of this anger.'

'Bastard,' Karl Oxen mumbled, and slipped a nicotine pouch under his lip.

'Exactly, Karl, good. It was hard to find a place up there with a good vantage point, but this spot was perfect. Partly concealed by the trees and yet it offered an unbroken view of the field where the boys were lying.'

Munch clicked for the next picture, which showed the view towards the location where they had found the bodies.

'Perhaps he picked the location first?' Katja van den Burg wondered out loud.

'Pardon?'

The Dutch woman looked athletic today, dressed in a blue Adidas tracksuit as if she had come straight from a run.

'Well, everything seems well planned, doesn't it? So the field may not have been chosen at random. Perhaps there's our answer. As to why he left the bodies there. Because he'd already found a good vantage point from which to watch.'

Low murmuring and nodding across the team.

'Good thinking, Katja.'

'This tells us quite a lot,' Anette Goli said.

'Such as?'

It was Karl Oxen again. Mia had had enough of this swaggering man. Strange, really, that the otherwise so intelligent Munch had picked him for his team.

'Surely you can work that out for yourself, Karl?' Katja sighed.

She folded her arms across the chest of the blue tracksuit top.

'Can't you?'

'Come on, people. Pull yourselves together. We haven't got time for this,' said Ludvig Grønlie from his seat by the wall. The old, greying investigator didn't say very much and, as a result, he had everyone's attention when he did open his mouth.

'What do you mean?' Oxen snapped, and turned.

'He wants you to shut your mouth,' Katja said, still with her arms crossed.

'And why the hell would I do that?' he growled, glowering at the Dutch woman. 'It's a fair question, isn't it? Why does it matter? If he found the place from where he'd be watching?'

Katja heaved a sigh and shook her head.

'We haven't got time for this, people.'

It was Ludvig Grønlie again.

Karl Oxen muttered something under his breath.

'Thank you, Ludvig,' Munch said by the screen. 'Near the place where he was standing, we found these . . .'

Next slide.

A small pile of cigarette butts. On the ground under the tree.

'Now, they could belong to someone else. But there's a fair chance that our man was standing there. The brand is Camel Lights and they have been sent off to Forensics. I've asked them to make it their top priority. Hopefully we'll hear if they can extract DNA from them perhaps as early as today.'

Smiles and nods again across the room.

'How easy is that, really?'

This time it was Anja who spoke. The bespectacled nerd didn't normally say much during team briefings.

'How easy is what?'

'Collecting DNA from cigarette butts. I thought that just happened on TV? Can you really do that?'

She gave a light shrug and looked around.

'I thought you went to Harvard?' Oxen chuckled.

'No, I went to . . . whatever: surely I'm allowed to ask?'

Anja looked mortified now.

'All biological traces left on a surface can be analysed,' Ludvig said. 'Blood, saliva, semen, skin, epithelium. The crucial bit is the amount recovered. If there's enough, we can generate a DNA profile.'

'Right? And is there enough on a cigarette butt?'

Mia's heart went out to the young woman, who obviously hadn't been hired for her forensics skills but for her IT expertise.

'If we're lucky, then we'll have found enough,' Munch said. 'We have twelve cigarette butts. I won't say we're home and dry, but we should be in luck. Like I said, I hope we'll hear back either today or tomorrow.'

'Fredrik?'

Munch nodded towards the besuited investigator, who got up and walked up to the screen.

'As I'm sure you've heard, I spoke to two boys at Finstad School yesterday.'

He took over the remote control from Munch.

'The boys reported that they had been in contact with a man who had tried to persuade them to entice Ruben up to the well house. With the help of a sketch artist we have produced these two sketches of the suspect.'

Two pencil drawings appeared on the screen.

'Hang on,' Oxen said, holding up his hand this time. 'Say that again? He didn't try to entice *them*?'

'No.'

'Oh, Christ. That must mean . . . that he only wanted Ruben?'

He looked around the room.

'Congratulations, Sherlock,' Katja said, taking a bite from an apple.

A muffled outburst from the others now.

'Yes, but—'

'Exactly,' Riis said, and continued. 'It's extremely important information, in my opinion. This man has evidently been in contact with several local children in the period leading up to the murders. And as Karl has insightfully pointed out, he specifically targeted Ruben—'

Oh hell, Mia thought, not realizing that she had spoken out loud.

Everyone's eyes were on her now.

'Yes, Mia?'

'Oh, sorry, I was just thinking—'

'Go on?'

'Well, the other boy. Tommy. He wasn't a part of that friendship group, was he? He was, I guess – how did you put it, Fredrik? – from the wrong side of the tracks, words to that effect?'

'Yes, indeed he was.' Riis nodded.

'So what are you thinking, Mia?' Munch said.

'No, it might not be very important, but the boys the man spoke to, they didn't do what he wanted, did they?'

'Do what?'

'They didn't take Ruben with them to the well house?'

'No, they were very clear about that,' Riis said.

'So perhaps Tommy did.'

The room fell silent.

'The other boy,' Mia continued. 'I'm thinking he is – *from the wrong side of the tracks*, maybe not quite so popular. We've already heard about his home life, on benefits, an absent mother – he might be more inclined to cooperate? A stranger approaches him, offers him money and much-needed attention?'

144

'Good thinking,' Munch said.

'That would explain a great deal,' Goli said. 'We were wondering about the relationships. I mean, Ruben and Tommy, they don't appear to have been friends.'

'It might also explain the crime scene,' Mia went on. 'The two boys. Positioned very differently. It was clear, or at least it was to me, that Ruben was the central character in the image. He was also the only one who had been fully undressed.'

'So Tommy was just—'

'A means to an end,' Mia said softly. 'Collateral damage.'

'This is excellent,' Munch said, nodding to Riis to indicate he could sit down again. 'OK, let's stay with this so it doesn't slip away. Two victims, one used to trap the other. Why?'

'Because he wanted Ruben,' Katja stated.

'But why? Why Ruben?'

There was silence in the room once more.

'The car crash,' Munch said, 'where Ruben was injured outside the Burger Bar, how are we getting on with that lead?'

'The e-group has been having some issues, but they're fairly certain they can provide us with a registration number later today.'

'Good. When we get it, that becomes our top priority, OK?'

Nods across the room.

'Again, why Ruben? Why him?'

'Perhaps we need to take a closer look at his family?' Goli suggested. 'That may be where the answer lies.'

'Good,' Munch said.

'We've already received several reports of concerns about his father,' Grønlie said.

'Yes, that's right, haven't we?' Munch said. 'I had decided to put them on the back burner, but now it seems relevant to investigate them. Ludvig and . . . Katja, please, could you follow up with anyone who phoned in?'

Nods from Ludvig and Katja.

'Don't forget Sweden,' Mia said.

'What do you mean?'

'The evidence suggests that he chose Ruben, yes, but which of the

145

Swedish boys did he choose? The answer can't just lie here in Norway with Ruben's family, can it?'

Low mumbling across the room once more.

'Unless there's no connection between the families in Sweden and those here in Norway?'

It was Karl Oxen speaking, and it was the first sensible thing he had said all morning.

'That thought has obviously crossed my mind too,' Mia said. 'But I haven't had time to go through everything from 1993.'

She looked up towards Ludvig, who continued:

'As I said, we have a ridiculous amount of material from Sweden. We're talking nearly—'

'One hundred thousand,' Anja said.

'Yes, almost one hundred thousand pages in the files, and where do we start? It's like looking for—'

'Start there,' Munch said firmly. 'Look for anything that might suggest a connection between the Lundgren family and the—'

He turned to Mia.

'Who do you think is the central character at the Swedish crime scene?'

'Oliver.'

'OK, so the Lundgren and the Hellberg families – go over everything we have and see if you can find something.'

Katja and Ludvig nodded.

'We can get you some help with that today,' Anette Goli interjected.

'Yes, of course, I nearly forgot,' Munch said, turning his attention to his team once more. 'Sweden has sent us a man to help with our investigation. A psychologist. He worked as a profiler for the three teams who worked on the case, so I think this is someone who could be very helpful to us. His name is—'

'Patrick Olsson,' Goli prompted.

'That's right. Olsson is arriving this afternoon, and then we'll make a plan for how we can best use him.'

'Maybe we could have him first?' Ludvig suggested with a nod to Katja.

'Exactly. Family leads. Is there a connection? Lundgren and Hellberg. Why did the killer choose Ruben? And Oliver?'

'If my young colleague is right,' Oxen remarked archly, with a nod towards Mia behind him.

'I think she is,' Munch replied with a faint smile. 'OK, so the families, what else?'

'The sketches,' Riis said, looking up at the sketches which had now been on display for some time.

'Yes, of course,' Munch said. 'As you can see, they are very different. That's because he looked different on each occasion when the boys met him. To be honest, I'm not convinced we will get very much from them; it looks as if he likes to disguise himself—'

'You think those are disguises?'

'It looks like it. Or at least one of them does. Let's discuss if we should release them to the public, and if we have the capacity to deal with the number of possible erroneous sightings of the two of them.'

He turned to Goli.

'I think we should make them public,' she said. 'I'll talk to the commissioner about getting more staff to answer the phones down at HQ.'

'Right, that's decided then. Release the sketches to the media during the day; hopefully it will add even more momentum to the investigation.'

He scratched his nose and thought for a moment.

'OK, does anyone have anything else to add?'

Riis stuck up his hand.

'Yes?'

'It's just a small thing. I don't know if it's important. It might not be true, for all I know, but something tells me that there might be something to it.'

'And that is?'

'When I spoke to the boys, they mentioned football. Manchester United. Our killer had used it as a conversation starter in order to engage with them. He also mentioned Ole Gunnar Solskjær. Claimed they had gone to the same school. They might even have played for the same football team. In primary school, I imagine. Something about a damaged knee. Our man was limping slightly. It might be nothing, but even so—'

'Definitely worth checking out,' Munch said.

'Clausenengen,' Oxen said.

'Come again?'

'Ole Gunnar Solskjær. He played for Clausenengen FC as a boy. In Kristiansund.'

'Great. You look into that, Karl. Old coaches. Old photos – you know the drill.'

'I'm on it.'

'Good. We have a lot to go on here. Let's get to work and we'll meet up again here tonight for an update, or sooner if we learn anything before then.'

Munch found a cigarette in the pocket of his duffel coat.

'Mia? You wanted a word.'

'Nothing, really. In private, please.'

'OK, my office shortly. Great, everyone. Good luck today.'

Munch smiled, stuck the cigarette in his mouth and disappeared off in the direction of the smoking balcony.

Chapter 26

The change had been a shock to the senses. Mia had been so consumed by her new job that she had almost forgotten there was a world outside, but it came back to her slowly as she left Karl Johans gate and walked up towards Palace Gardens. Big, beautiful trees greeting the spring with shiny, green leaves that fluttered in the light breeze. She couldn't see any birds and yet it seemed as if they were everywhere. Frenzied chirping, as if all the birds had gathered here to celebrate right in front of the home of Norway's royal family. The Royal Standard was flying, which meant the King was in residence. She had learned that as a little girl and, back then, her main concern had been how on earth the royals were able to find their way around such a big house. Just to go to the loo or to bed – you would surely have to walk so far that you would get tired, or what if you were going for breakfast? The King would have to plan every trip; otherwise, how would he manage it all?

They had gone there once on Constitution Day, on the day when the whole country donned national costume and cheered the royal family on the balcony. She had been so excited to see them, but it had been fraught. Hooting horns and stomping police horses, people clapping and hollering and waving their flags. It had started to make her feel anxious, being trapped in the street among a huge crowd of people, but her father's strong arms had been there for her. He had lifted her up on to his shoulders and the world had looked completely different. He wasn't a monarchist, not that he would admit to it, but he was certainly more supportive than her mother, who always complained about how much money was wasted on royal families. *Look at the UK. Where royals get married in silver*

149

dresses and golden thrones and pomp and circumstance costing millions, while people starve in working-class areas. How's that acceptable? Much better with her father, who smelled nice, wore freshly ironed shirts and whose wallet was always open. Later on there would be Constitution Day parades from Åsgårdstrand School, which were nice enough, but it was never quite the same.

A daddy's girl.

She felt slightly guilty remembering the label as she passed Grotten, Norway's honorary residence for artists, designed and built by Henrik Wergeland in 1841. Since then it had been the preserve of the very few artists deemed important enough to represent the country in an address next to the royal palace. The current occupant was the contemporary musician Arne Nordheim, with his plinky-plonk music, as her father referred to it, while her mother loved it. Of course she did. If something was elevated and a little elitist, she was always a fan.

He likes you more than me.

It was what Sigrid would say to Mia when she wanted to be horrid to her.

A daddy's girl.

Mia had always regarded it as a term of abuse. But she liked being in the garage while their father tinkered with the old, jade-green Jaguar which he had bought despite her mother's objections, and nearly every evening he was out there doing it up in the hope of one day getting it on the road.

A tomboy.

That was worse, but after a while, she stopped caring. About the girls in her class. Because she didn't hang out, as they did, at the Mobil petrol station, chewing gum and drinking alcohol while hoping for a ride in one of the cars up to the southern end of Lake Borrevannet to make out. Instead she bought herself a motorcycle, a red Honda CB100, which nearly gave her mother a heart attack.

What! Do you want to kill yourself? Are you out of your mind letting her ride it, Kyrre?

Her level-headed father also took her side then: *Surely she can spend her confirmation money on anything she likes? Sigrid does handball and horse-riding. Why shouldn't Mia have something of her own?*

Oh yes, a daddy's girl, that was probably what she was. Perhaps that explained why she had always got on so well with her paternal grandmother.

'Moonbeam.' The old woman smiled broadly and gave her a good, long hug.

Her grandmother had dressed up for the occasion. She had put her wild, black hair in a bun and wore make-up in fresh colours. She had on a fine red coat that Mia knew she loved, and her favourite ankle boots, gold-coloured with tassels at the back. Her dark, deep eyes gazed at Mia warmly as the old woman caressed her cheek with a wrinkled hand.

'You look nice, Granny.'

'No, you're the nice-looking one, Mia,' the old lady chirped and clasped her hands. 'Let me take a look at you. Imagine that. My little moonbeam has grown so tall.'

'You only saw me a few weeks ago, Granny.'

'I know, I know, but even so. Now you have a job and everything. No, this really is long overdue. Come with me. I've been looking forward to this.'

Her grandmother smiled, slipped her arm through hers and walked her up Parkveien and into the street behind it.

'This, my friend,' her grandmother said with a sly smile, 'is Inkognitogata.'

'OK?'

'There,' she went on, acting as a tour guide now as they walked down the elegant street, 'is the Korean embassy. And there's the Italian one. Right over there is the Prime Minister's residence. Further away we have the Chilean, the Swedish and the Cuban embassies. So this, my friend, is quite a location. And the King living next door doesn't do anyone any harm.'

The old lady winked, opened a gate and entered the small garden of a big, white building.

'Built in 1879, designed by the architect Stener Lenschow and, as you can see, it has an asymmetric facade in neo-Renaissance style.'

She said the latter with some exaggeration, as if she was starring in one of the programmes Mia's mother liked to watch on TV.

'We all have our little secrets, don't we? And this is mine.'

Her grandmother winked at her again and took something out of her pocket.

'From me to you, I love you so much.'

A key.

'What's this?'

The old lady smiled happily.

'There you go, my dear.'

Mia looked at the key, baffled. Again she looked up at the incredibly beautiful building and then back at her grandmother.

'In the 1950s,' the old lady chuckled, 'there was still life in these old bones. Swinging Oslo, yes, that was just the beginning. The post-war era made us all do – well, how can I put it? – somewhat rash and strange things.'

She laughed, then started to cough.

'Are you all right, Granny?'

'Yes, of course I am,' the old lady said.

'Is this . . . your house?'

'It is.' The old lady smiled slyly. 'Well, not all of it, or I would have had to have been much richer than I was back then, but all of the first floor is mine. All two hundred and fifty square metres of it.'

Again the key in front of her face.

'And now it's yours.'

'No, you can't—'

Mia was in shock. She was utterly lost for words.

'Oh, yes I can.'

Her grandmother took her arm again.

'No, really, Granny, you can't—'

'Come on.' The old lady smiled again, and started to climb the elaborate steps. 'Don't you want to see what it looks like on the inside?'

Chapter 27

Fredrik Riis had just picked up his lunch from the bakery in Wilses gate and was standing in the lift when his mobile rang. It was the e-group again. Fortunately, it was one of the senior staff this time.

'Hello, I'm Morten Olsen. Am I speaking to Fredrik Riis?'

'Yes?'

'I'm sorry that it took a while, we had a systems crash.'

'So I heard. But you were successful?'

'Oh yes, eventually. We struggled a bit with the last digit, whether it was a seven or a one, but we decided on seven.'

'OK,' Riis said. He had already forgotten that he was hungry.

They had found the van.

'I must admit that we were rather surprised,' the man on the phone said.

'You were?'

'Well, we saw the name on the request and thought perhaps it was a joke.'

'Because?'

The lift had reached the third floor. Grønlie appeared in the corridor and looked as if he wanted to have a word with him, but Fredrik waved him away and pointed to his phone.

'Your name *is* Fredrik Riis, isn't it?'

'Yes.'

'And you work with Munch?'

'Also yes.'

'And this isn't a joke?'

'Listen,' Fredrik said, starting to lose his patience, 'just tell me the name of the registered owner of the van, all right?'

'Sure. I just had to check. The white van on the video you sent us is registered to *you*.'

'What?'

'Or it's in your name. Do you own a business in Alnabru?'

'No.'

'Or do you have a namesake? The white Boxer has the registration number DK 87127 and is registered to Fredrik Riis Ltd, Verkmester Furulunds vei 12. So it's not yours, then?'

'Again, no,' Fredrik replied. He had now forgotten all about his lunch. 'Do you know what kind of business it is?'

'No. All we have is the name and the address.'

'OK, great. Thanks for your help,' Riis said, and ended the call as Ludvig Grønlie popped out his head again.

'Do you have two minutes?'

'No, not really. We have a hit on the van from the crash outside the Burger Bar. I'm going there now. Was it important?'

'Yes and no. Ruben's funeral has been moved forward to tomorrow.'

'So soon? Why?'

Grønlie shrugged.

'I don't know. What would you do if you were a parent who had lost a child? The grieving process has to start. Don't you think that's why? Munch wants us to send a team. Could you and Katja do it?'

'Of course. So what are we thinking? That since he watched us at the crime scene, he might show up at the funeral?'

'Something like that.' Grønlie nodded. 'The service is at noon in Lørenskog Church.'

'Right, thank you. I'll tell Katja.' Fredrik nodded and took the lift all the way down to the basement car park.

Fredrik Riis Ltd?

Had the circumstances been different, he might have found it funny, but he wasn't in the mood today. He had woken up to more text messages on his mobile, and this time he had chosen not to reply. Shit. How had he let this happen? Got himself mixed up in something like this? And now these coincidences? How was it possible?

A concert in Grünerløkka, a jazz trio; he couldn't remember the name of it. He had gone on his own. He often did; he didn't mind sitting alone and letting himself be enveloped by the music. Afterwards, in the lobby, he had been in a weird mood. Happy, yet a little sad, melancholic; the music had affected him. She had been sitting there. The lobby was busy and he had asked her politely: *Is this seat taken?* No agenda at all; he was just looking for a chair and somewhere to put his beer. Three hours later and he knew almost everything about her. Their conversation flowed effortlessly. First some light flirting. Music, movies, some politics, feelings, thoughts. The jazz club had closed and they had gone to another bar, as if it was the most natural thing in the world, more drunk now, but not excessively so, still thinking clearly, and then the sad stories had started. Fredrik Riis didn't know what it was about him, but there had to be something because people always wanted to confide in him. About their most private concerns. It was as if he had confessional DNA. Or perhaps he just exuded deep kindness; he wasn't sure, but it had been the case since he was a teenager. His schoolfriends entrusting their secrets to him in his room, invariably followed by: *You can't tell anyone*, and this had continued into adulthood. Ultimately that was what he had fallen for. Her grief. The petite creature in front of him who clearly needed a shoulder to cry on.

My husband isn't kind.

If it hadn't been for our daughter . . .

Not that he cares about her.

The soft, foreign body under the duvet at home in his bedroom.

Not until later.

The fourth time.

So what does your husband do for a living?

Shit.

He pulled up in front of the large warehouse and checked his mobile again, but there were no more text messages.

Thank God.

A small brass plate and a door leading up to the first floor; a row of offices, one after the other. He knocked softly on the first door and was summoned by an old woman who was sitting behind an old-fashioned reception desk. There was nothing to indicate what the business was, but it must have been going on for a while, because the interior looked unchanged since the seventies. The grey-haired lady smiled and ended her telephone call.

'Hello, my name is Fredrik Riis. I'm a police officer.'

The old lady laughed as she took his card.

'You're joking?'

'Oh, no, I—'

'Olav!' the old woman called out, and knocked on the flimsy partition wall.

A man the same age as her, wearing a waistcoat and corduroy trousers, came out.

'Yes?'

'Your grandfather's here.' The old lady smiled.

'Eh, really?'

'Fredrik Riis.' Fredrik introduced himself and held out his hand to the new arrival.

'Look.'

She got up and shuffled around from behind the desk to show him Fredrik's card.

'Good heavens.' The man in the waistcoat smiled and put on a pair of glasses hanging from a string around his neck. 'The police? Have we done something wrong?'

'I have a question about this van,' Fredrik said, and showed them a photo. 'It's registered to you. Do you recognize it?'

The old man hummed to himself, then led Fredrik down the narrow corridor. He pulled up a dusty blind in front of a window, smiled again, then pointed down into the car park.

'Do you mean one of those?'

Fredrik looked down at several rows of parked vans.

'We have thirty-two of them,' the old man smiled. 'So, yes, it might be one of ours.'

'What kind of business is this?'

'Commercial laundry,' the man said with pride in his voice. 'Forty long years next year. Would you like me to show you around?'

'No, I'm all right,' Fredrik said. 'Commercial laundry . . . as in?'

'Hotels. Six thousand hotel rooms across eastern Norway need clean linen every day. When my grandfather started the business, times were different. Back then we were located in the city centre, we were just ordinary dry cleaners, but one day, during lunch at Kaffistova, as it happens – you see, he had moved to the city from Seljord and he had no time for this *modern food*, as he called it—'

'Yes, impressive,' Fredrik gently cut him off. 'So that explains why you have so many vans?'

'We pick up dirty linen, we return it clean.' He smiled again. 'It could be our slogan. Every single day. Shuttling back and forth. Most vans go to the city centre, of course, but also to Lillestrøm, Gardermoen airport, Drammen—'

'But this van?' Fredrik said, holding up the photo once more.

The old man looked at it over the rim of his glasses.

'Yes, it might be one of ours. Have you checked with the drivers' office?'

'I haven't. And where is that?'

'Follow me,' he said, leading the way down a creaky spiral staircase and into a room on the ground floor.

It looked like a small café. Clearly the break room. A soft-drinks vending machine in one corner. A counter where, according to a sign, you could help yourself to coffee and crusty rolls, but: *Max three per driver. If you take more, please leave some money in the basket.*

A man with dark hair and a moustache who reminded Fredrik of a pirate put down his newspaper when they entered.

'Olav, what brings management down here to us mere mortals? Are you about to offer us yet another pay rise?'

Laughter from the other drivers, who were seated on a bench by the window.

'Not today,' their boss replied, seemingly unaffected by the obvious sarcasm. 'We're trying to track down a van.'

He nodded to Fredrik, who showed the picture to the man.

'DK 87127. Hmm.'

The man got up and went over to a list which was stuck up on the wall.

'Yes, it's ours. Why?'

He handed back the picture to Fredrik and wiped something off his moustache.

'Who uses that van?' Fredrik wanted to know. 'Does every driver have his own?'

The man turned to the other men by the window.

'Does anyone here know who drives . . .'

He looked at the registration plate again.

'DK 87127?'

Heads were shaken over the coffee cups.

'We have a rotation system,' he explained, nodding to the wall, where several keys hung under a sign saying AVAILABLE. 'If you need a van, you just pick up a set of keys.'

'So you don't know who—' Fredrik began, but was interrupted by a young man on the bench.

'Wasn't that the one that was nicked?'

More mumbling and nodding from the drivers.

'Bloody hell, it was, wasn't it?'

The dark-haired man ran a hand across his moustache.

'We're short of a van?' the boss exclaimed. 'Since when?'

The senior driver had been hoping for a pay rise, but clearly had no idea how to do his job, and was lost for words when yet again one of his colleagues came to his rescue.

'A couple of weeks ago.'

'So, around two weeks ago. I was just about to tell you, it needs to be reported, so we'll do that. You're a police officer? Can we—'

His boss was annoyed now, and stamped his foot on the linoleum.

'This is your responsibility.'

'Yes, it is . . . Only I—'

'Make sure you report the van stolen without further delay. Haven't I told you to get things in order down here?'

'Yes, yes . . .'

The man stared at the floor, ashamed now, while the drivers by the window reacted by grunting.

'So we're down a van. And nobody knows where it is?'

There was silence from the bench.

'Do it now.' Olav jabbed a finger on the table in front of his neglectful employee.

Fredrik and Olav went back upstairs, with Olav apologizing all the way up the creaking staircase.

'Again, I'm so sorry.'

'Do you have cameras out there?' Fredrik said, glancing down at the parked vans once more.

'Not out here. You need a key card to access the yard. But there are two cameras outside the gate. I'll check with the security guard to see if we have any footage.'

'Or a log of some kind? Surely the drivers have to sign in when they pick up a van?'

The old man heaved a sigh.

'Yes, that's how it ought to be. But you just saw for yourself. I'm too nice. My wife is always telling me. *You're too nice, Olav. You're not running a charity, are you?* My grandfather always said—'

'Please would you contact me if you find out who drove it last? Or if anyone remembers anything?'

Fredrik produced one of his business cards from his inside pocket and gave it to the old man, who nodded.

'Of course. I'll do my best.'

'Thank you. Nice to meet you.'

Fredrik nodded by way of goodbye, also to the old woman behind the reception desk, walked down the narrow stairs and back to his car.

Bother.

He had hoped to be able to ring Munch with good news.

Well, at least they now knew where the van had come from.

It was a start.

Fredrik had just got in behind the wheel when someone tapped on his window.

He recognized the face straightaway. The driver by the window who had told them that the van was gone.

The young man glanced furtively around.

'I know who did it.'

'What?'

'I know who did it, who took the van.'

159

Chapter 28

Mia Krüger wished that she could stop time for a moment and replay the last hour with her grandmother inside the apartment for ever. She was still in shock and didn't know what to say when the well-dressed old lady flung out her arms and executed a small pirouette under the ceiling rose in one of the many enormous rooms.

'As you can see, you can move right in,' her grandmother smiled. 'I have let it for years, but recently I've had the furniture I kept in storage moved back in. I'm not sure it's your style, but you can always replace it later. I thought it would be good for you to have something to get you started.'

'It's beautiful, Granny.' Mia smiled and carefully removed the dust sheet from a mustard-yellow sofa.

'Well, I'm not sure about that. It's not very modern, but it's better than nothing.'

'I love everything about it.'

'You do?' her grandmother said, tilting her head. 'Do you think you will be comfortable here?'

The world wasn't in tune with Mia's wishes right now, as her mobile rang in her pocket, interrupting the idyll. She walked into the massive kitchen, which had a view of the Italian embassy, and took the call.

'Hello, it's Holger. Where are you?'

Mia was temporarily wrongfooted.

Yes, where am I, really?

She glanced around the amazing apartment once more. She could still feel the joy bubbling in her stomach.

'I'm with my grandmother. I'm sorry, like I said, I had something to do. Is everything OK?'

'Yes, everything is fine. We have a hit on the white van from the Burger Bar.'

'You do?'

'Fredrik has done good. We're going to interview the driver now. That's why I'm calling.'

'OK?'

'I was supposed to meet the Swedish profiler, Patrick Olsson. He's on his way to Mariboes gate now, but we have to leave. Do you think you could come down here?'

'Now?'

'Yes, he'll be here any second. Do you have a car?'

'No, I'm walking.'

'Take a taxi.'

Scrambling in the background followed, and the line went quiet for a moment before Munch came back on.

'We're off now. Are you on your way?'

'I'm on it,' Mia replied, hung up and felt disappointed as she stuck her mobile into her jeans pocket.

'Work?' her grandmother asked.

'Yes, I'm sorry,' Mia replied. 'I have to run.'

'That's fine. I'll stay behind. Reminisce about my old life, if you don't mind.'

'Of course not. Stay as long as you like. We could even live here together. Wouldn't that be nice?'

Her grandmother laughed.

'You're very sweet, Moonbeam. But I prefer living by the fjord. And like I said, you can move right in. Do you have a lot of stuff in your flat?'

'No, hardly anything. I'll bring it down here as soon as I have a moment. As early as tonight, I hope.'

'That's lovely.' The old lady smiled. 'Did I give you the keys?'

Mia gave her another long hug, jingled the lovely bunch of keys all the way down the stairs until she was outside in the attractive street and ran as fast as she could to Bogstadveien to hail a cab. She was still out of breath as she got out of the cab after having frantically paid the driver, but it turned out there had been no need to worry. Patrick Olsson looked relaxed as he leaned up against the cream wall with his eyes closed. The taxi drove off and Mia watched him from a distance. A psychologist. That wouldn't have been her first guess. Perhaps some kind of creative profession. Architect. Designer. Something like that. He was stylish, that was why. A grey woollen coat over a black roll-neck jumper. Blue jeans. Brown suede ankle boots. Not bad. She was almost impressed. Few men understood shoes. Fine hands. Long fingers. Like those of a pianist. Blue eyes. Swedish. Obviously. But not blond. He had dark hair. Like hers, perhaps a shade lighter, and with a hint of grey here and there, something that suited him. How old had Munch said he was? Forty? That sounded about right. Too old for her, obviously, but even so. Definitely a handsome man. Could it really be him? The serial killer expert? The only member of the Swedish team who had been part of the investigation from the start? He looked more like a male model as he stood there, blowing his fringe away and glancing briefly at an attractive wristwatch.

There was only one way to find out.

'Patrick Olsson?'

She crossed the street and walked up to him.

His bright blue eyes lit up as he saw her.

'Yes?'

'Mia Krüger,' Mia said, and stuck out her hand.

'Nice to meet you.' He smiled as he picked up a suede bag from the pavement. 'Munch isn't here?'

'No, I'm afraid he's busy.'

'OK,' Olsson replied, slinging the bag over his shoulder.

'Is that all your luggage?'

He laughed briefly.

'Oh no. I've already dropped off my suitcase at the hotel.'

'They hadn't arranged a flat for you?' Mia asked, waving her card in front of the lock to the front door.

'I think they meant to, only it wasn't ready. It's fine. The Swedish police are paying. At least for now.'

A calm voice. He seemed trustworthy. She hadn't seen a psychologist since she was seven years old, but should it become necessary, this man would do. Lie down on the couch and tell him all her secrets. A charismatic glint in his eyes and still the hint of a friendly smile at the corner of his mouth as he stood patiently next to her in front of the lift.

'I've only just started,' she said, pressing the button. 'But I'm getting the hang of it already. I can sense him. If that means anything to you?'

The Swede's eyes lit up again.

'OK? So you are—'

'No, I'm not someone's assistant.' Mia smiled. 'Munch wasn't terribly specific when he hired me, but I guess you could say I'm a profiler. I'm not sure.'

'You're very young?'

He looked at her now. Sizing her up from head to toe, but it wasn't unpleasant in the way it could be sometimes when men stared at her.

'Yes.' Mia nodded and stepped inside the lift. 'A few days ago I was at the National Police Academy.'

Olsson laughed, still not in a way that was irritating, just friendly.

'Are you serious?'

'Yes. Like I said, I've only just started, but I'm making progress. Would you like to see what I've discovered so far? Or would you like the full guided tour first?'

'There's definitely no need for the full guided tour.' The Swede smiled broadly again.

'OK, great,' Mia said, pressing the button for the third floor again.

Chapter 29

Susanne Hval Pedersen hadn't waited by the door for her husband until he came home. Or, more accurately, she had tried, making herself comfortable in the hall on a kitchen chair with a cup of strong coffee and some magazines. But a few hours later it was like she was watching herself from the outside and seeing how absurd it was. There was no doubt that her husband was going through something – a phase, whatever – but they had always been able to talk about things before, hadn't they?

She had read an article in a woman's weekly some time ago: *Has your husband changed?* It had said that men often became distant and bored when they reached a certain age. A midlife crisis, apparently. The psychologist who had written the article explained that men often changed when they realized that there was more road behind them than in front of them. A house, a job and children, and on the wrong side of forty. That this was their lot in life, a daily rut of washing the dishes, paying the bills and watching boring Friday-night entertainment on TV. The long and short of it was your husband might seek consolation through infidelity. Often with a younger woman.

An affair? Please God, no.

She had felt sick at the realization, because he showed every sign, didn't he?

Was he often out at night? Tick.

Were his replies to her questions evasive? Tick.

Did he take less interest in their children? Tick.

Had he suddenly bought new clothes, started working out at the gym, got a new haircut, experimented with aftershave and developed interests other than his old ones? Er, no. Definitely no to that. The last time she spoke to him, two seconds in the corridor before he mumbled something and rushed out of the door, he had actually looked worse than usual.

So what was he up to?

Whatever it was, she was going to find out today.

She had driven Nora to nursery earlier than usual and had called in sick to work so she would be at home when he got up.

No chance for him to sneak out now.

What are you up to, Gunnar?

Nora misses you. I miss you.

Please, you can't go on like this.

Susanne hadn't missed a single day of work, but desperate times called for desperate measures.

She was going to get to the bottom of this.

Today.

There was movement outside the kitchen window again as she went to put her empty cup in the sink.

Yet another car with a photographer in the passenger seat. What was it with these journalists?

She opened the fridge and could feel it again now, the fear she had woken up with some days ago, a terror that refused to let go of her.

It could have been Nora.

No, don't even think about it.

Images had appeared in her mind, and she had run around the house again, hunting for the sedatives her doctor had prescribed, but she still couldn't find them.

He was going to be buried soon. Ruben.

She had decided against going. She knew Ruben's mother, Vibeke, a little, but it was really a nodding acquaintance. Vibeke's husband would say hello, but almost reluctantly, and only if she did it first. What was his name again? Jan-Ottar? Jan-Otto? Something like that. She had also heard rumours, not that you could trust them, but there was no smoke without fire, was there?

She fetched some eggs, whisked them together with a little milk, some thyme and chives, and poured the mixture into the pan on the cooker. A good but late breakfast. She would allow him that. Before he got a lecture. She was smiling faintly to herself now and turned on the radio as a car pulled up outside their house. Then another one. She twitched the curtain slightly. What was going on? A man with a reddish beard got out of the first car and gestured. He signalled something to another car which had pulled up across the road as he walked up their gravel path, followed closely by a younger man in a suit. Several cars had now arrived on the road behind the first two.

What on earth was going on?

Susanne quickly rinsed her hands under the tap and dried them on her trousers on her way out into the hall. She had just reached the door when the bell rang.

'Gunnar Pedersen?'

'Yes, he lives here, but he's asleep. Can I help you?'

'My name is Holger Munch. This is Fredrik Riis. We're police officers.'

'What? Has something happened?'

She could see movement further down the road now. The cluster of journalists making their way to her house.

'What—'

A piece of paper was thrust towards her.

'We have to ask you to wake him up.'

FOUR

Chapter 30

Eleven-year-old Kevin Myklebust was sitting in the back of the old Toyota Corolla, wishing the ground would open up and swallow him. How exactly that would happen, he didn't know, but it would undoubtedly be the best option for all concerned. Because Kevin believed that everything was his fault. It was his fault that his mother had to drive an old car which had broken down – yet again – in the middle of nowhere, with only trees around.

He had heard them again in the living room last night. His mother and Elsebet, one of her friends who would come over to watch *Big Brother* with her, and his mother had launched into her usual rant. *That could have been me on the telly. Not with this body, Christ, no, but the way I used to look. At least I didn't breastfeed him, that's always something.*

A long time ago his mother had been young and pretty, and she had turned heads, no matter where she went. Once, in Oslo, she had been stopped by a man who had asked her if she wanted to be a model. She would get a lot of money and live in New York, in a big penthouse flat, and not the crappy little basement flat they rented now. But, unfortunately, she had fallen pregnant with him and not done anything about it until it was too late, and now her life was ruined.

His mother finished her phone call outside and got back in the car with a sigh. She turned her face to the rear-view mirror and checked her lipstick was in place before she adjusted the mirror to look at him.

'Why am I stuck with this crappy life, Kevin? Can you tell me that?'

He gave a cautious shrug of his shoulders.

'This car? Eh? How's that fair? Why can't I have a decent car like everybody else? A new SUV. A four-wheel drive with a sunroof and a ski box, maybe a Mercedes. Wouldn't you like to see that? Your mum driving around in a big, fancy Mercedes?'

'Yes, I'd like that, Mum.'

'Yes, you would, wouldn't you? But do I have one? No.'

She shook her head and took her cigarettes out of her bag. She heaved a sigh when she realized only two were left in the packet.

'*Shit.*'

Kevin had looked at the cigarette packets in the shop many times and wished he had been tough enough to steal one for her, lots perhaps, so she didn't have to get upset that she could not afford to smoke as much as she wanted to. He knew that many of the other boys in his class did it, shoplifted, but his tummy had hurt even at the thought and he had felt shame on his way home. Not only was he a burden, he wasn't even tough enough to steal a packet of cigarettes.

The other children he knew had grandparents. Or most of them did. That would have been the answer, wouldn't it? Then he could have packed his bag and wouldn't even have had to say goodbye. He could just get on his bike or catch the bus. Gone to stay with one of his grandmothers. But he had never heard of either of them; he didn't even know if they existed.

No, it was very complicated.

'Well, at least we have breakdown cover. He forgot to cancel it before he bailed, didn't he, the idiot?' His mother smiled briefly in the rear-view mirror now and lit one of her cigarettes anyway.

The eleven-year-old boy nodded and attempted a smile as well. He liked it when he wasn't on the receiving end of her tirades. Sometimes he would do that when she got very angry, pretend to randomly ask about one of the men who had lived with them, because he knew she would start to slag them off instead.

'Bloody loser. Where are all the decent men? Well, they're not here, are they? Not out here in the back of beyond. If only we lived in Oslo. Why do I have to live out here? Why is life so unfair?'

No, he couldn't tell her why, even though one of his teachers had once explained to the class that all the money in the world was un-evenly distributed so that some people had a lot while many people had almost nothing, but he didn't think that was quite what his mother meant. Nevertheless, he had thought about it a great deal, but he didn't know what to do to make her life better.

'One whole sodding hour,' his mother fumed, and checked her wristwatch. 'What's the point? Why am I paying for roadside assist-ance if I still have to wait here for hours?'

Kevin was about to say that it was not her but Jan-Erik who had paid for it. Just like he had paid for everything else during the months he had lived with them. The rent and the electricity and the new television and clothes for his mother. And though his mother had said that he was just a goldfish and not a real man, she had cried a bit on the day he packed his bags and moved out. But not for long. Because a few days later, a man called Rune had moved in, and then one called Gunnar, but Kevin had liked Jan-Erik best, and he felt a bit sad when he left.

They never stayed.

Most of them were there only for a matter of weeks. To begin with, she was very keen on them. She would try very hard, put on a lot of make-up and laugh out loud at everything, flatter them. She would say they had big muscles, something which he knew she did care about, because she had commented on Ronny's muscles – Ronny was one of Kevin's friends – and said that he would probably be a good-looking man in a few years. And then she had twirled her fingers in his hair, and later Ronny's mother said that Ronny and Kevin weren't allowed to see each other any more. That was a real shame because in Ronny's basement was the world's biggest racing track, which his dad had built. And Kevin had loved being there, being allowed to race the really cool cars in the big room, but now that was no longer possible.

Kevin didn't know what he preferred. Living with his mother, just the two of them, but that invariably became problematic because every time letters arrived in the post she would burst into tears. Even though she didn't open most of them and just stuffed them in a drawer until she could barely close it. So it was probably better that someone moved in who could pay for things. Though they weren't all nice and seemed almost disappointed when they discovered a little boy had been hiding in his room while they were partying in the living room. Some would leave at that point, without even saying hello to him.

But not Jan-Erik. He had been so different from the others. Almost like a father.

Kevin had never met his father, but he was quite sure that he had one because from time to time when his mother was having a really bad day, she would say things to him like: *Stop looking at me with those eyes and freckles. You remind me of someone I definitely don't need to think about right now.* Which led him to conclude that a man who looked like that was probably his real father. A man with blond curls and freckles. And then he would do what he always did when things got bad, go to the bus shelter and stay there until it grew dark while he fantasized about what his father was like and, more importantly, *where* he was.

His mother rolled down the car window, flicked out the cigarette butt and looked briefly at the packet again, where only one cigarette remained now, and then she dropped it into her bag, only to change her mind, retrieve it and light it with an even heavier sigh this time.

'Christ, Kevin, what's going to happen to me?' she asked, studying her face in the mirror once more and shaking her head. 'Just look at me.'

His mother turned to him and pulled at the skin under her eyes and on her cheeks.

'I think you look nice.'

She turned back to the mirror and shook her head in despair again before suddenly reacting to something in the road behind them.

'Oh, finally. There he is.'

She quickly produced the lipstick from her bag, added a little extra red on top of the already thick layer and pulled down her jumper so that her shoulders were bare.

'Wait here.'

His mother opened the door and waved merrily at the man who had arrived in a yellow tow truck.

Kevin opened the window a tad to let out the heavy smoke. He could hear it in her voice now and see it in the way she moved her body. She was like a cat again.

'Right, what happened here?'

The man scratched his head as if he couldn't believe that anyone was still driving an old wreck like this.

'Well, I don't know. But you're my knight in shining armour, aren't you? You've come to help a damsel in distress.'

'Yes, I guess I have.' The man nodded and shook his head again.

'Wonderful.' His mother smiled and placed her hand on the man's arm.

Chapter 31

Katja entered the room, placed her coffee on a small table by the one-way mirror and positioned herself next to Munch, who was observing the man in his mid-forties sitting in the small interview room.

'We're letting him stew?'

Munch nodded.

'He needs some time to compose himself.'

'He looks bloody awful,' Katja said, and produced an apple from the pocket of her tracksuit top. 'Has he said anything yet?'

'Not a word in the car,' said Fredrik Riis, who had taken a seat at the far end of the room.

'And he doesn't want a lawyer?'

'No, so he says,' Munch said.

'How odd. He looks guilty as hell.'

Katja took a bite of her apple and moved closer to the one-way mirror.

'He's as white as a sheet. Look, he's shaking. He's guilty, if you ask me.'

'He might well be.' Munch heaved a sigh. 'But of what?'

He gave a slight shrug, took off his duffel coat and went into the interview room on his own. The man jumped out of his chair.

'Please stay seated, Gunnar,' Munch said, and also indicated that he could sit down again. 'Do you want something to drink? A cup of coffee? A glass of water?'

'No, thanks,' the trembling man mumbled. 'No, wait, perhaps a glass of water? My mouth is completely dry.'

'Some water, please?' Munch said, and gestured towards the mirror before flopping on to the chair opposite Gunnar Pedersen and pressing the button sunk into the table.

'The 24th of April. The time is 15.20. We're interviewing Gunnar Egil Pedersen. Present in the room are Pedersen and Holger Munch, head of investigation. Gunnar Egil Pedersen has declined his right to legal counsel.'

Munch looked at the man across the table.

'Please would you say it out loud, Gunnar?'

'Eh?'

He had zoned out and didn't look as if he knew where he was.

'For the microphone? You have refused a lawyer, is that right?'

'What? Er, no thanks. I don't need a lawyer.'

'OK,' Munch said, and opened the file he had brought with him. 'Gunnar Egil Pedersen. Born 2nd January 1956. Is that correct?'

'What? Er, yes.'

'Your address is 13 Timoteiveien? And you're married to Susanne Hval Pedersen and have a grown-up son and a daughter? Nora, aged five?'

Pedersen ran a hand over his furrowed forehead and nodded.

'Good. Then we have the right man. Let's start with a simple question. Do you know why you're here?'

The door opened. Katja entered, put a bottle of water on the table then left just as quietly.

Pedersen, too, was quiet; he still looked as if he was trying to make sense of it all. Wondering if any of this was real or whether he was still at home in bed dreaming.

'No?' he said eventually, and looked briefly up at Munch.

'No? That didn't sound very convincing, Gunnar. Let's try again, shall we? Do you know why you're here?'

The slim man chewed his lip then looked around for a window, which wasn't there.

'I . . . don't think so.'

'You need to make up your mind, Gunnar. You don't know why you're here? Or you don't think you know? Are you telling me that you have no idea? That we brought you in by chance?'

'No, maybe not by chance,' Pedersen said in a subdued voice, and stared down at the table again.

'Why don't we save ourselves some time, Gunnar? It's not much fun sitting here, is it? Why don't you just confess, and then we can all go home, wouldn't that be good?'

'Will I be able to go home?' Pedersen asked hopefully.

'Well,' Munch said with a nod towards the water bottle.

The man was so dazed he hadn't noticed that Katja had brought the water.

'That depends on what you tell us, doesn't it?'

Pedersen untwisted the cap, but his hands were trembling so much he struggled to raise the bottle to his lips.

'It wasn't . . .' he began, glancing cautiously up at Munch again.

'What wasn't?'

'Well, I didn't mean to. For it to turn out like that.'

His eyes found the floor again, in between his feet.

'All I thought was that . . . well, you know. It wasn't going to end this way. I never meant for this to happen.'

'You were just having fun?'

'Er, yes . . . or no, maybe not fun, but I thought that perhaps it was no big deal. Not at the start, if you know what I mean?'

Again, he glanced cautiously up at Munch.

'No, I don't understand, Gunnar. But at least it tells me that you know why you're here, can we agree on that?'

Pedersen screwed the cap back on the bottle with considerable effort, placed it on the floor by his feet and nodded softly.

'Yes? You know why you're here?'

'Yes. I know why.'

He sounded as if a weight had been lifted off his shoulders. His slender body expressed a strange kind of relief. He exhaled heavily and proffered Munch something that almost resembled a faint smile.

'But I never thought that . . . well, you know. That it would turn out as badly as it did.'

His ashen face looked serious once more. He cleared his throat and looked at Munch again.

'You were just having a bit of fun, was that it?'

'Yes. Or no, maybe I wasn't having fun, that's not the right word. But, yes, I was pissed off. Angry. I was. I wanted revenge. I had said that I would pay them back, hadn't I? But no, they refused to listen to me. And we weren't talking a lot of money, were we? Only a measly fifty thousand kroner. You don't give people the sack for that amount of money, do you? I had worked there for ten years. Do you think it was my dream job? Bookkeeper at a laundry? Hell, no. I've given them everything. I worked day in, day out—'

Munch interrupted him.

'What do you mean? Fifty thousand kroner?'

Pedersen looked up again, puzzled.

'Well, the money. Which I took. That's why I'm here, isn't it?'

'No, Gunnar.'

Munch took a photograph from the file and slid it across the table.

'That's why you're here.'

Pedersen looked at the picture and his eyes widened.

'What?'

The crime scene. The boys lying on the ground with the fox between them.

'Are you out of your mind? Surely you don't think that—'

'You were just having a bit of fun, Gunnar? To begin with? With the boys? Was that it? Inside the well house? A bit of fun, was that the plan? Get them drunk? Have some fun?'

'No, no . . . that . . .'

Pedersen's eyes widened even further and he shook his head frantically.

'But then things went wrong, didn't they? Did they die inside, Gunnar? Or was it later? Were they still alive when you brought them to the field?'

Pedersen's face was red now and he struggled to sit still on the chair.

'No, no, no . . .'

He recoiled and covered his face with his hands.

'Take it away. Take it away.'

'So you didn't do it?' Munch asked him calmly, placing a new picture next to the first one.

'No.'

Pedersen turned away from the images.

'No?' Munch said, placing a third picture on the table. 'You didn't kill Ruben?'

His finger pointed to the boy's naked body.

'And Tommy?'

Pedersen was trembling so much he could barely keep his face covered.

'I want one after all,' he whispered.

'What do you want, Gunnar?'

'A lawyer,' the shaking man mumbled. 'I want a lawyer.'

Chapter 32

Mia Krüger was sitting in Mother India on Pilestredet, in front of a bronze statue of Shiva, and realized that she felt tense because she had been unable to read the Swedish psychologist. She had done the talking. For almost two hours she had stood in front of the photographs at the office with a sense of having repeated herself to the point of boredom, and during the whole monologue, Patrick Olsson hadn't said one word. His grey coat was draped over the chair next to him. A pair of reading glasses under a furrowed brow. A few nods here and there. A notebook in his lap, which he would occasionally open and scribble something in, but he said nothing.

Finally, when she couldn't take it any more, she had folded her arms across her chest and asked him directly, 'So what do you think? Am I on to something?'

The Swede had merely smiled to himself, returned his glasses to their case carefully and said, 'I think we need something to eat. Do you happen to know if there's a good Indian restaurant nearby?'

Under normal circumstances she would have been annoyed. Standing like this, a little nervous, new to the job and sharing her thoughts with someone who had worked in the profession for a long time: *Come on then, man, say something. Am I getting close? Do I understand the perpetrator? Or am I on a wild goose chase?* However, something about him caused her not to flare up. He was so calm. So friendly. So trustworthy. His stillness was like the most natural thing in the world. And more importantly perhaps, at no stage in her presentation had she had the feeling that he wasn't treating her as an equal. Even though she'd only had this job for three days. Even though everything she knew came from library books – a lot of books, true, but even so, this case was different. These pictures were not from an American reference book. *Columbus, Ohio, 4 April 1987. Notice that the two prostitutes, just like in the previous crime scene, are placed facing each other, with the fingernails removed, and their hands on each other's hips.* Nothing like that. This was real. But if he had thought at any point during her lecture that she wasn't up to this job, he had not mentioned it.

'Coriander Chicken curry sounds good,' the Swede said from behind his menu. 'Have you eaten here before?'

'Once.' Mia nodded.

'What did you have?'

'Lamb korma. Number 53.'

'And was it good?'

She was getting twitchy; she couldn't bear to wait any longer.

'Absolutely. But I hear that everything is good here.'

'You can't go wrong with a tikka masala,' the Swede said from behind his reading glasses as his eyes returned to the menu.

And a memory surfaced, the one she hadn't thought about for a long time.

Seeing a psychologist.

She had been seven years old, and she hadn't understood very much. Early one Sunday morning, both her parents awake for once, even her mother, who usually enjoyed a lie-in.

We want to talk to you about something, Mia.

A seriousness she had never seen in her parents before, and the obvious thought had flashed through her mind. Had she done something wrong? What might it be? The thirty kroner in loose change which had been in the jar by the front door? It had been Sigrid's idea, but she had joined in, so she felt a knot in her stomach. They had bought sweets at the corner shop, which they had hidden in a secret place in the attic. Or was it the broken basement window? They had played croquet in the garden and she had been unlucky. She had missed the last hoop and her ball had gone astray. The window had cracked, but it hadn't smashed, fortunately. It was just a hairline crack; had they noticed it? Even though it was almost invisible?

Except this didn't feel like a telling-off.

Both her parents were so calm, their faces friendly; a pancake with jam on a plate was waiting for her.

'You know, Mia, that you sometimes seem to . . . disappear?'

'What do you mean, Daddy?'

'Well, you know, when you disappear from us?'

'Disappear?'

Her parents exchanged glances.

'Daddy means when you stare. It's not good.'

'When I stare?'

And then the pancake didn't taste as good as it usually did; it was just a cold lump in her stomach.

'You know what we're talking about, Mia.'

'Don't worry, it's no big deal, but we thought it might be a good idea for you to talk to somebody about it.'

Her father's warm hand in hers, fortunately.

'Do you know what a psychologist is?'

And then, once every fortnight over the next six months, young Mia would sit in the big chair, which smelled funny, in front of this strange adult who was trying to be nice, but she could see that he was just pretending, that he was mostly curious. It was always this question, as if he didn't care that he was asking her the same question over and over: But what do you *see*, then, when you stare at these things for hours?

A waiter arrived, the Swede made up his mind at last; finally the time had come for her to hear his verdict. The psychologist rested his spectacles on his nose, took his notebook from his bag and placed it next to his plate.

'OK,' he said with a smile. 'The first thing I have to say is wow.'

He leaned back in his chair, clapped his hands, then said it again.

'Wow. I am, to put it mildly, hugely impressed. No, that doesn't cover it, it's more a case of . . .' He laughed, showing her a row of pearly white teeth. 'Shock. Can I use that word? I've been working in this field for almost – well, how long is it now?'

The Swede was interrupted by the waiter, who had returned with a jug of water.

181

'Fifteen years? And you have been doing this – how long?'

Mia could feel herself getting hot under her jumper, almost a little embarrassed.

'I've read quite a lot.' She smiled. 'I practically lived at the library for a while—'

'Sure, sure, but what you have . . . your eye . . .' He pointed to one of his own eyes. 'You can't get that from books.'

'Oh, I don't know.' Mia smiled again and swallowed a large gulp of water to distract herself.

'I'm already a fan,' the Swede chuckled. 'How old did you say you were?'

'Twenty-two, almost,' Mia said.

'Good heavens. Again, quite incredible, seriously impressive. I can't wait to see you in action again.'

The Swede continued to chuckle as the waiter returned and poured him a glass of wine.

'Are you sure you don't want some?'

'Wine?'

'Yes?'

Mia shook her head.

'I don't drink alcohol.'

'You don't?'

'Well, not very often. There's nothing I need to numb myself. I like the world as it is.'

The latter had come out wrong. She saw him frown and the expression on his face changed as if she had reminded him of something.

'But again, that's just *my* body and *my* head. Most people I know drink, the whole world drinks, so that's what people do, isn't it? They drink? So I guess I am abnormal. In that respect?'

He was back again, the smile was in place, but he looked a little awkward as he tasted his wine.

Dear God, Mia.

Seriously.

Do you always have to speak your mind?

She turned away, a little embarrassed, and pretended to study the statue behind her. Shiva. Married to Parvati. The god of opposites, male and female, ascetic and animal, creator and destroyer. Suddenly she had a flashback to Sigrid in the classroom. Religious Education. The teacher sighing because she had asked yet another question. Creative and destructive. Mia cleared her throat and looked at the Swede out of the corner of her eye, hoping that she hadn't just done exactly that, destroyed their relationship before it had even started. After all, they would be working together, closely, for quite a while, until this was over, but the psychologist appeared to have taken it well. The notebook lay open now; he had his pen in one hand, wine glass in the other.

'Would you like to hear my feedback?'

He looked at her almost a little provocatively over the rim of the wine glass as an aroma of freshly roasted spices and curry wafted towards them.

'Yes, please.'

There was an abundance of food between them now, with sizzling scents from another world.

'Shall we eat first?'

'No, do we have to?'

'You want to hear my feedback right away?'

'Absolutely. I can't bear to wait any longer.'

He laughed.

'Are you always this honest?'

'Yes. I'm afraid so.'

'How refreshing. I think we're going to enjoy working together. I'm looking forward to our next session.'

The psychologist smiled, raised his glass and slid his notebook carefully across the white tablecloth towards her.

'Do you see this?'

'Yes?'

'I think you're a hundred per cent right about that.'

Chapter 33

Fredrik Riis had sat so long behind the one-way mirror facing the interview room that his body was getting stiff, but events on the other side had absorbed him so much that he had been unable to leave his seat. At the start of the interview, he had been excited because he had been sure that they had the right man. Gunnar Pedersen had been shaking like a leaf, his face ashen and his body slumped, ready to confess his sins, but once his lawyer turned up and Gunnar Pedersen managed to string a sentence together, Fredrik began to see that it wasn't quite as simple as he had originally thought. Gunnar Pedersen was guilty of something. But not of murdering the two boys. That had become increasingly clear. Fredrik could tell it from Munch, too, whose conduct was highly professional during such interviews. The more Pedersen was able to explain himself, the softer the investigator's voice became. They were at the final stage now, and Fredrik had just decided to stretch his legs and fetch himself a cup of coffee when Anette Goli appeared in the small room with two paper cups, one of which was for him, thank God.

'How is it going?' the lawyer wanted to know as she took a seat next to him and studied the scene in the interview room.

It was almost strange to see her like this. Sitting down. He knew that Anette Goli had been Munch's first choice when it came to hiring staff for the new unit, and he could well see why. Down at Police HQ she had been nicknamed the Duracell bunny; strictly, she was there to provide legal advice to her colleagues, but there didn't seem to be a job she couldn't do. He had hardly ever seen her sit down in all the time they had worked together. She was always on the go, a phone practically glued to each ear. It was common knowledge that Munch didn't get on with the commissioner at HQ, the old or the new, so Anette had taken on this responsibility as well, keeping the lines of communication open, making sure that there was a functioning level of cooperation. He was bowled over by her ability.

'Is he our man?' she asked in a soft voice as she pushed the paper cup across the table towards him.

'No, I'm afraid not.'

'We're sure?'

A hint of disappointment in her voice, echoing his feelings.

'Yes, unfortunately. Or at least I think so. And it looks like Munch agrees. Still, we'll keep him here overnight, though his lawyer is trying to get him back to his family.'

Goli furrowed her brow and sipped her coffee.

'So what's his story?'

Riis shook his head wearily.

'It's a bit sad, really.'

'Sum it up for me,' Goli said, glancing at one of the mobiles in front of her. 'Quickly, please. I have to run soon.'

'OK. Gunnar Pedersen. Bookkeeper with Fredrik Riis Ltd.'

Goli smiled at the name of the company.

'I know! What an odd coincidence. Perhaps I was meant to work there.'

'I'm pleased you're here with us,' Goli assured him as she quickly responded to a text message she had just received.

'Anyway, I don't know if he was bored with his marriage or with life in general. However, we now know he developed a serious gambling addiction over the last few years.'

'Go on?'

'Not sure exactly how, but it's to those fruit machines you find everywhere. You insert a bit of change, it flashes and you hope to get three lemons in a row or something.'

Goli ignored a new text message.

'So he was hooked on fruit machines? A grown man?'

Riis shrugged.

'It appears to be more common than you would think. A general

185

sense of being depressed, I guess. Then a fleeting burst of happiness. A dopamine rush. What do I know?'

'How sad.'

'It is, isn't it? And there were other issues, I believe. A poker game he had taken part in where he thought somebody had cheated him—'

'So money problems is what you're saying?'

'Yes. And in a desperate moment, he had put his hand in the till, not a great amount, I think, fifty thousand kroner. But he was caught and got the sack, and that's when it all unravelled for him.'

'But he was the driver of the van? That hit Ruben.'

Fredrik nodded and sipped his coffee.

'While intoxicated. Not sure how it all adds up; he hasn't been in trouble before, then suddenly he's in a lot of trouble. He doesn't remember very much; I think he was quite drunk. But he admits to stealing the van from the laundry, an act of revenge, possibly, and he accepts that he drove under the influence on that day, or at least he thinks so. He hit the car in which Ruben was sitting; he woke up the next morning with a broken nose and blood on his clothes, so he thinks it must have been him.'

'OK.' Goli nodded and glanced at her mobile again as a defeated-looking Pedersen and his lawyer got up from the chairs in the interview room.

'Well, at least that lead has been exhausted,' Goli said. 'It's yet another thing we can cross off our list.'

'Have we got the DNA results yet? From the cigarette butts?'

Goli shook her head.

'Sometime tomorrow morning, they say. Sorry, I really have to take this.'

'Yes, Goli speaking?'

The police lawyer nodded to him, smiled and then hurried out of the room.

186

Chapter 34

Munch parked his car outside the garage in front of the white house, turned off the engine and sat behind the steering wheel in quiet contemplation. A house. A garden. An amazing wife. A lovely fourteen-year-old daughter. On days like today, he wondered why he was so wedded to his job when he could be at home instead. Listen to a symphony. Open the windows to the back garden. Water the roses. This autumn he would turn forty-three, but he felt much older. And today had done nothing to alleviate that. Human misery. Some poor guy just looking for a bit of excitement in his life, who took a few wrong turns, lost his job and almost ended up a killer. It was pure luck that he had avoided the latter.

Munch shook his head wearily, got out of the car, lit a cigarette and stopped to gaze at the sky. April in Oslo. Brighter days. A soft, pleasant veil of twilight over the city and the scent of spring. Had it been a mistake? To say yes to this? His own unit? He could see her inside now, as he walked across the gravel and closer to the windows. On the sofa. With her legs curled up under her. The light from a lamp on a book that had almost slipped from her hands. She had fallen asleep. Exhausted from the day's work, no doubt. Asylum-seeking children fleeing all the misery of their world, and now her job was to teach them Norwegian and help them find their feet in a new country, in a totally different world. He loved her for this. For being this person. For helping others. Without asking for anything.

Munch went over to the hedge, threw his cigarette butt out into the road and had just lit another cigarette when his mobile rang.

'Hello, Mia.'

'Hello, Holger. Is this a good time?'

'Sure, sure, of course it is. Are you still working?'

'What?'

'Are you still at the office?'

'Er, yes.'

'You know you don't have to. You need to take a break every now and then. This is a marathon, not a sprint. I need you rested, understand.'

'Yes, I just want to finish something Patrick and I started.'

Patrick Olsson. The Swedish profiler. He should have been there himself to welcome him, of course, but it hadn't worked out that way. Besides, tomorrow morning's team briefing would offer Olsson a good opportunity to introduce himself to everyone. Still, it was good to hear that Mia and the profiler were on first-name terms already.

'How did it go?'

'How did what go?'

Munch couldn't help smiling to himself. The young woman hadn't been part of the team for more than a few days, but he felt he was already getting to know her. Chronically absent-minded. *She* had called *him*, but it seemed as if she had already forgotten that. He could almost visualize her. Her long black hair. Her blue eyes gazing intensely at the photographs on the wall as if she expected them to come alive for a brief moment and did not want to miss it for anything in the world.

'Mia, are you still there?'

'What? Yes, I just had to—'

'So it went well with Olsson? Has he settled into the flat?'

'No.'

'No?'

'It wasn't ready, I believe, so he has checked into a hotel room.'

'OK, I'll see what I can do.'

Munch made a mental note and placed it at the back of his already overstuffed mind. *Ask Anette about Olsson's flat. Make an appointment to see Dreyer. Read through today's notes from Anja and Ludvig. Brief Katja and Fredrik about tomorrow's funeral: photographs/camera in car/ask Katja to wear something other than*

the blue tracksuit. Ask Anette to finish her report on Ruben's father.
Rumours/is there anything in it/should we bring him in for an
interview?

'And yes,' Mia said.

'Yes, what?'

'It's going well. With Patrick. We started in the office for a couple
of hours. I explained what we or I had been thinking so far, then we
went out for something to eat, then he went to his hotel and I've
been here at the office ever since. There's something that doesn't
quite add up . . .'

And she disappeared again, but then came back.

'What is it?'

'I can't quite put my finger on it. Patrick said something about us
not having all the relevant photos from Sweden. I tried to ask Ludvig, but I couldn't get hold of him. Would you know anything about
that?'

'About Ludvig?'

'No, about missing photographs from the Swedish investigation?'

Another mental note landed in the pile with all the others.

'I'll look into it. Did he say anything about which pictures?'

'No . . .'

And she was gone again. He could hear her rearranging something in the office.

'Mia?'

It was getting darker around him now. Tonight's sunset was over
and the streetlights came on. He looked into his neighbour's garden
with envy. There was a blue glare from the television and he could
see the family in the living room. Together on the sofa.

'But he brought something with him.'

'What?'

'Patrick. He has brought quite a lot of material from the Swedish
investigation, and I'm wondering if we can't just use that. Don't you
think that would be better? Rather than Ludvig and Anja spending
days sifting through the files we were sent?'

'Of course. Good idea,' Munch said, lighting a new cigarette
from the previous one.

'And, yes, that's the real reason for my call. Or rather two things, but I need to think about it first, OK?'

'What do you need to think about?'

'If I ask you about both of them or just the one.'

Munch smiled to himself again. Her honesty was quite simply refreshing. He made another mental note to send Yttre at the Police Academy something to thank him for recommending Mia to them.

'OK. So ask me about the first one while you think. It's getting quite late, isn't it?'

'I got myself a new flat.'

'Good heavens, congratulations. Was that your question?'

She disappeared once more, but she swiftly came back.

'It's quite cramped here. There isn't room for everything. So I'm thinking, the walls in my new flat are enormous. Like big white canvases. Perhaps it would be good for me. To start over. In my flat. Look at everything with fresh eyes, if you know what I mean. And perhaps Patrick could have some walls as well. For his things. Then we could compare notes. Could we do that, do you think?'

She was sweet now, and he reminded himself of something he absolutely must not forget: even though she was clever, talented and apparently strong, she was still a fragile young woman.

'Listen, Mia.'

'Yes?'

'You're not at the Academy any more.'

'What do you mean?'

'It means that you can do pretty much what you want. It's great that you report back to me every now and then, about where you are and what you're doing, but you're in charge, OK? If you want to move everything into your new flat, then do it. I think it sounds like an excellent idea. As does combining it with everything Olsson brought. Perfect. I feel twice as blessed for having you both. But keep your mobile on, OK?'

'Aha,' Mia said in a distant voice.

'Did you hear me?'

'What?'

'I need to be able to contact you, that's all I'm saying.'

'Of course. Listen.'

'Yes?'

'How is Tommy Sivertsen's mother?'

'A staff member from our consulate visited the hospital in Alicante today, but she wasn't able to talk to her.'

'That's a shame. Do we know when she might be able to?'

'Anette is in contact with them. Why?'

'No, it's just that I—'

'Spit it out.'

'Tommy has some marks right above his ankles. I didn't see them at first because you can't see them properly when he is lying on his back, but I have just got the photographs from the post-mortem, and there, yes . . . oh, I don't know . . .'

'What kind of marks are you talking about?'

'Well, just some . . . dots . . .'

'Any mention of them in the post-mortem report?'

'I haven't read it.'

She disappeared for a moment again.

'Check it to see if there is. And I'll have a look at it tomorrow when I come to the office, OK?'

'OK . . . Do we have a team briefing tomorrow morning?'

'Yes, at nine o'clock.'

'I'll try to be there, but if I'm not, I'll leave a copy of the pictures in your office. How about that?'

'Great, Mia.'

He waited a moment for her to ask the next thing.

'Was there anything else?'

There was silence down the other end now.

'The second thing? The other question you had for me?'

More silence before she came back to him in a quiet voice.

'Perhaps some other time. Not tonight.'

'OK, Mia. Well done, good night.'

'Good night, Holger.'

Munch dropped his mobile into the pocket of his duffel coat and entered the house as quietly as he could in order not to wake Marianne.

Chapter 35

The church bells had long stopped tolling, but the sound still echoed when Fredrik Riis checked the cameras they had attached to the inside of the car. One on the dashboard facing the church and one at the top of each window to cover the street to either side.

'He's a good-looking guy, our Swedish psychologist,' Katja said with a teasing smile.

'Oh, you think so?'

'Sure, he's definitely my type. Almost makes me want to see a shrink.'

Katja giggled, then rolled down the window.

They had had a morning briefing some hours earlier, everyone rather excited. Another new member of the team and, not only that, someone who had worked on the Swedish investigation. It could have gone either way, but even Oxen had sat still and allowed himself to be impressed.

Quiet, pleasant and, yes, Fredrik had seen for himself that the charming profiler had looks on his side.

'It's good, I think,' Katja said.

'What is?'

'That he came here. With all his experience, I mean. She's really bright, our little student, but even so—'

'What do you mean?'

'Well, we've already had this conversation. She has some good ideas, but we can't base our entire investigation on her – how can I put it—'

'Intuition?'

'No, that's not what I meant, it's more that—'

'Munch is still in charge.'

'I know, I'm just saying that I think we're better off with Patrick here.'

'Because he's so good-looking?'

'Ha-ha.'

She pulled a face, then punched him on the shoulder.

'No, I meant because he's an experienced profiler. Someone who knows what he's doing. It's reassuring. I feel that we're in safe hands.'

Fredrik poured himself a cup of coffee from a Thermos flask and looked towards the church.

'How long is the service, do you know?' Katja said, and checked her mobile.

They were waiting for the service to end. The two of them and the uniformed police officers who were on duty outside, mainly to keep the press at bay. A spokesperson for the family had been on the news last night and asked for privacy. The words had been chosen with care, but everyone could read between the lines. Could journalists please stay away, for pity's sake? Not that it seemed to have had any effect. There may not have been hordes of them, but there were enough for the officers, who were now pacing up and down the pavement on the far side of the street, to have put up a cordon and shut the road to regular traffic. Three cars were already lined up near the old church steps, ready to drive close family members away. It looked a little like Hollywood. Lørenskog Church. With room for one hundred and forty. Except many more had turned up. It was almost like a whole nation mourning a head of state; groups of crying people who didn't know what to do with themselves once the church doors had shut, and piles of flowers, pictures and candles. Photographers were waiting with big tripods and long lenses aimed at the cemetery, hoping for the most evocative pictures of grief-stricken faces as the coffin was lowered into the ground, but Fredrik knew something they didn't. For security reasons it had been decided that Ruben Lundgren's family wouldn't carry the coffin out of the church. This would happen, unofficially, tomorrow morning, in the hope that the family could have a private moment to say their last goodbyes to their son.

'No idea,' Fredrik said, and drummed his fingers lightly on the steering wheel. 'After all, they didn't get started until – one o'clock, was it? And just getting everybody out of the church will take at least—'

'Yes, I know, but family and closest friends will be leaving first, won't they?' Katja said, gesturing towards the file which Grønlie had given them.

A complete list of all family members, close and distant; they had ticked off most of them, but some still remained unspotted.

'Did we see him?'

Katja pointed to a photograph of a man with glasses and a moustache.

'Who is that? An uncle on his mother's side?'

'Yes. Loki. Who the hell calls their kid Loki? Now you probably know your Norse mythology better than I do, but Loki? Wasn't he a trickster? A mischief-maker? It's like naming your kid Judas, isn't it?'

'Norse mythology? How on earth would you know anything about that? Is that on the Dutch school curriculum?'

She squirmed in her seat; she was already uncomfortable. Munch had asked her to wear something other than a tracksuit to represent the police force at the funeral. She looked as if she had borrowed Anette Goli's clothes, and didn't like them.

He laughed. 'What? Norse mythology? Tell me more.'

Katja heaved a sigh.

'Well, we didn't learn much about it at school, but I had this boy-friend once.'

'Go on?'

'Seriously? Are you going to make me tell you?'

'Of course I am. I'm even more curious now. How long ago was it?'

'Oh, six or seven years.'

'Wow, that's recent. So go on then. Norse mythology?'

She squirmed in her seat again, and not just because the skirt was clearly uncomfortable.

'Why don't we go through these?'

'We've been through them. Everyone is here, aren't they? Except for those who said in advance that they couldn't make it. The maternal grandmother who is in hospital. His aunt, who lives – where was it again?'

'In New Zealand.'

'Exactly? So what about Loki?'

He smiled again as if to tease her about it. It had been a long time since they had last hung out. Everything had stagnated, so to speak, since the time he had misread her signals on the sofa. It had not been a complete disaster, but even so, it was nice to share this moment with her, as an antidote to the tragedy that was unfolding in the white building in front of them.

Katja heaved another sigh.

'I don't want this going around the office, is that clear?'

'Of course. Now I'm even more curious.'

She shook her head.

'So I went out with a guy, OK? He liked black metal. From Norway. *Mayhem. Burzum. Dark Throne. Immortal.* And not just the music, but everything that went with it. Helvete, the record store, Norse mythology, and so on. So what do you do? You try to be the girlfriend who takes an interest, don't you? Let's put it this way: I have seen my fair share of Satanists.'

She winked at him and took a bite of the apple she had put next to the gear stick.

'Wow. I would never have guessed that.'

'My dark past.'

She laughed briefly.

'So what are we talking about here? I mean, body piercing, black hair?'

'The whole caboodle.'

'You went to concerts looking like a corpse?'

'And that's enough for today.'

'Are you serious? White make-up?'

She mimed a zip across her mouth.

'Oh, come on! Is that why you always dress like Sporty Spice now? Are you compensating?'

This time she punched his shoulder so hard that he winced, and he was just about to deliver his next jibe when the church bells started to ring and the mood in the car went back to sombre.

Katja raised the camera to her eye and used the telephoto lens to have a look around.

'Where are you . . .? Where are you . . .?'

The cigarette butts they had found in the forest were the primary reason why Munch had decided on this surveillance.

He likes to watch.

Observe his creation.

What's better than a funeral?

'You like this, don't you? Come to Katja now.'

The sound of the shutter and the mirror lifting so that images could fix on the sensor was reminiscent of a machine gun.

The doors to the church opened and the mourners appeared. Heads bowed. Black clothing. A sobbing mother, who had to be supported in order to walk. Restlessness among the journalists now, a sea of lenses pointed at the mourners as they made their hesitant way down the steps, towards the waiting cars, and then it happened.

It was like a scene in slow motion.

A photographer had managed to get past the cordon. Arms trying in vain to stop him. The alarm on the grieving faces when they suddenly found themselves staring into his camera, and then something the mourners would talk about for a long time afterwards.

The uncle.

Loki.

'Give me that camera, you evil bastard!'

One hand snatching the camera from the photographer, the other punching him in the face until he collapsed on his knees with blood pouring down his shirt and he lay curled up on the tarmac.

'Is that what you like? Harassing people?'

The uncle raised the camera into the air before he smashed it with huge force into the head of the man who was already on the ground. Then he did it again.

'So how do you like this? Is this fun for you?'

A foot aimed through the air towards the already bleeding face, but by then she had reached them.

Katja.

She subdued Loki, put him on the ground, then nodded to Fredrik.

Get them out of here.

And he was in the middle of them.

He could see everything close up.

The sunken eyes. Tears pouring down cheeks.

'That's right. That's it. Just get in the cars.'

A few moments later it was over.

Red rear lights disappearing in the distance.

Katja sitting astride Loki's back, looking sternly at the uniformed officers who were only now coming to their aid.

'Where the hell were you? Get the squad car up here *now*.'

Fredrik Riis didn't realize that he had blood on his shoes until he stepped aside, feeling rather shaken up, and called for an ambulance.

Chapter 36

Mia Krüger took a few steps back to take in, almost with a sense of pride, the new wall she had created. It had been messy in the small office. This felt much better. A fresh perspective. Smiling, she skipped across the old parquet floor into the kitchen and brought a cup of freshly made coffee back to the living room. The apartment was enormous, but she had decided to start small. Inhabit a couple of rooms first. She had made three trips last night, taking the tram up to Torshov and back down to the Nationaltheatret, and had discovered that she didn't own very much. Her old room was practically empty. What was left of her stuff could stay there, she didn't care; someone was bound to want it. As she walked out of the door for the last time she had thought how fed up she had been with the poky flat share and how wonderful it felt to be going to this beautiful apartment. Her very own? She could hardly believe it. She would have to have a word with her grandmother. It was too much. She couldn't accept such a generous gift. Perhaps she could rent it from her? Pay her own way. After all, she was earning now. Her first month's salary had already been paid into her bank account. It stung a little that she probably wouldn't get back the deposit she had put down for the flat share, but OK. Never mind.

Her grandmother had left some items of furniture behind, old and attractive chairs and tables covered by dust sheets, but she had carried everything into one room and closed the door. The apartment was now otherwise empty. Amazing, really. Nothing to disturb her. She had picked a bedroom overlooking the garden. A big bed in the middle of the room; nothing to disturb her there either. Two large living rooms and an attractive kitchen. That would do for now. This was her priority: the images stuck on to the walls that surrounded her. Everything else was on hold. Life could wait. She sat down, barefoot, on the floor and put down her mobile. She had sent him a text message, but he hadn't replied. She had smiled as she watched it being sent. *I'm ready.* That was exactly how it felt. That she was awake. Present. But sharper than she had been for ages. All her senses on full alert. Like a hunter tracking her prey. She had barely been able to sleep. She had lain, excited, in the big white bed, waiting for the light, for dawn to break. Of course she felt guilty for not having wandered the streets, searching. But she had been out there for such a long time, hadn't she? She had handed out flyers everywhere. If Sigrid was in Oslo, she must know that Mia was looking for her. Oslo wasn't a big city, or at least the junkie scene wasn't. After all, Mia already knew most of them, didn't she? For fuck's sake, Sigrid. Why are you doing this to me? She immediately felt bad about this too, that thought. Of course no one should feel sorry for her. That wasn't the point she was making, sitting here in her new palace, with her new job and everything, and her sister out there and—

She stopped herself. She refused to go there. It was a visual nightmare which nearly destroyed her mind. Distorted images of Sigrid – high, surrounded by . . . no, enough, she pushed it aside and fetched a second cup of coffee. She probably ought to eat something, but resisted the urge. Food made her drowsy. Lethargic. She much preferred this, a little sleep, a lot of coffee, her head completely clear, her nerves on edge, almost on the verge of what was responsible. She sat down, then got up to move two photographs from one wall and fix them to the completely bare wall facing the kitchen.

A dead fox.

A dead hare.

A fox. A hare.

One red. The other white.

White? Purity? Innocence?

She snapped off the cap of the pen she was holding with her teeth and ran to the third wall, which she had covered with plain sheets of paper.

White.

The child. Innocence.

Yes, definitely.

She was on to something.

So why do you like innocence? Vulnerability? Does it give you a feeling of power? Do you like being in control? For once? Is that something you don't typically feel in your life?

Those eight years?

Was that why?

Did they lock you up for eight years? In a psychiatric hospital? Where you had to do what they told you to?

Did they make you feel small again? Insignificant? So you had to show them?

Who you really are?

That you are not someone they can boss around? That you are . . .

She wrote THE WOLF in capitals, on its own on one of the large new sheets of paper.

It's a full moon tomorrow.

I'm scared of The Wolf.

From Oliver Hellberg's diary.

The blond angel in Sweden.

It was easy, of course; she hadn't even needed to check the case files.

28 May 1993.

She could just look up the date on the Internet.

A full moon.

She drained her coffee cup and ran back across the beautiful floor to make another pot; she waited impatiently for the water to boil, fearing she might lose her train of thought.

The Wolf.

That's your excuse, isn't it?

For killing someone?

It makes you feel better?

Doing what you feel compelled to do?

Patrick. In the restaurant. That was what he had written in his

200

notebook, which he had slid across the tablecloth, the point he believed she was right about.

You're just pretending. For your own benefit.

A wolf. Hunting its prey.

As if this is natural.

As if what you are doing is natural.

You're not to blame, are you?

She spilled coffee on her way back but didn't have time to wipe it up, not now; she hurried back to the wall.

He's pretending.

In order to justify himself.

Why Oliver? Why Sven-Olof? Why Ruben? Why Tommy?

She refilled her cup and sat down on the floor again.

No, no. This was all wrong.

Fredrik's interview with the boys, friends at school who had known him.

Ruben.

It was all about him. Tommy's role was purely to make Ruben go to the well house.

Had it been the same in Sweden?

She checked her mobile, but Patrick had yet to reply.

Sod it. She wished he was here now. Her brain was painfully slow. Because she already knew the answer.

She jumped up and ran to the wall, took down the photos of the fox and the hare and replaced them with two other pictures, the crime scenes. Both of them. Where she could see all the bodies.

Oh, get a grip, Mia.

It's right there.

You were the one who spotted it in the first place.

One boy naked, on his back, at the centre of it all; the other unimportant, not even completely undressed.

Quickly she scribbled underneath the pictures.

I want Ruben. I want Oliver. Why?

She crossed it out again and wrote in capital letters.

WHY?

She was shaking now. She could barely drink the rest of her coffee.

Look, Mia. It's right here. You must be looking straight at it. Now get your brain in gear.

Suddenly her mobile rang, an unknown number, but she didn't have the energy to take the call, not now.

Why Ruben?

Why Oliver?

She stepped back from the wall. And suddenly she saw it.

Dear God.

She ran across the floor once more, snatched the photos from the wall and held them up to the light from the window.

That's it!

Your brain is so slow it hurts.

It was staring you in the face all along.

Is it possible?

On the floor, her mobile buzzed again, and she pressed the red button impatiently to make the unknown caller go away, then she scrolled to find Munch's number.

'Yes, Holger speaking.'

'Hello, it's Mia.'

She could feel it herself now. How fast she was speaking. Her heart was pounding under her black jumper.

'Hello, Mia, is everything OK?'

'I know why, Holger.'

'Why, what?'

'How he picks them. Why he chooses those particular boys.'

'Are you in the new flat?'

'Yes.'

'What's your address?'

'Number 12 Inkognitogata.'

'Stay where you are. I'm on my way. Give me ten minutes.'

Chapter 37

Fredrik Riis felt ill at ease as he sat in the incident room with his shoes on his lap, rubbing the cloth against the soft leather to remove the blood. Katja was also in a bad mood, slumped on a chair next to him, while Ludvig Grønlie shook his head as he stuck up on the wall the last of the pictures she had taken.

'Not good.'

Grønlie heaved a sigh and repeated what he had just said, but this time he was addressing them.

'Not good.'

'But for heaven's sake!' Katja exclaimed, and threw up her hands. 'We weren't there on babysitting duty. It's not our bloody fault.'

'Whatever, it's not good.' Grønlie sighed again and pushed his glasses further up his nose. 'You know how this makes us look, don't you?'

'Like amateurs,' Fredrik mumbled as he studied one shoe, which fortunately was starting to look clean.

'Exactly,' Grønlie said.

Munch had just left the room, growling. Fredrik had rarely seen his boss as irritated as he was now, but fortunately Munch's mobile had rung and he had stormed out of the room to take the call before his mood deteriorated even further.

'The idiot will live,' said Katja, who had taken off her skirt suit and was back in her tracksuit. 'It's par for the course, surely? I mean, show some respect. Don't just shove your camera into the faces of those poor people.'

'That's not the point,' Grønlie said. 'I'm sure he got what he had coming; the point is that all of Norway's media were there, lock, stock and barrel. Have you seen the news? It's everywhere. What do you think the commissioner is going to say? She's always looking for a reason to blame us. Do you think Munch will be allowed to run this unit for ever? Oh, no. If it was up to her, she would . . .'

He trailed a finger across his throat.

'I know, I know, but Jesus Christ. We were just there to take some pictures. Munch was in charge of the uniformed officers, wasn't he? Or was it Anette? Don't blame us.'

'I'm just telling you. Munch has already been summoned.'

'Where?'

'To a meeting with our beloved Hanne-Louise Dreyer. Rumour has it that she wants to reassign the investigation.'

'No way.'

'No, seriously. That's what people are saying. I believe Kripos has already been put on standby. They're reading up on the case.'

Katja fell silent. Fredrik didn't know why, but Katja had left the Homicide Unit briefly after a previous case and worked for Kripos, Norway's National Crime Agency, for a while.

'OK, can we drop this now? And do the job that we're meant to be doing.'

Fredrik put his shoes back on and stood up. He walked up to the wall and nodded towards the photographs.

'So these are the spectators? How do we do this?'

Neither of the other two said anything.

'Oh, come on. If they take the case from us, well, they take the case from us, but until they do, we give it our all. And yes, Katja, I agree with you. No way we take the fall for this. Public order? No, that was never our responsibility.'

Katja's mood seemed to lighten somewhat and she, too, got up from her chair.

'Are these all the pictures, Ludvig?'

'That's everything I've got, yes.'

'OK, so where do we begin?'

Ludvig shrugged.

'Over there, perhaps? The press line-up? The photographers? I can ask around. Send the pictures to the news desks. Cross off your own journalists, your own photographers. See if we end up with someone we can't account for?'

'Good idea.' Fredrik nodded.

'No, it isn't, it's going to take us weeks.'

'No, days possibly, but what else are we going to do?'

'It's fine,' Fredrik said in an encouraging tone of voice. 'Let's make a start. How many people are we talking about? Fifty, maybe? That shouldn't take too long, I mean, I can personally identify nearly half of them.'

'My money is on this group,' Katja said, pointing to another picture. 'But where on earth are we going to start?'

The mourners with flowers, soft toys and photographs. Mourners who hadn't been seated inside the church.

'Well, like this perhaps,' Ludvig said, and took a pen out of his pocket. He walked up to the picture. 'Women, we can eliminate them, can't we? Now that is . . . what would you say? . . . Well over half of those present? So we're left with what? Forty males approximately. And if we then cross out children and teenagers, what are we left with? I'll do a quick count, twelve to fifteen men? We have to be able to identify them, don't you think, sunbeam?'

Katja pulled a face at him, but she nodded her approval.

'Yes, we should be able to do that.'

'Exactly. Like the Americans say: if life gives you lemons, make lemonade. Or perhaps they don't say that in the Netherlands?'

'No, we don't say that, but we have something like it.'

She took the pen from him.

'And what's that?' Ludvig prompted.

'Stop being so bloody positive and fetch me a coke, then I promise to be in a better mood when you come back.

'Good heavens. How poetic.'

'It is, isn't it?'

Katja pulled another face, a friendlier one this time, and started crossing off faces on the enlarged photograph. Ludvig hummed to himself as he left the room.

'He's right, isn't he?' Katja said. 'Take a look. Not that many adult men.'

Fredrik was about to join her when his mobile rang. When he saw the name of the caller, he stepped out into the corridor to answer it.

'Hello, Silje.'

'Hello.'

Her voice sounded anxious.

'Is something wrong?'

'I—'

'What is it?'

'I think I might have done something I shouldn't have. I didn't know who to call and—'

'I'm glad you called me. What is it?'

There was silence for a moment before she replied.

'You know Ruben's father?'

'Jan-Otto Lundgren? What about him?'

'Well, it's just that I feel really bad now, I don't think what I've done is entirely legal—'

The usually cheerful teacher sounded almost on the verge of tears.

'Relax. I'm sure everything is fine. So tell me what you have done.'

He closed the door to the incident room and walked even further down the corridor.

'You know, well, we talked about how his father might not be a nice man? That there had been rumours about him not treating Ruben right?'

'Yes?'

There was another pause.

'I have a friend who works for Social Services. I decided to take matters into my own hands and I asked her to tell me if they had anything on him.'

'A case file?'

'Yes.'

'And?'

'Well, she isn't allowed to do that, of course, but I know her well, we've been friends for a long time so—'

'Did you find anything?'

She disappeared again.

'Hello?'

'I'm sorry, listen . . . it doesn't feel right talking about this on the phone. Could we meet somewhere? Somewhere not in public? A more private place?'

'Where are you now?'

Ludvig was coming down the corridor, carrying a can of cola, and disappeared into the incident room with a smile.

'I'm in town, in Oslo. My mother is minding Siri, so I'm on my own. Where are you?'

'I'm at work. Do you want to come here?'

'No, I don't know—'

'Or my place? Would you prefer that?'

'Oh, I'm nervous. I shouldn't have done this.'

'How about I jump in a taxi and you do the same? We'll meet at my place – as soon as you can? I'll text you my address, OK?'

Another silence.

'Are you sure it's going to be OK?'

'Of course. I'm leaving the office now.'

'OK. Great. Thank you so much.'

'Don't worry about it. I'll see you soon.'

Chapter 38

Munch parked his car and was impressed as he looked up at the majestic white building. He wondered if Mia might have given him the wrong address. Inkognitogata? Surely mere mortals didn't live here, did they? He could make out the Prime Minister's residence a short distance away. Suddenly she called down to him from a window on the first floor.

'It's open, just come on up.'

He passed a bright green hedge which looked as if it had been trimmed with mathematical precision and was about to push the large front door when his mobile rang. It was Karl Oxen. Munch had had his doubts, to be perfectly honest. Oxen had a reputation for being impetuous and unnecessarily macho, but Munch had wanted diversity in his unit. A range of personalities. But perhaps the time had come to have a word with him. Katja had never been specific as to why she had suddenly requested a transfer to Kripos, but her brief exchange with Oxen during a recent team briefing had made him realize that Oxen might well be one of the reasons. A personality clash. It was something he should have addressed earlier, but everything was so fresh. The unit was so new. Nor had he wanted to admit defeat and make changes already in only its first year. But perhaps the time had come.

'Hello, Karl. What's up?'

He took a cigarette from the packet in his pocket and lit it, squinting against a sun which was peeking out from behind a cloud.

'Ole Gunnar Solskjær. I'm starting to see the big picture, but I'm still not sure. Something tells me I might do a better job if I flew up there to see for myself. Spoke to people in person.'

The boys Fredrik had interviewed at the school. The man on the drawing who had boasted of having played football with the Norwegian hero but whose injury had put a stop to his career.

'He always played for Clausenengen. As a kid, I mean, made his debut with their A-team at the age of seventeen. I wonder if I shouldn't jump on a plane and take a look at some old team photos. I spoke to one of his old coaches. What do you think, is it worth it?'

'I'm not sure,' Munch replied. 'It's just hearsay, and he might easily have made it up, but at the same time it's so specific that I think we should give it a go.'

'You mean, if he was lying, why lie about something like that?'

'Exactly. I think you can spend a day or two up there. Keep me posted along the way, OK?'

'Will do,' Oxen grunted, and hung up just as a puzzled-looking Mia came down the steps with a banana in one hand.

'So are you coming up or what?'

'Yes.'

Munch smiled and followed her inside the imposing building.

'Jesus. This is where you live?'

Mia gave a slight shrug.

'I'm still not sure what really happened, but I have a key, so I do for the time being. Please leave your shoes out here, would you?'

She tossed the banana peel on the kitchen counter and walked barefoot in front of him into an enormous white living room with a ceiling rose. The bright room was completely bare apart from the walls, which were plastered with photographs and notes.

'Good heavens!' Munch exclaimed. 'Perhaps we should have tried to get offices here.'

'Yes,' Mia agreed, without appearing to have heard him.

She was already facing one of the walls which had fewer pictures on it.

'So what have you got?' Munch wanted to know as he went to join her.

'Again,' Mia said, brushing some hair away from her eyes. 'I could be completely wrong, and after we spoke on the phone I

209

started to have doubts, but every theory is worth considering, don't you think?'

'Absolutely.' Munch nodded and switched his mobile to silent.

'I've heard from Patrick, by the way.'

'Aha?'

'He was going to meet me here after the team briefing, but he's unwell. Stomach problems. I hope it wasn't the curry. I feel fine. Anyway, he didn't think he would be out of action for very long, so I've reserved a space for his photographs over there.'

Mia pointed to a part of the wall which had yet to be covered.

'Go on then, try me,' Munch said.

'OK. So at first, I looked at the crime scenes. At how the boys had been posed. Why is Ruben completely naked while Tommy is still wearing his underpants? And it's the same in Sweden. Why is Oliver completely naked while Sven-Olof is in his underwear? And then there was something the schoolmates said to Fredrik. That he wanted Ruben specifically . . . by the way, have we heard anything more on that front?'

'Wilkinson and his team are still in the area,' Munch said. 'Knocking on doors, shaking people up a bit, you know. There's a lot of gossip, but very little actual information so far. We have some sightings, and we think they might be of our man, from a distance admittedly, but they're on the case, and I have great faith that Wilkinson will come back with something. Somebody always knows something, although they don't know that they know – or at least that's my experience.'

'Good. What about the artist's impressions? Anything there?'

'Oh, what haven't we got? Everyone is calling the incident line about anything from suspicious uncles to someone they might have seen poking around next door's garage. You know what it's like.'

'Not really.'

He smiled faintly.

'No, that's true. You've barely been here a week, but you're so professional that I keep forgetting.'

'Did you just compliment me?'

She turned and looked at him warmly.

'Perhaps I did.'

'Thank you. So back to the crime scenes. It would appear as if – no, that's too vague – it's quite clear that the killer is interested in one boy specifically, in both cases. Perhaps he likes killing both of them, but I have a feeling that he really enjoys killing one of them *in particular*. Do you follow?'

'I do.'

'So I had been staring at these pictures until I was practically blind when I suddenly realized that – hello? How dim can you be? The pictures I need to look at are *these* ones. Of the *living* boys, don't you see?'

She took some pictures from the wall, held them up to emphasize her point and then put them back.

'Take a look.'

She took a step to the side and gestured to the four photographs.

'Aha?'

Pictures of all of them alive.

'What am I looking for?'

'Take another look.'

She removed two of the pictures so that only Ruben and Oliver were left behind.

'No, hang on.'

Mia ran to the other wall and came back with a crime scene photograph.

'This one is better. I think the other was an old picture of Oliver. His hair looked like this when he died. It was longer.'

Munch swore softly to himself. He could see it now.

Mia smiled triumphantly.

'Isn't it remarkable how similar they are?'

'Why didn't I spot that earlier?' Munch wondered out loud.

'It's not easy to see. Because the boys aren't identical, that's not it. They just have the same – how do I put it? They give off the same vibe somehow, don't they?'

'Dear Lord . . .'

'They're both blond. Their hair is quite long, they have very blue eyes. And take a look at this. I didn't notice it at first because the

211

eyes lose their shine when you die, of course, and in this photograph of Ruben there must have been something wrong with the light. But in *this one*? And again, this picture of Oliver, look at his eyes. Bright blue. And look, here and here. Freckles. Ruben has many, not as many as Oliver, but he does have them, doesn't he?'

She pointed eagerly. Munch nodded slowly.

'And they're both of slim build. Delicate. Perhaps they were also shy, but what do I know?'

'What do you mean by shy?'

'Their character, how they came across. Many boys at that age, they're – how can I put it? They try to act tough, don't they? Just to show off. Some of them are a little feral. But I bet you that if we had met these two boys, they would have been gentle souls. Kind. Humble. And he likes that—'

'This is progress, Mia,' Munch said.

'It is, isn't it? It has to mean something. They look almost angelic, don't they? Like those pictures. What do you call them? Cherubs?'

'So he likes this type . . .' Munch said softly.

'Fragile, tiny, blond, humble, kind—'

'Great job, Mia.'

'I can't take all the credit,' Mia said, and darted to the kitchen.

She returned with a pot of yoghurt.

'Sorry, I need to eat something. I keep forgetting. I'm practically hollow.'

'Why not? Who is due the credit, then?'

'Jodie Foster.'

'Come again?'

'Have you seen the movie *The Silence of the Lambs*?'

'No, I'm afraid not.'

'Oh, seriously, Holger. You have to see it. Hannibal Lecter is a serial killer. He helps her and gives her a hint. *You covet what you see.*'

'Which means what?'

'You desire what you see. You *want* something, you *have* to have it, and you can't stop yourself – that's what it means. The movie was based on a real serial killer, Ed Gein. He lived in the US, of course.

212

In Wisconsin, in a small town somewhere in the countryside. When police searched his house, they found several items of furniture upholstered with human skin, masks made from real women's faces, a belt made of human nipples, a lamp shade made with the skin from a face. There were body parts everywhere: lips, fingers, genitals—'

'Jesus,' Munch said, and patted his duffel coat to locate his cigarettes.

'Exactly. And so I thought that it might be what we're dealing with here. That it's based on something real. I mean, he sees them . . .'

She tapped her finger on the photographs.

'He wants them. And he decides to take them.'

Munch stuck a cigarette in between his lips.

'But how?'

'You mean where does he pick them?' Mia said.

'I'm not sure. Schools? Football pitches?'

She hesitated.

'I have a hunch that it might not be so deliberate. That he happens to come across the children somehow and then he gets the urge. Otherwise there would be more victims, wouldn't there? If his urge is so strong that he practically chases them, combing playgrounds and other such locations for them.'

'You might be right about that.'

'Do you know what Ed Kemper said when he was first interviewed by professionals who were interested in why he had decapitated his mother and later had sex with the head?'

'Yet another serial killer?'

'Yes.'

'How much time have you spent studying them?'

'A lot. But anyway, he said: *It's like a sneeze. You just kind of have to, don't you?*'

'So it's like sneezing?'

'Yes. Because that's not something you can control either, is it?'

'Good grief.'

'Is it the same for the man we're looking for? Perhaps he didn't even know he was like that. Perhaps Sweden was the first time. He

213

saw Oliver, this attractive, delicate child – I don't know – and he just had to.'

'OK, but why wait eight years until the next time?'

'Perhaps he got scared afterwards. Scared of his own violence. If he was a total beginner.'

'But we don't know that.'

'No, but have you ever seen other homicides like these? Young boys, one of them naked, with an animal posed between them? So it could have been his first time. And how does it feel after the first time?'

She looked at him hard as if he was meant to say something, but he couldn't think of a reply.

'The first time?' she continued. 'An intense experience. No matter what it is. I mean, parachuting, sex, bungee jumping, free diving forty metres – a total rush, isn't it? A kick? But in contrast to the experiences I just mentioned, this is . . .'

Her finger jabbed the crime scene pictures again.

'This is different, isn't it? Killing someone. That release. It teaches you something about yourself. You might have suspected it deep down for a while. It's easy to deny as long as you don't act on it, but now you've done it, haven't you? So now you know who you are.'

'So you think he had himself admitted?'

'Bingo.' Mia nodded. 'Perhaps he got scared. Scared of who he really was. *I'm sick. I need help.*'

'At a psychiatric hospital?'

'Quite likely. And he's there for a long time, years. He feels better. Perhaps he even believes he's well. He returns to society. He might even get a job. Until one day. A bolt from the blue.'

She pointed to Ruben.

'And history repeats itself?' Munch said.

'Exactly.'

'A new desire.'

'*You covet what you see.*'

'Mia, I can work with this.'

'Yes?'

'Absolutely. You've done really well.'

He took the cigarette from his mouth and looked about him as her mobile vibrated on the floor.

'I need to get that. That same number has been trying to call me all day.'

'Where can I smoke?'

'Go that way, through a couple of rooms. There's a balcony at the back, on the corner.'

She waved him off, chewed her lip and looked as if she had to brace herself before she finally pressed the green button on her mobile.

Chapter 39

Eleven-year-old Kevin Myklebust was woken up by noises coming from the bathroom and realized that it had happened again. There was a new man in the house, and his mother would be a different person, at least for a while. Which he didn't mind, because whenever there was a new man in the house, she was always nicer and didn't complain to him as much as she usually did. His mother seemed to be lots of different people. Two, at least. One when she was alone and another when she and Elsebet drank red wine, because then she suddenly appeared to like him a little bit. Well, she did for as long as Elsebet was there. *You and me, Kevin, eh? We muddle along just fine, don't we? We don't need a man in the house to be OK, do we? You're the man of the house, aren't you?* He would join them and his mother would squeeze him tight, saying he could help himself to the can of cola in the fridge, though it was really hers, and it wasn't even a Saturday.

And that was what he had striven to be ever since that night. The man of the house. He wasn't sure what it actually meant, but he had tried to do what the other men who had lived with them had done. Like Rune. And Gunnar. And Jan-Erik, who had been the one he had liked best.

But it wasn't as easy as he had imagined. Being the man of the house. He had done everything he normally did. Get breakfast ready. Clear up afterwards. Tidy the living room when Elsebet or one of his mother's other friends had stopped by. Pick up glasses. Empty overflowing ashtrays. But the toughest job of all remained. Paying the bills. He hadn't been able to do that. No matter how hard he had racked his brains. He didn't have any money and the bottles he collected down by the foot-ball pitch for the deposits provided far from enough.

So perhaps that explained why she had brought a new man into the house after all.

He could hear them more clearly now; the walls were flimsy. His mother laughed and said things he had only ever heard on television. He stuck his fingers into his ears, then counted to ten thousand, and by then they seemed to be done. They were in the kitchen now. He could smell bacon and coffee, and that was his cue. He didn't want to see either of them naked – no, he really didn't – but it was probably safe for him to come out now.

Kevin got dressed, still lying in his narrow bed, then he entered the kitchen with a forced smile.

'Hello.'

'Oh, hello, darling. You remember Ulf?'

A hand was extended towards him.

'Yes, hello, hi. Of course I do.'

It was the man with the tow truck.

'Take a seat and I'll get you some breakfast, sweetheart.' His mother put on the affected voice she always used whenever there was a new man in the house.

'No, thank you. I'm not hungry. And I've got to go. I've made plans. I don't want to be late.'

'Oh, where are you going, son?'

He grabbed an apple as he headed for the door.

He wanted to say: I'm meeting Ronny – except I'm not allowed to see him any more because of you, but he couldn't make himself; he didn't want to be cruel.

'Just a trip to the library. We have a project at school. I'd like to do well.'

'Oh, what a good boy you are, Kevin.'

For some reason, she was wearing an apron. His mother came up to him and patted him on his head.

'Kevin is doing really well at school. I can't imagine where he gets it from. Certainly not from me.'

Giggling now, she slipped into the arms of the new man and kissed him on the cheek like a proper housewife would probably do.

'Good for you,' said the man whose name was Ulf. 'You don't want to end up driving a tow truck.' He erupted into raucous laughter and Kevin's mother punched his shoulder lightly.

'Oh, silly boy. There's nothing wrong with driving a tow truck. Coming to people's rescue.'

'Sure,' Ulf said with a slight shrug, then put his arms around her again and laughed as he groped her everywhere.

Kevin had had enough.

This time he didn't look back. He could drop his guard a little and not worry about her watching where he was going. The game was on again. And he knew how it would play out. It would be nice for a while. Until they found out what she was really like and left.

Kevin pretended he was walking down towards the road, just in case they were watching him after all, but when he reached the small shed he didn't turn right towards the town but crouched down instead. He waited a little while, then he made himself as small as possible, crept along the hedge, back towards the house, and ran as quickly as he could up the cart track that led towards the forest.

He had felt sad for a moment, but not any more, because he had a plan. A smile broadened across his small mouth when he thought of the discovery he had made.

A place of his own. His own home.

It could be, couldn't it?

He didn't know why he hadn't noticed the cabin before. Or, more accurately, it had been pretty much hidden; it was almost invisible behind the hill, which might explain it. His heart had skipped a beat under his jumper when he saw it for the first time, the dilapidated cabin between some dense trees. The light had fallen from the sky at the same time, a ray between the clouds, as if someone up there had shown him the way. *Look, Kevin. A secret place. Just for you.*

It didn't take him long to walk there. He smiled again. He was practically chuckling to himself: it was perfect. A tiny little house hidden deep in the forest. Known only to him. Kevin carefully opened the door and found the matches he had hidden, lit the candle and hung his jacket on a peg near the broken kitchen table. He had made several trips up here. Sneaking things into his rucksack. It was starting to look really nice. A sleeping mat in one corner that he had found in their landlord's garage. It was cosy now. There was no electricity, but there was a stove so he had carried some logs in his rucksack as well as an axe so he could turn the old, dying pine into firewood. A saucepan. A plate. A few bits of cutlery. The table had been there already, as had the chair. Both of them were a bit past it, but he could fix them. He went over to the cupboard, which lacked a door, and took out some of the tinned food he was storing there. Peaches. And baked beans in tomato sauce. He crossed the floor and stopped in front of the small mirror hanging on the wall. It was old, cracked and a little foggy, so he could only just make out his face in it.

A new life. Perhaps he, too, could become someone else?

Change his appearance? Cut his hair? Perhaps dye it another colour?

It was yet another thing they teased him about at school, but his mother liked his hair so much that he had been scared to do anything with it, because he enjoyed the praise.

His long, blond hair. Freckles across his nose.

He looked like a girl.

Toughen up.

Kevin Myklebust smiled broadly to himself as he took the apple from his rucksack, went back outside and turned his face to the faint spring sunshine.

Chapter 40

The taxi had stopped for a red light by Pascal Patisserie in Henrik Ibsens gate when the heavens opened and a torrential downpour hit the windscreen and the bonnet with such force that Fredrik Riis and the taxi driver both jumped.

'*Pakao!*' the young man behind the wheel exclaimed.

'Quite right,' Fredrik agreed, and looked through the window up at the pitch-black clouds that had ambushed the capital. 'Not that I know what it means, but it sounds about right.'

The taxi driver flashed him an apologetic smile in the mirror.

'Sorry.'

'No, no, don't worry about it. *Pakao?*'

'It means hell,' the taxi driver said. 'In Croatian.'

'Yep, that pretty much sums it up.'

Riis glanced at the sky once more as another cloudburst erupted. The light was green now, but the cars around them remained stationary. They'd been hit by a deluge in just a few seconds and water was already rushing through the streets.

He hoped that Silje had avoided it, or at least found somewhere to shelter, but it didn't look like it. The teacher was shivering under the small porch at the entrance to his apartment block as he ran from the taxi, trying to cover his head with his hands before he fumbled for the key.

'Unbelievable.'

'Yes, indeed.'

Drenched, they ran up the stairwell as lightning struck beyond the small windows, followed by a loud rumble of thunder.

'Where on earth did all that come from?' Silje Simonsen laughed, clutching her bag outside Fredrik's flat as the water dripped from her.

Finally, Fredrik managed to unlock the door.

'Well, that will teach me to wear make-up.' She shivered as she paused in front of the mirror in the hallway and took off her wet ankle boots.

'Judgement Day?' Fredrik quipped as he shook water from his hair.

Silje looked at him, her make-up rapidly dissolving, and winked back.

'Quite possibly. Still, not the worst way to spend Armageddon.'

Fredrik laughed and nodded to her handbag.

'Is the file in there? Did it survive?'

'I hope so,' Silje said, and shivered as she made her way to the kitchen, both of them leaving wet footprints on the beautiful oak floor. She put the bag on the table, raked her wet hair and looked down at herself.

'I know this sounds like a cliché and we've only just met, but do you think I could borrow some dry clothes?'

Half an hour later the worst of the weather had passed. The black clouds had dispersed and were now heading south to torment the tourists on the ferry to Denmark. A weak sun could be seen outside now; it fell across the kitchen table. All of a sudden it was like a scene from a rom-com as she sat there in his far too big, pale blue shirt, warming her hands on a mug of tea while logs crackled in the fireplace in the background; they had both been frozen to the bone.

'Sorry,' Silje said after a while, and then her face settled into a serious expression, similar to what he had detected in her voice on the telephone.

'Sorry for what?'

'For being such a nuisance. I'm sure it's my fault. For doing wrong.'

She gestured towards the rest of the storm now heading out across the Oslo Fjord.

'So that's what you believe? That there's someone up there? Meting out punishment for you? Who would that be? A meteorologist?'

221

She smiled wryly.

'Yes, why not?'

'A blonde woman waving her arms in front of a green screen, forecasting, talking about atmospheric pressure and from time to time dishing out punishments to humanity.'

She laughed.

He liked her laughter. He liked all of her, really. It was a strange situation. More than anything, Fredrik wanted to put reality on hold for a while. Savour this moment.

'You said Siri?'

'Pardon?'

'Is that your daughter?'

She looked down at the table and shook her head.

'Now I'll have to feel bad about that too.'

'Bad about what?'

'I lied to my mother. I told her I had an errand in town. I didn't, but I just needed some space. That funeral really got to me.'

'Yes, it was quite a scene.'

'You were there?'

He nodded.

'Did you see what happened?'

'Poor policing. It was probably our fault. I don't know.'

'He's in there.' Silje looked at him, then she nodded towards the file on the table.

'Who?' Fredrik asked.

'Ruben's uncle. Loki.'

'Are you serious?'

She nodded once more, then she sipped her tea.

'So you have looked into him too?' he said.

'No. But my friend Liv at Social Services told me. Gosh, we have been bad, haven't we? I'm sure we'll both get sacked.'

She set down her mug and glanced slyly around her.

'You wouldn't happen to have some wine, would you?'

'Sure.'

He got up and went to a shelf over the kitchen counter.

'How about a Pinot Noir?'

'Yes, please. I'm sorry, I think I'm a bit shaken up. I don't normally drink at this time of the day.'

'It's five o'clock somewhere, isn't it?'

He smiled and found a corkscrew in a drawer. Took two glasses from another shelf and poured wine for both of them.

'Do you have a picture of her?'

'Of whom?'

'Of your daughter. Siri.'

Her attractive face lit up again.

'Yes, I do.'

She took her purse from her handbag and slid a photograph across to him.

'Oh, she's a sweetheart. How old is she?'

'Five. She will be starting school this autumn. We have just enrolled her.'

'How exciting.'

'Oh, I don't know. I think she's too young. Poor kid.'

She stroked the picture before she put it back in her purse.

'And . . . her father?'

It sounded crass and he regretted it immediately, but from the look in her eye he could tell that she didn't mind.

'He was never around.'

'OK.'

'So I am – yes, a happy and contented single parent. How about you?'

He flung out his hands to indicate the flat.

'I'm single, as you can see. There is just me and—'

Patrik Sjöberg.

He had completely forgotten the bird. The poor thing must be terrified after the storm. He made his excuses and fetched the cage from his bedroom, removed the cover and released the cockatoo.

'Sorry.'

She smiled and raised her glass.

'No problem. So no children, no girlfriend?'

'A girlfriend, no. Children, I would like some, but the two often go together, don't they?'

223

'Yes, so they say.'

She laughed again.

'So.' He cleared his throat and looked down at the file. 'Shall we . . .'

'Do we have to? I'm still feeling very rattled.'

'No, of course not. Take as long as you like.'

'Are you sure?'

She took another sip of her wine and looked furtively at him across the rim of her glass.

'There is nowhere else I need to be.' Fredrik smiled, a little embarrassed, picked up his glass carefully and raised it in a toast.

Chapter 41

Emilie Skog was sitting on the rocks on the shore of Hvalstrand, feeling wistful because soon it would all be over. It was the middle of March and still cold out here in Asker, but she didn't mind because she liked wrapping herself in a blanket and going to the fjord to clear her mind in the morning before the others woke up. She was a student at Amund Andersen's Arts Academy, a private art school that offered a two-year course. Seven students were admitted each year, so there were fourteen people in the big house. Not all of them lived out here, but most of them did, students who had come from far away, like Emilie, who had come from the picture-postcard town of Grimo in western Norway. Soon, however, she would be making her way back home to her life's commitment. The farm. Her parents. The apples. She realized that she had always known it. That she would live out the rest of her life there. Not because she had to, but because she wanted to. She couldn't imagine another life. So why didn't they understand? Her wanting to have two years for herself first? Her parents had shaken their heads at her. To Oslo? Why? Everyone was baffled, even her friends: *Why would you want to do that?* Not that it mattered, because Emilie had already made up her mind. Two years. Just for her. At an art college. Afterwards she would come home and take over the farm, and not just because she had promised her father to do so.

Emilie had initially considered the Academy of Fine Art in Oslo but quickly dismissed the idea. Bloody gloves on a bare wall or dead mice in pickling jars weren't her idea of art. She liked painting. Nothing profound. Just re-creating what she saw. Creating it afresh. She loved the visual element. She liked how her hand moved across the canvas. How the colours morphed together on her palette and turned into new ones. She wasn't profound like Hansi, for example. His angst. His sense of emptiness. His existential grief at the human condition and his fear of death. OK, he was only nineteen, but even so. Hansi was from Trøndelag, and he was really nice, but also sad and not very good at looking after himself. He didn't want to eat, and he wouldn't drink water or apple juice or anything else that was healthy because: *That's not how life is, life isn't nice, life is hard and difficult, and in the end we're all going to die, and nobody knows why. And you want me to sit here and eat cake and drink cordial? I don't think so.*

She wrote 'Hansi?' in the notebook on her lap. Perhaps one of his ghost pictures?

That was what he painted. Figures so thin that you could see through them, their skeleton and everything. Watching him move in front of his canvas sent shivers down her spine. His brush technique was incredible. Sometimes she would pause her own work just to watch him paint.

But he was so unhappy. Poor boy.

She would buy one of his pictures before she went home. She had made up her mind. Hansi was the recipient of a grant from Andersen himself. He only awarded one a year and, two years ago, it had gone to Hansi. She wasn't going to tell him that she had bought one of his paintings. She would just sneak an orange sticker on to it.

Look, you've made a sale, Hansi!

Or possibly a painting by Amalie? Her near namesake from northern Norway? She wrote down the name in her notebook.

The academy's final-year exhibition. That was the reason she had come out here this morning. Because Andersen had given her this important job.

Listen, Vestland. That had been his nickname for her from the very first day.

'Listen, Vestland. Are you painting an elk in a sunset? Look at your light! It's terrible. Hopeless. Give me your brushes so I can burn them.'

Emilie smiled to herself and tightened the blanket around her as the sun peered over Konglunden on the other side of the now sparkling fjord.

226

Andersen could be like that.

An eighty-year-old eccentric who valued art above anything else in the world and who never minced his words when he gave his opinion.

Thank God he didn't speak to Hansi like that, because Hansi would have snapped like a twig and collapsed in a heap, but Emilie didn't mind.

'Vestland, I said light! Light, light, light, damn you!' A crooked finger jabbing at her canvas.

'What are you really doing here, Vestland? Go back to pig farming. I don't want to see your hideous efforts!'

And yet he had chosen her.

'Listen, Vestland.'

'Yes?'

'You know the final-year exhibition?'

'Yes?'

'We need a poster. I want you to design it.'

The poster for the final-year exhibition.

Seriously. Her?

Because she knew what it meant.

That you could choose your own painting and it would be on display this year and for ever.

Amund Andersen's Arts Academy. Final-year Exhibition 2001. This year's poster was designed by Emilie Skog.

Or possibly one of Amalie's pictures?

She was about to write down her friend's name but had second thoughts. She wondered why she had brought the notebook with her; she had already made up her mind, hadn't she?

Because it was impossible to choose between them.

She had approached Andersen with some reluctance: could she pick two paintings for the poster? But the old man had snorted with derision. He didn't want a bloody collage – what did she think this was? Kindergarten?

Emilie heaved a sigh and returned the pencil to her pocket. No, she would go with her first idea. The boy with the badger.

She had found the painting in the depths of the storeroom, which she had been asked to clear out. He was good at that, old Andersen, getting his students to do his work for him, whether it was cutting the grass or walking his dog. But anyway, the picture had been lying in a dusty corner.

A blond, naked boy. Gazing at her mournfully. Holding a badger in his arms.

She had asked Andersen for the name of the painter, but he had been unhelpful. *Some idiot. He was only here for a few months, couldn't afford the fees*. And since then it had hung above her bed.

Emilie Skog got up from the rock, stretched out her arms to the sky, smiled at the sun and then walked calmly back to the large house to start making breakfast.

FIVE

Chapter 42

A schism had erupted in the small religious community after the pastor's fourteen-year-old daughter had her vision. Admittedly there had been disagreements before that – if not actual rows, then at least heated discussions – but nothing like this. They were divided into two camps now: those who believed in her revelation, and those who denied it and regarded it as a false prophecy. And now the former had gathered at the viewing platform at the top of Marifjell.

If you looked closely, the wooden structure was reminiscent of the tower of Babel, and it had been erected on the highest point of the mountain, just a few kilometres from where they had built the new church less than two years ago. Because once the discussion was finally over as to whether the pastor's daughter's vision had been real, the part of the congregation who believed her had spent very little time debating where the assumption should take place. The viewing platform was a large part of the reason why people had been persuaded – why else had someone built it in the first place? And why in that exact spot? On Marifjell. What was the name of the pastor's daughter? Exactly, her name was Mari. And how high was the mountain? Seven hundred and eighteen metres above sea level. And what did it say in Matthew 7:18? *A good tree cannot bring forth evil fruit, neither can a corrupt tree bring forth good fruit.*

Karoline smiled to herself as one of the young men came over to the rock on which she was sitting and offered her some tea. The young man, Erik, was about her age, twenty-one. One of the consequences of the schism in the small community: it had divided them by age, the young versus the old. The unhappy situation had gone on for some time now without anyone addressing it publicly. It had

231

mostly been mutterings in the corners among the younger members of the congregation. *But these are old ideas. Surely they can't be right? Do you think God will send angels to fetch us if we behave like that?* In time, they had formed a small faction which obeyed the sermons as they had been told to, yes, but which had also started to meet in secret. In the evening. When the older members had gone to bed. They were led by Marius, who had come close to being ostracized from the community for his opinions, but after protests from – precisely – the younger members, he had been allowed to stay on probation. From now on, he was to follow the rules and do what the elders said. Because an ark would come. That was the core of the conflict. It was what God had promised *and* it was in the Bible, wasn't it? Noah's Ark. Before the flood, Noah chose two of every kind, and God had chosen the people. They had laughed out loud at this during their secret meetings, huddled together by candlelight on the floor of the small cabin. An ark. Yes, seriously. An enormous boat made from wood would appear all the way up here? With enough room for everyone? Doh. It had to be a *metaphor*, surely anyone could see that. Times had changed. They lived in the modern world now. And God was no Luddite, he was light itself and he was obviously not going to send them a boat.

'What about a UFO?'

It was Erik who had mentioned it first, in a quiet voice in the small cabin, whispering, the thought almost too dangerous to voice out loud.

And joy had rippled through them, a spirituality that couldn't be mistaken. They had all felt it – how the idea took up residence in them, making them almost euphoric.

'Yes!'

'Of course!'

'That explains everything, doesn't it?'

Because they had already discussed the possibility in the small church, not long after Marius said he thought he had seen something luminous fly across the ridge. He hadn't just seen light, he had also seen a vessel. It had been metallic and buzzing, with dazzling colours at the centre, almost like a nightclub – a comparison which had made the elders reconsider ostracizing him, because it was sinful. God would never do something like that. Flying saucers, little green men and extra-terrestrial life: everybody knew they were the devil's work on Earth to confuse mankind, to make them doubt the wonder of creation. But that wasn't the point Marius had been trying to make. He was saying that the UFO *was* God. But that only made things worse, and he had been given another warning. Fortunately, it no longer mattered.

What mattered now was what Mari, the pastor's fourteen-year-old daughter, had seen. She had been lying in her bed, fast asleep in the middle of the night, when a voice had woken her up and told her to go down to the river. Mari hadn't been scared, she had just felt, as she put it, a warm sense of comfort, and she had obeyed the voice. Wearing only her long, white nightdress, she had walked barefoot through the forest, and as she later said: *I didn't have any shoes on, but I was fine. Whatever I stepped on didn't hurt, it was as if God Himself had made a path of cotton wool, just for me.*

On her way through the forest, she had been able to hear wonderful music all around her – a choir of angels and violins – and she had been so moved that tears had trickled down her cheeks. Then she had reached the river and it was running fast after the spring floods, but the voice had ordered her to step into it anyway. And then, imagine, even with the water roaring and frothing around her, she had stood firm. And that was when she saw it. In there. In the water.

The burning numbers.

24040424.

'And there can't be flames underwater, can there?' Erik said as he sat down on the tree stump next to Karoline and turned his face to the sky.

The phrase that had become their secret signal.

There can't be flames underwater, can there?

The meaning being: *who is the only one powerful enough to produce such a sign?*

It was obvious.

GOD.

A debate had ensued and everyone had taken part in it, as had been the custom ever since they moved out here some years ago. Where will God come from? When is God coming? And what do we do to make sure that He picks us to enter heaven?

As regards the latter, they were all convinced that question had been settled. Because they were the chosen ones. No one served the Lord better than them.

And where would He come down to them? Well, they had their answer now, hadn't they? Mari. Marifjell. It could not be a coincidence that the pastor had chosen this very forest in which to build the new church, could it? No, of course not. Now only one question remained: when?

When will it all happen?

When will we get our reward?

24040424.

'What if it means 24 April? At 04:24 in the morning?'

Another explosive revelation inside the small cabin and Karoline had almost wept from joy.

She had rarely felt such a truth.

'That's very soon.'

'A matter of weeks.'

'We have no time to lose.'

And so they had started.

In secret again.

To gather their things.

What little they needed.

And now they were waiting here, trembling with excitement.

Fourteen young people.

It was ink-black outside; just a few stars lit up the mountains and the little group that had instinctively huddled together.

4.20

4.21

She felt her heart race under her jacket, her hands starting to clap.

4.22

4.23

4.24 . . .

4.25 . . .

But . . .?

4.26 . . .

Wasn't that . . .?

They looked at each other, baffled, then at the endless sky above them.

Marius was the first to spot it.

'Look!'

Eager fingers pointing to the flames coming from the forest.

Small at first, then bigger, fiercer.

Smiles now as they realized what was happening.

The viewing platform on Marifjell.

It wouldn't be landing here.

Of course, it wouldn't.

This was the point from which they would see it!

Karoline let out a small yelp of delight as she quickly gathered up her few belongings.

Then she started running as fast as she could down the slope towards the burning sign.

Chapter 43

Holger Munch got out of the car and lit a cigarette as Fredrik Riis came walking up the narrow path through the forest. The young investigator wasn't wearing a suit for once and had wisely chosen an outfit more appropriate to his surroundings.

'Is it far?' Munch wanted to know.

He opened the boot of his car and took out his wellington boots.

'Just under one kilometre.'

'Have we cordoned off the area?'

'Yes, what little we needed to. Not many people live out here, as you can see.'

Riis nodded towards the woods that surrounded them: Marifjell nature reserve by Lake Hurdalsjøen. It was only a ninety-minute drive north of Oslo, yet it felt as if they were deep in the wilderness. They had received an early-morning phone call from the local police, who had been clever enough to spot the connection. A white Peugeot Boxer van. Just like the one they had been looking for.

'So who found it?'

Riis hesitated before he was able to answer Munch's question.

'A group of young people. They said they were out here camping, but I'm not sure. I didn't see any tents and they were all wearing crucifixes around their necks, something which tells me that they were out here to – well, who knows, and I don't think it matters. Anyway, they noticed the fire and alerted us, so I guess we were lucky that they were here. The fire had pretty much been extinguished when I turned up.'

Munch followed him down the track. It was a long time since he had been so far outside the city. The scent of the Norwegian landscape. Air so fresh that it almost challenged his lungs. It was probably doing him good; he had been smoking pretty heavily recently. Marianne had looked at him anxiously when she helped him into the passage.

Your breathing is very heavy when you're asleep, Holger. Don't you think we should make another doctor's appointment?

He had let them down again, having previously promised her some family time at breakfast.

I've packed you a snack.

A squirrel ran down a tree trunk and darted across the track in front of them.

'But we think it's our man?'

'We can't be sure,' Riis said. 'But why would you drive an almost brand-new white Peugeot van so far into the wilderness and torch it? At worst, it's suspicious. I'm impressed that the local officers linked it to our investigation so quickly.'

Munch was panting now. He was struggling to keep up with his younger colleague.

'Why didn't we drive down there?'

'What?'

'If he could drive his van down there, why can't we?'

Riis stopped, turned and smiled.

'You don't mind a little exercise, do you?'

'Of course not, but there are limits.'

'You'll see why once we round this bend.'

Two hundred metres on and Riis stopped in front of a big pine blocking their path.

He pointed to the fresh wood at the end of the trunk.

'I see,' Munch mumbled.

'It seems like overkill, but he would appear to have cut down the pine in order to block the track.'

'How strange.'

Munch took a cigarette from his duffel coat pocket and lit it.

'Why here?'

He looked about him.

'Does it mean anything?'

'What do you mean?'

'That he cut it down right here. Is it important?'

'I hadn't thought about that.'

Riis glanced around, then gave a slight shrug. 'I suppose it's a coincidence, don't you? It could have been any tree. Surely he was just trying to stop other people driving down here? Delay their access to the burnt-out van? I mean, it was four thirty in the morning. We were just lucky that the young people were in the area, whatever they were doing. If they hadn't been here, it might not have been discovered for weeks.'

'No. Nothing this guy does is by chance,' Munch mumbled, and rolled the cigarette between his fingers. 'How did he get back?'

'Eh?'

'He drives the van out here. To the middle of nowhere. So did he walk all the way home? Was someone waiting for him back on the road?'

'Good point,' Riis said, and studied the ground until he found what he was looking for. 'Do you see this? These are fresh, and there are several of them, all the way down the track.'

Tyre tracks in the wet earth.

'I think he must have had a quad bike in the back. He drove down here. He torched the van. And then he left the scene on the quad bike. At least, that's one theory.'

'And how many hours ago, did you say?' Munch looked about him again.

'The witnesses said around four thirty. So roughly five hours ago.'

'Are there any other roads that lead here?'

'Only the one you came up on, according to the local officers. But if I'm right that he had a quad bike, he could in theory have left the area anywhere.'

Riis shrugged and continued along the track as Munch's mobile rang.

Anette.

'Yes, Holger speaking.'

'Hi, are you there yet?'

'I'm at the scene now. Any news?'

'We've just heard from Forensics. We have a hit on the cigarette butts. A DNA profile. He's in our system. I think they might even have found our man, Holger. I'm looking at his picture right now.'

'Stay where you are,' Munch said eagerly. 'I'm on my way.'

He called down towards Riis.

'I have to get back. We have a match on the cigarette butts. You keep following the quad tracks and call me if Forensics find anything in the van, OK?'

'Absolutely.'

Munch dropped the mobile into the pocket of his duffel coat, took a final drag on his cigarette and half ran back up through the forest.

Chapter 44

Mia Krüger had had a terrible night's sleep and woke up feeling distraught. The bed was on its own in the big white room, and that was how she felt, overcome by loneliness. She had dared to hope again. When her mobile kept ringing. Showing the same number.

Sigrid?

But no, of course it wasn't her.

Hi, I'm calling from—

Just a stupid cold call.

Mia forced herself to get out of bed and shuffled to the kitchen. She grabbed a pot of yoghurt from the fridge. She felt nauseous, but she had to eat something. She jumped when her mobile rang again, but fortunately this time Munch's name came up on the display.

'Yes, Mia speaking.'

'It's Holger. Are you at home?'

'Yes.'

'We have a match to the cigarette butts from the forest.'

'Seriously?'

'I'm on my way to yours now.'

'I'll come down to meet you.'

And then, not long afterwards, a feeling that something was wrong as she got into the black Audi. Munch was staring vacantly through the windscreen. It wasn't the reaction she had been expecting. If they had a match on the cigarette butts, why hadn't he already arrested the suspect? And why that face? There was no sign of joy, only these narrowed eyes which eventually woke up and looked at her as she put on her seatbelt.

'So tell me?'

'Sorry?' Munch said. He sounded almost surly as he started the car. 'Who is it? Who is the match?'

He nodded to a slim file between them, pulled calmly out into Parkveien and continued up towards Majorstuveien. For some reason, he had all the time in the world.

Mia took the papers out of the file.

'Paul Iverson?'

She looked at the picture. A man in his mid-thirties. His head was shaved. Tired eyes. Tattoos – one next to his eye and several down his neck. The picture had clearly been taken as part of an arrest process, and carefully documented every physical detail. Several scars on his chest and across his thighs. From a knife, perhaps.

Munch stopped at a red light. There was still nothing to suggest that he was in a hurry.

'Do you remember a case from some years ago?' he mumbled when the car was moving again.

'What case?'

'A bank robbery in Lillestrøm. It got nationwide publicity, not because they got away with a lot of money, but because they didn't get very far.'

A quick, brief smile now before he grew serious once more.

'Oh, is that him?'

She remembered the case well. Her family had been glued to the television as the bank robbery became classic Saturday-night entertainment. It went on for weeks; even after the news programmes had forgotten about the case, the comedians had taken over. The world's worst bank robbers. Worst getaway driver in history. She remembered how they had laughed that summer in Åsgårdstrand. Being back home again had been wonderful. CCTV footage had flickered repeatedly across the screen. Showing inside the bank where the robbers had brandished their weapons, and ordered people down on the floor. The alarms were turned off: it was a truly professional job, like in the movies. So far so good, but then there was the footage from outside the bank. The getaway car had arrived at speed and pulled up outside; the driver had killed the engine. Action as the robbers in balaclavas ran out of the bank, still waving their weapons, only to find the car at a standstill. The driver got out, his face uncovered. He even managed to look straight into one of the security cameras. He opened the bonnet. Tinkered with the engine. Eventually he got in, succeeded in starting the car, only to veer across the street and plough right into a lamppost.

The shortest bank robbery in the world.

'Is that him?'

Munch nodded and turned into Sørkedalsveien.

'He was the getaway driver?'

'Paul Iverson was the getaway driver, yes. He got eighteen months, mostly for being an idiot, I think; anyway, that's why we have his DNA in the system. He's out now, on benefits. He lives up in Østerås.'

'And?'

'And what?'

Mia still couldn't work out what was going on.

The cigarette butts?

From the vantage point?

From the clearing.

Hello?

Flashing blue lights?

Why on earth had Munch stopped to pick her up first?

Munch frowned, opened the window and lit a cigarette when they stopped for another red light.

'OK,' Mia said. 'And we're sure? It's his DNA on the cigarette butts?'

'Forensics say it's a complete match.'

'So it is him?'

'So it would appear.'

But what the hell, Munch?

'And we know where he lives?'

'Eiksveien 88C. Second floor.'

'Have we sent a car up there already?'

'No.'

'So how do you know that he's at home?'

'I called him.'

'You did what?'

'He said he would put the kettle on.'

'You called him to tell him we were coming?'

'Yes.'

She gave up at this point.

'So why aren't you happy?'

'What do you mean?'

'We have a DNA match on the cigarette butts. Yet you're driving like a Sunday driver. And why did you bother stopping by to pick me up?'

Munch furrowed his brow again.

'Because I wanted you to see it for yourself.'

'See what?'

'You'll find out when he opens the door.'

Chapter 45

His strange mood had now lasted days and, though Lydia Clemens had considered that it might be her fault, she decided then it couldn't be. It happened once a year. Because she was a minor. But surely her grandfather could see that it wasn't her choice that the *spies* were coming to visit? That was something *the government* had decided, not her. *Try to cheer up, Grandad*, she had said, almost a little cheekily during breakfast, but that had only made him moodier. Oh well, she wasn't going to waste any more time worrying about it, because she had worked all winter, toiling in front of the heavy sewing machine, which wasn't powered by electricity but had a kind of pedal that you needed to step on, and she could barely reach it so she had had to tie a big wooden block to it. But it didn't matter much now because today was the first day she would wear it and show it to someone.

The dress.

Lydia smiled and could feel her cheeks grow warm. It was already hanging in the wardrobe, but she hadn't wanted to take it out. She needed an occasion. Not that the *spies* visiting was something worth celebrating, but there was no point in showing off a dress if there was no one to see it, was there? And her grandfather didn't care about such things. There was a reason for that, obviously, and she knew it. Because the fashion industry was one of the reasons the Earth was broken and why *the long time* would soon arrive. If people had just made do with the clothes they *needed*, nature would still be alive. But people were not like that. People were silly, self-obsessed creatures. *For some reason, greedy people are very clever, and that's very bad for the rest of us*. She thought that was wisely put and had made a note of it in her book where she tended to glue things she found or scribble down her thoughts. Like if she had been out on a hike and seen an eagle which was so impressive and beautiful, and soared so majestically in the sky that she had wondered why eagles were not in charge on Earth.

So Lydia had done what her grandfather had always taught her: *Before we make something new, we must first use up what we have.* That had proved difficult to begin with because all their clothes were made either by Lydia or her grandfather, and most of them were pelts from animals they had shot or from sheep wool. Lydia had pondered this for a long time before the solution had come to her. She knew very well that she shouldn't because *the forbidden chest* was just that, forbidden and off limits as well as locked, and its contents were secret and no one would look at them again, not ever. But then again she knew where her grandfather kept everything. He had made a system and everything had a place of its own. Including secret things, such as the key to *the forbidden chest*. And she knew very well that she shouldn't, that it was forbidden, but it had been such a lonely, dark winter.

So she had done it.

One day when her grandfather had gone to Vassenden to buy the goods they couldn't grow or make themselves.

Even though she wasn't allowed.

She had climbed on to a stool, fetched the key from the old cigarette case at the top of the cupboard, then gone down the steep ladder to the cellar, where she removed the blankets with trembling fingers before she opened the pink chest. She had done it once before, and that was why she knew that they were there. The floral curtains. The first time she had only dared sneak a peek, but during the last winter, she had grown bolder because she had turned twelve. Twelve years, that was an important age. Because at that point a child could make her own decisions. It had felt very grand. Her birthday. Her grandfather had got up even earlier than usual, baked a cake and cleaned the whole house, and when she had blown out all the candles, he had started to cry, stroked her hair and said: *You're the most wonderful girl*, and she had felt warm all over and the feeling had stayed with her for days.

She was trembling with awe as she took the dress from the wardrobe and let her deerskin clothes fall to the floor. The mirror was small and quite filthy, but she could just about see herself in it as she carefully put on the floral dress and stood below the window where the light was better.

Wow. How pretty she looked. She twirled around and smiled. Should she knock on her grandfather's door and show him how nice she looked?

No. Best not to.

She was going to savour this.

Lydia Clemens smiled broadly as she skipped out into the passage, pulled on her boots and ran all the way down to the gate.

In order to wait.

Chapter 46

Fredrik Riis was hunched over the ground where the wet track turned into a slightly harder gravel track, relieved that for once the weather had been on his side. The rain had made both this muddy track and the gravel track wetter and, having studied the ground for a while, he finally spotted them. The quad bike tracks. He walked back to his car and spread the map out across the bonnet. It was like looking for a needle in a haystack. He was surrounded by forest on all sides. Northbound the gravel track led to Gullenhaugen nature reserve before turning westwards down to Øyangen, and then to route 120 by Lake Hurdalsjøen. At that point the killer could have gone anywhere – down to Eidsvoll, up to Hurdal; what was the size of the petrol tank of a quad bike? His uncle used to own one. It hadn't been that big, had it? How much could it take? Three litres? At most. Of course, different models might have different sizes, but they weren't built for long trips, so how far had he really been able to drive? Fredrik straightened up and looked at the forest about him.

The bastard was out there somewhere.

Nearby.

He bent over the map again. The exit from Gamle Hurdalsveg. What was the distance from here to there? Three kilometres? Six? OK. So he had approximately six kilometres until the tarmac road began. Where the tracks would disappear. It had to be up here. On the gravel track. How many exits had he counted on his way up here? One leading to a felling area with big piles of lumber at the end. One to something that seemed like a reservoir; there had been some local authority signs. The last he had merely reversed out of, having almost got stuck.

Fredrik Riis checked that he could still see the quad bike tracks, then got into his car.

He could still smell her.

Her soft skin under the duvet.

Her smile on the pillow afterwards.

The teacher. Silje Simonsen.

Damn it, Fredrik, as if your life isn't complicated enough as it is.

One bottle of wine had turned into two. The world on hold for a moment at the kitchen table, and he had allowed himself to be carried away by how easy it was to chat to her. The old cliché: it was as if they had known each other all their lives. He had become quite dizzy after a while with the soft music playing in the background: Billie Holiday, the same track on repeat as her fingers edged across the table towards his.

The Social Services file hadn't turned out to be as bad as he had feared. Bad enough, yes, since Ruben had turned up at school with bruises on several occasions, enough for the headteacher to finally take action. A meeting with his father. Not enough to accuse him of anything, but the case worker's conclusion had made an impression on Fredrik. *The father appears to lack empathy and it is my firm recommendation that this case be followed up.* There was a suggestion with a date for another meeting, but it did not seem to have ever taken place. Fredrik had already felt uneasy when he learned that Ruben had stayed in the car while his father bought food only for himself, but murder? No, he had found nothing in the file to indicate that. He would have to have a word with Munch. It certainly could do no harm to interview the father. Unless they had already found the right man, that is. The cigarette butts. A perfect DNA match. From the clearing. He still couldn't understand how she had managed it. How she had thought of it. This student. Mia Krüger. There had been mutterings in the corners on her first day, but they had ceased now. She had charmed all of them. Even Oxen had stopped grumbling.

Oxen.

No, he didn't have the energy to think about that now.

He swore softly to himself over the steering wheel as the quad bike tracks he was following suddenly disappeared. The road surface was too hard. He got out of the car and knelt down.

Nothing.

Sod's law.

A pond right by the exit to Gamle Hurdalsveg temporarily made him feel more optimistic, but he could find no quad bike tracks on the tarmac.

He was interrupted by a text message.

Hello, handsome. Taking a sickie today. Thinking about you. S.

He stared up at the trees.

Had he missed something?

Had he overlooked an exit?

Ah, well, he would have to start over.

Fredrik Riis slipped the mobile into the pocket of his fleece jacket, got back behind the steering wheel and turned the car around, driving slowly back up the narrow gravel track.

Chapter 47

Munch almost felt sorry for Mia as she slumped against the bonnet of the Audi, her hands plunged into the pockets of her black leather jacket. He reminded himself that he had to take care of this young woman, that she was fragile and nowhere near as tough as she tried to come across. She seemed almost transparent now as she raised her gaze and looked towards the housing blocks in front of them. Anette's voice came from the mobile against his ear, but he had almost stopped listening.

'Dreyer is furious. Have you seen today's newspapers?'

'Sorry, what?'

'Please, Holger. She wants you to go and see her. I've told her that you're coming down to Police HQ sometime tomorrow. Is that OK?'

Munch heaved a sigh and lit another cigarette.

'Me coming to her office? Why?'

Anette heaved a sigh of exasperation.

'For heaven's sake, Holger, have you been listening to anything I've been saying? Have you seen today's newspapers?'

The front pages of every national newspaper.

Police stumped after boys murdered.

No comment to the media.

Police cover-up?

'What did you say?'

'Seriously, Holger. You know how much she cares about PR. Us looking good. Serving the public. I personally couldn't care less, but for some reason this has become my job, acting as your go-between with her. How about you take her calls from now on? I've had enough.'

Anette sounded as if she had got out on the wrong side of the bed. That is, if she had had any sleep at all.

The media?

What the hell did that have to do with anything?

'Are you there, Holger?'

Mia continued to stare at the housing block they had just left.

'Calm down. I'll meet with her tomorrow, all right?'

'Don't you tell me to calm down.'

'Fine. I'll do it, Anette, OK?'

'So I can organize a press conference for this evening?'

'Why?'

'*Why?*'

He could hear her take a deep breath on the other end of the line.

'Set it up if you must, but I don't want to talk to anyone. I'm not a media darling, I have a job to do—'

'I know, but this is how these things are done—'

'You handle it. Let Oxen do it, or how about Ludvig?'

'But, Holger—'

'No, that's the end of it. I'll go and see Dreyer tomorrow, fine, but that's all I'm prepared to do. Did you do the other thing I asked you?'

There was silence for a moment as the lawyer took another deep breath.

'Yes, I've spoken to Ullersmo Prison.'

'And?'

'Just so I'm clear. You'll go and see the commissioner tomorrow? I can tell her that?'

'Sure, sure.' Munch lit up a new cigarette with the last one.

'So he really does need a wheelchair?' she asked.

'Yes.'

'Christ.'

'Quite.'

'So how did his cigarette butts end up in the forest?'

'I have no idea. Are we absolutely sure they're his?'

Anette sighed.

'For the umpteenth time, I've now spoken to Forensics three

times, they have retested everything – again – and yes, Paul Iverson is our man. His DNA is on not just one but all thirteen cigarette butts we found in the forest.'

'Shit.'

'So what are we thinking? How did they end up there?'

'Well, that's the million-dollar question. I want Katja to get some officers from Police HQ and see if Iverson can give us a list of any criminals he might know. He was quite drunk. His flat stank, empty bottles everywhere. Maybe we shouldn't be surprised.'

'You think somebody might have taken the cigarette butts from his flat?' Anette said.

'It's possible. Where else? I don't know, but whatever it is, we're up against something other than what I first thought. I also believe that we need to be more vigilant than we have been so far.'

'What do you mean?'

'The whole thing seems much more calculated than we initially assumed. He's much cleverer than I thought. The well house shows us that it wasn't a crime of impulse, but even so, this is next level, isn't it? It's almost as if he's toying with us. We need to be on our toes from now on. I want to be alerted immediately to any reports that might potentially be a missing persons case, OK?'

'Sure. Boys and girls aged eight to twelve?'

'Yes.'

Munch glanced at Mia's slumped back once more.

'Or rather, no. Only boys. He likes boys. And they need to be blond.'

'What do you mean?' she asked.

'No, include all boys. Age range eight to twelve years is fine.'

'Do you want this information released to the media? Issue a public warning?'

Munch mulled it over.

'No, not yet. I might discuss it with Dreyer tomorrow.'

Anette laughed with derision.

'Oh, I would love to see that.'

'But about Ullersmo Prison? That was where he broke his back?'

'Yes. In the gym. Their records list it as an accident, but I seriously doubt that. They found him with a twenty-kilogram weight wedged into his lower spine.'

'Christ Almighty.'

'You can say that again.'

'A punishment for something? Do we have any inside information?' asked Munch.

'The prison staff I spoke to were not particularly up to speed, and I didn't find anything in the files they sent me either. Perhaps it was payback.'

'For the bank robbery?'

She heaved another sigh. 'I don't know. Whatever, it probably makes little difference to us. Have you spoken to her? To Katja?'

'Yes, she's on her way here. Do we have a time?'

'For what?'

'From Forensics? For how old the cigarette butts are? How long they had been lying there?'

'No, but perhaps that's more your field than mine. We could always test the ashtrays on your smoking balcony. See how much they have deteriorated since you started smoking out there last autumn.'

'Ha-ha.'

'I doubt they can give us a precise age, but I will ask.'

'When did Iverson get out?'

'Six months ago.'

'OK, see if they can give us something from before or after he went to prison.'

'Will do.'

There was silence down the other end now.

'Yes?' she said eventually.

'What?'

'Try: thank you, Anette. For everything you do for me.'

'Sorry, of course. Thank you, Anette. For everything you do for me.'

'See. That wasn't so difficult, was it? Team briefing here at six o'clock?'

Munch checked his watch.

'Let's make it seven.'

'OK.'

He had barely had time to press the red button before his mobile rang again.

This time it was Fredrik Riis.

'Hi, Fredrik, how did it go?'

A breathless voice on the other end.

'I've got him.'

'What?'

'No, not like that, but I have him. On CCTV.'

'Where are you?'

'I'm at an Esso petrol station in Maura. Are you at the office?'

'I'm on my way there now.'

'OK, I'll see you there.'

Chapter 48

Mia Krüger got out of the car outside her new apartment in Inkognitogata and walked around to Munch's side.

'You're meeting Patrick now?'

'Yes, he's already here. We're comparing notes. Going through everything together.'

'Great.' Munch nodded. 'We have a team briefing at seven tonight, but you don't have to be there. Just focus on what you need to do now.'

'Thank you,' Mia said, and pulled her jacket around her.

It wasn't very cold outside and yet for some reason she felt chilly. Munch looked at her closely.

'Are you sure you're all right?'

'Yes, of course.'

'Did you get anything out of it?'

'Anything out of what?'

'Our meeting with Iverson? I guess I should have explained the circumstances to you in advance, but I wanted to, well . . .'

He gave a slight shrug behind the steering wheel.

'You wanted what?'

'Well, I wanted to see if you had any insights, I don't know . . .'

'Visions?'

He laughed briefly.

'No, but yes—'

'That's not how it works, Munch.'

'No, I guess not. I don't know what I was thinking.'

He scratched his forehead and looked at her apologetically.

'What did you think? That I would have been shocked when I

255

saw him in his wheelchair, that I would have collapsed on to the floor, started shaking and speaking in tongues? *The one-armed man did it.* Words to that effect?'

Munch laughed again.

'Oh, I don't know, Mia.'

'I look at things and I realize things. Sometimes it works. Sometimes it doesn't.'

'Of course, Mia. I'm sorry, I should have warned you. That would have been better. So what are you thinking?'

'About him being in a wheelchair? And yet we still found his cigarette butts in the forest clearing?'

'Yes?'

She shrugged.

'The same as you. Someone must have planted them there.'

'Yes, they must have, mustn't they, but isn't that in itself unusual?'

Munch frowned and took out another cigarette from the packet, seemingly reluctant to let her go.

'Is there something you're not telling me,' he said at last.

'What do you mean?'

'Now, I haven't known you for very long, but I haven't seen you like this before. It's my responsibility to make sure that you can handle this. Did you see something in the mind of this guy that you haven't told me about? Is this too much too soon for you? Perhaps you need to go back to the Academy? I'll always have a place for you. After all, this has come about very quickly. We could pick up where we left off next year? Would you prefer that?'

'Thank you, but I'm fine. Send me the footage from the petrol station, the one that Fredrik found, all right?'

'Of course.'

She could feel his eyes on the back of her leather jacket as she walked away.

Might he be right? Was this too much too soon for her?

She closed the front door to her apartment behind her.

No.

Hell no.

It was time to grow up.

'Patrick, are you there?'

'I'm in here.'

The Swede was standing in the middle of the floor, cradling a cup of coffee, his face turned to all the new photographs.

'Then let's get to work,' Mia said, and turned to the photographs on the wall.

Chapter 49

Fredrik Riis was not a vain man (though everyone thought so because of the suits he wore to work) but he relished the looks of approval he got in the incident room. Even Oxen had deigned to give him a small nod.

'OK, everyone,' Munch said up by the screen. 'We have all watched the CCTV footage, and we'll obviously view it again, but first, we need to go back to the beginning. Because although we might think we're making progress, we aren't really, are we? According to the media, we're all idiots, even though the investigation is only one week old, but I'm aware of it, of course, and I'm sure that you are too: we're no longer in the driver's seat. Our leads fizzle out and, if the video that Fredrik has found for us is to be believed, this case might be about something other than what we had first assumed. It seems that it was planned in even greater detail, doesn't it? I won't go as far as saying he's actually toying with us, but he's certainly much more calculating than we thought. I mean, he's aware of us specifically and of how to wrongfoot us. The thirteen cigarette butts in the clearing, for example. I have given Mia time to work with Patrick tonight and I really hope that they can get us back on track, because right now I have to be honest and say I feel somewhat at a loss.'

Munch looked across the team and nodded to Ludvig Grønlie, who turned off the light.

'So this is what we're going to do. We're starting over. No one is going anywhere. If you have commitments other than this, consider them cancelled. We're going to stay here until we feel we're back on track.'

Grumbling across the room, especially from Oxen, but Munch ignored him.

'Right,' he said, and switched on the projector.

Pictures from the crime scene again.

Back to day one.

'Sunday morning we find Ruben and Tommy dead in a field. We now know that before that they had been to the well house, that the killer had drugged and later strangled them.'

New slide.

'We don't know how many hours he kept them up there, but it's clear that he took his time.'

Munch clicked the button again.

'This was found by Forensics up there.'

A pair of underpants in an evidence bag.

'We now know that these belonged to Ruben and that he was wearing them on the night he disappeared, so . . .'

Back to the bodies on the ground.

'We don't know how long he was up there, but we can surmise the following course of events.'

The red well house appeared and Fredrik had a flashback. The smell. The nauseating feeling that the oppressive room had given him.

'If Mia is right, then this man likes to watch. There is something about the optics that gives him a thrill. Again, as we can see . . .'

Munch clicked back to the field, to a picture taken from further away this time.

'. . . the staging of the bodies seems important to him. He might be trying to re-create some kind of artwork, or maybe this *is* the artwork. Perhaps the latter is more likely. If we're trying to understand him, we need to try to understand this. How does he get his kicks? What is it he likes? I don't know if you remember Dennis Nilsen?'

Some people in the room nodded.

'The London serial killer who murdered at least fifteen young men in the seventies and eighties. He was gay. But also into necrophilia. He was originally a police officer but had been kicked out of the force after being caught interfering with bodies at the mortuary.'

'Gross.'

'He made contact with men who were often homeless or addicts, sometimes both, invited them to his home, they drank together, had a nice time, and then he drugged them before he strangled them.'

Fresh murmuring across the room now.

Munch clicked back to the well house.

'But our killer didn't interfere with the bodies in that way?' Anja Belichek asked in an almost pleading voice.

'No, that wouldn't appear to be what our man likes. Again, as Mia says, the optics are how he gets his kicks, his release, if you like. But to go back to Dennis Nilsen for a moment. After having killed his visitors, he would often do things with them. He took a bath with one body, they slept together, they watched TV—'

'Er, after they were dead?'

'Yes, with their corpses. Until – still in his own flat – he would dismember them, boil their heads and bury them in the garden. Most of them couldn't be identified.'

'Christ almighty.'

'I appreciate that this might be too much for you, Anja. But please, close your eyes rather than your ears. I want us all here. It's important that we have a shared understanding of this.'

Munch pointed to the well house on the screen.

'So this is where it happens. Something he has presumably been looking forward to for a long time. It is for him exactly as it was for Dennis Nilsen – it makes him feel like himself. OK?'

More nodding.

'So he sets the trap in here. Porn magazines and fizzy pop. Valium and Rohypnol. Again, and I think this is important to notice, these substances aren't fatal. But they're so strong that the children have no chance of defending themselves and – this is what we hope, obviously – that they were unconscious and had no idea of what was happening to them.'

'I need to . . .'

Anja, the computer geek, got up and left the room.

'OK. We have tiptoed around this for a while, but now the time has come. The time for us to work out who this man really is. The way I see it, it's not the killing itself which gives him a thrill. I think he enjoys the time while they're still breathing, when he can do whatever he likes with them.'

He clicked back through the images on the screen.

'As you can see, they have been cleaned up. Or at least Ruben has, and Mia believes he is the main character in this macabre performance, and I think she's right. He has combed Ruben's hair. Cleaned his fingernails. He cleaned his toes – did you notice that the first time? Every scratch has been cleaned. Forensics found traces of antiseptic, and I didn't understand why at first, but when you think about it, it makes sense: completely clean. So that's what he's doing in there. I want you to . . .'

The interior of the well house.

'Yes, Karl, I know we have all seen and talked about this before, but now we're doing it again, so you can take that look off your face. We're going to be here for a long time.'

Munch was clearly in a combative mood tonight.

Oxen nodded and straightened up in his chair.

'Take a look at this.'

Munch's finger jabbed the screen again.

'There's a lock on the inside. He locked himself in, so no one could enter and he could enjoy this for as long as possible. As you know, we found the remains of candles in there and, if they were new – and we don't know if they were – but if they were and he lit them when he started, he was in there for . . .'

He looked towards Anette.

'Approximately five hours,' she said.

'Thank you. According to his family, Ruben climbed out of his window around . . .'

'Sometime after ten thirty the previous evening,' Fredrik said.

'Exactly. Let's say Ruben waits for a little while. Until his parents have gone to bed. So the killer starts around midnight. It might take twenty minutes or even half an hour before the boys are unconscious. So he begins, he takes about five hours, so now the time is – let's say – six a.m.'

A new slide, back to the field.

'The moment has passed. At least, the initial pleasure has. But now the second stage arrives. We didn't know that then, but we know now that he hasn't finished yet. He moves the bodies to the field in the white van. He needs to hide it somewhere, and we assume that it's his van which was spotted behind the tyre garage.'

'What tyre garage?'

Fredrik leaned towards Katja, who rolled her eyes and whispered back.

'It came from Police HQ today. A member of the public reported it, but HQ has only just logged it.'

There was a map on the screen now.

'As you can see, the tyre garage is here. It might have taken him perhaps thirty minutes to walk back, then onwards up to here . . .'

The clearing now.

'Where he must have sat down to wait for us.'

'Sick bastard.' Oxen shook his head menacingly.

'But how on earth did he get past us? If he was up there at the same time we were?' It was Anja Belichek, from the doorway.

'Yes, good point, there are a number of possibilities. He probably wouldn't have got past us – or he might not have dared to, but if you look at the map, there are several paths through the area. One here, for example; we can see that it's leading down towards the field, and look here, he could easily have walked to the tyre garage and driven away.'

'But why?'

'Yes, Katja?'

'No, I'm just wondering, why run the risk? I mean, we were right there?'

Munch gave a shrug.

'A calculated risk, perhaps? Again, if Mia is right about the significance of watching, then that was almost as important to him as the murders themselves. Watching us discover his work of art. Like a cat bringing in a mouse it has caught. Pride. Look at what I have done.'

'For pity's sake . . .'

'And at this point I think we should make a brief detour and discuss what we saw on the CCTV today, especially at the end. What does he do once he has filled the jerry cans with petrol? He's still wearing his helmet, but even so.'

They looked at him now.

'He pauses in front of the camera,' Munch went on, 'with a jerry can in each hand. He assumes that we will find this footage and he's sending us a message, isn't he? And what's the message?'

Munch looked across his team.

Everyone's eyes turned to him again.

'*I can drive as far as I want to; if you think you're going to find me, you're wrong.*'

'Exactly,' Munch said, and pressed for the next slide.

A photograph of the Lundgren family.

'So everything afresh. Every single detail. We start with the next of kin. Fredrik?'

'Yes.'

Fredrik Riis took out his notes from his briefcase and walked up to the light from the projector.

Chapter 50

Mia was sitting on the floor with an empty coffee cup in front of her, feeling that Munch might have had a point when he suggested that it might be too soon. That she wasn't ready yet. She thought she had seen it in Munch's eyes: a hint of doubt. *Yes, you have talent, but this isn't the library reading room, this is real life.*

'You're very quiet?'

Patrick looked up from his notes.

Mia chewed her lip and didn't know whether to speak her mind, but eventually she gave into it.

'I don't think I can do it.'

'What do you mean?'

Patrick put his notebook on the armrest of his chair.

'Oh, I don't know.' Mia nodded towards the photographs on the wall in front of her.

'I don't seem to see anything any more. No connection. My mind is completely messed up.'

'That can happen to the best of us, Mia.'

Patrick got up and opened the window behind them. The sound of the city outside, so near and yet it seemed far away. Having him here made her feel strangely safe. They had known each other for less than a week, but she felt that she could trust him already. And that wasn't like her. Not usually. She was generally distrustful of humanity. It took her a long time to let anyone get close to her. Too long in most cases, which might explain why she had so few friends.

'Perhaps we should take a break?'

'No,' Mia said with grim determination, and got up.

She walked up to the wall again and started taking down the pictures.

'What are you doing?'

'Starting over. I can't see anything. Perhaps everything is in the wrong place.'

He came over and stood close to her.

'Why don't we clear our heads? Go for a walk? Get some fresh air?'

'No,' Mia said again, and started sifting through the pictures on the floor in front of her.

Damn it.

It was here somewhere, wasn't it?

'What is it that you can't see?' Patrick wanted to know, and placed a friendly hand on her shoulder.

'Why.'

'Why he does it?'

She turned to him, walked barefoot across the floor and flopped down in the chair he had just vacated.

'It's not always as simple as why,' Patrick said. 'It's so typical for us, this.'

He smiled faintly as if to console her.

'Who is *us*? What's *typical*?'

'People like us. Healthy people. People who wouldn't want to harm anyone. We get scared, don't we? Who would do such awful things? Murder eleven-year-old boys? We need an explanation. So that we can find the courage to get out of bed in the morning, and step out into the street without being scared. We need to find the words to explain the *why*, it helps us, but it's not always like that, is it? Sometimes evil is just evil. Why do you think they invented religion?'

'Go on, enlighten me.'

'To create an illusion that there's something good up there which will triumph in the end. So that normal people like us can function in our daily lives. If we lose faith in goodness, we lose everything, don't we?'

'How very profound,' Mia said.

This sounded sarcastic, although she hadn't intended it to and she immediately felt guilty.

Because it wasn't his fault.

He was the only positive thing in here.

Damn it, Mia.

What is it you can't see?

'You're quite sure you don't need a break? How about we go for a walk in the park?' he suggested again.

'No.'

'OK,' Patrick said, leaning up against the now half-empty wall. 'Let's attack it together. His motive. What do you think so far?'

'I'm just speculating and guessing, that's how it feels. There's no substance.'

'Oh, come on, Mia.' Patrick sighed, and for the first time he sounded exasperated. 'You're the one who has spotted most of the clues so far. The ear of the fox? The capital letter?'

'Yes, but—'

'No, listen to me.'

He took a marker pen from his trouser pocket and went over to the wall with the notes.

'Eleven years old. All the boys were eleven years old. What associations does that evoke in you?'

Come on, Mia.

This isn't like you.

She pulled herself together.

'Perhaps something happened to him?'

'What do you mean?'

'When he himself was eleven. Perhaps there's something he wants to relive?'

'Good.' Patrick smiled and put pen to paper.

'An extreme incident? Perhaps he's exploring it? Wanting to observe it from the outside? Perhaps that's why everything is so stylized? Distanced? Perhaps he's trying to create distance from an incident where he was the victim?'

'Right, now we're getting somewhere . . .'

266

Patrick smiled and scribbled fast. 'Anything else? Any other thoughts?'

'The arts,' Mia said, straightening up in the chair.

'Go on? What about the arts?'

'Well, we as a society revere artists, don't we? They're mysterious, different. People used to think that artists were in touch with the divine, didn't they?'

She grew more animated now.

'Yes, go on . . .' Patrick waved his pen in the air.

'I mean, Edvard Munch's pictures sell for hundreds of millions, people queue for hours every day to see a tiny *Mona Lisa* . . .'

Mia got up from her chair and started pacing around in circles.

'What if he—'

She broke off.

'What if he what?'

'Well, maybe it's really simple?'

'Simple how?'

'Perhaps he's a nobody. With grandiose thoughts. He wants to be someone important because he isn't. Perhaps that's where we need to start looking?'

'Where?'

'For a nobody. Somebody who isn't anyone. Or thinks he isn't.'

'Are you thinking about . . . his job?'

She shrugged. 'Yes. That is if he even has a job.'

'Good, Mia.' Patrick smiled again. 'You're on to something.'

'Really?'

'Absolutely. Go on, keep talking.' Patrick looked as if he wanted to give her a hug.

Mia returned his smile. 'All right, but first I need more coffee.'

SIX

Chapter 51

VG journalist Alf Inge Myhren, aged forty, was still processing the announcement he had received two days ago, about the newspaper's local office in Molde being earmarked for closure. He reached for his alarm clock, turned it off and lay staring, wide awake, at the ceiling. Thirty full-time posts would be cut across the country. The whole organization was being slimmed down and those who contributed the least would be the first to go. Myhren got out of bed and went to the kitchen. Found the ingredients for his breakfast – eggs, milk and juice; he had bought rolls the night before.

Molde was such a beautiful city, as was the whole region. Mountains plunging into shimmering fjords inland or straight into the sea along its coastline. He wasn't that interested in the local football team; he had always been a loyal Vålerenga supporter, but it undoubtedly added local colour. And then there was the jazz festival, of course. Europe's finest? Quite possibly. Every year during two weeks in July, the otherwise quiet little town practically turned into Rio de Janeiro, with parades through the streets and global stars headlining. Miles Davis. Twice. Those interviews were regarded as his greatest achievement as a journalist. The series he had written about Davis's chauffeur had also been very well received. *VG*'s management hadn't given a date by which the job losses would be announced.

Alf Inge Myhren laced up his trainers, walked down the stairs with a yawn and had just stepped outside when his mobile rang.

'Alf Inge speaking.'

'Yes, hello. Is this *VG*?'

The voice belonged to an old man.

'Yes, it is. Who is this, please?'

'My name is Olaf Eriksen and I'm calling from Kristiansund.'

'Hello, Olaf, what can I do for you?'

'Is it true that your paper will pay a thousand kroner for a tip-off?'

'It is, but you'll need to ring our tip line. If you have a copy of our newspaper, you'll find the number on the back.'

There was silence for a moment.

'Yes, I saw it, but that's an Oslo number, isn't it?'

'Yes, it—'

'Oh, I don't want to talk to them.'

'I don't blame you. What did you want to tell us?'

'You could give me the money, couldn't you?'

Alf Inge considered this for a moment. 'Yes, I probably can, but we don't pay everyone who calls, only those with a tip-off that turns into a story we can publish. What have you got for us?'

Another silence, a little shorter this time.

'I was Ole Gunnar Solskjær's coach when he was young.'

'All right? Now I'm not sure if—'

'Yes, yes,' the man went on, sounding irritable. 'I know, but that was why he visited me, that policeman from Oslo. It was about those boys. The two who were found in that field.'

And it was at this point that the newshound in Alf Inge Myhren woke up.

'Right, so you've just had a visit from a police officer working on the case?'

'Yes.'

'And did he give you a reason for his visit?'

'Yes, something about a man with a limp.'

'Go on?'

'Well, they suspect a guy. A guy with a limp, who said he played football with Solskjær when he was little.'

'Right?'

Alf Inge Myhren turned around, ran up the stairs and found his notepad on the kitchen counter.

'And what was his name?'

272

'Who?'

'I'm sorry, the name of the police officer who visited you?'

'Oxen. Karl Oxen. An unpleasant man. He couldn't wait to leave, if you know what I mean.'

'I'm not sure I follow, but he asked you if you knew—'

'If any of the boys on the team were of the same calibre, yes. As Ole Gunnar Solskjær. If any of them might have been just as good but had had an injury that wrecked their career. Like I said, I didn't take to him. And I couldn't think of any. At least, not at the time. But then, as I was looking through some old team photos, it hit me. There was one. I suddenly realized who he was looking for.'

'Someone with an injury, someone with a permanent limp, was that it?'

'Yes.'

'Remind me, where are you calling from again?'

'Kristiansund.'

'Would you mind if I paid you a visit?'

'No. That would be all right. When were you thinking of coming?'

Alf Inge Myhren kicked off his trainers, took out a shirt and a pair of jeans that lay folded in his wardrobe and glanced at the clock by the fridge.

Kristiansund? One hour and twenty minutes?

'I can be there just before ten. Is that convenient?'

'Yes, that's fine. See you then.'

'Good. Thank you for calling. I'll see you soon.'

Chapter 52

Mia Krüger stepped out of the icy shower and stood naked and shivering in front of the large mirror. Fuck. It was a painful reminder. Of why she never drank alcohol. She liked her body being fit. Her mind being clear. Clean blood coursing through her veins. Her head was pounding so badly that she had to lean against the wall for support. Was she about to throw up? She bent over the lavatory bowl, but there was nothing in her stomach. They had forgotten to eat yesterday. Two days now, Patrick and her. Toiling away in the large apartment until they finally hit a wall.

'How about we open this one? See if that helps?'

'What is it?'

'The Queen of all Armagnacs. A Domaine de Pantagnan 1965 Labeyrie. It's thirty-five years old. I know you don't drink, but—'

'You'll find glasses in the top cupboard. Bring two.'

Mia turned on the cold-water tap and gave her face a second go. Oh, God. She staggered naked into the bedroom and rummaged around in her bag for some clothes. Black leggings and a tracksuit top. Time for a run. It was the only remedy that would help her now. Rid her body of this crap. The door to the living room was wide open. She could hear him snoring in there. She had found a mattress in one of the rooms. A blanket and a pillow. There was no point in him going back to his hotel. They were so deep into it. Two days now. They had lived on takeaways and caffeine. They had been so close, so very close it felt, but every time the killer seemed to slip through their fingers like sand.

'No, that just can't be right.'

'What can't be?'

'That he is shy. That he doesn't feel he fits into society. That he's a victim of some kind. We have to stop doing that. *You* have to stop doing that.'

'Me?' Mia had protested.

'Yes, you, with your bleeding-heart therapist's hat on. You want to *understand* him. Work out what *happened* to him. How hard it must have been for him. Screw that.'

'But that's not what I'm saying—'

'No, but that's what you're looking for. An excuse. This guy washes and grooms sedated children before he puts them, naked, on his lap and kills them with a fucking cord for his own satisfaction. So screw that. We're not looking there any more. Forget about his bad childhood, I don't give a toss about it.'

'How about we order some food?'

'No, but is there any more coffee?'

'Perhaps water would be better?'

Mia put on a black baseball cap, hid her red eyes behind a pair of big sunglasses and staggered to the kitchen. She stuck her head under the tap and filled her dry mouth. She cursed the night before. Drinking? No, never again. No matter how fancy his armagnac had been. Not that it was his fault, of course. She had raised the glass to her lips herself.

'What pictures are these? I haven't seen them before.'

'That's Oliver in front of his house. Some months before the murder.'

'A new car?'

'Yes, he's excited, as you can see. He liked cars. Anything to do with engines, really. He wanted to be a Formula One driver.'

'Do you have other pictures of him at home? Or any of Sven-Olof?'

'No, I just found these in the archive.'

'Do you see it now?'

'See what?'

'I'm right, aren't I?'

'Right about what?'

'He picks them based on their appearance. The blond curls. The freckles. Slim. Skinny. Innocent. Weak. He likes it, doesn't he, the bastard? Children who can't defend themselves?'

'How about some fresh air, Mia? I don't think you're looking at things objectively right now.'

'Fuck off. I've never seen as clearly as I do now.'

The bright light slammed into her brain despite the sunglasses, and she stopped and leaned against the entrance door for a moment before she finally managed a few stumbling steps out into the front garden.

Cars. Noises. Exhaust fumes. People.

Mia pulled the baseball cap further down her forehead, buried her hands in the pockets of her tracksuit top and started running towards Uranienborgveien. Stupid people everywhere. Why couldn't they just stay at home? And where was nature when she needed it? Lovely swaying trees? Moors? A brook babbling, but quietly, please?

OK then, Frogner Park it was.

It would have to do.

What had he really put in that bottle?

Thirty-five-year-old devil's brew? Poison from Mordor?

She jumped as a car sounded its horn at her. She had veered into the road without looking.

Hell no.

This was definitely the last time.

Never again. No alcohol for this body.

'OK, so what if it isn't the same man?' Mia had suggested.

'Hello? Why not?'

'We agreed that we would take everything apart and look at it afresh, didn't we? So let's look for evidence that it might *not* be the same man.'

'I don't think that'll work.'

'Humour me, please. Look here. The arms of the Swedish bodies haven't been arranged at the same angle. Neither Oliver's nor Sven-Olof's. Now look at the Norwegian crime scene. It's much – well, how can I put it? – tidier somehow.'

'More perfected.'

'Oh, shit.'

'What is it?'

'You just said it yourself. He's getting better. He's becoming more aware of what he wants. Take a look at this.'

'But he waited eight years.'

'Yes, you're right. Not because he wanted to, though, but because he didn't have a choice. That would be my theory.'

'So you still think he was locked up somewhere?'

'Absolutely. And so he had time, didn't he? To perfect it. Home in on it. Do it exactly the way he wanted. He must have yearned for it. He must have been desperate—'

Another car sounded its horn; Majorstukrysset this time. Again she was just as startled as the last time. Why, God? How could people do this to themselves? Every single week? Was this really the social lubricant in this country? Alcohol? No, forget about trying to regulate it, just ban alcohol altogether. It's no good for anyone. Ever.

She had reached Frogner Park at last and could launch into a proper run. Though calling it a run was an exaggeration. She felt more like a pensioner behind a Zimmer frame. Her temples smarted every time the soles of her feet hit the tarmac until, finally, she was forced to slow down. Baby steps for now. Her head bowed under the baseball cap. Her shoulders slumped under the training jacket.

'Have you read his diary?'

'Yes, several times.'

'Strange, really.'

'What is?'

'That The Wolf is only mentioned on the last page. And there's nothing disturbing anywhere else either. Everything in the garden is lovely, racing cars and motorbikes and – no, I just don't get it—'

'Get what?'

'That there's no other mention. Why only on the last page? What happened that day?'

The peal of church bells rang out from her pocket and she stepped away from the path and into the shade of a tree to take the call.

'Yes? Mia speaking.' Her voice was rusty, almost refusing to talk.

'Hello, it's Anette here, how are you?'

'Yes, I'm . . . good—'

'I don't want to be pushy, but have you made any progress? Found anything?'

'No, unfortunately . . . no . . . we haven't . . .'

A dog owner had allowed its dog to defecate under the tree and the stench hit her right in the face.

'Are you there, Mia?'

'Yes, I just had to move from where I was. No, we haven't found anything. Nothing, in fact. What about you?'

'Slim pickings here. We have gone through everything with a fine-tooth comb. It's frustrating.'

'And Munch?'

'Not saying much today. He just sits in his office.'

'Dreyer?'

'Well, Munch didn't turn up for the meeting with her that I had organized. No surprise there. And, as a result, Kripos called. They're ready to take over the case. Dreyer has already prepared them.'

'Yes, but it has only been . . . well, not very long—'

'I know. But she uses Sweden as her argument. She doesn't want us wasting eight years as well and thinks we might as well grab the bull by the horns. Rip the plaster off quickly. Words like that. I don't know – no one has had much sleep around here. Call me if you find something, OK?'

'Will do.'

She bought two bottles of water in the kiosk at the entrance to the Frognerbadet pool complex. Don't look at the newspaper head-lines. You're not responsible for everything. Step away. Drink your water. Try a bit of running. You'll feel better soon.

She risked another cautious run on the tarmac. Slightly better this time. A kind of jogging. There were people everywhere today. Out in the nice weather. Like frisky cows in a meadow after a long winter in the barn.

She had reached Vigeland Park.

The pride of Oslo.

She had loved coming here as a little girl.

The city had expanded rapidly; every patch of land in the centre had been developed and property prices had skyrocketed. But in the past some people had had the foresight to create this oasis.

She was forced to stop again.

Yesterday's excess was on its way up from her stomach.

Sinnataggen, the Spitfire sculpture.

The famous angry little boy was surrounded by tourists from all over the world, taking pictures of him.

There were lavatories nearby, weren't there?

A café with outdoor table service.

Flat beer and happy faces. It had been a long winter.

Gentlemen. Ladies. Both occupied. And with long queues.

She couldn't face throwing up in public so she retreated from the crowds and into the shade.

Among the tall trees.

A wall of posters.

Elton John performing at Oslo Spektrum.

A Korean production of an Ibsen play at the National Theatre.

Dog-walking services advertised. Cheap and reliable.

She cupped her hand over her mouth and glanced at the queue, which didn't seem to be moving.

She started drinking her second bottle of water.

Feeling better now.

Mia was just about to raise the bottle to her lips again when she saw it.

What the . . .

She moved closer, still with her mouth open.

A poster.

Amund Andersen's Arts Academy.

Final-year exhibition 2001.

She let the bottle fall to the ground, pulled her mobile out of her jacket pocket and found his number with shaking fingers.

A painting. Of a blond boy. Surely that was . . .

Yes, indeed it was.

'Munch speaking.'

'Hi, it's Mia. Get in your car.'

279

'Eh?'

'Meet me outside Vigeland Park.'

'I have to—'

'No, right *now*. I'm looking at a painting of Oliver Hellberg. The Swedish victim.'

'What?'

'He's naked. And holding a badger.'

'Which exit?'

'Majorstuveien. Where the tourist coaches park.'

'I'm on my way.'

Chapter 53

The house Alf Inge Myhren arrived at was beautifully maintained and occupied an attractive location with a view of Dalabukta some kilometres from the centre of Kristiansund. It was big and painted white, just to his taste; it wasn't too unusual, but nor was it just like all the other houses in the area. He really liked this particular one. The journalist parked his car on the verge, walked up the gravel path and into the well-kept garden. Good heavens. He stopped in his tracks and bent down to check that he was not mistaken. Austin roses? This far north? A bright yellow Teasing Georgia, was it? He took his Nikon camera from its bag and took a picture of it, which turned out rather well. *VG*'s regional office used to have a photographer of its own whom he could call whenever he needed to, but that post had fallen victim to cuts long ago so Alf Inge Myhren had been forced to teach himself this skill as well. He wasn't a pro, but from time to time his pictures didn't turn out too badly. The door opened behind him and a voice called out.

'Oi! What are you doing in my garden?'

Alf Inge Myhren jumped, then he quickly picked up his camera bag from the lawn.

'I'm sorry. I'm Alf Inge Myhren. The journalist from *VG*. Are you Olaf Eriksen?'

The rather forbidding face softened.

'I am. I didn't mean to be rude, only I've had problems with young people trespassing at night. I've just had this put up.'

The old man with the spectacles pointed towards a camera mounted above his door.

'I'm seriously impressed,' Alf Inge Myhren said, nodding towards the beautiful flowers.

'You are? You like roses?'

A high-pitched voice called out from inside the house.

'Olaf, will you be wanting coffee?'

A gentle-looking woman about the same age as Olaf Eriksen appeared in the doorway, drying her hands on a tea towel.

'Marit Eriksen.'

Alf Inge Myhren smiled and shook her hand. 'Alf Inge Myhren from *VG*.'

'Oh yes,' she chirped. 'How nice to have a visitor. Are we going to be famous?'

'Marit,' the husband grunted, embarrassed.

'What? Surely I'm allowed to pull your leg. Would you like coffee inside or out?'

Her husband looked towards Alf Inge Myhren.

'Thank you. I would like it outside, please. It's a lovely day.'

'He likes the roses.'

'Oh, yes?'

The woman flung the tea towel over her shoulder and planted her hands on her hips.

'I'm responsible for them.'

Her husband reacted instinctively. 'No, you're not.'

She laughed heartily.

'No, indeed, I'm not. I wouldn't be able to get green fingers if I stuck my hands into a tin of green paint. I'll bring you your coffee.'

Her laughter followed her into the hallway.

'So you like roses, do you?'

'Oh yes. I've tried growing that one myself. For years, actually.'

'Which one?'

Olaf Eriksen slipped his feet into a pair of clogs and followed him across the lawn.

'The Austin rose. I'm sorry, I took some pictures. I know I should have asked for permission first, but I just couldn't help myself.'

'That's all right.' Eriksen nodded proudly. 'Yes, that took time and skill, believe me.'

'Oh, I do. Do you have any tricks you would be willing to share with me?'

'Well, now, I don't want this on the national news, you understand—'

'No, no, my lips are sealed. This is just for my own benefit, for the next time I try.'

'Do you have a big garden?'

'Yes. Or no, not any more. But I used to. And I hope I will have again.'

'Right, let me show you.'

Olaf Eriksen smiled knowingly and led the way to a freshly painted shed which was in just as good condition as the rest of the property.

'I guess you've tried growing it in a greenhouse?'

'Oh yes.'

'It didn't work?'

'No. Total failure.'

'Well, it would be.'

Eriksen chuckled and shook his head at the same time.

'It doesn't thrive next to other plants, that rose, you know. It's an oddball. Like me. It wants things just the way it likes them. It doesn't grow alongside other plants, lumped together in a greenhouse. The light isn't right and the air gets too humid. No, if you want to grow Teasing Georgia, you need to treat it like a frightened child, perhaps even more carefully.'

Alf Inge Myhren peered curiously through the open shed door.

'Do you see this?'

'Yes.'

'I built it myself. I call it my non-greenhouse.'

'Eh, what?'

Eriksen chuckled to himself again.

'It's a greenhouse, yes, but it's no ordinary greenhouse. I made it especially for David Austin roses. The roof is full of small louvres that can be opened according to the humidity. They're connected to the hygrometer there. And the heating is thermostatically controlled, of course. If the temperature drops below a certain degree, hey presto, the heating switches itself on.'

He closed the door to the non-greenhouse solemnly and turned the padlock dial several times.

'Where outside would you like your coffee?'

Marit Eriksen had opened a kitchen window and was calling out to them.

'We'll have it on the terrace,' Eriksen responded.

A few minutes later they were sitting in comfortable chairs under a large parasol with coffee and three types of biscuit on the table between them.

'So you had a visit from the police?' Alf Inge Myhren began as he took out his notepad from his bag.

'Yes, a big, strong fellow, a really unpleasant man.'

'And he asked you about Solskjær? About a former fellow footballer of his, am I right? Would you mind starting at the beginning, please?'

'Of course not,' Eriksen said, and dropped a sugar cube into his coffee.

Chapter 54

Holger Munch saw a creature practically crawling towards his car and didn't realize who it was until she opened the door. Her face was covered by a baseball cap and a pair of large sunglasses and her breath stank.

'What the hell happened to you, Mia?'

'Don't shout,' she growled, and covered her mouth.

'I hope you're not going to throw up in my car?'

She shook her head and thrust a rolled-up poster at him. Munch spread it out on the steering wheel and did a double-take.

'Wow.'

The likeness to one of the Swedish victims was striking.

'What did I tell you?' Mia said.

'Amund Andersen's Arts Academy?'

'It's in Asker.'

'Have you got the address?'

'Hvalsbakken. Take the exit to Holmen. Do you know where it is?'

Holger nodded and started the car.

They had been house hunting out there, Marianne and he, a very long time ago. Imposing old houses with gardens by the fjord that near the capital? Clearly not within their budget. He could still remember her disappointed face in the car as they drove back.

'There's a hotel out there, isn't there?'

Mia nodded and tentatively removed her hand from her mouth.

'Holmen Fjordhotell. But that's not where we're going. Turn right now.'

Munch turned right and headed towards Skøyen.

'How do you know so much about this area? Have you been there before?'

Mia nodded gingerly.

'Just to visit. A long time ago I had a . . . friend, who was considering going to that art school if he got a grant. He didn't. And so he couldn't afford it.'

'So it's a private college?'

Mia rolled down her window and stuck out her head.

'Yes. It was founded by the painter Amund Andersen a long time ago, back in the seventies, I believe. His parents had left him a large house and he needed money to do it up.'

She stuck her head even further out.

'Oh, hell.'

'Late night?'

'I've no idea what time we finished. I can't remember the last few hours. Patrick had brought along a bottle of something, God knows what it was called. Pure poison. I'm giving up alcohol for good after last night. Yuck, what gut rot. Tell me, do people actually choose to drink?'

Munch smiled to himself and then thought back to his father's cherry brandy.

'Yes, it's very popular, I believe.'

'So what do you think?'

She nodded towards the poster, which was lying between them.

'It has to mean something, surely?'

Munch really wanted to say that the hairs on the back of his neck had stood up when he saw the image, but he was trying to stay calm. They had hit enough walls recently. His mind couldn't cope with yet another dead end, not today.

'There is a similarity,' he conceded.

'Yes?'

'A strong one, but even so . . .'

'What?'

'What are the odds?'

She looked at him with irritation.

'What do you mean? What are the odds of what?'

'That he's our man?'

Munch joined Drammensveien and settled in the fast lane.

'Seriously? What are the odds that our guy who makes art using dead bodies and clearly gets a kick out of the optics went to art college? And painted Oliver Hellberg naked with a badger?'

'Yes, what are the odds?'

'The odds are . . .'

She covered her mouth again and closed the window as the exhaust fumes from an articulated lorry became overpowering.

'Well, who knows? I certainly don't. Do you mean mathematically?'

'No, I mean, what are the odds of you dressing up like a cartoon burglar and stumbling across that very poster in Vigeland Park with an image of Oliver Hellberg?'

'Unlikely, I admit.'

She sat very still until they reached the exit to Holmen.

'So what you're saying is: don't get your hopes up,' she said at last.

'Yes. Let's calm down for now. Wait and see what we find. The last few days have been . . . I just can't cope with another disappointment, do you understand?'

'I understand,' Mia said, and looked at him with kindness.

'And another thing . . .'

He nodded towards the glove compartment.

'You stink like a brewery. You'll find some breath fresheners in there.'

She pulled a face at him, but she still opened the glove compartment, found the Läkerol and popped four pastilles into her mouth before pocketing the packet.

'Here we are,' Munch said, turning off the ignition.

They could hear laughter and music from the far side of the large, attractive house. It looked like the house of Pippi Longstocking, only with a slightly more conservative colour scheme. Two girls in smart dresses were flanking the entrance gate and balloons were tied to the trees. They seemed to have arrived at just the right time.

'It's today?' Mia said, and unfurled the poster again.

'Perfect,' Munch said. 'Let's hope there's food. Will you be OK? Are you able to stand up?'

Mia climbed out of her seat and leaned against the Audi for support.

'I'm good.'

'Sure?'

'Yes, I am. I'm twenty-one rather than . . . remind me how old you are?'

'Forty-two.'

'That's right, and it's one of the advantages of youth: we get over a hangover quickly.'

She reached into the car and finished off her second bottle of water.

'Ready?'

'Yes.'

'How about losing the sunglasses?'

'No. Oh, all right, then.'

She took them off slowly and raised her hand to shield her eyes against the sun, then blinked a couple of times before leaving her sunglasses on the passenger seat.

'There. Happy now, boss?'

'You need that stuff for your eyes.'

'You mean Clear Eyes? Which turns red eyes white?'

'Yes.'

'That has been banned, I believe, but I agree it would have come in handy right now.'

She popped another pastille into her mouth and led the way down to the flags by the open gate.

Two girls, possibly nineteen or twenty, both wearing colourful dresses, came towards them with a smile.

'Welcome, welcome. The buffet is in the back garden. You pay for your own drinks by leaving money in an honesty box. All the pictures have been painted by the final-year students, and they're all for sale. Should you decide to buy something, we would be so happy.'

They were each given a piece of paper listing the paintings, their titles and price.

'Thank you, but we're here to find someone,' Munch explained, and showed them his warrant card.

The young women looked at each other.

'Aha? Who?'

'The man who painted this,' Mia said, and held up the poster.

They both frowned.

'Him?'

'Yes?'

'Emilie did that.'

Munch and Mia exchanged a quick glance.

'Emilie?'

'Yes, Emilie Skog. Our lovely girl from the west. The Apple Queen.' They smiled broadly.

'Right, and she is here? Emilie?'

'Oh yes, she's in charge of the punch. You'll find her by the orange punch bowl. She's wearing national costume, so you can't miss her.'

More guests arrived behind them.

'Welcome, welcome. The buffet is in the back garden . . .'

Mia looked at Munch again as they walked down the spring-green avenue. The party was already well underway behind the house. Cheerful music poured softly from speakers placed in the open windows as smartly dressed young people circulated with glasses of bubbly.

They certainly could not miss her behind the table in her fine national costume, red and black, with a big, shiny filigree brooch on her chest.

'Emilie Skog?'

Munch produced his warrant card again.

'Eh, yes?'

'We're from the police. Could we have a word with you?'

The blonde young woman looked quizzically at them as she ushered them away from the table.

'OK. How can I help you?'

Mia unfurled the poster again.

'Did you make this?'

'Eh, yes? What about it?'

'So you painted this picture?'

'Sorry?'

It took a second before she understood what they meant.

'Oh, no, no. I didn't paint the picture. I just designed the poster.'

'So who is the artist?'

'I've no idea.'

'What do you mean?'

'I found it when I was clearing out one of the store rooms. It was painted by a former student, I believe. I think you had better talk to Amund.'

'Are we supposed to help ourselves?' said a smiling young man in a suit and sunglasses down by the punch bowl.

'No, please wait, let me serve you—'

The young woman looked apologetically at them.

'Is that all? I think I need to—'

'And where will we find Amund?' Mia asked, and looked up towards the house.

'He's hiding,' the young woman replied. 'In the boathouse. He has barricaded himself in with his sherry. He hates this part. That we'll all be leaving him soon. It makes him so sad. He isn't a bad guy. Everybody thinks he is, but he has a big heart.'

Emilie Skog smiled and placed her hand on the bodice of her national costume.

'Sorry, do you mind if I just—' said the young man again.

'I'll be right with you.'

She turned to face them again.

'Just follow the path over there down towards the fjord. The boathouse is on your left.'

Fifty metres further down by the jetty, where the sun glistened on the quiet fjord, was a small building, a miniature replica of the main house.

'Amund Andersen?'

Munch knocked softly on the door.

'Go away!'

'Could we have a word with you?'

'Just go away!'

290

It took a few seconds, then there was some noise from inside before an old face with a large white mane of hair appeared in the doorway.

'What?'

'Holger Munch, Homicide Unit, Oslo Police. Are you Amund Andersen?'

'Yes?'

He looked at them from under his bushy hair with an expression of confusion.

'We're looking for the man who painted this image,' Mia explained, and held up the poster again. 'Is he a former student?'

Amund Andersen put on a pair of spectacles hanging from a string around his neck and glanced briefly at the poster.

'Oh, hell. I knew there was something not right about that guy.'

'So you know who he is?'

'Oh, yes,' the old man said, and stepped out into the sunlight with his sherry glass in his hand.

Chapter 55

Ludvig Grønlie carried his mug of tea back to his desk and flopped into his chair in front of the screens. Anja had sighed as he left the room and she sighed again as a ping announced the arrival of another email on her computer.

'Oh, hell, when will it end?'

'More files from Stockholm?'

'How many case files do they have? I've just about had enough. My degree costs me an arm and a leg, and here I am playing secretary. We have to have a word with the boss, Ludvig.'

Anja leaned back and unwrapped a Snickers bar.

'You mean Munch.' Ludvig smiled and blew on his tea to cool it down.

'Yes, or Anette. She's the real captain of this ship, isn't she?'

'Depends on what you mean by being the captain,' Grønlie said, and opened one of his own emails. Not quite so exciting: an invitation to enlarge his penis.

Grønlie had no desire to enlarge his penis or any other body parts for that matter, so he decided to delete it but wasn't sure which basket to drag it into.

'What's the difference between my recycle bin and my junk mail?'

Anja laughed out loud and raked a hand through her tight curls.

'You're such a sweetheart, Ludvig.'

'What?'

'You remind me of my dad. He doesn't get computers either. I was on my mobile earlier today trying to teach him how to store pictures in a file on his desktop. Thirty minutes later, when he still hadn't managed it, it occurred to me that he might think I meant the actual desk on which his computer was standing and that he had fetched a paper folder and was ready and waiting.'

'Hilarious,' Ludvig said, and took a sip of his tea.

'So it's just as well that you have me, isn't it?'

The Polish woman put her feet on her desk and interlaced her fingers behind her head.

'We're lucky to have you, Anja.'

'And I would have died of boredom without you here, so that makes two of us.'

She blew him a kiss, then swore when yet another email arrived.

'We don't want to hear from you any more! We have enough files from Sweden. I can't bear it!'

Anja stuffed the rest of her Snickers bar into her mouth and wiped her fingers on her chequered skirt.

Ludvig's mobile vibrated on his desk.

It was Munch.

'Hello, Ludvig, I have an urgent job for you.'

'OK?'

'I need everything you can find on a man called Frank Helmer.'

Ludvig put his hand over the handset and said to Anja:

'It's urgent. What do we have on a Frank Helmer?'

Anja nodded and got to work on her keyboard.

'I can find two men, one who lives in Alta, a Frank Robert Helmer, retired, he's seventy-one years old. Then I have one living in Manglerud . . . Frank Helmer, aged thirty-six. Two addresses, a home address and a business address in Lysaker, it would appear to be a pipe-laying business . . .'

'Are you there, Ludvig?'

'I am. We've found him. I'm guessing you're not looking for a pensioner in Alta, so I'm sending you what we have on a Frank Helmer who lives near Oslo. We have his home and business addresses.'

'Super, Ludvig. Send them to Mia as well as me, would you?'

'Will do.'

Anja opened a can of cola and raised her eyebrows.

'Finally.'

Ludvig smiled.

'I think you should stay with us, Anja.'

'Perhaps I should,' she replied, and pushed her glasses up the bridge of her nose just as someone knocked on the door frame.

'Excuse me?'

It was the Swedish psychologist.

'I'm sorry for interrupting you, but Mia isn't answering her mobile. Would you happen to know where she is?'

Chapter 56

Eleven-year-old Kevin Myklebust was sitting by the round break-fast table in the small basement flat and didn't know whether to be happy or sad. On the one hand, it was good that his mother had cheered up. She was practically beaming as she sat there, and she had bought fresh bread and cooked bacon and eggs. She had also tidied herself up and got dressed properly. But now it was different, of course, because there was a man in the house. A real man rather than young Kevin trying to be a man. Ulf with the tow truck had stayed over again. He had heard them giggle and make a plan behind the thin wall, a plan they now intended to present as if it was for his benefit, but he knew what they really wanted to do and why they wanted him out of the house.

'Listen, Kevin,' his mother said in a saccharine voice, and poured coffee into the cup of the new man of the house.

Kevin didn't want to be there at all. They were groping and touching each other, and his mother was acting strange; she kept covering her mouth with her hand when she giggled and she sat properly on the chair rather than putting her feet on the table. Nor was he very hungry. But his mother was so happy that he felt he ought to try so he put some fish roe on a slice of bread and ate it slowly in very small bites.

'Listen, Kevin,' his mother said again, having stroked his arm and offered him sugar lumps from a bowl which Kevin had never seen before.

'Yes, Mum?' Kevin said.

'Ulf and I have had a great idea.'

She sat upright on the chair and adjusted the apron she had put on, with stitching that read 'Sweetest Cook in the World'.

'OK? What kind of idea?'

Kevin was just playing along with it, of course. He already knew where this was heading. He had heard them from his room, even though he had had his head under his pillow.

'Yes, we were thinking,' his mother said, and put her hand on the hand of the man whose name was Ulf. 'Why don't Ronny and you go camping? Pack some snacks, spend the night in a tent. Wouldn't that be fun?'

'Yes, that sounds like fun,' mumbled the man whose name was Ulf, and then he drank some of his coffee.

'Yes, it does, doesn't it? You could take some torches? Maybe the fishing rods?'

'But what about Ronny? We're not allowed to play together any more?'

He washed down the bread with a little milk.

'Oh, I'll sort that out.' His mother smiled, her mouth a little fixed now.

Kevin concluded that his mother hadn't told her new man the full story, and he wasn't surprised.

'I'll speak to his mum today. After all, we're good friends. There's no need for people to fall out, is there?'

'No, it's better when people get on,' the man called Ulf said, then he cleared his throat and put mackerel in tomato sauce on the slice of bread he had already buttered.

'Sure,' Kevin said when he had finally managed to swallow his food.

'Well, that's great.' His mother beamed.

'Yes, you'll have a good time,' Ulf said.

'I'd like to do it if it's all right with Ronny,' Kevin said.

And he meant it. Because he missed Ronny. He saw him at school, of course, but it wasn't the same.

'I'll fix it.' His mother kept smiling and poured herself some more coffee.

He had spotted his opportunity now; he couldn't manage any more of that stupid breakfast.

'I'm full.'

'Right. And what do we say?'

More playacting, except this time he genuinely didn't understand what she meant.

'And what do we say, Kevin? When we have finished eating? Thank you for . . .'

'Oh yes, thank you very much for breakfast,' Kevin said, and got up.

He tied his shoelaces over by the door and felt that he had to say something now.

'Listen, Mum?'

'Yes, Kevin?'

'We don't have a tent.'

There was a flutter of panic by the kitchen table before she suddenly remembered.

'Why don't you ask old Wennberg? He's bound to have a tent, don't you think?'

Old Wennberg?

Kevin squirmed.

'I don't know, Mum—'

She got up at this point and practically shoved him out of the open door.

'Sure, he won't bite. And I guarantee that he has a tent. He keeps all sorts of things in his shed.'

She nudged his back gently, but still he lingered, somewhat at a loss, outside the house.

Old Wennberg.

The man upstairs who owned the house in which they lived.

Normally Kevin was under strict instructions from his mother not to go near old Wennberg because she thought he was an odd-ball, and it had never been a problem before because Kevin didn't have the slightest desire to visit the old man. It was enough to hear his shuffling footsteps through the ceiling. Or the screaming and the strange noises from the movies he always watched. If he saw old Wennberg down by the mail boxes, he would rather make a detour through the forest than risk bumping into him.

'But, Mum—'

'Ulf and I are going shopping later and we'll be gone for a while. He's taking me to Strømmen shopping centre, can you believe it?'

His mother untied her apron and blew Ulf a kiss.

Strømmen shopping centre. He would have loved to go there.

He had often heard the other children at school talk about it. It was supposed to have more than a million shops and they sold everything from the most delicious ice cream to the most expensive radio-controlled cars in the world, and some of the other children had been there many times, as many as ten, but it looked like Kevin would have to wait because his mother had shut the door behind him now.

Old Wennberg.

He walked in a circle around the house, taking care to keep well away from the windows as he didn't want the old man to see him; then he stopped on the gravel path outside Wennberg's front door.

He took a step forwards. The gravel crunched.

He quickly stepped back on to the grass.

No.

He didn't want to do it.

Ask Wennberg if he could borrow a tent.

But then he had an idea.

Genius.

If they had set him up, surely he didn't need to tell them everything either, did he?

Kevin smiled broadly to himself as he sneaked down the path behind the house and then ran towards the forest as fast as his legs could carry him.

Chapter 57

Anja fetched the printouts that had just emerged from the printer and stuck them up next to each other on the board on the wall.

'This is what I found,' she said, and took a step back.

'On Frank Helmer?'

'Yes.'

Ludvig got up to join her.

'And who is he?'

'Well, that's a good question. We don't have a great deal on him, but I did find something.'

'Does he have a criminal record?'

She hesitated.

'No . . . or possibly yes. He was no choirboy when he was young. Fighting, ABH, some vandalism, a couple of car thefts, but everything happened before he turned eighteen so there shouldn't really be anything because it's wiped automatically.'

She took a lollipop out of her skirt pocket, unwrapped it and stuck it in her mouth.

'But after that?'

'Nothing except this . . .'

Ludvig cleaned his glasses on his shirt tail and walked closer to the wall.

'Do you see?'

'A court case?'

'Yes, but he was just a witness.'

'What was the case?'

'Handling stolen goods, smuggling of a controlled substance – anabolic steroids – but he wasn't the defendant. That was a friend of his, apparently. Frank Helmer appeared as a witness for the prosecution.'

'So he's a snitch?'

She laughed.

'Now that's jumping to conclusions, wouldn't you say?'

'But what if he moved in criminal circles?'

'He's not a hardened criminal. Frank Helmer is now – let me check – thirty-six years old, and the earlier offences happened almost twenty years ago. Youthful indiscretion?'

'I know, I know, but even so—'

'Now don't be so prejudiced, old man.'

She yawned and then popped the lollipop back into her mouth.

'Then I found some information from Companies House. He set up a business in 1992 called Helmer Finance. Not a great success apparently. The business failed to file accounts for two years and he declared himself bankrupt in 1993. I didn't find anything else until 1996. Then he sets up a new business, Helmer Pipe Laying Services, and that would appear to be still trading in Lysaker, even though there are issues with the tax office here as well . . .'

She glanced up at the wall and returned to her screen.

'Did I not print that out? I did – here it is. Yes, tax owing from last year, 300,000 kroner, which doesn't appear to have been paid, as far as I can see. That's pretty much it. Did Munch say anything?'

'About what?'

'Frank Helmer? About why we're suddenly interested in this guy.'

'No, but it seemed important.'

'And we're the last people to be told anything, as usual.' Anja heaved a sigh and rolled her neck. 'We're nothing but hamsters running on the wheel, powering the lightbulbs at the top.'

The Swedish psychologist passed in the corridor once more, this time with his mobile pressed against his ear.

Anja leaned towards Ludvig with a nod of her head.

'The Swede and Mia? Do you think that they're . . .'

She raised her eyebrows.

'What? That they're . . . No, I can't imagine that. He's twenty years older than her.'

'I know, but even so.'

She leaned back in her chair.

'Attractive, isn't he? He is wasted on psychology with looks like his.'

'So what do you think he should have been doing?'

'What do I know? Modelling, perhaps? Scantily clad? On a bear-skin in front of a fire? In my house?'

'I didn't know you had a fireplace.'

'Ha-ha, Ludvig. Whatever. He's very good-looking. But, yes, he would have to be at least ten years younger.'

'I thought you were seeing someone?'

She let out a sigh.

'Yes, but you know me. I get bored easily. Most of them are so dull. A dental student? What the hell do I do with him? Did she also ask you, by the way?'

'Who?'

'Anette. She wants all the paperwork from Sweden that mentions him. The Swedish psychologist. But I haven't seen any, have you?'

'Not that I can remember.'

'OK, well, she wants it. If you do come across anything with his name on, send it to me, please? Then I can pretend to have done what I was told.'

'Of course.'

'Thank you.'

She opened another can of cola and studied the tattoo, a heart, on her wrist.

'I'm thinking of getting another one. What do you think? Do you think I should get a new tattoo?'

She pulled her blouse down over her shoulder as she turned around.

'Here, on my shoulder blade. That would be cool, wouldn't it?'

'Yes, why not?'

'I'm thinking a white eagle. Poland's coat of arms. Golden crown, red background. Do you think that would work, or is it a bit – how do you say? – nationalistic, in a bad way?'

She got up and went with her shoulder still bared to the small mirror by the coat pegs.

'I thought you were Polish?'

'Yes, I am. That's why I've been thinking about it. I think it might be super-cool.'

Ludvig reached for his mug and was about to get up when Anette Goli came running down the corridor and stopped, out of breath, in front of them, her mobile pressed to her ear.

'Where did you say?'

Anja took out her lollipop and straightened up.

Goli covered her mobile.

'Look up *VG*'s online edition. Now.'

She returned to her mobile call.

'Yes, absolutely, of course, Commissioner. No, don't mention it, we're on it. Yes, I'll speak to him immediately. Of course. OK, I'll call you back.'

'Oh, shit!' Anja exclaimed as Ludvig looked up the same website on his screen.

'How bad is it? Is it bad?'

Anja quickly skimmed the article.

'It's bad.'

'How bad?'

The normally very composed Anette Goli pushed the young Pole out of the way and stood in front of the screen. Her jaw dropped.

'Oh, no.'

POLICE BLUNDER IN HUNT FOR KILLER. SUSPECT IS CHILDHOOD FRIEND OF OLE GUNNAR SOLSKJÆR

'Oh, shit.'

'I didn't think Oxen had discovered anything up there?'

'Neither did I,' Goli hissed, and tapped her mobile hard.

'And they've got his name,' Ludvig said.

'What?'

'The name of the boy who was injured. Whose career was wrecked.'
Anette moved to look at his screen.

'Where?'

'There.'

'Roger Lørenskog? Haven't we heard his name before?'

'Not to my knowledge.'

'Get me everything you can, everything we have on Roger Lørenskog. And organize another interview with the coach, the man in the photo in front of the flowers. Sod it, Karl, you had just one job to do. Must I do everything around here myself?'

She was shouting at her mobile now, even though no one had picked up her call.

'Roger Lørenskog, originally from Kristiansund. Absolutely everything you can find on him, understand?' said Goli as she ran out of their office, now dialling a new number.

'I'm on it,' Ludvig said as his fingers hit the keyboard.

Chapter 58

They found the sign saying *Helmer Pipe Laying Services* at the entrance to a run-down commercial property near the CC Vest shopping centre in Lilleaker, but the office itself proved a bigger challenge. Munch lit a cigarette as Mia reappeared from a building, in better shape now. The water and especially the adrenaline seemed to have perked her up.

'Nothing?'

'No, I've knocked on two doors, but nobody has heard of him.'

'How odd.'

'Did you check over there?'

He nodded.

'Both entrances are locked.'

'But this is the place, isn't it?'

A pale green delivery van came down the road and stopped by the entrance, and a young man in a pale green, slightly too tight shirt, got out.

'Excuse me. Do you make many deliveries here?'

'A fair amount, yes, why?'

'Helmer Pipe Laying Services, do you know where that is?'

The young man scratched his head and looked around.

Munch had a horrible flashback to his student days, when he had briefly worked for a delivery company. The pay had been miserable and he had been forced to wear the company's orange uniform, which hadn't come in XL or bigger.

'That rings a bell,' the young man said, and stuffed a nicotine pouch under his upper lip as he had another look around.

'Yes, there.'

He smiled as he pointed to the sign by the entrance.

'Ha-ha,' Mia said with a shake of her head. 'But the actual office, do you know where that is?'

'Isn't it in there?' the young man said. 'After all, there's a sign.'

'Thank you,' Munch grunted, and waved the young man away.

'Happy to help.' The young man smiled, raised his hand to his baseball cap and whistled as he went through the door with packages to be delivered.

'What if the company doesn't exist?' Mia suggested. 'What if it's just a sign?'

'It's possible,' Munch said. 'Let's pay him a visit at home. Remind me of the address again?'

'Number 25 Skuronnveien, Manglerud.'

Mia put her sunglasses on and got into the car.

'Sweet, aren't they?' Munch said once they were back on Drammensveien. 'The street names in Manglerud.'

'What do you mean?'

'Well, it's a part of Oslo now, a part of the city, but the street names still suggest that we're in the country. Rugveien, Byggveien, Grasveien . . .'

'Yes, great,' Mia mumbled, and opened the window.

'. . . Skigardveien, Plogveien, Treskeveien.'

'I said great. What's really going on here?'

'I'm trying to think.'

Munch opened his window a little and lit another cigarette.

'And how do street names in Manglerud help you do that?'

'I came across something similar once before, many years ago.'

'What?'

'A sign. On a mailbox up there. In Treskeveien. Larsen's Import. And it was my job to watch it. So I did. In the city or in the countryside, whatever you want to call it, I sat staring at that mailbox for almost a week.'

'And what happened?'

It started to rain as they passed Skøyen and soft drops landed on the windscreen. Munch threw his cigarette butt out of the window and closed it.

'After six days, a car arrived and a guy jumped out. He went over to the mailbox, removed the sign and drove off. I followed him all the way up to a farm in Hadeland, and there—'

His mobile rang. He placed it in the holder on the dashboard and pressed the speaker button. 'Hello, Anette. What's up?'

'Have you seen *VG*'s online edition?'

'No, why?'

'That idiot Oxen . . .' She was breathless and it sounded as if she was running. 'He didn't find anything up there, did he? Did he say anything to you?'

'Up where? In Kristiansund? No, nothing. Why?'

'It's everywhere now. The commissioner is furious—'

'Calm down. What's everywhere?'

'The man who was injured as a boy. The limping man in Finstad. Who said he used to play football with Solskjær. The story is true. A reporter has spoken to the old coach and done a better job than we have, evidently.'

'What the hell?'

'Yes, precisely. Hang on—'

She stopped, covered her mobile for a moment and came back. She was on the move again now. 'He lives in Oslo. We have an address.'

'So we also have a name?'

'Yes, Roger Lørenskog.'

'What? Not Frank Helmer?'

'No, listen to me. His name is *Roger Lørenskog*. He lives in Oppsal. I've dispatched a car. I'll text you the address.'

'OK. Thank you, Anette.'

He ended the call.

'Bloody Oxen!' Munch fumed.

'Oppsal? Helmer's home address is on our way, isn't it? Why don't you drop me off there and we can do a house each?'

'No, I'm not letting you loose on a suspect single-handedly.'

'What? Oh, go on, I'm not a kid any more.'

'All right, very well. But don't go inside. You're just there to hold the fort until I've worked out what's going on, understood?'

'Understood.'

Munch swore, opened the window, reached under the dashboard and stuck a blue light on top of the roof of the car, pulled into the fast lane and floored the accelerator.

Chapter 59

It was Natalie Sommer's second appointment with her psychologist, and she felt slightly better than she had the first time, when she had mostly sobbed and struggled to utter a single word. When she had finally asked her GP for a referral, she had hoped it would be to a female psychologist. Because it would feel simpler to tell this whole – well, bizarre – story to someone of the same sex. She had been allocated a man, and she had had her doubts, but the man turned out to be on sick leave and his replacement was a woman, and then it had felt like a kind of sign that she was doing the right thing. That it was time for her to talk about the incomprehensible events of the last few years.

Natalie Sommer had always regarded herself as the most normal person in the world. From the world's most normal family. Her father had worked for the post office, and her mother at the library. She was an only child, but that was perhaps the only thing that distinguished her from her fellow pupils and friends in the neighbourhood. The detached house in Helge Sollies vei in Oppsal had a beautiful, large garden with a small playhouse where she and her friends would gather. She looked forward to every single day. Going to school, coming home, playing in the afternoon, going to bed next to the beautiful lamp that her mother had made. Her bedroom was pink and safe, and every night her parents would sit down with her, read to her and sing until she fell asleep. When she became a teenager and her friends started hanging out with boys down at Manglerud Shopping Centre or drinking beer and smoking cigarettes on the benches down by Lake Østensjøvannet, she didn't join them.

She would rather be at home. She loved her family. She could see no point in roaming the streets at night. While her friends eventually drifted apart, went backpacking or moved to other parts of Norway, Natalie stayed in Oppsal in her bedroom. However, it was no longer pink and she moved up into the attic when she went to college. She had a view of the apple trees in the garden while she completed her teacher training course, specializing first in sports, then as a special needs teacher, because that was where her interests lay.

Three years ago, at the age of only twenty-four, she had been appointed to her first full-time job teaching at Skøyenåsen Continuation School. She still lived at home – after all, she was only a few hundred metres from work – but she was starting to want a place of her own and she had recently viewed a flat with a balcony in Ulsrud and decided to make an offer. She would never forget the moment, of course, sitting on the sofa when her aunt had rung.

'How are you today, Natalie?' the psychologist said in a friendly voice as she pushed the box of tissues gently across the table.

'Thank you. I'm not really sure.'

She reached for the box and took a couple of tissues, just in case, although she had made up her mind to be stronger today. Not to cry so much. Because if she did, she would not get to say any of the things that had burdened her for so long.

'How about we pick up from where we left off?'

'Yes, OK.'

She could feel them coming all the same. Natalie covered her eyes with her hand and tried to stem the tears. Fortunately, she managed to breathe through them – for now.

'So your parents were going on holiday, was that it?'

'Yes. It was Dad's present on his fiftieth birthday. He had always wanted to go on a cruise and now was the time.'

'It was a cruise with Hurtigruten.'

Natalie nodded and sniffled a little, but so far her cheeks had stayed dry.

'But your parents changed their plans?'

'Yes. They were due to sail all the way up the coast from Bergen

309

to Kirkenes. But they decided that they would also visit my aunt and uncle.'

'They lived in Stavanger, am I right?'

She nodded. The psychologist carefully wrote down something in the notepad on her lap.

'And that was where it happened?'

Natalie nodded again and had to press her hand against her eyes now.

'It's all right,' the psychologist said gently. 'Take as long as you like.'

But that wasn't entirely true, and it had upset her the last time. She had been sobbing her heart out when suddenly the psychologist had checked her watch and said: *Well, that's us done for today. That will be 285 kroner. Cash or card?*

'I didn't even know they were catching that ferry.'

'The Sleipner?'

'Yes. I remember I was watching TV when they interrupted the programme: a ferry had run aground. Sixteen passengers were dead. In Norway? It had to be a mistake, surely? That was my first thought. Dear God, those poor people. In this country? A huge tragedy like that. It can't be happening?'

'And when did you learn that your parents were on board?'

'Later that evening, when my aunt called me.'

They came after all, the tears, and this time they refused to let themselves be stopped. But Natalie pulled herself together; she didn't want to waste this hour as well. Because they hadn't reached the nub of the matter, the issue she really wanted to talk about.

The big secret.

After the funerals some weeks later, while she was still living alone in the big house, which was crammed with flowers, the lawyer in his gloomy office had delivered the news.

'I have your parents' will here. They leave everything they own to you. The house in Helge Sollies vei, their cabin in Solbergstrand, both their cars, all their savings, everything except a considerable sum which your mother had in a separate account in her name only.

310

The balance of that is 1,270,000 kroner. This entire sum will go to your brother, Roger Lørenskog.'

'My . . . what?'

'Your brother, Roger.'

Sheets of paper were slid across the desk towards her.

'I have . . . a brother?'

Natalie sat with the tissues in her lap and could feel it return, the rage that had been building up inside her. Who were these people really? Her parents? If they had lied to her about that, what else hadn't they told her? Had her entire life been nothing but a lie?

'So you knew nothing at all?'

'No.'

'They had never talked about him, mentioned that he existed?'

'Not a single word.'

'So what did you do?'

The gravel under her feet. The wind in the trees. She had been nervous outside the red-brick building. But she had made up her mind, come what may. Gaustad Psychiatric Hospital. In Ullevål, near the centre of Oslo, and again this rage. How long had he been here? So close by? Her brother? Locked away?

A friendly care assistant had led the way through the corridors. Natalie's palms had been sweaty, and she had been relieved that she didn't have to open the doors herself; she had come close to turning back several times, but then he was there.

Gangly. With dark circles under his eyes. His gaze dull. A shy, wondering smile across pale lips.

'Hello, I'm Natalie.'

'Hello, Natalie. I'm Roger.'

And at that point she had lost it and the tears had trickled quietly down her cheeks.

'I'm so sorry.'

'Why?'

'For all of it. I don't know . . .'

He was gazing through the window, his legs pulled up underneath him, arms hugging his skinny body protectively.

'Has she . . . passed?'

'Yes, I'm afraid so.'

'I'm sorry to hear that. I've always wondered how it would be.'

'How what . . .?'

'The day she came back for me.'

Natalie lost track of the time. The psychologist looked hazy in her chair as words and emotions spilled out of her. How she had visited him nearly every day since. How he had refused, said he didn't want to be any trouble, but she had insisted. He would come and live with her. Of course they would live together. After all these years. They were still young, weren't they? They could start over. Reclaim all that had been lost.

Bother. She had braced herself for this moment, but clearly not well enough.

The psychologist's gaze veered towards the small, red clock to indicate that Natalie's hour was up.

That will be 285 kroner. Cash or card?

Outside, unlocking her bicycle, and the air felt different.

Purer. Fresher.

She had just pushed her bicycle up to the start of Helge Sollies vei along the pedestrian street and could make out her house in the distance when a man suddenly appeared with a camera.

'Are you Natalie Sommer?'

'What?'

Several others behind him. The clicking sound of camera shutters.

'Hey, Natalie, look over here!'

'Where's your brother?'

'Over here, Natalie! This way!'

Cars, aerials, microphones, more cameras, people with mobiles, a sudden swarm of arms and legs charging at her from every direction.

She pushed her bicycle the last hundred metres as quickly as she could.

'Natalie!'

'Look this way!'

'Is he at home?'

'Where's Roger?'

A black car, two shadows forcing their way through the crowd towards her, a tall woman in a navy tracksuit and a young man in a suit.

'Natalie Sommer? My name is Fredrik Riis. This is Katja. We're from the police. Could we have a word with you?'

Chapter 60

Number 25 Skuronnveien in Manglerud was a colourless, rectangular semi-detached house from the late sixties, when the practical necessities of housing the city's ever-growing population had taken priority over beauty. Nor had anyone maintained it either, at least not this property, which lay at the end of the road and where she found his name written in ballpoint pen on a scrap of paper next to the bell.

Frank Helmer.

Mia pressed the bell a second time and reminded herself yet again of something which her brain had been shouting at her all morning. Avoid alcohol. It does you no favours. She had left her apartment with no thought other than to detox her body, and she felt a little uncomfortable as she stood there with sweaty armpits, still in her running clothes.

It wasn't an outfit she would have chosen when visiting a suspect; she hadn't even brought her warrant card.

It had to be him, didn't it?

It was him, surely?

With the painting.

Of the blond boy with the badger.

Got you!

Mia could feel her heart pound under her tracksuit top, and she smiled to herself, barely able to wait for the door to open.

Her first case.

And they had solved it in how many days?

OK.

Easy now.

You haven't got him yet.

Wipe that smile off your face.

Look normal.

She pressed her finger against the bell again.

Hello, my name is Mia Krüger. I'm from the police. Are you Frank Helmer?

There was still no sound coming from the run-down house.

Damn it, he wasn't in.

Mia walked down the road and studied her surroundings. She could hear Munch's voice clearly in her ear, the instructions he had grunted at her before he had continued in haste up to Oppsal.

'*You don't go in, understood? We've no idea what this guy is capable of. You wait on the doorstep. Ring the bell, hello, hello, got it? Pretend you're at the wrong address or that you're selling lottery tickets – whatever you want. If he's at home, you make your excuses politely, then you calmly walk away and you call for back-up, understood? If he's not at home . . .*'

He had glanced at her running clothes.

'*Well, then you can run up to join us, or do whatever you like, but under no circumstances . . .*'

Yada, yada.

It was like being back in the headteacher's office.

Shit.

Did she just see a curtain twitch?

Mia arched her back, then bent to the ground, pretending to stretch. It wasn't such a bad idea after all, her outfit. She didn't stand out; no one would take any notice of a random runner up here. The thought had crossed her mind recently. If a man had ridden his bicycle past her in head-to-toe Lycra, helmet and hi-vis jacket, straight from the crime scene, no witnesses would have noticed him. After all, Oslo was full of them. It was the perfect disguise, wasn't it?

It certainly was.

Was there someone in the house after all?

In that window up there?

Mia jogged a little further down the road, then she turned again and bent down as if tying her laces.

She viewed the house from a different angle.

A hand.

A curtain being closed.

No.

OK.

Not his side.

His neighbour's.

Stars and planets on the fabric.

She had seen a bucket and spade on the doorstep, and an old plastic tractor on the gravel.

A child lived next door.

She did some more stretching, rested her hand on her hip, then walked back down the road until the house lay behind her. Then she stopped. She had a better view now. Of the back. Trees and bushes clustered together in front of the old, dilapidated fence which bordered the property at the back.

The temptation was too great.

She left the road and ventured in between the trees.

A runner caught short.

Needing a wee.

Whatever happened, it would be more embarrassing for him than for her, were he suddenly to appear on the derelict terrace.

Sorry, sorry . . .

I just had to . . .

She looked about her and approached with caution.

No one on the road.

No neighbours in sight.

She could see the garden more clearly now.

Though calling it a garden was an exaggeration; it was more just an area between the house and the fence.

She heard her mother's voice in her head now.

You can tell the owner of a house by looking at the garden, Mia. Do you see that? Her finger pointing through the car window. *Depression, poverty or both. No, keeping your garden in order is important. And it's not as if it's difficult, is it? Choose plants that are easy to look after. Perennials will come back year after year.*

No loving green fingers here. An overgrown patch of moss which might once have been a lawn. Dried-out shrubs, some rotting planks of wood and a couple of black bin liners covering a gap where the fence had practically collapsed.

Mia walked cautiously towards the fence and crouched down. She glanced about her again before risking a peek. Steps leading up to a garden door. Large, dark windows on the ground floor. Three smaller windows on the first floor, all with curtains, or at least fabric that covered them. She slipped carefully under the trees and knelt down by the gap in the fence.

It couldn't be, could it?

She took a chance and straightened up, craning her neck in order to see better.

It wasn't locked?

She spotted the hasp on the garden door. Some smart supplier must have made a fortune out of them, because almost every house she had ever visited had one. And they were rubbish. Her parents had a door like that leading to their back garden. The frame had warped, making it impossible to lock. The handle wouldn't go all the way down; it stayed at an angle. That was how she had sneaked in and out of the house when she was a teenager.

She quickly made up her mind, slipped through the gap in the fence, crouched down as she ran through the garden and tried the handle tentatively.

Exactly.

Unlocked.

Before she had time to think about it, she was inside the house.

Shit.

OK.

She forced her heartbeat to slow down and pressed her lips together in order to stifle the sound of her frantic breathing, and that was when she detected it.

The smell.

Oh, hell.

She pulled her running top over her nose.

She looked around the place as professionally as she could. The man who hadn't looked after his garden had no great love of house-work, either. An old sofa, a coffee table laden with empty bottles, plates of leftover pizza, ashtrays. A painting of an African woman with large earlobes which hung crookedly and failed to cover the tear in the wallpaper.

Dear God, what was that stench?

A TV. A sideboard with green glass doors, full of rubbish and papers. A round dining table. Two mismatched chairs; an attempt had been made to paint one of them. A box with the top cut off by the door.

Oh, right.

A litter tray.

More excrement than granules.

One cat. Or several.

She pulled the top from her nose, forcing herself to embrace the smell.

The kitchen through the door; dirty plates everywhere.

She took a cautious step into the passage.

A pair of old boots.

A woven rug lying askew.

A jacket dumped on the floor.

Some photographs on the wall.

One of a car with stripes.

Exhaust fumes and tarmac.

A car race.

Men on a trip.

Showing off the catch.

Grinning teeth. Cans of beer.

Mia took the picture from the wall and returned to the living room, where the light was better.

Arms around shoulders.

And there it was.

The tattoo.

A big, grey, howling row of teeth down a muscular arm.

The Wolf.

She took out her mobile and suddenly felt vulnerable where she was.

318

Her heart was pounding under her jacket now, Munch's voice-mail in her ear.

You have reached . . .

'Holger. It's him. It's Frank Helmer. He has a tattoo. Of a wolf. And he painted the picture of the boy with the badger. It's all connected . . .'

She was whispering, but still thought her voice sounded far too loud.

'Please come down here. Call me. Send someone, OK?'

She found Anette Goli's number and was just about to call her when a thought occurred to her.

Mia turned and stopped, almost calm now, in the middle of the filthy floor.

Where were all his paintings?

The man was an artist, he knew how to paint; she had already seen evidence of it. The painting of the boy with the badger was fascinatingly beautiful, and if she hadn't known the story behind it, she might easily have been absorbed by it, the brushstrokes, the light.

But there was no art on the walls.

Only a kitsch painting which looked as if it had come from a skip.

No, this didn't add up.

At that moment she heard a car on the gravel outside and froze.

Could it be him?

No, it was the family next door. A little boy jumped out and ran off, laughing, followed by his angry mother. Carrier bags from the boot of the car. Soon she could hear them indoors, behind the thin walls. An ordinary day. Home from work. Time to cook dinner.

Shit.

She couldn't stay here.

She looked up Anette's number once more, but again she had second thoughts.

A tattoo.

Lots of people had those.

But combined with his boy-with-the-badger painting?

What were the odds?

No, damn it, it had to be him, if only she could find . . .

A half-open door that led to a dark staircase.

Of course.

Hidden away.

That was how he worked.

In the basement.

Bingo.

Mia returned her mobile to her pocket, opened the door fully and tiptoed softly down the creaking steps.

Chapter 61

Munch could hear the sound of clicking cameras behind him as he gently put his arm around the terrified young woman and led her inside the large, attractive house.

'My name is Munch,' he said once they were finally inside the hallway. 'We're from the police. I gather you have already met Katja and Fredrik?'

The blonde woman just stared at him. Then she said: 'Yes, hello. What on earth is going on?'

'You've not seen the news?'

Munch gestured to indicate that they should walk upstairs to get away from the hallway. The young woman nodded and walked up the staircase ahead of him, almost in a trance.

'The news?'

She looked to be in her mid-twenties, and she was beautifully dressed, in a white, freshly ironed shirt and a pink vest, a knee-length skirt and a pair of lace-up shoes which, in her confusion, she had forgotten to take off. She would not appear to be someone who wore shoes indoors because everything inside was extremely clean.

Munch was so taken aback that he almost forgot to guide her to the sofa. The floor was polished; the old joke about it being so clean that you could eat your dinner off it was no exaggeration in this house. The windows sparkled as if the cleaner had left only ten minutes ago. The books on the bookshelves were organized according to colour. The sofa looked as if it had just been cleaned and the Persian carpet under the glossy table looked as if it had come straight from the dry cleaner's. On the glass coffee table was a glittering crystal bowl with fresh white lilies. Marianne would occasionally take him to interior design fairs out at Fornebu, but none of the showrooms he had seen there came even close to this.

He looked down at his dirty, ugly shoes and took them off at the top of the stairs.

'What's going on?' the young woman demanded to know. She stood, confused, in the middle of the room, her face turned towards the crowds outside.

Munch walked slowly past her and closed the curtains.

'Why don't you sit down? Would you like a glass of water?'

As if this was his house and not hers, but he had spotted it immediately. She was in shock. The young woman didn't even know where she was.

'Yes, please,' she said, and finally let herself flop on to the immaculate cream sofa.

Munch went to the kitchen and found a glass in a cupboard, whose contents were not, surprisingly, organized with military precision, as was all the other kitchen equipment, and returned to the living room.

'The news?' the young woman repeated, and stared into space with the water glass held in front of her mouth.

'I'm here to ask you some questions about Roger Lørenskog. Is he your boyfriend?'

'Pardon?'

She had yet to taste the water, the glass still frozen in mid-air in front of her.

'Roger Lørenskog,' Munch said again. 'Is he your husband? Your boyfriend?'

Finally she seemed to wake up and understand his question.

'Roger?'

'Yes?'

'What do you want with Roger?'

'Is he your husband?'

She tasted the water now, finally present, and then she shook her head gently with a faint smile on her lips.

'No, no. He's my brother. Or rather, my half-brother.'

322

Fredrik and Katja had joined them now, quietly and discreetly, and sat down on some chairs further away. Again he was reminded why he had selected them for his team; not like that bull in a china shop, Oxen, who couldn't even do his bloody job. Munch pushed it aside. He would have to deal with Oxen later.

'What do you want with him?'

The young woman had come back to life, the colour had returned to her cheeks. The glass stood empty on a coaster on the shiny table in front of her.

'Why don't we start with a proper introduction,' Munch said politely. 'So, my name is Holger and this, as I said earlier, is Katja and Fredrik. And your name is?'

'Natalie,' the young woman said. 'Natalie Sommer.'

'So your surname isn't Lørenskog?'

She smiled a little wistfully.

'No. We were half-siblings.'

'Were?' Munch said, looking cautiously towards Fredrik and Katja.

Fredrik shrugged.

'Yes.'

'As in?'

'Roger is dead,' the young woman said, almost in a whisper. 'He took his own life. Six months ago.'

Chapter 62

Mia walked further down into the darkness and could feel the steps almost give way under the weight of her body. Their creaking spooked her. Her heart was pounding harder now as she stopped halfway in order to let her eyes adjust to the lack of light. Once she reached the bottom of the stairs, she stopped and fumbled blindly for a light switch, but found nothing on the cool basement walls in the small passage; instead, her fingers found a handle and she opened the basement door slowly.

A rectangular room.

No windows.

The smell was stronger in here, of something rotten, almost pungent. Another litter tray somewhere, perhaps.

No, this was worse.

She pulled her running top up over her nose again and stepped carefully into the room. She trailed her hand along the walls on both sides of the door and felt relieved when her fingers found what she was looking for – a light switch – and a flickering, crackling fluorescent tube in the ceiling slowly came alive.

She couldn't help but jump when she saw them.

The cats.

Hanging by their hind legs from a string attached to the ceiling.

Three of them.

The soiled litter tray upstairs.

Where were all the cats?

Hanging from the ceiling, that's where they are.

In the basement.

Mia pressed her lips together and steeled herself. She fought her instinctive urge to turn around, run back upstairs, into the light and out into the fresh air. She breathed calmly as she scanned the room. Concrete floor. Some woven rugs. Filthy. One had a large stain in the middle. A Formica table with some tools. A small saw. A hammer. A long, slim knife. An ice pick. A spool of fishing line. Some needles. Various colours of sewing cotton. A pair of gardening gloves. Cardboard boxes in one corner. Many of them. Buff-coloured. Sealed with broad, blue tape. Neatly stacked on top of each other. A door at the far end of the room. More solid. Mia dreaded to think what might be behind it, but he had certainly done what he could to prevent anyone from finding out. It was reinforced with steel and had a large metal bolt with a massive padlock.

OK, Mia, you can't stay here.

Get out now.

Call Munch.

There was a desk in one corner. A green Ikea reading lamp, a copy of a seventies design classic. She crossed the room carefully and turned it on, but the bulb didn't work. Piles of paper. A chipped plate, a stale slice of bread, half eaten. A black laptop, an older model, half open, but not connected to a power cable. She picked up an envelope from the desk and held it up towards the flickering light. Frank Helmer, 25 Skuronnveien. The logo in the right-hand corner.

Gaustad Psychiatric Hospital.

OK.

It was all starting to make sense now.

She carefully returned the envelope and resumed her examination of the room.

But where were the paintings?

The easels? The paints? The brushes?

Had he stopped?

Was that why?

After his time at the arts academy?

After he had been thrown out, had he dropped it altogether?

Quit painting?

And instead turned his dreams into reality?

Maybe.

It made sense.

Didn't it?

But even so.

Something was off . . .

She had just pulled her mobile out of her pocket when she spotted it.

Up in a corner.

A security camera.

Shit.

It had been too good to be true, hadn't it?

The unlocked garden door? Gaining access to the house? And the basement?

Suddenly she heard creaking from upstairs.

Mia stood very still.

She listened.

No.

Yes, sod it, there it was again.

Someone was moving. But very quietly.

So that she wouldn't notice a thing.

Images in her head now as she tried to remember. Upstairs? Had there been any cameras there? And how long had she been inside the house now? Twenty minutes, perhaps? Then it suddenly struck her.

He didn't live here, did he?

The smell.

The rotting food.

She glanced quickly at the bolted door with the padlock.

This was about something else, wasn't it?

This was a place he was watching.

Cameras.

Upstairs and downstairs.

He had seen her enter.

And now he was here.

Again she heard noises.

She heard wood creaking.

The stairs.

He was on his way down to the basement.

Softly.

Shit, shit, shit.

Mia looked about her frantically, but there was nothing: nowhere to hide, no escape, no windows. She was trapped. The only way out was the door through which she had entered.

The door handle moved down softly, then suddenly there was a bright light in her face and a dark, horrible voice.

'Who the hell are you?'

Mia shielded her eyes with her hands, the torchlight blinding her.

'I'm sorry, it's a misunderstanding.'

He approached her.

'Oh yes? Did Boromir send you?'

'Eh?'

'Empty your pockets.'

'Sure, just calm down.'

Mia lowered her hands. The light was hurting her eyes. She turned the pockets of her running jacket inside out and realized too late what he had made her do.

A baseball bat through the air.

He had tricked her.

Tricked her into not protecting her head.

'Tell him I said hi.'

Mia just had time to pull her hands out of her pockets and raise them desperately in front of her when the first blow hit her.

Chapter 63

Munch was outside on the balcony, his mobile pressed to his ear. Ludvig Grønlie was on the other end. He was desperate for a cigarette, but couldn't bring himself to smoke because where would he throw away the cigarette butt? The outside of the house was even tidier and more pristine than the inside. The garden below reminded him of a scene from an English manor house; even the tablecloth on the table under the parasol was freshly ironed. He stuffed the cigarette packet into the pocket of his duffel coat as Ludvig's voice came back.

'No, I can't find it.'

'So we don't have him registered as deceased?'

'No. Definitely not. According to my computer, he's alive and well. Roger Lørenskog, born 18 March 1967. His address is Helge Sollies vei 3, Oppsal.'

'Thank you. That's where we are now. Could it be a mistake?'

'What do you mean?'

'A blip in the system?'

'It's possible, of course, but I've never come across it before.'

'All right.' Munch heaved a sigh. 'Check it out. Even if you have to go down to the records office and find the death certificate yourself. If that man is still alive, I want to be told immediately, understand?'

'But he is alive,' Grønlie ventured cautiously.

'I want to know if somebody made a mistake. Was it the morgue? Issues with the paperwork. Was there a suicide six months ago, at this address? That's what I want to know, OK?'

'Right,' Grønlie said, and ended the call.

Munch decided to smoke anyway and stuck a cigarette into his mouth. He looked into the living room, where Fredrik Riis sat with his notepad open; Natalie Sommer was on the sofa facing him. He found his lighter in his pocket and glanced at his mobile, mainly to make sure it was still on silent. It rang constantly and he had wanted to create as much calm around the young woman as possible. Mia had called him several times and sent him a text message. Munch was just about to read it when another message from her flashed up.

What the hell?

Trapped in the basement. He is here. Come.

Munch tore open the balcony door.

'I have to run.'

Eyes widened with surprise in the living room, but he didn't see them. He was already halfway down the stairs and had forgotten that he was running into a lion's den, into all the photographers and journalists, but to hell with them all.

In the basement?

He muttered curses under his breath as he ran as fast as he could across the lawn.

Idiot girl. He had made it quite clear that she was not to . . .

Camera lenses and microphones.

'Munch!'

'Have you arrested a suspect?'

He waved them away and threw himself behind the wheel. Grabbed the blue light, plonked it back on to the roof and revved up the engine. There was some commotion in the crowd behind him and, not surprisingly, he saw other cars being started, doors being slammed shut.

Shit.

He stamped on the accelerator.

An old woman with a dog started crossing the road in front of him at a snail's pace.

'Get a move on!'

He hammered the steering wheel, sounding the horn as he steered the car around her.

OK, easy now, Holger.

He was in a residential area.

He had hordes of journalists at his heels.

He was forced to stop again; three children on their bicycles this time. He sounded his horn, drove up on to the pavement and turned into Haakon Tveters vei as he tried to remember the route he had taken to get here.

Skøyenåsen.

Down to Østensjøveien.

Would he have to drive all the way down to Bryn shopping centre?

Or was there a shortcut?

Think, Holger.

Think.

He reached for his radio and was shouting into the microphone when he was forced to stop again: another pensioner, a man this time.

Munch gestured frantically at him through the windscreen.

'Duty officer.'

'Yes, Foxtrot 13, it's Munch. I need immediate assistance.'

'OK, 13, where are you?'

'I'm near Østensjø School, but I'm not the one who needs assistance.'

'OK, 13, what do you want and where do you want it?'

The old man had almost crossed the street. Munch hit the accelerator and turned into the main road, where the other drivers had, fortunately, seen his flashing blue light and were pulling over.

'The address is 25 Skuronnveien, Manglerud. I repeat: Sierra, Kilo, Uniform—'

'13, received.'

'Do we have any cars in the area?'

'I have two cars in Ryenkrysset. Dealing with a suspected stolen vehicle. They have stopped the driver—'

'Forget that. Redirect them immediately. I have an officer trapped in a house with a potential suspect. Potential danger to life. I repeat, potential danger—'

The duty officer went away for a micro-moment.

'I confirm that Foxtrot 20 and 23 dealing with an incident in Ryenkrysset have been redirected and are now making their way to the address 25 Skuronnveien.'

'How long?'

The duty officer went away for a moment.

'ETA four minutes.'

'Good, but tell them to hurry up. And have their firearms at the ready.'

'13, can you confirm the last instruction?'

Bloody rules and regulations. Norwegian police officers were allowed firearms, but they were kept locked in the boot and could be deployed only on a direct order. He couldn't imagine how that would go down in the centre of Los Angeles.

'Yes! Get their firearms ready. I have an officer in danger. Didn't you hear me?'

'Message confirmed. Foxtrot 20 and 23, the use of firearms has been authorized. ETA is now three minutes and thirty-three seconds.'

'Tell them to get a bloody move on!'

Munch tossed aside the microphone and threw the car into a roundabout. He was forced to brake suddenly when a white BMW nearly collided with a red Volvo.

'Get out of my way, you moron!'

Easy now, Holger. Let's try not to kill anyone.

He glanced up at his rear-view mirror and he could see them clearly now.

The media vans with their logos.

NRK. TV2. *VG. Dagbladet.*

But there was nothing he could do about it.

She took priority.

Obviously.

Mia, Mia, Mia.

What do you think you're doing?

It was his fault, of course it was – again. Hiring somebody straight from the Academy.

'Get out of my way, you stupid . . . !'

A truck with an Ikea logo stopped at a red light at the junction by Manglerud shopping centre, and it wasn't going anywhere. Munch reversed his car, wrenched the steering wheel and drove into the lane of oncoming traffic, where another car was forced to slam on the brakes in front of him. He saw a woman's terrified face behind the windscreen; he could hear and see the two police cars now, 20 and 23, howling sirens on their way towards him. Munch turned into Plogveien and they drove right behind him. A procession of blue lights and journalists while people on the pavement watched with open mouths.

Why, Mia, why?

He was forced to reduce his speed again.

He was in a residential area.

Signs on both sides of the road.

Children playing.

His knuckles gripping the steering wheel were white and he had to exert extreme self-control in order to not just floor the accelerator.

Come on.

The road was clear again, thank God.

Just a few hundred metres to go.

At last.

He slammed on the brakes and the car screeched to a halt across the road. He opened the glove compartment and took out his gun.

OK.

What did the protocol say?

Wait. Assess the situation.

But screw that now.

She was in danger inside that house.

Enter from the front? Or at the back?

The two other police cars had pulled up behind him. Blue flashing lights across the neighbourhood. Four officers jumped out, four equally confused faces, and then another cluster of vans behind them; journalists and photographers spilling out of their doors. Munch crouched down behind his car and waved the officers towards him.

'It's the right-hand house of those two. I have an officer trapped in the basement. The suspect is down there with her. I want two officers to go to the back, to the garden door you can see over there. Two officers at the front. Kick down the doors if you have to—'

And then he was stopped.

First by one police officer.

Then the other.

Their eyes widened. Someone nudged his shoulder and pointed to the garden of the nondescript house.

For the next three seconds he, too, watched in incredulous silence.

The garden door was flung open by a man in his mid-thirties. He wore a white vest, he had a tattoo on his shoulder, his head was shaved and his hand was pressed against what looked like a bloody nose. He ran as if he had the devil at his heels, scaled the fence, tripped as he landed, and looked over his shoulder, terrified, as he scrambled to get back to his feet.

Because there she was.

Mia.

She came out of the door like a panther and leapt over the fence. The man had just about got up when she flew through the air and crashed into his back. The man buckled and collapsed like a sack of potatoes on the ground with the supple girl on top of him.

Munch reacted instinctively. He ran towards them as fast as he could and pressed the muzzle of his gun against the back of the man's shaved head.

The four police officers were still standing by their patrol cars, their mouths hanging open.

'Could someone bring me a pair of handcuffs? Now, for God's sake!'

Mia stood panting in front of him. She was bleeding from her mouth and one arm was hanging limply by her side.

'Are you OK?'

She nodded.

'Frank Helmer, I'm arresting you for the murders of Ruben Lundgren and Tommy Sivertsen.'

Chapter 64

The office was quiet, but an atmosphere of excitement mixed with relief filled the corridors. Ludvig Grønlie checked the time on the clock on the wall and then on his mobile. He had done little else for the past four hours, and it might be time to call her again. Though he doubted it would do much good. The woman from the records office he had spoken to had been gruff, bordering on obstructive. She had reminded him of a librarian in Nordstrand when he was a boy, who would tell the children off if they forgot their library card. She was notorious, and the children ended up stealing books and then sneaking them back into the library in order to return them. The librarian's face had come back to him as soon as he heard this woman's sour voice on the phone. *Well, in that case, you need to complete form AR-18 with attachments ARF-1 and 2, and then we will get back to you, usually within three weeks.* Three weeks? Grønlie used his stern voice, the one he didn't put on very often, and asked her if she had watched the news recently. This case was of national importance and he needed a reply within two hours at the most, and that had been nearly two hours ago now.

There was a cautious knock on the door and Katja popped her head round.

'Are you busy?'

'No, no.'

He gestured for her to take a seat in Anja's chair, as she had gone for the day. He liked Katja. He didn't know why she always dressed as if she was on her way to the gym or a member of the Spice Girls, but what did he know about fashion? He had dressed the same for the last thirty years and had no plans to change. Not until the shop

334

he bought his clothes from went bankrupt and he was forced to find another, something which reminded him that it might be time for some new purchases, a few shirts and pairs of socks at least, in order to keep the old menswear shop going; it, like all the other shops where he lived, was threatened by the chain stores that had taken over the country.

'Did you hear?' Katja said, pulling out a stress ball from her pocket and starting to play with it.

Grønlie nodded.

'It would be hard to avoid, wouldn't it?'

'I've never heard Munch so angry.'

Ludvig had gone to the break room. He had nearly spilled his coffee when it started, the noise reverberating from Munch's office. A tirade lasting a few minutes, and then a crestfallen Oxen had slinked out, his face bright red. He had gone straight to his desk, put all his personal belongings into a cardboard box and left.

'I'm guessing you're heartbroken,' Ludvig said with a smile.

'Oh, gosh, yes, I'm really going to miss him. Lovely guy. So knowledgeable. Respectful towards women. No, seriously, Ludvig. If he had provoked me once more, I would have . . .'

She raised her hand and squeezed the red stress ball hard.

'What did it look like down there?'

'You mean Frank Helmer's basement?'

'Yes.'

Katja shook her head.

'Bizarre. It was straight out of a horror film. Dead cats hanging from the ceiling. Stained floor. We needed an angle grinder to open the bolted door. You said he had been a witness in a smuggling trial recently, didn't you? For the prosecution?'

Ludvig nodded.

'So that must have been what it was.'

'What was?'

'All the stuff we found in there. Pills. Boxes of them. All shapes and sizes. Mostly anabolic steroids, but also pharmaceutical drugs. Including Rohypnol.'

'Which he used to drug the boys?'

'Possibly. I don't know. Like I said, the quantities of drugs we found were industrial, and our killer would only have needed a little. This was much bigger, more organized. I think it has to do with the trial. It explains why he was willing to testify for the prosecution.'

'In order to rid himself of a rival?'

'Looks like it.'

Katja put the stress ball back in her pocket and got up.

'Are you coming? Fredrik has set up a screen in the incident room. We have a live video link to the interview room. They're starting shortly. We're just waiting for his lawyer.'

'I won't be long,' Ludvig said, and checked the time again, then he looked at the yellow Post-it note and rang the number.

It took a while before someone answered.

'Yes? Ragnhild speaking.'

'Yes, hello, it's Ludvig Grønlie from the Homicide Unit in Mariboes gate calling you back—'

Background noises, children shouting, a sports hall.

'You know it's outside office hours, don't you?' the grumpy voice said.

'Yes, of course, but like I said, I need an urgent answer. Did you find what I was looking for?'

There was silence for a moment, as if she was strongly contemplating ending the call.

'Yes, and I have sent you my reply.'

'What do you mean?'

'His death certificate is in the post.'

'OK, so he really is dead?'

There was some cheering behind her now, a referee blowing their whistle as if someone had scored a goal.

'Yes. I had to search for a while, but I found it eventually. I don't know what happened. One of our staff must quite simply have forgotten to enter the information into the database.'

Precisely. And Ludvig had a strong feeling of just who that member of staff might have been.

'So Roger Lørenskog really is dead?'

336

'Yes, he's dead. And the relevant information can be found on our system now. I've obviously made sure of that.'

Great, wonderful, thank you. For finally doing your job.

'OK, thank you.'

He pressed a button to end the call.

OK, good. Done and dusted.

Ludvig arched his back, then got up from his chair. He could see that they had already started. Katja and Fredrik were watching Munch on the screen; Frank Helmer and his lawyer were sitting on the other side of the table. Ludvig went to the break room to fetch himself another cup of coffee and took it with him as he joined them.

'How is it going?'

'Shhh, they've only just started.'

'How long did you study at Amund Andersen's Arts Academy?'

'What?'

The man with the shaved head snorted with derision.

'Come again?'

Munch slid a piece of paper across the table towards him.

'Am I right in thinking that you painted this picture?'

'Eh?'

Helmer was laughing now and looked at his lawyer.

'Painted? Are you out of your mind? I can't even draw a stick man!'

Chapter 65

Kevin Myklebust sat dressed and ready on the sofa, watching his mother take her new treats from Strømmen shopping centre out of their bags. Ulf would appear to have spent a lot of money on her, and they were going to have a fancy dinner later. Lasagne, which Ulf was apparently very good at making. He had his own recipe with real pasta sheets and proper sauces. Not like the package ones they sold at the Co-op to which you just added water. Like his mother had done the one time she had tried. Kevin had given up hope of there being anything for him in the shopping bags. Because his mother could be like that sometimes; she would completely forget to ask if there was something he might like, even though he had dropped several hints, most recently when he had walked them down to the car earlier that day.

A remote-control car.

He had tried slipping it into the conversation so it wouldn't be too obvious, so it didn't sound as if he was begging, because if there was anything his mother hated, it was beggars. There were no beggars where they lived, but there were in Oslo, and they didn't work or anything, they just lied and begged and then spent the money buying fancy houses in Romania. Whereas people like her, proper Norwegians, barely qualified for unemployment benefits.

'I've spoken to Ronny and he's really looking forward to going camping tonight. Only it's sad that his remote-control car is broken because we were going to play with it. That would have been really nice, but, whatever, I guess that's just what happens.'

She had emerged from the shower with a towel wrapped around her head.

'Do you think I should have my hair cut?'

'What?'

'When we go there? To the shopping centre? I bet the hairdressers there are much better, don't you think?'

'Yes, they're probably good.'

And then, a little later, as she tried on various outfits in front of the mirror.

'What do you wear for a trip to a shopping centre, Kevin?'

'I'm not sure, Mum.'

'A dress – is that too much, do you think? I don't want to stand out like a sore thumb either, *here I come, look at me in my dress*.'

'It's nice that dress, Mum. I like the sequins. They sparkle in the light.'

'Oh, please, what am I thinking? I'm not going to a party, am I? Jeans and a T-shirt are better, don't you think? Maybe that tight, roll-neck black jumper? Smart casual, it's just a regular day, but elegant all the same, eh?'

'That's a good idea. It reminds me of the jumper I had when I was little, do you remember it? It was blue and had a car on it. And that guy, Ivar, used to pretend that he could remote-control me and I would run around and turn this way and that, left, right, stop, reverse, I had to do as he said.'

'You know we don't talk about Ivar in this house, Kevin. Oh, now I know. Big sunglasses. Tight jeans, black roll-neck jumper and those sunglasses? Perhaps I could put up my hair, backcomb it and wear it in a high ponytail like Angelina Jolie. What do you think?'

'Yes, Mum, you'll look really good.'

He had made a final attempt as they got into the car. Ulf's expression had been distracted, like with a lot of the other men. Because they wanted his mother, at least for a while, except he was in their way all the time.

'OK, have fun. I hope you have a nice time. Now don't crash the car on your way. Because the guy who would come to your rescue is right here, so who would tow away your car? No one will come. Now let me remote-control you down the drive.'

He had positioned himself in front of the car and pretended to hold a remote control, but they hadn't noticed him. Ulf was busy looking over his shoulder as he reversed down the drive and his mother was touching up her make-up in the mirror.

And there was nothing in the bags for him.

'So when will Ronny be here?' his mother said impatiently, glancing at the clock on the wall by the fridge as if that could tell her.

'He'll be here at seven.'

'OK. Well, that's not long.'

She came over to him and pinched his cheek, like she tended to do when she wanted something.

'Kevin, darling, please sleep in the tent tonight. I'm sure you'll have fun. But listen? Couldn't you wait for Ronny outside or down by the road? I just need to tidy everything up and get myself ready. I can't have the place looking like this when the master chef gets here – what would he think? Please?'

'OK, Mum.'

He got up from the sofa and put on his rucksack.

'Have a nice time.'

'Thanks, Mum.'

Fortunately, it wasn't raining outside.

SEVEN

Chapter 66

Munch sat in his duffel coat outside the big corner office on the fourth floor at Oslo Police headquarters, experiencing for the first time for as long as he could remember a sense of defeat. He had had a terrible night's sleep. Tossed and turned in his bed, got up several times, paced up and down the living room, bashed both his shins on the new dining table Marianne had bought. That was how she passed the time, and who could blame her? He had barely been at home these last few weeks.

The brass sign on the shiny door, *Hanne-Louise Dreyer, Commissioner*: very grand. And she let him wait; of course she did. He could stew out here. He had flown too near the sun, scorched his wings and was now in freefall. Newspaper front pages had mocked him in the corner shop in Borggata; it was the second time in less than a week that he had made her look like an amateur – and himself, of course, but personally, he couldn't give a toss what some idiot thought. She, however, felt differently.

Hanne-Louise Dreyer. The Dragon. In some ways, Munch could be naive; he had actually believed that he might finally end up with a boss he liked. But no luck this time either. He quite simply couldn't stand her. She represented the exact opposite of everything he had fought for within the police force for almost two decades now. She wasn't even a police officer. She had degrees in law and economics and had been headhunted from another senior management position in order *to get every single department in the Oslo Police Force straightened out once and for all*. Straightened out? Munch swore softly under his breath and regretted not having smoked a third cigarette outside. His body was already screaming for another.

Straightened out – what the hell did that mean? What kind of ship did she think she was sailing? The police force wasn't an insurance company, or wherever it was they had found that witch, where only one thing mattered. The bottom line. Money. Profits for already super-rich shareholders – was that the new goal for the police? Savings here. Cuts there. Less of this. Fewer of these. And then those bloody lick-spittle toadies everywhere in their fancy uniforms, as if what they wore meant anything at all. Not surprisingly, he had been unable to control himself. *So what do we do about the more than 27,000 reported robberies and burglaries in Oslo last year, of which more than 85 per cent were abandoned? People are assaulted in the street, mugged, their cars are broken into, they walk home at night, scared, but you don't want us to care about them, is that what you are saying? Last year we were allocated 2.5 billion kroner. And yet we don't solve these cases? Where do you think we should make cuts? And why? All research proves that the more money we spend on policing, the greater the benefits to society. Where the hell can we make cuts?*

It might have been the swearing that did it. Or simply the fact that he had opened his mouth. The Dragon had certainly never forgotten the humiliation.

'Didn't your mother teach you to always read the small print?' Anette Goli had said last night after the disastrous interview with Frank Helmer, where they had failed to make any progress at all.

'What small print? What the hell are you talking about?'

'Your own unit. Complete freedom to hire your staff. Run the investigation any way you like. But you seem to have forgotten that we're being evaluated in July. And you have heard about this concept called budgets, haven't you? I think you genuinely believe it's possible to live on thin air and love, Holger, but who do you think chairs the committee? Who do you think decides how much money we'll get next year?'

'The Dragon?'

'I think you would be wise to stop calling her that, but yes. Of course Dreyer is on the evaluation committee. And on the budget committee. So we're agreed, aren't we? You turn up at her office tomorrow morning at nine a.m. You dress well. You are cheerful.

I'm not saying that you need to lick her backside – no, wait, that's exactly what I'm saying. If she says jump, you jump, if she says roll over, you—'

'All right, all right.'

'Nine a.m. tomorrow morning. And try to look smart. A shirt and tie wouldn't hurt for once.'

The time on his mobile was ten minutes past nine.

Let him wait out here. Show him who is in charge.

He was briefly tempted to just get up and leave, step out into the sunshine, have a cigarette or two. Surely he had better things to do, a case to solve.

Munch popped a piece of nicotine chewing gum into his mouth and shuddered as his teeth sank into it. Who the hell had decided that this was a good idea? Invent something that tasted like mint-flavoured exhaust fumes to persuade people to quit smoking? Bloody idiots. He spat it out, stuck it discreetly under the sofa and washed away the disgusting taste with water from a plastic cup by the watercooler.

Shirt and tie, my arse.

He had just sat down again when the door opened and the Dragon stuck out her head.

'Holger Munch. There you are. Come in, come in.'

Who really got appointed to these posts, and why? Uncaring cynics, egotists adept at climbing the greasy pole and to hell with everyone else, in his experience.

OK, take a deep breath now.

Remember your budget.

Munch plastered something he hoped resembled a smile on his face and entered the extravagant office. A panoramic view of the city. A massive teak desk. A tall chair, which reminded him of something from a Formula One racing car.

Why don't you start by making a few cuts here rather than let the public suffer?

He swallowed his remark and sat down like a good boy in the chair she was offering him.

'Would you like something to drink? Coffee? Tea? Or perhaps some mineral water?'

'No thanks, I'm fine.'

'Pastry?'

She slid a small plate towards him.

'No, no, I'm watching my weight.' He patted his tummy.

'Holger, listen. Well, where do I begin?'

She leaned back in her chair and pressed her fingertips together.

'You tell me. I'm a bit busy, so it would be great if we could—'

The apparently warm face changed into its true self with cold eyes and pursed lips; an index finger was pointing to the newspapers on the desk in front of her.

'We certainly need to talk about this. Assaulting an innocent man? Using firearms? In front of Norway's media? I mean, this is extreme, even for you. And who is this *student police officer* I hear you've hired? That's her in this picture, isn't it?'

She held up a newspaper to him. 'She hasn't finished her training yet and already she's on active duty? No, no, Holger, it's a real shame. It was all so promising to begin with, wasn't it? Innovative. An independent unit. It would be hugely disappointing if we had to close you down after just one year—'

'I just need to—'

'We'll return to that,' the Dragon said, and put on her fake smile again. 'But first I want that report I've been asking for – for two weeks, is it now? And let's start at the beginning.'

She opened a file which was lying on the desk in front of her.

'Like I said, we have—'

'We will stay here until I'm satisfied, Munch. Then we'll decide. Anette has probably informed you that Kripos has already been put on standby. One phone call from me and they take over the case. She's very clever, incidentally. Anette Goli. I think we must find her a better job. So, on to Frank Helmer. You spent several hours interviewing him yesterday, am I right?'

'Yes.'

'Bring me up to speed.'

Munch heaved a sigh and unbuttoned his duffel coat.

'We've found a painting that resembles the crime scenes.'

'A painting?'

346

'Yes. A poster which led us to an exhibition. There we had it confirmed that Frank Helmer had painted it and, as a result, we searched his house in Manglerud.'

'You mean you broke in. Without any kind of evidence. Without a warrant. You know that he may get away with it purely on procedural grounds, don't you? *If* it turns out that he is the man we're looking for, something he appears not to be, am I right? He isn't our man?'

'My officer found several grounds for suspicion and so decided to enter the property in order to prevent the destruction of evidence.'

'I see? What kind of evidence?'

'A photograph.'

'Which she could see from the outside?'

'Yes.'

'And this was a photograph of . . .?'

'Helmer. And one of his tattoos. A wolf on his shoulder.'

Dreyer smiled an ironic smile.

'Yes, so I've read. That you're looking for a wolf. One that kills during a full moon, if I have understood it correctly? Or does he turn into a wolf, is that your theory, with fangs and everything? You're clutching at straws here, Munch, aren't you?'

'If you'll just allow me to—'

'Yes, be my guest. I'm enjoying this.'

'My officer—'

'You mean Mia Krüger, don't you?'

'Yes.'

'The *student* police officer.'

'Yes.'

'Whom you hired before she had finished at the Academy, finished her training and her probationary year of service, which all rookie police officers must complete so that we can see how they interact with the public, how well they are suited – *if they are suited at all* – to this extremely important service to society, am I right?'

He nodded.

'Thank you. I just needed you to confirm that. Go on.'

'In the basement, she found some dead cats, a locked room, and she was about to leave the scene and, following protocol, she called me, her superior, but she was then surprised by Helmer in the basement and he attacked her with a baseball bat.'

'Whereupon she assaulted him, chased him through the house and overpowered him in full view of the assembled press?'

'That's correct.'

Dreyer sighed and shook her head. 'And what was the result of your interview with Frank Helmer?'

'He didn't paint the picture.'

'No?'

'No.'

'Anything else?'

'Nor was he ever a student at the arts academy.'

'And we know this how?'

'We went there last night. With a photograph of him. No one recognized him. He was never a student there and, consequently, he didn't paint the painting.'

'But the student at the arts academy called himself Frank Helmer?'

'Yes.'

'And do we have any other Frank Helmers who might fit the description? Because you have sent a sketch artist to the arts academy, haven't you? In order to be sure that the next time we let someone loose on a suspect, then he actually looks like the man we're hunting?'

Munch accepted this. Her suggestion was a good one. He should have thought of it.

'We have nobody else by that name who fits the profile, no, and yes, we have dispatched an artist.'

'So he was there under an assumed name?'

'Yes.'

'It's still rather far-fetched, isn't it? A painting? Who came up with that idea? Hey, this painting looks like the dead boys, let's beat up some random man?'

'I did.' Munch cleared his throat.

'OK.' Dreyer heaved another sigh and took a sip of her coffee. 'It was a stroke of luck that Frank Helmer didn't turn out to be a law-abiding citizen who might sue the police force for what we did to him. In fact, he turns out to be . . . a smuggler . . . is that what we think?'

'Pills, steroids.' Munch nodded. 'Whether he does the smuggling or is just the middleman who stores the product, we don't know, but we have passed the file to the drugs team and they're looking into it.'

'OK, good. So are you saying that you have eliminated Helmer from your investigation completely?'

'No, not entirely.'

'Really?'

'Frank Helmer has been admitted to Gaustad Psychiatric Hospital on several occasions.'

'And this is important because?

'It fits the profile of our killer. And the gap between the murders in Sweden and here. We think he might have been hospitalized somewhere.'

'Still rather far-fetched, but OK, so why—'

Munch leaned forwards and pointed to the newspaper.

'This man.'

'Oh yes.' Dreyer heaved another sigh. 'That's also on my list: you had an officer fly all the way up to Kristiansund. And still he failed to get you the information you needed. That job ended up being done by *VG*. I mean, really, Munch—'

'I take the blame for that,' Munch said. 'And I've already dismissed the officer in question.'

She looked at him as if she was wondering whether he had told her the truth or perhaps she was more surprised that he was capable of making such a decision.

'OK, fair enough. But I mean, Ole Gunnar Solskjær? You do realize the press will have a field day with this, don't you? They'll make us look like total idiots.'

'Yes, I understand. But it was relevant.'

'Why?'

'Two boys described the killer; they had met him by the football pitch in Finstad. He was limping. He told them his injury was something that had prevented him from having a career as a top footballer.'

'And you believed that?'

'Not necessarily, but all leads are worth pursuing and this was the only witness observation we had.'

'OK, and this led you – or rather, this led the journalist from *VG* – to this man?'

'Yes. Roger Lørenskog.'

'And where is he now?'

'He's dead. Suicide.'

Dreyer shook her head again and let the file fall on to her desk.

'What have you really got, Munch? Just nonsense? Just smoke and mirrors? Fairy tales and ghost stories about wolves and full moons and old friends of legendary football players who end up limping before they kill themselves? No, this won't do. I had intended to ask you how a bank robber in a wheelchair managed to be watching you in the forest when you found the bodies, but I think I've heard enough.'

'If you would just—'

She held up her hand and leaned back in her chair again.

'I'm going to be completely honest with you, Munch. I don't like you. I have never liked you. Not just because you act and look a mess, but because you don't respect your superiors. There's no room for people like you in my organization. The way I see it, you're a source of shame to us all. But—'

She took off her glasses and cleaned them with a cloth on the desk.

'I've looked through your files, and you have had a remarkably good clear-up rate these last few years, close to one hundred per cent, and that's why—'

She put her spectacles back on.

'I'm going to give you thirty seconds to convince me why I should let you continue the investigation. Why I shouldn't pick up the phone right now and reassign the case to Kripos.'

Munch leaned forwards. He turned two of the newspapers so that they were facing her.

'Roger Lørenskog. And Frank Helmer. Both men with mental

health issues. Both admitted to Gaustad Psychiatric Hospital. On several occasions. At the same time.'

'And why does that matter?'

He suppressed his anger.

'Someone is pretending to be Frank Helmer. While hinting at the same time that he might be Roger Lørenskog? Do you think that's a coincidence?'

She sat very still now in her tall chair.

'Have you visited the hospital yet?'

'That's where I'm going next. I have a car waiting outside.'

More silence from the stern face. Then she said, 'I'm giving you two days. And I want reports from you on everything this time, and I mean *every* little detail, do you understand?'

'You'll have them,' Munch said.

She gestured for him to leave.

'Good. You can go now.'

Munch got up from his chair, stuck a cigarette in between his lips and left without closing the door behind him.

Chapter 67

When Camilla had gone to that appointment, she had concluded that the man behind the desk was mad. Or at best that he was lying. At first, she had been convinced that he only said what he said in order to make her feel better; it was what they usually did when you were in hospital.

It's going really well, Camilla.

You're making great progress, Camilla.

'I've managed to get you a job. Interested, Camilla? Re-joining society?'

Her? Work?

Camilla had returned home from the local hospital that day with butterflies in her tummy.

She had never had a job in her life.

She had left school at the age of sixteen and since then she had been in the system.

Hospitalized and sectioned. For four years.

Although it was really against policy; no one was hospitalized for four years at Gaustad these days. In the past, yes, when patients were restrained with straps and lobotomized. In these same rooms. Which had become her home. Well, not a *home* exactly, just a place to be, a safe place for everyone when the voices in her head became too bad.

Four years.

Hazy days in a fog of medication, forever new types. And when the pills had stopped working, they had locked her up. It was no longer called isolation. It was called a secure unit, *for her own safety and that of other people.* And then she would stay there for a while until they worked out why and she was prescribed new drugs.

And then it was back to the ward.

To the fog.

Where she would wander up and down the corridors without feeling anything at all.

January, February, March, April, May, June, July, August, September. The green velvet curtains, the white mattress, the picture of the cute dog she had cut from a magazine, toast for breakfast, the same every day, which they made sure she ate. *There you are, well done, now have a little juice.* October, November, December.

Until one day.

She ought to remember his name because he had changed her life.

Egil, was it?

No, that wasn't it. But it was like that.

It started with an E. Camilla struggled to remember people's names.

She had read somewhere that it might be a condition, in addition to all her other ones, though not as dangerous, just a minor, innocent one.

Named dyslexia.

Not like the others listed in her medical records.

So many. One after the other. Several pages.

But then this man had arrived. He was new to the ward. With different ideas to the old staff. And she had been prescribed new drugs, as usual. No, that was wrong, less of what she was already taking, that was more accurate. And less again, right until she was practically taking nothing at all, and all the time this man and the others he had brought with him, the woman with the curly hair, the slightly younger woman with the almost purple glasses, new conversations, different methods and then the miracle had happened.

'We've got you your own flat, Camilla. And from next week we're transferring you to the local hospital as an outpatient. What do you say to that?'

What?

She had been terrified those first few days in the flat, of course she had, alone, out in the world, but it had helped that it was so near the hospital that she could return there whenever she wanted to.

And then, some months later.

Interested, Camilla?

A job at Rema 1000 supermarket. Her first job.

And they had called today. As they did nearly every day.

'We're getting a delivery in half an hour, Camilla. Are you free to come to work?'

Of course she was. The first times she had been nervous about going there, she had almost turned back in the park, but her feet seemed to have a mind of their own even though her head and lungs didn't want her to go.

She had forced herself to go to work to begin with.

Trainee.

The badge on her shirt still said so. A dark blue T-shirt with the name of the supermarket, Rema 1000. Dark blue, somewhat stiff trousers. She liked her uniform. At first she had been afraid that it might make her stand out in the store, that she would be too visible, and so she had asked her boss if she could not wear it.

What was her name? Berit? Bente?

Whatever.

Her boss had smiled and said, *I'm sorry. Everyone who works for us needs to wear a uniform, but it doesn't make you more visible, in fact, it makes you invisible. People don't notice your face when you wear a uniform; they see the uniform and assume they already know who you are. Police officers, posties, shop assistants – the customers just think: ah, there's a member of staff, not a person, so you become anonymous to them, and isn't that what you want?* Yes. That was exactly what she wanted. She didn't want to talk to the customers. Perhaps someday, but not now. Her boss was wise. She talked about many things in new ways. And she was understanding and kind, almost as if she knew who Camilla was. She had given her the badge. Pinned it to her T-shirt, almost as if it were a medal. Look, now the customers won't even ask you where things are. No one asks someone with *trainee* on their badge; it takes too long.

There were three of them who were being trained by her. The boss.

Was her name Belinda?

No, though that was more like it. To Camilla, the letters looked like green flowers that floated around and jumped out of the water whenever a bird flew by.

Beatrice.

That was it, wasn't it? Something like that. Whatever.

Her boss.

And the guy with just one arm. And the short woman with the flat hair who couldn't pronounce the letter S.

'Tomato oup, cauliflower oup, fruit quash, OK? Oups go here and until here, fruit quash there.'

Learning it was easy. She had got it immediately. It wasn't difficult at all. She tried as hard as she could not to speak out loud to herself. For example, when she stacked shelves with crisps and popcorn and cheese puffs and potato sticks and Twiglets and cola and Fanta and mineral water and lemonade and ginger beer and semi-skimmed and skimmed and full-fat milk and single cream and whipping cream and double cream. But a few words would escape every now and then because there was so much to celebrate. Only once had some teenagers commented that she was talking to herself, but then she had just taken out her mobile and talked to that, which seemed to fix it, so there was no need to panic. Not any more. Not here.

Or anywhere else really.

Who would have thought it?

Her? Holding down a job?

Camilla smiled and entered the code on the door.

She knew codes now.

The clock above the sink in the staffroom showed five. It was only twenty minutes since they had called. She liked getting there early so she had plenty of time to change.

She put on her trousers and was just about to pull the T-shirt over her head when she saw them.

The newspapers on the table.

What? But surely that was . . .

Astonished, she walked closer, her T-shirt only half on.

On both front pages.

Practically the same photographs.

But surely that was . . .

Him? The gangly boy? Who was always so friendly?

And the other guy. With the tattoo on his shoulder.

But why?

She quickly flicked through the newspapers.

It wasn't just on the front page, but on several inside pages.

Roger.

That's right, that was his name.

He had been admitted repeatedly. They had been there at the same time. At Gaustad.

As had the other one, but not for as long.

Learning social skills.

Being in the activity room with the others. The two of them were always together; they used to play cards.

With that third guy. The one with the ring. Now what was his name again?

She couldn't remember.

The door opened now and her boss appeared with a smile in the doorway.

'Hi, the delivery is here. Are you ready?'

'Coming.'

Camilla pulled down her T-shirt, slipped on her white shoes, checked in the mirror that the badge on her chest was in the right place and followed her boss into the store.

Chapter 68

Fredrik Riis carried his baguette and cola into the incident room and sensed immediately that the mood had changed. The overhead light was on. There was nothing on the screen. The projector had been turned off. And Munch was practically slumped across the table further up with his cigarettes next to him and a cup of coffee in his hand. It was not until this moment that Fredrik realized how much space Oxen had physically taken up at nearly two metres tall and weighing more than a hundred kilos, and not least by his provocative behaviour. He took a seat next to Katja as Munch got up and folded his arms across his chest.

'Hello, everyone. We're going to do things a little differently from what we normally do. I'll be the first to admit that we have hit several bumps in the road recently, and it's time to reassess, to think about where we are now and how we should proceed.'

Munch took a sip of his coffee, scratched his beard and looked as if he was mulling something over before he went on.

'First, an update on Mia. She was discharged from the hospital last night and I have told her to stay at home for a few days. All things considered, she's in good shape. She has two broken bones in her forearm and her arm is in plaster, she has a few stitches to her temple and has sustained some hairline fractures to her jawbone, but apart from that she's fine. She says hi to you all. Obviously, she wanted to come back today, but I've told her that she needs to rest.'

'We had a meeting with senior management yesterday,' Goli began, but Munch cut her off.

'No, I'll handle that one, Anette.'

He turned towards them and threw up his hands. 'All right. Like

Anette just said, I had a meeting with the commissioner earlier. I was summoned for a dressing-down by her, something that was probably long overdue and that's entirely on me—'

'So is Kripos taking over?'

Katja's remark caused ripples of protest across the small gathering.

'The commissioner has threatened this, yes, but I managed to buy us a little time, so we carry on as normal, at least for now. I was forced to tell her a white lie, but—'

'Wait? What?' It was Anette again.

'Well, she didn't leave me with much choice. She wanted a good reason why we should be allowed to carry on, so I gave her one.' Munch shrugged.

'So what did you say?'

'I said that we have an appointment at Gaustad Psychiatric Hospital, that we have access to their patients' medical records.'

'But we don't, Holger, do we?'

'No.'

'Why don't we?' It was Anja Belichek this time.

Anette heaved a sigh. 'Medical records, especially those of psychiatric patients, are very hard for the police to access. It's impossible, to put it mildly. Living patients have to give their permission—'

'And Helmer hasn't done that?'

'No. And even when a patient is deceased, we need to submit an application to a judge, then it goes to the family for consideration and they have the opportunity to appeal. It could take weeks—'

'Especially when there's no evidence to suggest that either of them is the man we're looking for. They're not even suspects any more.' Katja took out her stress ball from her pocket and shook her head.

'Exactly.' Munch nodded.

'So Helmer and Lørenskog are no longer on our radar?'

'They still have our full attention. The way I see it is that we have nowhere else to look and we should definitely continue doing some digging there. If I'm wrong, feel free to suggest other ideas. I might not have made the right decisions recently and, again, that's on me.'

No one said anything.

'OK, this is what I'm thinking. A student calling himself Frank Helmer painted the picture of the boy with the badger. Katja, you went to the arts academy last night, didn't you?'

'With a photograph, yes. Andersen confirmed that the man in the photo isn't the man who painted the picture. He had never seen him before.'

'And have you dispatched a sketch artist?'

'She'll be going there shortly. I'm guessing we will have an image later today, I hope.'

'OK, good. At the same time, there is Roger Lørenskog, who we now know is definitely deceased. Thank you, Ludvig.'

'Of course, don't mention it.' Grønlie nodded. For once, he was also sitting down.

'So,' Munch said, and took another sip of his coffee, 'we had two witnesses who told us about a man with a limp who used to play football with Ole Gunnar Solskjær; VG finds out his name in Kristiansund.'

He had expected a tart quip from Katja here, but it never came.

'Now that's an odd story, isn't it? Or it would be if it hadn't been for the student at the arts academy. Because there's a pattern, isn't there? Or at least there is in my head. It's about pretending to be someone else, isn't it?'

There was another ripple of murmuring across the tables. Fredrik hadn't considered that theory either.

'We have someone *pretending* to be Roger Lørenskog. And we have someone *pretending* to be Frank Helmer. We're assuming this is the same person.'

'That is, if the painting has anything to do with this at all, and we can't be sure of that, can we?' Anja interjected.

'That was my initial thought,' Munch said, putting down his coffee cup. 'But if we look at it from a different angle, then I believe that Mia is right. Because why would anyone at the arts academy pretend to be someone they're not? And how did that person come across the name Frank Helmer?'

'Complete coincidence?'

'Yes, that's a fair point, but when you add Roger Lørenskog to the mix, then what? Why does he choose those two specific names? Why does he steal those two particular identities? If we didn't have Helmer as well, then it could be anyone who knew Lørenskog's story, I agree. An old friend, a teammate, anyone, but combine it with the name Frank Helmer? What's the only thing – as far as we know – that these two and our man have in common?'

'Gaustad Psychiatric Hospital,' Katja said.

'Exactly.' Munch was gaining speed now. 'I spent all night mulling it over until suddenly the penny dropped. It's simple, isn't it? The chances of our man knowing Roger Lørenskog's football story and at the same time also knowing Frank Helmer are tiny.'

'Yes, but—' Katja tried to interrupt.

'True, it could still be a coincidence. Lørenskog, Helmer and our man. They might have met in the same bridge club or been involved in Helmer's drugs trade.'

'They might have met in some bar – perhaps they support the same team. Went to see a match—'

'Exactly. Thank you, Katja, and that's what I want to brainstorm. Firstly, are we all agreed that it's highly likely that there is a connection? That our man is somehow associated with both Lørenskog and Helmer?'

'Without a doubt.' Grønlie nodded.

The others followed suit.

'OK, good. And we know that Lørenskog and Helmer were at the same psychiatric hospital on several occasions, I believe it was in Ward 21, the psychosis unit.'

'He *has* to be from there,' Katja said.

'That's what I think, but let's keep an open mind. So that's the first thing. Now let's see if we can come up with something else, something new, something we haven't thought about before.'

'And is it absolutely impossible for us to gain access to Gaustad's patient records?' Anja said, turning to Anette.

'In theory it's possible, of course it is.' Goli heaved a sigh. 'But like I said, it's quite a process. First we need reasonable grounds for suspicion of the person whose records we want, but even then it will take a long time.' She changed her voice slightly: '*Hello, this is Oslo police. We suspect someone who used to be a patient of yours. Unfortunately, we don't know their name so please could you make the medical records of absolutely all your patients available to us?* Now that's obviously never going to happen, is it? So we have to come up with something else.'

Anette glanced at her vibrating mobile and dismissed the call.

'So,' Munch said. 'Any ideas?'

'What about someone who works there?' Grønlie suggested. 'Someone who was there during the relevant dates.'

'That's a good idea,' Munch said.

'No, it isn't,' Anette said, dismissing yet another call.

'Why not?'

'Because members of staff have a duty of confidentiality. They can't discuss their patients. They'll lose their job at best; at worst they risk prosecution.'

'Sure, sure,' Katja said. 'But that's not our problem, is it? If one of them accidentally gives away some information, I'm certainly not going to tell on them.'

'No, that's—' Anette began, but Munch talked over her.

'That's definitely an idea. Within limits, of course. We can't twist anyone's arm, but should we find somebody who is happy to talk, we'll obviously accept the offer. Do you think we can get a list of all members of staff at the hospital?'

'No chance,' Anette said.

'Right, then we'll have to be creative. How do we get in touch with people who have had contact with these two men during the periods in question?'

'Helmer might be able to help us,' Fredrik suggested. 'After all, he was very forthcoming to begin with. The only reason we know the dates when he was a patient at Gaustad is because he told us so himself.'

'And because Mia found correspondence from Gaustad in his basement,' Katja interjected.

'Without a warrant,' Anette muttered.

'Sure, but even so—'

'Helmer was happy to chat, he was,' Munch said. 'Right up until his lawyer realized how little evidence we had and told him to shut up. Since then he hasn't said anything, but it's obviously worth another try.'

'I really have to take this,' Anette said, and left the room with her phone pressed against her ear.

'What about Lørenskog's sister?' Katja ventured. 'Natalie. She might know more. Who he was with – he might even have made friends with some of the other patients, kept in touch after they left the hospital?'

'Good, Katja. Will you follow that up?'

'Absolutely.'

'Right, this is great, people,' Munch said, reaching for his coffee. 'Any more ideas? How can we—'

He was interrupted by Anette, who returned to the room, out of breath.

'We have another missing persons case. Two boys. Eleven years old. Didn't come back from a camping trip last night.'

'Where?' Munch said. He had already stood up.

'Løvstad, a residential area near Hakadal. The local police discovered an old cottage in a nearby forest. The remains of porn magazines which had been burned on a small fire outside, empty bottles of fizzy pop found inside.'

'Katja, Fredrik. We're going there in three cars,' Munch ordered them, as he grabbed his duffel coat and ran to the door.

Chapter 69

Mia Krüger was wrapped in a blanket on a chair in front of the walls with all the pictures, struggling to keep her eyes open. At the hospital, they had given her some pills for the pain and they had insisted that she took them, but she had said no, she was done sabotaging her own brain. But then the pain in her temple and jaw had woken her up in the middle of the night, the room spinning like a merry-go-round, and so she had given in, staggered to the bathroom and stood swaying in front of the sink. *One tablet when needed.* She had swallowed three. She had passed out a few minutes later and woken up to a sleepy sun with a head that absolutely refused to play ball.

Crap.

She got up gingerly and shuffled to the kitchen. Her body was hurting all over. She really fancied a cup of coffee, but opted for tea instead, carried the mug carefully back to the warmth under the blanket, sat down and resumed staring vacantly at the walls.

Come on, Mia.

It has to be here somewhere?

Her mobile pinged. Again. It had done so all morning. Her mother, this time. Her daughter was on the front page of every newspaper and her parents had probably talked about little else with their neighbours and colleagues. So is it finally all right, then? Me wanting to join the police? She brushed it aside. She was being petty. Of course she could allow her mother this. Her daughter in the limelight. She knew that such things mattered to her. Important people who stood out. Got attention. Preferably in the media. Mia, personally, could have done without it.

It had all happened so quickly that she hadn't had time to think.

She had just reacted on instinct, raised her arms to shield her head and heard the fragile bones smash in her forearm. The pain had seared through her, explosions of light in front of her eyes. She had barely managed to stay on her feet. The second blow had hit her head, just brushing her temple, fortunately, and that had allowed her to retaliate, as his body had been leaning forward after the heavy blow. She had jammed her knee into his stomach with all the strength she had, followed it up with a kick to his groin and an elbow over his neck. The tables were suddenly turned: she was no longer the prey. She was the hunter. The stunned look on his cowardly face when he realized that she wasn't just anyone, and then he had legged it.

You could read the rest in the newspapers.

Shit.

Munch had given her a strange look, outside on the ground in front of Helmer's house.

A mixture of admiration, but also doubt.

Who the hell did I just hire?

She got it. Of course she did.

Her phone pinged again, and she switched it to silent. An unknown caller this time. Probably a journalist, yet another one.

Zero impulse control. She had felt like an animal. Bared her teeth. She had done what anyone would do to defend themselves. Of course she should have let him run. Avoided this circus. But she hadn't been able to help herself.

She blew on her tea and tried to concentrate on the walls.

Patrick had reorganized the photos.

Down to the least likely connection.

Because there had to be one, hadn't there?

What connects all these images?

Two boys in Sweden. Oliver and Sven-Olof. Oliver was the chosen one because he fitted the mould.

But how?

Where had he met him?

Ruben and Tommy. Ruben was the chosen one.

Now here she had more information: a man had made an approach, tried to trick other boys into helping him.

364

He had pretended to be someone else. Where did that fit in? He had pretended to be Helmer as well, hadn't he?

OK, don't think about that now. You already know this. He must have been in contact with both of them. He must have encountered them at some point.

The connection. It must be here somewhere.

The animals. The cigarette butts.

Where did he get the cigarette butts from?

The arts academy?

We need to go back there. Talk to the students.

Slowly her eyelids began to close again. She nearly dropped the mug and decided to place it on the floor.

Pull yourself together, Mia.

She rubbed her face with the palm of her hand. She went to the bathroom and stuck her head under the tap, came back with a wet T-shirt, but there was nothing but fog everywhere now. She could barely see the photographs on the wall. Her mobile flashed again, but she didn't even have the energy to check the name of the caller. Her eyelids were leaden, and she tightened the blanket around her cold body and finally gave in to the urge to sleep.

She didn't know how long she had been out, but it couldn't have been long. The sun still cast the same shadows across the room, towards Patrick Olsson, who was now standing in the doorway with two takeaway coffees and a worried expression on his face.

'Are you all right?'

He stepped tentatively into the light in the room. She could only see his silhouette now. Her head was still hurting and her body didn't understand why she had woken it up. It was desperate to return to the warmth.

'What?'

'Are you all right? I let myself in. I picked up coffee on the way. Do you want me to leave?'

She pulled herself together, surfacing slowly from the deep. She took the coffee and sat up carefully in the chair.

'No, no.'

'Are you sure?'

'Yes, it's fine. I'm just a bit tired.'

She pushed the blanket aside and got up with some effort while the room continued to spin around her.

'I don't mind coming back later,' the dark shadow said. 'The most important thing is that you recover. That you get enough rest.'

'No, no,' Mia protested again, and staggered across the floor to the photographs she had chosen and pressed her finger against them.

'This,' she began slowly. 'This is what it's all about. If we find the link between these pictures, we find him.'

He came closer. She could hear his breathing, but she still couldn't see him properly. Her head drooped towards the floor as another wave of nausea came over her. An arm on hers now, and soon she was back in her chair with the window open and fresh air wafting across her warm face.

'We're not going to work now,' said the voice behind the silhouette. 'You need to take it easy.'

'No, I—'

'Yes, I insist. Have you had anything to eat?'

She shook her head slowly.

'But that won't do, Mia. You need food. Have you anything in the house that I can cook for you? Or can we order in?'

She mumbled some words even she didn't recognize and pointed feebly in the direction of the kitchen.

'Back in a sec,' the shadow said, and disappeared into the light as her mobile flashed yet again.

A long number. Country code 61. Who the hell could that be?

She could hear a tap running in the kitchen, water going in the kettle, the fridge opening, cutlery being taken out from a drawer.

Her phone stopped ringing, only to start again.

61?

Eventually her curiosity got the better of her, she pressed the green button and lifted the phone carefully to her ear.

'Hello?'

A man spoke, then there was silence on the line. He seemed very far away.

'Are you Mia Krüger?'

366

'Yes.'

'With the Norwegian Police?'

'Yes. Who is this?' Her voice sounded as if it was coming from somewhere other than her mouth.

'My name is Wilfred Hansen. I'm calling because you visited my old workplace recently. With a picture of my fox.'

'Your fox?'

'You spoke to my old boss, Dr Dobrov, up at NINA, am I right?'

Slowly it started coming back to her. 'Oh, yes, yes, of course, hello. Are you—'

'I'm the PhD student who let everyone down by going to Australia, yes. Nina Dobrov sent me the photograph. She wondered if I knew anything. And I do. The fox you found killed is my fox. My special friend, Lisa. I can't believe that anyone would do that to her, it's . . .'

Swearwords she couldn't quite make out somewhere far away.

'OK,' Mia said, starting to wake up a little.

'What did you want with her?'

'I was trying to find out her territory,' Mia said, getting up. 'I was hoping she might be tagged with an active transmitter so that we could pinpoint the area where she was killed.'

'She wasn't,' the postgraduate student said.

'No, so I gather. Unfortunately.'

'But I know where her earth was.'

'You do?' Mia staggered to the windowsill, found a pen and a piece of paper.

'Oh yes, I know exactly where she lives. Or lived. I've been there many times. It's practically my second home. Lisa was an incredibly devoted mother. You know that foxes will roam, sometimes for miles, but not Lisa. Lisa stayed close to her home. Always. So we became firm friends, the two of us. I've got some lovely pictures of her and several of her cubs, if you want to see them.'

'Yes, please,' Mia said. 'Where was her earth?'

'It was in Ålsbygd. Near a lake called Vassbråa. Do you know where that is?'

'No, I can't say that I do.'

'OK, no worries, I know the GPS coordinates. You can't miss it.'

'How far is it from Oslo?'

'It's about ninety minutes unless you get stuck in traffic.'

'Could you send them to me, please? To my email? The coordinates and the pictures?'

'Of course.'

Mia put down her pen and paper and gave him her email address.

'I hope I've been of some help.'

She could barely hear him now.

'You have, absolutely, thank you so much.'

'My pleasure.'

Mia stuck her mobile into her trouser pocket and stumbled towards the hallway.

'Where do you think you're going?'

Patrick followed her with a sachet of instant soup in his hand.

'I have found the fox.'

'What?'

'The murdered fox, I know where she lived.'

'But—'

'No, we're going there now. But first, we need to go to Mariboes gate to pick up a car. Do you have a driving licence?'

'Er . . . yes?'

'Great. Then put on your shoes.'

Chapter 70

Ludvig Grønlie was sitting at his desk, glancing at Anja, who hadn't said a single word since the meeting with Munch in the incident room, something which was very unusual for her. Normally she chatted away constantly, mostly to herself, about something on the screens in front of her, and at the start it had irritated him. Until her arrival, he had worked on his own very comfortably, but it hadn't taken long before he had grown to like this girl, her company, and now he wouldn't want to be without it.

'Can I help you with—' he began, but she held up her hand.

'Sssh, I'm thinking.'

'OK, sure.'

She smiled and closed an imaginary zip in front of her mouth; their roles had been reversed for once. Suddenly his mobile buzzed and he was surprised when he saw the name of the caller.

'Hello, Mia, how are you?'

'What? Hello, fine. Listen, how do I go about borrowing a car?'

'What do you mean?'

'How do I get hold of one of our cars?'

'They're all parked in the basement. The key is in the ignition. You know the code for the door down there, don't you? It's the same as up here. But I thought you were—'

She was already gone.

Anja swore and took off her glasses.

'What is it? Can I help in any way?'

'No, I don't think so. I'm just trying to remember something.' She ran a hand across her eyes.

'What is it?'

'Gaustad Psychiatric Hospital. My sister had a friend. A neighbour who would often visit us. Until one day she just disappeared. And I think that was where they took her.'

'To a psychiatric hospital?'

'Yes. I'm sure it was Gaustad. I think my sister visited her there a few times – but no, I can't remember her name.'

She picked up her bag from the floor.

'Listen, I'm just popping out. I won't be long, OK?'

'OK,' Ludvig said as he, too, got up. He needed a cup of coffee now for what he was about to do.

The Swede.

Why didn't his name feature in any of the files which had been sent to them?

Ludvig didn't want to waste time brewing a fresh pot so he poured himself the dregs of the old one, returned to his screen and opened the folder with the vast number of files from Sweden.

Where to begin?

He mulled it over for a minute before an idea came to him.

He clicked on various documents, and it took him some time, but it was there.

A list of contacts. Important people. From the Swedish investigation.

He picked up the landline and rang the first number on the list.

'West Sweden Police, Karin speaking.'

'Hi, I'm Ludvig Grønlie from the Homicide Unit in Mariboes gate, Oslo Police. I'm looking for information about a man who worked with the investigation into the murders of Oliver Hellberg and Sven-Olof Jönsson.'

'I see? There were so many of them. Who exactly are you looking for?'

'A profiler, Patrick Olsson.'

There was silence on the other end.

'No, that name doesn't ring any bells. Hang on.'

She held her hand over the phone and called out something into the room before returning to him.

'No, there's no one by that name here. Certainly not anyone

370

who works for us. Have you tried the National Crime Agency in Stockholm?'

'They're next on my list. Thank you very much.'

'You're welcome.'

He soon found the number and waited for his call to be answered with a growing sense of unease.

Surely it couldn't be . . .

No, that was impossible.

'National Crime Agency, Stockholm. Stefan Holm speaking.'

Chapter 71

Rain spattered on the windscreen of the black Audi as they passed Sinsenkrysset and left the city behind. A very localized shower, which was over even before they passed Bjerke racecourse. Mia had been there only once, a craze her father had a long time ago; she might have been ten years old. Horse-racing. That had been his latest fad. Gambling on horses. Three hours and a thousand kroner from their holiday budget later they had driven home with their tail between their legs and she had never seen nor heard him mention anything to do with horses or racing ever again. They went back to Saturday nights on the sofa with their regular lottery ticket instead. And she could still remember the warmth in his eyes, their little secret. We only gamble for pennies in this house; we wouldn't dream of wasting money on betting. Twenty years of hoping, five correct numbers plus a bonus number was the goal, and the reason they continued every week, ever eager and hopeful, she had no idea why, but it was always the same ritual. Pizza ready on the table. Fizzy pop for the children, shushing should anyone dare to speak because here are this week's lottery numbers. It was possibly one of her most treasured childhood memories. Companionship and togetherness. The balls whirling around until they popped out, one after the other, her mother screaming every time she had been lucky enough to get a few numbers right. And the movie afterwards. Saturday movie night. Her parents hadn't always picked a good one, but it didn't seem to matter. The smell of her father as she curled up to him with her bowl of popcorn on the sofa. Sigrid, who invariably laughed at anything and everything, even things which weren't funny at all.

Patrick had eventually discovered how to operate the windscreen wipers; it evidently wasn't easy to find out how they worked. *This spaceship of a car*, he had complained as they drove out of the basement car park. She couldn't see what made it so special, it was a standard four-wheel drive Audi 4.2 Quattro; the latest model, but perhaps that explained it. The psychologist probably drove an old banger. Something nostalgic which suited him better. It might even be a classic car. She could easily imagine him wearing a cloth cap and a tweed coat behind the wheel of an open-top MG, perhaps a red two-door 1961 roadster, with a pipe and his scarf fluttering in the wind behind him. No, maybe not. It was much more likely to be something simple. Less flashy. Possibly an old Toyota Corolla, beige or something equally boring, with rust stains here and there, and not enough air in the tyres, so it struggled going uphill even in first gear. She smiled faintly at her own train of thought. The desire for sleep crept up on her as the sun came back and after she had managed, with much waving and pointing, to finally get him back on Trondheimsveien. He wasn't a very good driver, the Swede, as he pressed the wrong button on the modern steering wheel again, and yet again washed the rear window, not that it mattered. Christ, they lasted a long time, these pills. When had she got up? Could it have been four or five a.m.? She was still struggling to keep her eyes open. First no pain medication at all, then three pills at once. It was so very like her. Again, zero impulse control. Another light shower as they passed Groruddalen. Very fine this time, the calm, viscous sweep of rubber across the windscreen, the rhythm sending her to sleep. She sat upright in the seat and shook herself to wake up. They had stopped at a Shell petrol station to buy water and nicotine pouches for the Swede. She twisted the cap off the bottle and downed half of it, trying to shake off the effect of the drugs. Nicotine pouches? Yuck, how could he? It was pretty much the most revolting thing Mia knew. These new tins of pouches in the shops were one thing, but people who stuck their fingers into loose *snus* and then stuffed it under their lip? Who had brown slime running over their teeth and mouth: gross.

'Do you know how to use this?'

She strangled a yawn and nodded towards the hand-held GPS

unit she had found in the glove compartment, along with a map, a torch and a list of items that had to be kept in the car at all times, including a first-aid box in the boot. Someone from the police force had done a thorough job here. Complete understanding of the fleet of cars and what a police officer of her calibre would need for a regular day on the job. She smiled to herself. Hell, it seemed to come in waves, the effect of the pills. It felt as if it was rolling over her again, yet another wave of bliss against the pain, except the pain didn't seem to ease at all. There was a light grumbling from her stomach and she dreaded having to eat something soon. She had tried an energy bar at the petrol station, but her jaw had refused to cooperate. It would have to be soup. But not for a while, obviously. It wouldn't be easy to get a takeaway around here. They had left the suburbs behind and could see what many tourists found surprising. Here's the capital. And hey presto, ten minutes later you're in the middle of nowhere.

He hadn't heard her. He was in a peculiar mood today, Patrick. He wasn't his usual cheerful and positive self. His eyes stared right in front of him through the windscreen. His hands gripped the steering wheel hard. He had barely said a word since they got in the car. Perhaps something had happened at home? Come to think of it, where was his home? It struck her that they had spoken very little about him. His life. He was no longer married, he had no children; that was all she knew. Her mistake, probably. She had been so focused on the pictures.

'Do you know how to use this?'

She picked up the grey GPS from between their seats and held it towards him.

'I don't think it's very difficult,' the Swede mumbled. He really wasn't himself today. 'You just enter the coordinates and follow the arrow.'

'The arrow?'

'Yes, or the sound or the lights – I don't know which model it is. Do you think you could move it out of my way? I'm trying to concentrate on the road.'

Oh well, so much for a sociable chat and a pleasant drive. She could have driven there on her own, obviously, but not right now, not with this head, this body, so she had no choice but to put up with a boring, distant and rather incompetent driver.

'And we're going straight on here?' he asked her, his neck stiff. He didn't even turn to look at her, as if taking his eyes off the road for a nanosecond would cause the universe to collapse.

'I said straight on all the way. It's a ninety-minute journey. There's not a single exit until we get to Roa, and we won't get there for at least another hour. Then we need to turn right. So straight on for an hour. Then we're going right, OK?'

It was happening for real now, her trip to the land of Nod, and this time she couldn't delay it. The monotonous, beautiful landscape outside. Trees rushing by. The hum of tyres against tarmac.

'I think I need to rest. Wake me in an hour, would you?'

He glanced quickly at her now, the first time since they had left the city centre.

'You're going to sleep? Now?'

'I'm sorry, but I'm exhausted.' Mia yawned and closed her eyes. *God, how wonderful.*

'One hour, OK?'

She barely heard his voice reply from far away in the distance.

Chapter 72

Munch got out of his car and was met by a sturdy man in uniform and a police-issue leather jacket. A rough voice under a well-trimmed moustache, gloved hands.

'Ruud, head of operations.'

'What do we have?' Munch wanted to know as he looked up towards the white Block Watne house which someone had built out here in the forest on its own rather than near the other houses, as would have been more normal. The rest of the development lay around the bend in the road, a short distance away.

'Two boys, Kevin Myklebust and Ronny Eng, last seen near the white house up there where Kevin lives with his mother, who is – well . . .' The officer ran a hand over his head. 'A little confused, and that's entirely understandable. She said the boys were going camping, but as far as we know they didn't have a tent. However, we did find a strange place up in the forest. You may have been informed about that?'

Munch nodded and took a cigarette out of the packet.

'The same scene you found near Finstad?' the policeman asked, clearly curious. 'Do you think there might be a connection? With the murdered boys in that field?'

'It's possible,' Munch said as he lit his cigarette. 'And the other family?'

Ruud pointed. 'The Eng family live in the development around the corner. Red house, first on your right. Hysterical, of course. We've asked them to stay at home and wait for information, but I don't think it's working. I believe the boy's father is a member of the

Red Cross and they have already organized a search party. As you can see, there are people on their way already.'

He gestured towards the road, where a handful of adults were striding towards something, a meeting point evidently, in the opposite direction.

'And what steps have you taken?'

'We have summoned all personnel available to us down in Nittedal. I have eleven officers out knocking on doors and searching the woods up here.' He let out a sigh and ran his hand over his head again. 'But as you can see, this isn't exactly the centre of Oslo. It's miles from anywhere. Forest on all sides. Those boys could be anywhere. They could be sleeping behind a boulder, for all I know. But I've been in contact with Kripos, just to be sure.'

'And?'

'Now I know that they don't take missing person cases seriously until at least forty-eight hours have passed, but I thought that since what we have up here resembles the reports we got from you—'

'Absolutely,' Munch said. 'Have you sent them to the lab?'

'Sent what?'

'The bottles you found up there?'

'No, not yet. I thought you might want to have a look for yourself first. See the scene as we found it. But our forensics team has been in there: standard sweep for fingerprints, hair – yes, you know the drill.'

'Yes, fine.'

Munch turned to Katja, who was approaching from her car. 'Kevin lives here; the other boy, Ronny, around the corner. Please would you talk to his family? Eng, that was their name, wasn't it?'

Ruud nodded.

'Get an account of their son's last known movements. Find out if anyone has seen a stranger out here recently, anything different, anything unusual.'

'OK,' Katja said, and ran back to the car.

'Because you would notice that out here, wouldn't you?'

'Sorry, what?'

'Anyone who stood out. If anything unusual happened.'

Munch took another drag on his cigarette and looked across the landscape. Forest. Hilltops. Cultivated fields. Not much happened out here. Which suited them fine. If anything out of the ordinary had occurred in the last few days, people would have noticed it. And if they hadn't?

Then the bastard might be a local.

'Anything else?' Munch said as he grabbed his wellington boots from his car.

'Such as?'

'Anything unusual? Did anyone say something? Did anyone point something out? We're in the countryside, and the locals like to talk about one another, don't they?'

The police officer hesitated, then he glanced up towards the white house.

'Well, I don't know whether we should pay much attention to it, but the man who also lives up there, the Myklebusts' landlord, people talk about him a lot.'

'Do they? And who is he?'

'His name is Wennberg. He lives alone in the upstairs flat. He's an older man, as far as I can gather.'

'And what do people say?' Munch asked as he threw away his cigarette butt and pulled on his wellingtons.

'Oh, it's just gossip. That he's a weirdo. That he looks at children. That he stuffs animals. People are scared to visit him.'

'Right, and have you spoken to him?'

'No, he's not in,' the police officer replied, and led the way up the gravel path to the house. 'Do you want to talk to the mother first?'

'Kevin's mother?'

'Yes.'

'No, we'll do it later. Just tell her to stay at home. I would like to see the scene of the incident. Where you think the boys spent the night, is that what you said?'

They rounded the corner of the house and made their way up through the dense forest.

'They were going camping, supposedly. But like I said, we haven't found a tent, but we did find some sleeping bags and a few snacks in there, so we assume that they were there at some point.'

'When did they set out yesterday?'

Munch stepped over a small brook and ducked to avoid a heavy branch.

'Around seven p.m. Kevin's mother had sent him outside to wait for Ronny, then she had a shower and, when she came out, both boys had gone.'

It was damp now, muddy underfoot. Munch took a step away from the path, pushing aside even more branches.

'And when were they reported missing?'

'We had a call at eleven this morning. From Ronny Eng's mother. The boy was supposed to have been home by nine because they were going off to celebrate the birthday of a family member. He was under strict instructions. Yes, you can go camping, but you need to be home no later than nine a.m. The boy had even taken his alarm clock with him. We found it up there.'

The ground was slightly less wet now. The sun suddenly shone on them through an opening in the treetops, but apart from that they were surrounded by dense forest. There was a ringing from his pocket, and he stuck his hand into it and turned off the sound on his mobile.

'And Kevin's mother?'

'It took us quite a while to rouse her. When she finally did wake up, she didn't understand very much. It was almost as if she had forgotten that her son wasn't at home. She certainly hadn't missed him. She was a little dazed, to put it mildly.'

'Neglectful?'

'What do you mean?'

'I mean, what was your first impression of her? Her home? Is she a responsible parent with everything in order or is she more the type who might not have noticed if her son didn't come home at all?'

The police officer looked at him somewhat curiously.

'The latter, possibly. Does it matter?'

'Everything matters, obviously.'

Munch stopped to catch his breath.

'How much further?'

'It's just over the hill up there.'

Ruud took a step to the side and continued walking in front of him across the heather.

Chapter 73

Anja Belichek was standing outside the pale green tenement block on the corner of the junction of Kierschows gate and the busy Uelands gate, reminiscing about her childhood from the time when she, her sister and her mother had left Poland so they could finally be with her father again, who had been gone for such a long time in the cold north. Not entirely positive memories. Fortunately for the people who lived there now, the tenement block had undergone a total renovation, it was in much better condition than when they had arrived, but the location was still as bad. On a roundabout, with the number 20 bus and lots of other traffic going right past the windows. A ground-floor flat, and the funeral parlour was still right next to it. She used to have to reassure her sister often, holding her tight and comforting her under the duvet in the narrow bed. *Dead people live in this building. No, Zofia, no. Yes, it says so on the windows, it says funeral, that's when people are put in the ground, in between them dying and going to heaven. They lie next door and they talk to me.* Her sister had been six and she had been eight and, for some reason, her younger sibling had learned this new language quickly; she had spoken it fluently with everyone she met after just a few months. For Anja it had been a struggle. She had felt strange, an outsider at the otherwise very nice school. She had gone from being the centre of attention in her class back home in the small town of Weselno to being a mere spectator in this big, strange city.

But it had all worked out in the end. Slowly, but surely. The new normal. She had adapted to the novelty; in fact, she had started to like it.

She smiled to herself and walked up to the front door, scanning the nameplates displayed there.

Camilla.

The name had been on the tip of her tongue all along. She had only called her sister in order to jog her memory.

Camilla Holt.

She took her mobile out of her bag and found her sister's number.

'Zofia speaking.'

'Hey, I thought you said she still lived in our old block? I can't find her name on the door.'

'OK? No, I don't remember exactly. Yes, I do – you're looking for the name of a business or something. Its name is still on the bell. Mofiss? Lofiss? Could it be something like that?'

'Slowpace Ltd?'

'Yes, that's it.'

'But that's nothing like what you said. Mofiss?'

'Ha-ha. By the way, why do you want to talk to Camilla?'

'I've already told you.'

'No, you said that you couldn't tell me, that it had to do with your job?'

'Exactly.'

'Oh, come on.'

'No, maybe later, but not now.'

'Meh. Listen, if she's not in, she sometimes works in Rema 1000 in Mogata. Right next to Salon Habib. Do you know where that is?'

'I do, thank you.'

Her sister stayed on the phone.

'Go on, tell me.'

'No.'

'Oh, come on. Is it about the two boys found in the field?'

'Some other time,' Anja said, ending the call and dropping her mobile into her handbag.

She studied the names next to the doorbells once more.

Slowpace Ltd.

She pressed her finger against the bell and waited.

Nothing.

She tried again, but there was still no answer.

OK. Next stop Rema 1000 in Mogata.

She had just crossed the pedestrian crossing and was making her way through the park when she saw a figure coming towards her.

Skinny. Cautious. Hidden under a big hoodie.

The young woman jumped when she called out her name.

'Camilla?'

With frightened eyes, the young woman stopped in front of her and glanced around.

'Yes?'

'Do you remember me? I'm Anja. Zofia's big sister?'

Slow recognition on the young woman's pale face.

'Oh, yes? Hello. It's been a while. Do you still live here?'

'No. I'm here to talk to you.'

'Me? Why?'

'Do you have some time now? Perhaps we could go to your flat?'

Chapter 74

The distances between the houses grew longer and, once they had left route 4, there were hardly any houses at all. A few had been built here, for no obvious reason, because it really was the back of beyond. The nearest inhabited village was Gran, but the Norwegian Automobile Federation guidebook Mia had found in the glove compartment said that the place was also known as Vassenden. No one knew why, but at least there were people living there. A touring holiday with her family was nothing without the NAF guidebook. Another memory from her childhood came back to her, or several. It was like a journey from when she was between eight and fifteen, when her family took an increasing number of driving holidays because they didn't go to the Mediterranean like normal people. No. Oh no, they were going to traipse up and down the country. The traditional Norwegian holiday. Waterfalls, wide expanses, deep forests and tents that never kept the rain out. Her mother leading the way, always the most enthusiastic of them all. Reading aloud from the red NAF guidebook about all the places they passed. Mia had eventually realized that it was her mother's way of adding interest to these incredibly dull, long holidays, but at the age of thirteen she had finally rebelled. *Please, Mum, I can't cope with any more local knowledge. Yes, but it says here that this waterfall has a vertical drop of over two hundred metres. Imagine, girls, a two-hundred-metre drop? I know, Mum, but do we have to hear about it? Can't we just look at the waterfall once we get there?* Mia had no intention of taking over her mother's role and lecturing the Swedish psychologist on local Norwegian topography; she was only consulting the guidebook because of its map.

They had passed Gran, also known as Vassenden, ten minutes ago. There was nothing out here now. Except for one house. For some reason. A grubby-looking house and a workshop. A garage and tyre depot. Well, why not? Surely the rent out here was practically nothing? And you could repair cars anywhere. It was a good idea, though probably rather lonely. But after that there was nothing. The road narrowed, and it was as if the forest consumed them now. They continued at a snail's pace between dense spruces, and from time to time she caught a glimpse of a glittering lake or a small river. What an amazing landscape. She reached for the water bottle again. What *was* in those pills? The drowsiness seemed to come over her in waves, as it had done all day.

'You're allowed to drive faster, Patrick. I think the speed limit here is eighty kilometres an hour.'

'What?'

Patrick was still staring straight ahead. He really wasn't having a great day. Perhaps his stomach was playing up again. Mia didn't want to ask; she didn't know him well enough. In fact, she didn't know him at all.

'Eighty,' Mia said in a rather impatient tone, pointing both index fingers at the windscreen. 'It's only twelve kilometres to our destination, but at this speed we won't get there till the weekend. Do you think you could hit the gas a little harder?'

'What? Eighty?' The speedometer on the dashboard showed barely fifty kilometres an hour.

'Yes, eighty. An eight followed by a zero.'

'I thought it said thirty earlier on?'

'Yes, when we passed a school, but there's no one up here, so floor it. You do have a driving licence, don't you?'

'What?' He turned now, at first a little irritated, but then he softened into a smile. His first one today.

'Oh, you're so funny, Mia.'

She kicked off her shoes and put her feet on the dashboard.

'Yes, I am, aren't I?'

'Yes, very funny. But you're not wrong.'

'What do you mean?'

They passed a sign with a picture of an elk. Mia had heard that these were popular with campers, who unscrewed them and took them home as trophies. The locals didn't get it, but it was probably the equivalent of her excitement at seeing a sign depicting a kangaroo.

'No, it has been mentioned.'

'What has?'

Patrick let out a small sigh. 'Well, my optician said that perhaps I should start wearing glasses, not just in front of the computer, but also for driving.'

'What? And you're telling me this now?'

'I'm all right as long as I drive slowly.'

'Oh, great. So this is your max speed?'

'We're not very far away now, are we?'

'No, we're not.'

Mia closed the window as the clearing ended and the dense forest enveloped them once more. The road was, if possible, even narrower now, and then suddenly the tarmac ended. Stones were thrown up by the tyres as they drove on to the gravel track.

'I ought to sign your cast,' Patrick said with a nod to her arm.

'I prefer it white.'

'No W?' He proffered a wry smile.

'I don't think that would be appropriate.'

Another wave of drowsiness came over her without warning and she had to open the window again.

'What the hell is wrong with these pills?'

'Do you feel sick?'

'It seems to come and go. I'm all right for a while and then they suddenly get me.'

'Perhaps they are sustained release.'

'What's that?'

It was Patrick's turn to laugh now.

'You don't know what sustained-release pills are?'

'No?'

'You take one pill and its effects last for twenty-four hours. It releases its dosage steadily over that period of time.'

'Eh, what?'

'Seriously, you don't know what I'm talking about?'

'I don't take painkillers very often. I don't think I've had one since I was twelve.'

'What did they give you?'

'Tramo something or other? Or was it trama?'

'Tramadol?'

'It might have been.' Mia took another gulp of water and leaned against the head rest.

'OK. Good luck with that. That's an opioid. When did you last take one?'

'Take one?'

'Yes?'

'What if I took three?'

Patrick almost slammed on the brakes.

'What?'

'Hypothetically, yes.'

The wonderful tiredness came back as the forest opened up and the sun fell across her face.

'You took *three* Tramadols? Today is going to be a long day, I think. You just go back to sleep, Mia.'

Chapter 75

Munch emerged from the forest as Fredrik Riis came up the gravel path past the white house.

'What does it look like?'

'It's our man, no doubt about it,' Munch said, and took his cigarettes out of his pocket.

'Are you sure?'

'The exact same MO. Porn magazines in the cabin. The boys wouldn't appear to have liked them because they burned them on a campfire, but there are bits of tape on the walls.'

'Shit,' Riis mumbled. 'And there's fizzy pop and so on?'

Munch nodded. 'Four or five bottles. Two of them on the doorstep; the weather was good last night, wasn't it?'

'It was in Oslo, but out here? I don't know.'

'I'm guessing it was the same here. They probably sat outside. Enjoyed the sunshine. Maybe they slept there too. He must have moved them during the night. You found tracks from a quad bike up by the burnt-out van, didn't you?'

'I would recognize them anywhere.'

'Good, there's another path up there, not far from the cabin. He must have got them out that way. The ground is fairly dry, so I didn't see any tyre marks, but try to follow it anyway.'

'I will,' Riis said, and disappeared up into the forest.

Munch lit a cigarette and walked to the front door of the white house.

The old man the locals gossiped about.

It said Wennberg on a worn nameplate by the door.

Wennberg? W?

Munch walked up to the windows, but he couldn't see very much. A gruff voice behind him made him turn round.

'Excuse me, what do you think you're doing?'

An ageing face. Greying hair. Dark eyes scowling at him. Rolled-up shirtsleeves, tattoos on his forearms. A German shepherd on a leash, which, like its owner, didn't seem fond of strangers.

'Munch, Oslo Homicide Unit.' Munch introduced himself and produced his warrant card.

The man studied it. 'What do you want with me?'

The dog bared its teeth.

'Do you live here?'

The man nodded.

'You've heard what has happened?'

The man nodded again, placed his hand on the dog's head and made it sit quietly.

'Can't say I'm surprised.'

He passed Munch and walked up the quivering metal steps. He stuck the key into the lock and let the dog in.

'What do you mean?'

The man closed the door behind the dog and came back to Munch.

'What I said. I don't know about the ginger boy, but I know Kevin well. They've been my tenants for a long time.'

'OK? And you have obviously no idea where they are?'

'No, I don't. Or I wouldn't be standing here.'

'And how do you know that the other boy has red hair?'

The man laughed out loud. 'Oh, is that your strategy, Mr Clever Detective from our great capital? Of course I know what Ronny looks like. He's Kevin's only friend.'

He sat down on the bottom step and started pulling off his heavy, muddy boots.

'Do you have much contact with them, your tenants, I mean? Kevin and . . . she's a single mother, isn't she?'

The man snorted with derision.

'*Mother* is pushing it. Single? Once a month, perhaps. It's like a revolving door down there. I've stopped trying to keep up.'

389

'Do you get on with them? They haven't bothered you in any way, have they?'

The man scoffed again.

'You're suggesting I might have kidnapped two boys because the mother of one of them never pays her rent on time? I don't think so, young man. I don't think so.'

He got up and spat into the gravel.

'Is that all? I have things to do.'

'Sure,' Munch said. 'No, there was one more thing. Did you know there's an old cabin in that direction up in the forest?'

The old man looked up through the trees.

'Was that where they went? The hunting lodge?'

'The hunting lodge – so you know about it?'

'Of course I do. I was the one who fixed it up for him.'

'You fixed it up for Kevin, the boy who lives in your basement flat?'

'Yes.'

'May I ask why?'

The man stared at him now, then he ran his hand across his chin. 'Do you have a father, Detective?'

'Not any more, but yes, I did – why?'

The man placed a coarse fist on the door handle and looked up towards the forest once more. 'I didn't have one, and neither does Kevin. And someone has to look out for him, don't you think?'

'I understand.' Munch nodded.

'Was that it?'

'It is for now. Thank you.'

Munch put out his cigarette against his boot and was on his way back around the house when his mobile vibrated in his pocket again. He took it out this time and saw all the missed calls. He sighed, lit another cigarette and answered the call.

'Make it quick, Ludvig. I'm right in the middle of something up here.'

Chapter 76

Patrick held the GPS up towards the sky as the weather changed around them. Grey clouds drifted across the vast landscape. Spring had yet to arrive this far out into the wilderness, at least in the form of milder temperatures. Mia pulled her jacket around her as the Swede checked the display again.

'It's supposed to be around here.'

'Here exactly, or somewhere nearby?'

'You try.' Patrick sighed and passed her the grey gadget.

She shook her head and took in the terrain about her. Fortunately they had not had to walk very far from the road. She had had the foresight to bring her hiking boots, but Patrick was dressed as if he was going to a wine bar.

'Does it really matter?' he complained.

'What do you mean?'

He walked across the heather to join her.

'Well, she was somewhere in this area, wasn't she? The fox? I used the coordinates from the guy in Australia, and so we've done it now, haven't we?' Patrick blew on his hands to warm them up.

'We've done what? What are you saying?'

'Does it really matter if we find her actual earth now that we know this was the place?'

She gestured towards the trees around her. 'He killed her here. And that means he must be from nearby.'

'Except it doesn't, does it?' Patrick said. He had already started walking back towards the car. 'He could have come from anywhere.'

Mia avoided a hole in the marshy ground and followed him.

'No, it doesn't,' she said firmly. 'Because he wanted a fox, didn't he?'

'Yes.'

'No, don't just say "yes" like that. He *wanted* a fox. He *needed* a fox, and where do you find foxes?'

'You buy them.'

'No, don't be so negative. He couldn't risk it. What if the seller recognized the fox from the crime scene? So he obviously couldn't do that.'

'OK,' Patrick said, and clicked the key to unlock the car.

'So he must have known where she was, mustn't he? And so he went fox-hunting. How many people do that in this country, to your knowledge? Er, none. Nobody. Because you won't find them. Foxes are experts at hiding. So he must have been local or at least known about this place. Had a cabin nearby, something like that, don't you think?'

'I think I'm going to catch my death from cold if we don't leave soon,' Patrick grunted, and started the engine.

'But you can follow my train of thought, can't you?' Mia said as she got into the passenger seat. 'You saw the marks on her? A snare or something similar? He must have set a trap. There were no gunshot injuries, am I right? He wanted her intact. For the image. No, he must be from around here. Or, at the very least, he must have come to this *particular* place. At various times. To set the trap. To check if she had walked into it. I guarantee you. He knows this area.'

Patrick almost reversed into a ditch, but finally managed to turn the car around with some minor skidding on the gravel road before they started the drive back.

Mia was growing increasingly frustrated with Patrick because he didn't share her enthusiasm, but then again he had been a little out of sorts all day, not quite himself.

She leaned back against the head rest as the effects of the pills started to kick in again.

'You're absolutely right,' he said eventually. 'I'm sorry. What do you think we should do now?'

'We need to get some people up here.' Mia yawned and rested her head against the window. 'Or rather, we need to talk to Munch. Sit down with all of them. Tell them what we have seen. Let them make the decision. Possibly tonight?'

'Tonight?'

'We need absolutely everyone up here. A helicopter, possibly the army. Organize a search party, knock on every door, although there aren't many of those—'

'Do you seriously think Munch will deploy the army and a helicopter because you have found the vixen's earth?'

'Totally. He likes me.'

Patrick laughed. 'Yes, I'm sure he does, but that doesn't mean he's willing to blow his entire budget on this.'

'Just you wait and see.'

Again they drove past the tyre shop with the world's cheapest rent. A yellow-and-red tow truck was parked outside the filthy windows now.

Mia felt warm all over and struggled to keep her eyes open as the garage disappeared around the bend in the wing mirror.

Shit . . .

'Stop the car!'

'What?'

'Stop the car. I mean it, stop it now.'

Patrick slammed on the brakes.

'What are you——'

'Be quiet.'

'But—'

'No, shh, not a word.'

'What do you think you're—'

'It's him.'

'What?'

'The tow truck. That's the connection. Bloody obvious now. Every traffic accident.'

Mia opened the door as quietly as she could and climbed out of the car, then she sized up the white garage before crouching down and half-running along the road.

She reached the bend and could now see the name on the truck.

Ulf Holund.

Of course.

Damn it, why hadn't she understood it until now?

Ulf.

W.

Wulf.

The Wolf.

It wasn't until she understood the implication of the name on the truck door that she realized this might not have been the smartest move she could make.

She was unarmed.

With a head that wasn't working and a body that wanted nothing more than to sleep.

Keep going, Mia.

She exhaled heavily and paused to listen out.

Nothing.

Was he even here?

She crept up to the tow truck and touched the bonnet. It was warm.

So he had to be around here somewhere, surely?

The Audi came slowly round the bend now, and Mia gestured to make Patrick go away.

Get out of here.

A civilian police car.

He is bound to spot it.

Patrick leaning close to the windscreen, waving his arms frantically.

No, no, go away.

She didn't understand what Patrick was trying to do until he slammed his hand against the steering wheel.

The horn echoed in her ears.

No, no, what the hell do you think you're—

A warning.

She barely had time to turn around. She caught a glimpse of the spade. Reflected in a filthy window.

No.

She tried desperately to raise both her arms, but the plaster cast refused, her body didn't listen.

Damn it, Mia.

Then all sounds disappeared.

394

Chapter 77

Munch parked his car in a disabled bay below Oslo Police head-quarters and half ran up the slope to the entrance, where Anette Goli was waiting for him.

'Any news?'

The lawyer shook her head and opened the door.

'Nothing since the last time you asked. We can't find her. Or the Swedish psychologist. To be quite honest, I don't even know which hotel he was staying at.'

They showed their warrant cards at reception and walked over to the lift.

'And Mia hasn't been in contact with you?'

Anette pressed the button to call the lift, then she shook her head.

'Her phone is turned off. Ludvig last heard from her this morning. When she asked if she could borrow a car.'

'A car? One of ours?'

The lift pinged as the doors opened.

'Yes, one from the basement.'

'Can we track it in any way?'

'No, I'm afraid not. Any news from the scene? Anything about the boys?'

'No leads yet, but they're on top of things up there. The local officers seem up to the task. The Red Cross is organizing a search party and a family liaison team is on its way to support the parents.'

Anette got another call but dismissed it. Munch caught a glimpse of his face in the mirror. Drawn, exhausted, he looked as if he hadn't eaten or slept for a long time, which wasn't far from the truth. He regretted not having had a cigarette before coming inside. This might take some time.

'He's already in the interview room.'

Anette gestured down the corridor with her mobile.

'And it was him who wanted to talk to us?'

'Yes. His lawyer called. Said they might have information which could be of interest to us – if we would do something for them in return.'

'Like us dropping the charges for possession of the pills?'

'Something like that.'

'Could we do that?'

She considered it for a moment. 'Possibly. I'll need to talk to the public prosecutor.'

'OK, call him now,' Munch grunted, and entered the interview room.

Frank Helmer looked more alert this time, well kempt, as if he was about to face a jury. A shirt, suit jacket, his hair brushed back. He nodded politely to Munch and half got up from his chair as the investigator entered.

'Right, what do you want?' Munch said with a sigh as he flopped on to a chair.

'My client—,' the lawyer began, but Munch cut him short.

'I want to hear it from you. Straight.'

'So,' Helmer began, then he ran a finger along his shirt collar and glanced at his lawyer, who spoke again.

'I have learned that my client has information which might be beneficial to—'

'Christ on a bike,' Munch said. 'So you think it might be *beneficial to us*? That your client in all probability knows who brutally murdered four boys and currently has two more in captivity? Is that what you want, Frank? To have two more lives on your conscience?'

Helmer was sweating now, clearly uncomfortable.

'I—' His gaze flitted towards his lawyer once more.

'We ask' – the oleaginous creature cleared his throat – 'that all charges against my client be dropped. Furthermore that he receives substantial compensation and, more importantly, a public apology for the assault on him—'

Anette suddenly popped her head round, her phone pressed against her chest.

'You need to hear this.'

'Now? Seriously?'

'Definitely.'

Out in the corridor again, she smiled faintly before passing him her mobile.

'Yes, hello? Who is it?'

'Hello, Munch, it's Anja. Anja Belichek. I know who it is, I know who he is.' The Polish woman talked without drawing breath. 'My sister had a friend who disappeared, and I remembered that she was admitted to Gaustad Psychiatric Hospital. I eventually tracked her down and she now lives in the block where we used to live, would you believe it? But, anyway, I asked her about Lørenskog and Helmer, if she had seen the newspapers, if she remembered them. And she said she did. Then I asked if she could remember a third man who might be linked to the two men at the hospital. And she said it was strange that I was asking her that because she had just been thinking about him—'

'What's his name, Anja?'

'Well, that's it, that's why it took some time. Because Camilla, that's the woman I'm talking about, couldn't remember it. I think it's a condition – name something or other, whatever – we needed to call another friend who—'

'Anja?'

'Er . . . yes?'

'Great job. What's his name?'

'Eh . . . Ulf Holund.'

'You're sure?'

'One hundred per cent, because—'

Munch passed the mobile back to Anette, and the voice of the clever young woman could still be heard down the corridor when he returned to the interview room and calmly sat down.

'Like I said . . .' The lawyer cleared his throat again.

Munch ignored him and shoved a piece of paper and a pen towards Helmer.

'Ulf Holund.'

'Say what?'

'We might be willing to look at the charges against you. *If* you write down absolutely everything you know about your good friend Ulf Holund. Where he lives, what he does—'

The lawyer protested vociferously.

'Ulf Holund,' Munch insisted, jabbing the paper with his finger.

'No, no, I demand that all—'

'Shut up,' Helmer snarled, and grabbed the pen on the table.

EIGHT

Chapter 78

Lydia Clemens couldn't get the badger out of her mind. It had kept her awake all night. Thinking about how awful it must have been. For the beautiful animal. Being trapped in that tiny cage. Last night she had felt so enraged that she had got up, put on her clothes and had been halfway out of the door before she stopped. She had her bow across her chest and her knife in her belt, but it had been so dark outside, and the wind had howled and shaken the treetops so she turned back. Crawled into bed, almost on the verge of tears. Because what if he captured it again? Or if he captured some other animal?

She had liked him to begin with. The man up in the dilapidated cottage. His TV. All the excitement. And she had assumed that he was lonely because every time she had seen him, he had been alone, like her, with no friends. But then she had remembered that she had her grandfather and had decided to feel sorry for him. But no more. Not after the badger. Those feelings were gone. She would be going up to the cottage soon, and she would release the badger if he had trapped it in the cage again. She might even burn the cage.

She had got out of bed early that morning intending to leave as quickly as she could, but then remembered that she couldn't. Because today they were digging a ditch. From the brook and into the house. It would provide them with running water so they wouldn't have to go to the well when the jugs were empty. They had talked about it many times before, but never actually done it. Because her grandfather hated plastic. *Plastic is an incurable cancer on nature*, he would often say, and one day the earth would stop breathing altogether because everyone had been strangled by plastic. But then he had an idea. He had been to Vassenden one day and seen a skip with some old plastic piping sticking out, and it was as if a light bulb had appeared over his head. Aha, he had thought, these plastic pipes will either be landfill or burned and toxic fumes will go into the sky. It's better that we reuse them for something. Lydia had been so happy at the mere thought. Imagine turning on a tap and the water would come when she needed to clean her teeth, just like it happened in the lavatories at the library.

Apart from that, her grandfather had been in a bad mood ever since the *spies* had last visited. The people from the government who only fed them lies and fantasies about how wonderful everything was, how nothing bad would ever happen. Though they obviously knew it wasn't true. They had sent someone else this time. Not the sour people from the previous visit, who had laughed at her when they thought she wasn't looking. No, this person had been very nice. An older woman, possibly twenty-five or thereabouts, Lydia wasn't entirely sure, but anyway, it had been a much nicer visit than usual. Lydia had shown her around and the woman had praised many things, how well kept the goats were, the attractive fleeces on the sheep, that she had never seen a pigsty so clean before, that their hens had the prettiest feathers she had seen in a long time. She had said lots of nice things, and Lydia had been happy, delirious inside, and had almost been sad to wave goodbye to her down by the gate.

But even so, her grandfather remained grumpy and Lydia thought that it really was about time he snapped out of it. Improved his attitude. She had been good, hadn't she? With the government spy? And hadn't she toiled all day with her hoe and spade, digging up heather and turf, moving boulders until the sweat was pouring off her? So that they could lay the pipes?

Yes, she jolly well had.

She decided she would have a word with him when she got home tonight. But not now.

Lydia tied her bandanna around her head, stuck the knife into the sheath, lifted the quiver from the wall and checked that the tips of her arrows were sharp. She twanged the bowstring a few times to check that the tension was in order before she put on her deerskin shoes and stepped outside, out into the beautiful afternoon.

Chapter 79

Fredrik Riis had just stepped out of the lift in Mariboes gate when Ludvig came rushing down the corridor towards him.

'We've got him.'

'What?'

Ludvig gestured for him to follow him into the incident room, where he stopped in front of the big map and tapped it with his finger.

'That's where he lives.'

'What do you mean? Do we have him? For real this time?'

'Haven't you talked to anyone?'

'No, I've just come from Hakadal.'

'His name is Ulf Holund.'

Fredrik had never seen the normally calm investigator so excited before.

'Easy now. Tell me again. We got him? Seriously? Who found him?'

'Anja,' Ludvig said proudly.

The grey-haired investigator then ran out of the room, returned quickly with a file and spread the contents across the table between them.

'This is what I've found so far. I've only had ten minutes. Munch has just called from Police HQ, we have it from two sources—'

'Hang on, Ludvig, did you say Anja?' Fredrik smiled and pushed his glasses further up the bridge of his nose.

'Indeed I did. What about it? Or perhaps you didn't think that we pen pushers had it in us? That we just spend our days playing spider solitaire on the computer?'

'No, of course not, but—'

'Ulf Holund. He has a garage. Ten kilometres north of Vassenden. And he drives a tow truck,' he said triumphantly.

'What?'

'Exactly!'

The pieces slowly fell into place in his head.

The tow truck. The cigarette butts.

He must have taken them from someone's car ashtray.

At a traffic accident.

The Burger Bar.

The collision.

A car crash.

He had seen him on video.

A long time ago. In the background.

But he hadn't looked closely.

Not closely enough.

'And that's not all,' Ludvig said, and shook his head. 'You know Patrick? Our Swedish profiler?'

'Yes?'

'He's not who he says he is.'

'What do you mean?'

'I traced the number that rang us,' Grønlie said eagerly. 'The Swedish number, you know? He was *recommended* to us, wasn't he?'

'I don't follow?'

'No, neither did I! When I called that number, I got hold of an old man who didn't know who or where he was. He banged on about Ingmar Bergman being stuck in his basement. I managed to calm him down eventually. It turns out that our man Patrick is his psychologist. He persuaded his patient to pretend to be from the police. He called us, he convinced us to work with Patrick—'

'Good God, but why?' This was too much for Fredrik now. He had to sit down.

'Patrick Olsson is none other than Patrick *Hellberg*.'

'*Who?*'

'He's Oliver Hellberg's father,' Ludvig went on. 'Oliver. The first victim. In Sweden. It must have tormented him beyond imagination, don't you think? First, his son is murdered. Then his wife kills herself. His whole world gone in a second. Because of this bastard. He must have seen our case and thought: I *have* to be a part of it, join in the hunt, find him, look him in the eye. Respect, if you ask me. We certainly fell for it.'

Fredrik Riis continued to be lost for words.

'So what are you still doing here?' Ludvig said, and threw up his hands. 'Munch wants all units up there now.'

'Where?'

Ludvig was back by the map on the wall. 'Here. Gran Tyre Service. They've already set off. Get out of here now.'

Fredrik Riis got up and ran down the corridor. He hammered at the button, though he knew it wouldn't make the lift arrive any faster, but he needed an outlet for his adrenaline.

Come on, come on, come on . . .

Yes, there it was.

For some reason, the basement car park seemed darker than usual. Had a fuse blown somewhere?

Not that it mattered now.

He ran to his car, found the key in the pocket of his jacket and was just about to unlock the door when a tall figure stepped out from the shadows.

'Oi you, Casanova.'

Fredrik jumped as he saw Karl Oxen swaying in front of him.

He had a bottle in one hand and was waving something in the other.

'So you like getting off with your workmates' wives? Are the slags you normally pick up not enough for you?' Oxen sneered, took a gulp from the bottle and came closer.

A pistol?

Fuck.

Fredrik raised his hands protectively in front of him and took a step back.

'Karl, I'm sorry. I really am. I didn't know who she was. It was pure chance, I thought—'

'Oh, shut up.'

He could see him more clearly now. The dark eyes were flashing. Oxen was so drunk he could barely stand up.

Oxen waved his gun again.

'Karl, seriously. I didn't mean it. I just—'

He didn't have time to react. The former boxer was lightning quick on his feet, the bottle came towards him in the dim light and there was a sudden flash in front of his eyes.

'Please, Karl—' The taste of blood in his mouth. His knees hitting the concrete.

'Did you enjoy it? What? You bloody rookie. Was it good?'

A kick to his head.

His neck jerked back.

And then another kick. And another.

It felt as if the roof had collapsed on top of him.

He could smell something. Alcohol.

It trickled from the neck of the bottle and all over him as Oxen raised his foot again.

Chapter 80

Something was dripping. To begin with, she didn't realize that the drops were landing on her face. Mia wasn't there. She was elsewhere. Golden drops from a waterfall? Rain from the sky, the colour of which she had never seen before. Another drop now. It trickled from a forehead, which was leaning against a brick wall, down to a nose that could smell mould and rot, to a mouth that refused to open, whose teeth were loose. The cold drop finally crept in between her lips, and that was when she opened her eyes.

A faint ray of light. From a small window somewhere. The plaster cast resting limply on her thigh. Her other arm was attached to something. Mia tried to turn her head to see what it was, but regretted it immediately. The pain seared through her temple, into her jaw and down her spine.

Oh, hell.

Don't do that again. Keep your head very still. She tried opening her eyelids very carefully this time. OK, so one was stuck, but not the other.

Easy does it.

'Are you awake?'

She was now able to see Patrick across the room. Both his hands were tied above his head and fixed to a pipe below the window.

'Where are we?'

'The forecourt of hell.'

She had to close her eye again. She didn't have the energy to keep it open.

His voice floated across the earthen floor.

'And we're not alone. There are children here. Two. In the other room. They were calling out at one point, but they're quiet now. He came downstairs. I hope he just taped their mouths shut. Or did something else to keep them quiet. Because I'm guessing he will kill us first? He has a ritual, doesn't he?'

She disappeared again, floated towards the beautiful sky that had no beginning and no end, towards colours that didn't belong on this side of reality.

Another golden drop.

This time she woke up as it hit her forehead.

The light was faint in the one eye she could open. His voice again, along the cold brick walls.

'I'm not who you think I am, Mia. I was never a part of the investigation. I'm Oliver's dad. And I've seen him before. The bastard up there. We were involved in a traffic accident. He drove the tow truck. He was much younger then, but it is him. I can die now, Mia. I can finally be at peace because now I know.'

What was he talking about?

These words?

Letters drifting apart. Which had no sounds. Only shapes.

In and out of the cracks in the earthen floor, in the smell of rot coming from the walls, out into the passage, up the stairs, along the stomping feet, in between the footsteps, around the key which was inserted into the lock, through the cracks, out of the window, into the fresh air, out into the light, the little house far below her.

Bliss.

She need never be scared again.

Chapter 81

The sun hung low over the vast forest when Munch arrived at Gran Tyre Service and got out of the car. Katja came rushing across the yard towards him as she pointed to a black Audi Quattro at the end of the house.

'Mia was here. We found her mobile inside the car. And Patrick was with her.'

'What? But how did she—' Munch located a cigarette in his duffel coat, but let it hang between his lips.

'I don't know,' Katja said, shaking her head.

A local police officer emerged from the house and greeted Munch.

'There's no one here, as far as we can see. His cabinet is open and, if it's normally full, then one is missing.'

'One what?'

'Sorry, a shotgun. The keys are still in the lock, so he must have left in a hurry.'

'And who are you?'

'My name is Martinssen, Gran Police. We came as soon as we were alerted. There are four of us. Two are on their way to the nearest houses some kilometres away to find out if anyone knows where he is or where he might have gone.'

'Is he known to you? Has he come to your attention before?'

Martinssen shook his head. 'It's a small town, but the region is large. If you want to be left alone, it's easy to hide. There's nothing in our files. Do you have anything?'

'We haven't managed to check yet,' Munch said as he lit his cigarette.

He took in the landscape around them. Mighty trees close to

each other; he had felt uneasy the further they had driven from Oslo. You would be hard pressed to find anyone in this area. Up here it would be possible to hide for months.

'Both vehicles are cold,' Katja said, indicating the Audi and the red-and-yellow tow truck. 'So no one has been here for hours. Which means that they could be anywhere.'

'Any tracks from a quad bike?'

Martinssen called out to his colleague, who was still inside the garage. 'Have we seen a quad bike?'

The officer stuck out his head and replied, 'No, but there are jerry cans here. And a set of small tyres by the table at the back, so he may very well have one.'

'Unless they're for sale,' Katja remarked with a nod to the crooked sign above the door.

Crap.

He felt even more uneasy now.

What had she been doing up here? How on earth had she tracked down Ulf Holund? And why hadn't she alerted him?

He looked at the deep forest again and had to spend a moment fighting a feeling of hopelessness. How the hell were they ever going to . . .

'What are we going to do?' said Katja, as if she had read his mind. 'If he has them. And the boys. He must be keeping them somewhere?'

'Have we searched the immediate vicinity?'

'There's nothing here except what you can see. Those two buildings. No basement. No other buildings nearby. This is all there is.'

'So he doesn't live here?'

'Not as far as I can see.'

'Shit. And we have no other address than this?'

'I'll double check with Ludvig.'

Katja went over to Munch's car and contacted the office via the crackling police radio.

She soon came back, shaking her head.

'Nothing. This is his registered address.'

'Family? Anyone else?'

'Ludvig doesn't have anything. Just a lot of printouts from the garage website. It's clear that Holund sold spare parts online from this address. Tyres, hub caps.'

'But nothing else, no known—'

Munch had forgotten about his cigarette. He almost burned his fingers and dropped it on to the gravel.

Katja folded her arms across her chest and looked at him anxiously. 'Where the hell do we start our search?'

'I don't know, Katja.'

The whine of an engine could be heard coming from around the bend in the road and then a teenager on a Suzuki moped pulled up in front of them. The boy took off his helmet and looked around, confused.

'Jesus, what's going on here?'

'Can we help you?' Munch said, walking up to him.

'I was just . . . Is Ulf here?'

'You were just what?' Katja asked him.

'He has my Shimano Stradic.'

'Shimano?'

'It's a fishing reel,' Katja explained to Munch.

The young man nodded. 'He's borrowed it from me, and I'm going up to Lake Randsjøen tomorrow, so—'

'Do you know him well?'

'What, Ulf? No, not well, but—'

'Do you know where he lives? He doesn't live here, does he?'

'No, no, he lives in his cottage.'

'And where is that?'

'It's all the way up by Brekkåsen.'

'Is it far?'

'Oh, yes.'

'Take us there.'

'What?' The teenager looked at them strangely. 'Now? But we need wheels. We can't walk it.'

'Then we'll *run*,' Katja said, and shoved the gangly boy across the yard.

Chapter 82

She had black lines drawn in ash under her eyes like the Native Americans used to have when they went hunting, when the sun hung as low as it did now, in order for them to see their prey better. Lydia crept through the trees and across the heather like a wildcat until she could finally make out the small brown house in the distance. She had to be careful. She was no longer the sweet girl in the forest, who walked up to the window to watch funny cartoons. No, this time she was on her guard. All her senses were heightened as she made her way to the badger hunter's house. This was serious. She crouched behind a juniper bush and raised her small binoculars to her eyes. There was activity over there. Normally he would sit still and she couldn't see him until she was closer to the window. With a beer on the table. Eating food from a tin with a fork. But not today. He was walking back and forth. He made a trip across the yard to the quad bike parked on the forest track. In through the door to the house and then out again, and this time he was carrying something. What was it? Crikey. A gun. A double-barrelled shotgun. She crouched down and crept across the moor. This time he wasn't going to get away with it. If he had put the badger back in the cage, he would get a taste of his own medicine. Did he think that she was just some ordinary twelve-year-old girl? She had caught trout with her bare hands. She had killed a deer with only a knife after hours of waiting. If that man had caught the badger again, she was going to show him.

Who she really was.

She crouched down again, kneeling on the damp ground now, the smell of sulphur and metal rising from the knolls around her. She raised the binoculars to her eyes once more; this time she could see the cage. She breathed a sigh of relief. There was nothing in it. The door was still open, as she had left it. Should she do it? Burn the cage? Destroy it? She had matches and her grandfather's lighter fuel in her rucksack.

Lydia let the binoculars flop on to her chest and was about to sneak closer when something happened near the house.

People were emerging from the basement.

Two, no, three of them. Two at the front and the man behind them.

So did he have some friends after all?

Oh, no.

He was walking behind them with the shotgun.

She quickly raised her binoculars to her eyes again. The people disappeared for a moment, but then emerged from the other side of the house.

And started walking slowly across the moor, straight towards her.

A young woman. Dark hair. Blindfolded. She wasn't able to walk on her own. The other person was trying to support her.

A man. Somewhat older. He, too, was blindfolded, and his hands were tied in front of him.

The blindfolded man turned and said something, but was nudged in his back by the muzzle of the shotgun, driving him on.

They were nearing her now as they stumbled across the moor. She didn't need her binoculars any more; she could see them with the naked eye.

The man ordered them down on their knees.

He took a step back and aimed his shotgun at them.

And that was when she got up.

She had snatched the bow from her shoulder and one arrow was already nocked.

'Hey!'

The man jumped and looked about him, confused. He couldn't work out where the sound was coming from.

'Over here!'

She strode towards them, the ground soft under her feet.

He had spotted her now. Frantically, he aimed the barrel of the shotgun in her direction, but her arrow had already left the bow.

Two hundred kilometres an hour; he spun around and groaned loudly as the arrow pierced his shoulder.

His gun went off, it echoed across the sky, a murder of crows screeched as they took off from the trees and she launched her second arrow.

She hit him again.

She saw his hands clutching his neck.

Lydia Clemens took out a third arrow from her quiver, but there was no need.

The man slumped to his knees. His arms hung limp along his sides. Then he collapsed on to the moor, dead.

NINE

Chapter 83

Fredrik Riis woke up to the sound of distant brass music and continued to lie still in the big hospital bed with his eyes closed. It was how he had spent the past week. He was scared to open them, scared to realize the state of his body, but his condition was slowly improving. Internal bleeding, a ruptured spleen, two fractures to his neck. He had woken up in the ICU, still hazy after the anaesthetic, and had not understood where he was. Drugged. Unable to feel anything at all. The pain had come later. Hit him hard. As if his mind and his body had worked it out at the same time. He had called the nurses constantly. *Give me some more pain relief, it's not working.* Pressed the button on the drip by his bed, the tube sending drugs into his left arm and then back to oblivion. Wake up. Pain. More pain relief. Repeat. But he felt better now. Much better. The marching band outside was coming closer, brass instruments and drums, clarinets and flutes, jolting, screeching, mostly out of step, but that was the charm, wasn't it? May in Norway. They would be celebrating soon. The country was one hundred and eighty-seven years old, wasn't it, or maybe that wasn't right, not according to the Vikings, who would have challenged that statement, raided the hospital and chopped him to bits. On 17 May 1814 Norwegian men had sworn an oath at Eidsvoll and drawn up the country's first constitution. To celebrate that occasion, the Uranienborg School orchestra, which had included young Fredrik playing his trumpet, had marched every year for many years up Karl Johans gate to the Royal Palace, playing their hearts out while the Royal family waved to them from the balcony. The Uranienborg School orchestra with its rather disappointing uniforms. Why did everybody else get to wear ones with gold buttons and bright colours while they had to wear sailor suits? With sailor caps? Like little white-and-blue sailors who had just come ashore? And he hadn't played the trumpet, it was a cornet, but his family couldn't tell the difference. A cornet – what's that? It looked like a trumpet, so surely it had to be a trumpet, and in time he had started calling it that himself.

His sister had been there. Sat by his bedside while she wept and clutched his hand.

He hadn't been able to say anything at the time – they hadn't unwired his jaw – but he had tried to communicate with his eyes.

It's all right. I'm all right.

Thank you so much for coming.

Finally he opened his eyes. Pale sunlight filtered through the gauzy curtains, and now he could see that someone was sitting in the chair.

'Hello,' she said softly. 'Are you awake?'

'Just about.' Fredrik smiled and pressed the button to raise the bed into a sitting position.

'My name is Silje Simonsen. I'm a teacher at Finstad School. Nice to meet you.'

He chuckled. 'Hello, nice to meet you.'

'Just in case you can't remember who I am.'

She smiled and got up from her chair. She went over to the window and stood with her back to the windowsill. It might be the drugs, but seeing her made him feel warm all over.

'How are you feeling?'

'Oh, I'm good. I'm going dancing tonight. Fancy coming with me?'

She giggled. 'I would love to. But I think we might need to wait a while.'

She came all the way over to him now, and he could smell her delicate perfume. Then she perched on the edge of his bed and caressed his hand.

'Is this OK? Does it hurt?'

'No, no, it doesn't hurt.'

'I've missed you,' Silje Simonsen said, and looked at the floor.

'I've missed you too.' Fredrik smiled again, then he had to close his eyes again and rest for a moment.

'Would you like me to leave?'

'No, no, I want you to stay.'

She came even closer, her breath against his skin.

'All right. Then I'll stay,' she whispered, and softly kissed his cheek.

Chapter 84

Lydia looked at the table in front of her to check that she had remembered everything. Packed lunch, tick. She had baked the bread herself. A wholemeal loaf with proper yeast. She had also churned her own butter. Usually, they got milk from the goats, but it wasn't suitable for anything other than drinking so they got jugs of milk from a farm in the valley and that was what she used if she was making butter or needed cream. Perhaps she was most pleased with her jam. There was an abundance of raspberries where they lived, so many that she need hardly move before her baskets were full, and she had found a way to make jam without sugar and still make it taste quite nice. Blueberry jam, of course, it was hard to choose between the two. She hadn't known what to use for her lunchbox, but then she had an idea. There was an old wooden box in the cellar. Wrapped in plastic, a material her grandfather hated, so it had to be valuable. It was small and pale blue and had pretty, hand-painted roses along the sides. On the bottom someone had written a name and a year: *Magdalena, 1980*. It had been perfect. Water in a metal bottle, tick. A jacket, in case the weather changed; after all, she would be walking some distance, tick. Spare socks, always a good idea, tick. A towel, in case she fancied a swim along the way, tick. Yes. She planted her hands on her hips. It was all there. Lydia carefully packed everything into the old green army rucksack and placed it by the door. She went to take a look at herself in the mirror. She was wearing her dress. The one with the big flowers. The one she had made herself. She had also done her hair. She had put it up in a bun, but changed her mind now, took it out

420

and let it cascade over her shoulders. It was better this way. OK. She was good to go.

She knocked on the door and entered his small bedroom.

'Grandad?'

It was dark inside. She went to the window and opened the curtains.

'Grandad? Are you awake?'

The old man pulled the duvet over his head and turned his back to her. He had been like that for some days now.

'Grandad? I'm leaving. Don't you want to say goodbye to me?'

Total silence, but she could see that he was breathing.

'Oh, give over, Grandad. It's not the end of the world. I won't be gone for ever. I'll be back this afternoon. Do you want me to bring you something?'

He shook his head under the duvet.

'I'm twelve years old now. I can make my own decisions. I need to go now. Don't stay in bed too long – you know it gives you backache – so get up. There's work to be done.'

She was almost at the front door, and she stopped to listen out for him coming after her, but there were no shuffling feet across the floor.

Ah, well. It would pass.

It was brilliant weather outside. As if someone above the trees wanted to celebrate with her.

She smiled towards the sun.

I'm going to school. Imagine that.

Chapter 85

Mia was sitting at the kitchen table by the window facing the street with a cup of tea in her hands as she watched the Italian embassy. Someone was working in the garden down there. Gloved hands over lilac bushes, under the handsome trees, and she thought: perhaps I need to be doing that soon. Gardening. Did she even have a garden? She had forgotten to ask. Her mobile vibrated softly on the table in front of her and she moved to press the red button. She definitely didn't want to talk to anyone but changed her mind when she saw the caller's name.

'Hello, Holger.'

'Hello, Mia, how are you?'

'I'm fine, and you?'

'I'm good, I'm at home. Did they discharge you yesterday?'

'The day before yesterday. Everything is looking good. I still have some ringing in one ear, but that will pass, I guess, if I don't have to talk on the phone.'

Munch chortled. 'Good, Mia, good. Have you spoken to Anette?'

'No?'

'I thought we might meet again in a few days. For a debrief. Would that work for you?'

'Yes, that's fine.'

Munch fell silent for a moment.

'Listen, I have to ask. Anette said that you haven't signed your contract yet. I hope it's just a formality. You are planning on staying with us, aren't you?'

Mia smiled over the rim of her cup. 'Yes, I am. That is, if you want me?'

He sounded relieved when he replied. 'Of course, Mia, of course. We have many good years ahead of us. Did you get the flowers?'

Mia looked at the lilies on the kitchen table.

'Yes, who were they from again?'

'Ronny Eng's family. They were overjoyed. They wanted to meet you. Thank you in person. I said that wouldn't be appropriate. That's right, isn't it?'

Mia nodded. 'I'm quite tired.'

'Yes, of course you are. I'll leave you in peace. I just wanted to hear how you were.'

She could hear noises behind him. He was outdoors; someone was calling out to him.

'So I'll see you in a few days?'

'By the way—'

'Yes?'

'You forgot to tell me how it ended.'

'How what ended?'

'Up at Manglerud. When you were watching that mailbox?'

A young voice behind him somewhere.

Dad, are you coming? The barbecue is hot now.

'Some other time. Life is calling.'

'OK. Thanks for ringing.'

She put the mobile back on the table. The gardeners seemed to be done. They picked up their tools from the grass and strolled up towards the attractive building. She was just about to boil the kettle again when she spotted someone in the street.

Long blonde hair under a cap.

Skinny arms hugging a gaunt body.

Good God.

Sigrid.

Mia jumped from the table and ran barefoot down the stairs and outside.

'Sigrid!'

Her sister was almost unrecognizable. Her face was pale. She was trembling. She could barely utter the words:

'Hello, Mia. Is this where you live?'

423

'Yes, come on in. You can't stay out here.'

She put her arm around her sister's fragile shoulders and supported her into the garden and up the stairs. Sigrid was close to collapsing. She barely had the strength to take off her filthy shoes.

Into the bedroom, down on the bed.

Mia helped her carefully out of her clothes.

'Where have you been, Sigrid? I've missed you so much.'

The tears came now, rolling down her cheeks. 'I'm so tired. I can't talk.'

'You don't have to say anything, darling. We can talk later.'

She got her settled. Tucked her in with love. Then she went over to the window and closed the curtains.

'Mia?' Sigrid reached an arm towards her through the air.

'Yes, darling? Don't talk now. I'm here. I'll take care of you.'

'I feel so dirty, Mia. On the inside.'

Mia sat down on the edge of the bed and stroked her twin sister's hair.

'You're not, Sigrid. You're the finest girl I know. No one is as pure as you. You're as white as snow.'

A faint smile now across the beautiful, pale lips.

Before her eyelids slowly closed.

And she fell asleep.